MARIANA

★

'Mary is a delightful heroine—completely
natural and unaffected . . . her final finding of happiness with the man she really
loves, is described with charm and skill,
and the people who surround her are
drawn with a sure hand and a humorous
understanding of human nature.'
(Scotsman)

'This is first-rate stuff without a single
spot in it that is weak. . . . Her descriptions are brilliantly amusing. Her
character-drawing beyond question is superb. Miss Dickens
has genius.' PHILIP PAGE
(Daily Mail)

Titles now available

MONICA DICKENS
*One Pair of Hands
*One Pair of Feet
*My Turn to Make
    the Tea
†Thursday Afternoons
†The Happy Prisoner
†No More Meadows
†The Fancy
†Mariana

AGNES KEITH
*Land Below the Wind
*Three Came Home

VICKI BAUM
†Danger from Deer
†Headless Angel

C. S. FORESTER
†The African Queen
†The Ship
†Mr. Midshipman
    Hornblower
†The General
†The Earthly Paradise
†The Captain from
    Connecticut
†Lieutenant Hornblower
†The Happy Return
†A Ship of the Line
†Flying Colours
†The Commodore
†Lord Hornblower

SIDNEY HARRISON
*Music for the Multitude

V. SACKVILLE-WEST
*The Eagle and the Dove
†The Easter Party

JOYCE CARY
†Mister Johnson

REGINALD ARKELL
†Old Herbaceous

PAUL GALLICO
†The Lonely
†Trial by Terror

DANE CHANDOS
*Abbie

H. E. BATES
†Colonel Julian
and other stories
†The Purple Plain
†Love for Lydia

RACHEL KNAPPETT
*A Pullet on the Midden

ERIC HODGINS
†Mr. Blandings Builds
his Dream House

BERGEN EVANS
*The Natural History of
Nonsense

**BRIGADIER JAMES
HARGEST**
*Farewell Campo 12

RUMER GODDEN
†The River
†The Dolls' House

ANNE SCOTT-JAMES
*In the Mink

†*Fiction*   *Non-fiction

MERMAID BOOKS

MONICA DICKENS

Mariana

London
MICHAEL JOSEPH

First published by
MICHAEL JOSEPH LTD.
26 Bloomsbury Street
*London, W.C.*1
JULY 1940
SECOND IMPRESSION AUGUST 1940
THIRD IMPRESSION MARCH 1948
FIRST CHEAP EDITION APRIL 1952
FIRST PUBLISHED IN MERMAID BOOKS (RE-SET) 1955

Made and printed in Great Britain by Purnell &
Sons, Ltd. Paulton (Somerset) and London, and
set in Times New Roman type, 9 point solid

TO
HENRY & FANNY

Chapter One

MARY sometimes heard people say: 'I can't bear to be alone.' She could never understand this. All her life she had needed the benison of occasional solitude, and she needed it now more than ever. If she could not be with the man she loved, then she would rather be by herself.

She had thought she could be alone in the little house in Marguerite Street, but London seemed to be still full of people who felt that they must ring up or drop in at all hours to cheer her loneliness. She could imagine wives saying to their husbands: 'My dear, we really must do something for poor Mary. The servants have had a lot to do lately, and it'll mean using that bit of butter I was keeping, but it can't be helped.' Then they would reach for the telephone and say to her:

'Now I shall be very hurt indeed if you don't remember that you can come to us *whenever* you like. Which day will you dine next week? Monday, Tuesday, Wednesday, Thursday. . . .'

So she and Bingo had come down to Little Creek End for a long week-end of solitude. Nobody here but herself and the dog and a thousand memories of the week-ends when there had been two people and a dog in the lonely cottage on the Essex marshes.

'You're mad,' her mother had said, 'to rush off to that desolate spot. Far better come and stay with Gerald and me if you're feeling low. You'll only brood down there.' They had had quite a row about it. Her mother did not understand that she wanted to brood; she did not want distraction. She wanted to fill the waiting-time with thoughts of him, and to keep herself aloof, as if she were holding herself in trust until he returned.

People were kind and friendly and amusing, but they thought that companionship and conversation were synonymous, and some of them had voices that jarred in your head. There was a lot to be said for dogs. They understood without telling you so, and they were always pleasing to look at, awake or asleep, like Bingo. He slept now, with little whistling snores, in his basket at the side of the fire, his stubby legs and one whiskery eyebrow twitching to the fitful tempo of his dreams. At the other side, with a cup of coffee on the arm of her deep chair, Mary lay relaxed, her silk dressing-gown slipping off her crossed knees, one

7

slipper dangling from her swinging toe. Beyond the inconstant firelight and the beam of the oil lamp at her side, the rest of the room was in shadow; not the sort of shadow that makes you keep looking over your shoulder, but a quiet, withdrawn friendliness, as if the unseen objects were waiting until they were needed again. Beyond the room, the night was lashing itself to an impotent fury of wind and rain. Mary thought how strange it was to think that only a few inches of wall separated the placid cosiness of the sitting-room from the howling, streaming darkness. Houses were very defiant things.

She had had her supper on a tray in front of the fire, reading while she ate, and her book now lay open on her lap, but she found her gaze more often drawn to the flames that leaped from the glowing foundation of the fire to lick round the black, unburnt coal above. Tomorrow, she thought, I'll dry some of those logs in the outhouse and have a wood fire. She twisted her finger idly in a strand of hair, lifting it from the long, dark bob that hung loosely almost to her shoulders. It was ages since she had been to a hairdresser and had it properly set. There didn't seem any point these days in doing anything more than just not looking a mess.

She was small and thin and very pale, with long, deep-set eyes and a mouth that drooped a little sadly in repose, but could grin from ear to ear like a boy.

She glanced at the clock on the wall that was made like a blue and white china plate. In London, at this time she would just about be hurrying into the hall at the snap of the letter-box to see whether there was a square, white envelope with 'RECEIVED FROM H.M. SHIPS' stamped across the corner. Supposing there were one tonight? She would have to wait until Tuesday to see it. There was nobody to forward it to her, because she had given Doris the week-end to go and visit her family at Dalston East.

In her mind she could see the letter quite clearly, lying crookedly, very white against the dark mat just inside the front door. The more she thought about it, the more certain she was that it was there. It was tantalizing to have to wait; she should have thought of this before. And supposing there were anything important?

Sitting up, she shut her book and put it on the table. I'll ring up Angela, she thought, and ask her to look in tomorrow and see if there's anything. She knows where the back-door key's hidden, under that flower-pot. It may be silly, but I really can't wait for that letter. There might be something in it, too, that he wants answered straight away.

She pushed herself out of the chair with an effort. She was stiff from the long, wet walk that she and Bingo had taken that afternoon, before the storm had blown itself up to this gale. Bingo opened one eye and thumped his tail as she picked up the lamp and walked through to the

8

other part of the room, under the framework of beams where there had once been a wall. It was cold away from the fire. The telephone was on the table by the window, and as she picked it up, she could hear the gusty spatter of rain on the glass, and the moan of the wind that had come all the way across the marsh to howl about her house.

The telephone was dead.

'Hullo. . . . Hullo. . . .' She clicked the receiver rest, but no peevish female interrupted her knitting to say, accusingly: 'Weatherby. Number plee-ase?' No buzzing. Just silence. The gale must have brought the lines down. Damn. She walked back thinking, her slippers clacking loosely on the wooden floor. Stepping over Bingo, she sat down again, biting her finger, pushing back her hair, and then leaned back, with her legs stuck out in front of her, and her chin on her chest, frowning. It didn't really matter, and there could hardly be a letter from him so soon after the last, but it was annoying. Tomorrow morning she would walk down to the cross-roads and catch the bus into the village and telephone from there. That would be just as good, because nothing could have been forwarded tonight in any case. She relaxed with a sigh and picked up her book again. That was what she would do tomorrow. I hope it's fine tomorrow, she thought.

When the blue and white plate struck nine with its gentle note, Mary automatically stretched out a hand and switched on the wireless. I ought to get that crackling seen to, she thought, hearing the first words without listening to them. But it's such a——

'The Admiralty regrets to announce that the British destroyer *Phantom* struck a mine and sank early this morning. A number of survivors were taken on board by two merchant ships that answered her SOS but it is feared that three out of the seven officers and twenty of the crew have lost their lives. The next-of-kin of the missing men have been informed. The *Phantom*, which was launched in 1927, was a thirteen-hundred-ton destroyer of the X Class. . . .'

Mary stretched out her hand again and switched it off, and when the words ceased, there was nothing to show that they had ever been uttered. She was still sitting in the yellow spotlight of the table lamp, with the half-empty coffee cup balanced on the arm of her chair. The fire was still leaping, orange and yellow, with little spurts of flame hissing out of corners of the coal; Bingo was still lying with his legs in a galloping position, his head screwed sideways and one ear standing straight upwards; the blue and white clock was still ticking. Nothing had changed, yet nothing was the same. In a lull in the storm there was a hush on the air, as if the room were waiting, holding its breath, to see how Mary would take it. While she sat there, with the chill of realization creeping over her, she kept saying to herself, with less and less conviction: 'It isn't true, it isn't true.'

9

Next-of-kin have been informed. So there might be something lying on the mat inside the front door; but not a white envelope—a yellow one, and she had got to wait until morning to know. Unreasonably, unfairly, the thought came into her head: Well, now Mummy will be able to say 'I told you so.' I was mad to come here.

It was funny that she did not feel like crying. She felt quite calm, except for the thick thudding beat of her heart. She could actually see it pounding under the thin silk of her dressing-gown.

'Bingo,' she said, 'Bingo, something ghastly's happened.' The little dog hopped out of his basket, shook himself, yawned, stretched, and pattered after her as she went to the front door. A swirl of wind and rain hit her in the face as she opened it and peered out into the wild blackness. She shut the door hopelessly, shivering. Her impulsive idea had been to walk to the village and knock up somebody with a telephone—ring up Angela, the Admiralty, anybody. But she would never get there in this storm; it was more than five miles. She would never even find her way. Even if she did, she would have to go to a strange house; she would have to explain; there might even be somebody in the room with her when she telephoned.

The clatter and crash of a tile falling from the kitchen roof into the yard deepened her despair. It was a wild storm. She had got to wait. To wait—and try not to think. She went back to the other part of the room. Perhaps if she sat down again and picked up her book, everything would be all right again. Time would click back, and she would find that it had never happened.

But this couldn't have happened to her—not to *her*. Tragedies happened to other people, not to oneself. Four officers were saved, and, of course, he was one of them. 'I'm lucky, I always have been.' Hadn't he said that in the Casino at Cannes, that lovely night when—was it only last May? It might have been another life.

'Oh love, we two shall go no longer to lands of summer across the sea.'

Not to think, that was the only way. She busied herself carrying out the coffee to the little stone-floored kitchen, lighting another lamp, fetching the kettle from the side of the fire, and washing-up her supper things. It was cold out there, so she went and got her coat to put on over her dressing-gown. In the cupboard where her camel-hair coat was hanging there was a pair of huge rubber boots, a battered old yachting cap, and a shapeless, oil-stained pair of grey flannel trousers. She shut the door with a quick, frightened movement, and went back to the washing-up, trying to keep her mind on details like what time she would have to start in the morning to catch the early bus, and whom she should ring up.

10

When she had finished, she didn't want to sit by the fire any more. She would go up to the room with the uneven floor and the yellow chintz curtains, and lie down in bed where it would be warm and soft and dark, and wait for the morning.

'Come on, Bingo.' She tipped the basket and spilled out the little Cairn, sleepily resentful. 'Come on, you can sleep on my bed tonight.' When she had filled her hot bottle, and cleaned her teeth and brushed her hair—just like ordinary nights—she turned out the light and crept in between the clean-smelling sheets, feeling very small. She lay on her back under the low ceiling, with the warm weight of the dog on her feet, staring into the darkness with wide-open eyes, fighting the thought that she had been forcing away ever since the apologetic voice on the wireless had shattered her security. The thought that perhaps, never again, never again. . . .

She could not let herself think of that, not of the future. The past, the certain past, was the thing to hold on to. It was safer to look back than forward. While she lay and waited, watching the vague, agitated shape of the curtain at the mercy of the half-open window, hearing the wind and rain, and the barking of a foolish dog across the marsh, she thought of the things that had gone, the years that had led up to this evening—the crisis of her life. All the trivial, momentous, exciting, everyday things that had gone to make the girl who lay in the linen-scented darkness waiting to hear whether her husband were alive or dead.

Chapter Two

IT was the smell of clean sheets that reminded Mary of what, when she was a child, she called the Charbury Smell. It was the first thing you noticed as you went in at the front door of Charbury; an indefinable pot-pourri of all the fragrant things in the house—roses, woodsmoke, polished floors, bread, and lavender-kept old linen. You were only conscious of it when you first came down from London. Once you had been there some time, it became a part of your country self, like the ragamuffin clothes you wore, and the grazes on your knees, and waking on Saturdays to the sound of the gardeners sweeping the gravel drive with brooms.

Sometimes when she was in London, at school, or in the flat near Olympia where she lived with her mother and Uncle Geoffrey, she would get a whiff of something that would bring the Charbury Smell to her imagination, and the whole of her small being would ache with nostalgia, and her eyes would fill with tears of longing for the holidays and the low, grey Elizabethan house in Somerset that was just the right size—large enough for everything except grandeur.

For Mary, everything at Charbury was unquestionably perfect. Even her most unlikeable cousins were acceptable because they were there. Without analysing the charm of the place, she was deeply conscious of enchantment, and it was with a shock of pitying surprise that she realized, in later years, that the grown-ups had missed the paradise which the children found so easily.

'Oh, terrible,' her mother told her, 'the family rows we had. There was always somebody being offended and creating an atmosphere, and then everyone had to go about apologizing to everyone else and saying: 'No, no, it was *my* fault.'

'But what a waste of time,' Mary said incredulously. 'I never realized all this was going on. Not all the time, surely?'

'Oh, no, of course not. We had a lot of fun, really. It *was* a heavenly place, wasn't it? But, somehow, you know how it is, there was always someone who wanted to make plans for the day at breakfast-time, and someone else who wanted to do things on the spur of the moment, and wanted everyone else to do them with him, and by the time we'd all settled what we were going to do, it would be lunch-time, so we couldn't do it, anyway. You were lucky, you children. You didn't know anything about the servants always giving notice because they had nowhere to go on their half-day, and Aunt Mavis discovering that the drains were bad, and raising a typhoid scare, and Uncle Lionel always complaining that the shooting was so poor, and telling your grandfather that his gamekeeper was a poacher—why, I even heard him say that he was thankful when Grandpa got rid of the place!'

Even when Mary heard all this, long after Charbury had been sold, none of it could spoil the perfect memory that stayed with her through the years, glorified, almost to legend, because it was a time that could never come again.

Charbury House belonged to Mary's grandparents, whose second son, George Shannon, had been Mary's father. Mary could not remember him, for he was killed in the hand-to-hand fighting at Thiepval, in 1916, when she was a year old. The photograph which her mother had given her to hang over her bed showed her a very young man in uniform with a round face and light curly hair, and the smile on his mouth repeated in his eyes. It looked like a face that was made for smiling, Mary thought, and she had told her mother this one night when she came to tuck her up, and Mrs Shannon had turned out the light and gone out of the room very quickly, as if she were cross about something. She never talked to Mary about her father, but Mary used to study the photograph intently and often, kneeling up on the pillow to get a good view of it, for it was very interesting to have a father who was dead. She never thought of it as sad until she went to the genteel private school in the Cromwell Road. Miss Carson, the Head Mistress, had asked her about her father, and when Mary said proudly, 'He was killed in the War,' Miss Carson had made a clicking noise with her teeth and had taken her into the study, which was so full of ferns and palms and bamboo furniture that you could hardly breathe. There Miss Carson, who smelt of bread-and-butter, had taken Mary on to her lap and stroked her hair, and told her that it was very, very sad to have no Daddy, but she must be a brave girl and not cry for him, as he had made the supreme sacrifice, which made Mary burst into tears and sob heart-brokenly into Miss Carson's modesty front. After this, she could hardly bear to look at her father's picture any more, for he had become one of the things, of which there were many, that made her cry. Although she had no idea what they meant, the two words 'supreme sacrifice' seemed to her the saddest in the world. She never told her mother when she was crying because of this; she pretended it was for one of the other things, like seeing the picture in *Peter Pan* of Wendy on the ground with the arrow in her breast, or not being allowed to see Uncle Geoffrey shave.

Geoffrey Payne was Mrs Shannon's elder brother. When he came back from the Army of Occupation to take up the frail threads of his stage career, he had moved into his sister's flat, and somehow or other never moved out. He specialized in 'Silly Ass' parts, which were booming in the early twenties, and chiefly because of his appearance, he had a certain success. He had a face like an egg, that slithered backwards at the forehead and chin, an inconsequential nose, and front teeth that pushed themselves forward at the expense of his lower-jaw. He was for ever beginning to grow a sandy moustache, and for ever shaving it off before it had a chance to be more than an embryo. On the stage, and frequently off it, he wore a monocle, in alternate eyes, high collars, bow ties, and suits that called attention to their pattern rather than their cut. He was amiable, in a passive way, and was quite genuine in his often-expressed wish that he could earn more so that his sister should not have to work.

'I wouldn't stop working if you were earning five hundred a week,' Mrs Shannon would say. 'I like it. What on earth should I do all day?' And she would laugh and click her fingers for him to throw her a cigarette.

When Mary's father died, Mrs Shannon had gratefully refused the offer of an allowance from his parents, who owned the famous 'Shannon's Restaurant' in Trafalgar Square. Her own parents could not help her, but she wanted to be independent, she said, and earn a living for herself and Mary. By the time Mary was eight years old she had established a secure niche for herself in a prosperous but stagnant dress-shop, which she abandoned in exasperation one day to bluff her way into the job of teaching dressmaking at a large Domestic Science College in South Kensington. Mary heard all about this later on. At the time she accepted the fact that her mother 'went to work' just as she went to school, and she was deeply surprised when she first discovered that all mothers did not leave home in the morning and return in the evening. Mrs Shannon was free for nearly the whole of Mary's holidays, which, in company with most of the rest of the Shannon family, they always spent together at Charbury House.

There they were, the mother and daughter, at Paddington Station on the Thursday before Easter, threading their way through the maddeningly loitering crowds, with only three minutes to catch the ten-thirty to Taunton. At a first glance they might have looked alike, for they were both small and dark and pale, but they were not really alike at all. Mary, at the age of eleven, was a shrimp of a child with no natural colour, so that people said triumphantly, she looked delicate. When she grinned she looked like a gnome, with her narrow chin and little pointed ears that were uncovered by her hair. It was drawn back behind them, and fastened with a slide in the nape of her neck before it fell tidily, half-way down her back. Mary's hair had an elusive tinge of chestnut, whereas her mother's was almost blue-black, and Mrs Shannon's eyes were much darker than Mary's, and small and round like energetic buttons. Her head and face were disproportionately small, hardly larger than the child's, but the delicate line of her jaw was square, and her under lip straight, following the line of her chin, while Mary's chin was pointed, and her big mouth matched none of the contours of her face. 'You'll have to grow to your mouth,' Granpa always said.

They pushed their way on to the platform, and ran alongside the train, where porters were already slamming doors and people poking their heads out of the windows for one last good-bye.

'In here, in here,' Mary kept saying, tugging at her mother as they passed half-full third-class carriages, and every minute she thought the train would start; she could see the guard standing by the luggage van, with his whistle even now at his lips. Mrs Shannon was always convinced that she would find something better farther up; when she went on a picnic she was always seeing 'the perfect spot' just beyond the place where everyone had settled. At last, to Mary's relief, they came up to the guard, and he said: 'Better get in, lady, if you're going,' and raised the arm that held the flag, so in the end they had to bundle into the very next carriage, which was full of glaring people. It was not a corridor train, so they had to stay there, and the people had to shift along the seats to make room.

14

By dint of saying that Mary might be sick if she didn't sit by the window, Mrs Shannon secured her a corner seat, and as she sat down herself, in the middle of the opposite side, she sent Mary a triumphant wink. Mary smiled back, but reservedly, for although it would have been agony for her not to look out of the window, she could not approve of her mother's tactics of making a nuisance of herself until she got what she wanted. Mary, being shy, saw everything in terms of herself. It was not what people would think of her mother that concerned her, but what they would think of Mary in connection with her.

There were five other people in the carriage; three unexciting women, who did not seem to belong to each other, a youngish, ugly man, who evidently belonged to one of them, because he only grunted when she spoke to him, and, in the corner opposite Mary, a comfortably fat old man, with an overblown white moustache, who looked as though he might dress up as Father Christmas for his grandchildren. They were already settled into apathy journey induces in some people, but Mrs Shannon could unwilfully stir up the most sluggish atmosphere. Even when she was sitting still, which was not often, there was still about her the sense of alertness that accompanied her wherever she went, as if she were living at high pitch. Before they got to Ealing, her eye was on the window, where the steam was already forming, and you could almost see the thoughts moving in her brain.

'May I?' She got up and stepped over the old gentleman's feet to get to the window. 'Just an inch—it's dreadfully hot in here, isn't it?' She looked round enquiringly at the other people, who didn't care one way or the other. All they wanted was to be allowed to read their papers in peace. Mary drew her legs out of her mother's way, and went on looking out of the window, her chin on her hand.

'Oh dear, *could* you help me? I'm afraid it's stuck——' The old gentleman prepared to be slightly irritated, but she turned on him such a dazzling flash of smile that he immediately felt twenty years younger, and chivalrous into the bargain. He puffed and panted at the window, and eventually sent it crashing all the way down. He and Mrs Shannon sat down quite pleased with one another, and started a conversation. One of the nondescript women shivered ostentatiously, and her husband made the motions of turning up his collar, without taking his eyes off his paper. A large smut blew on to Mary's nose and settled there. She could see it out of the corner of her eye, looming enormous, and she kept squinting at it as she gazed out of the window at the things that went by so fast, they made you squint, anyway.

'Perhaps that is a little too far,' said Mrs Shannon, getting up again. She wrestled with the strap with a frail impotence that put the old gentleman on his feet once more, and by the time they had got it fixed

15

to her satisfaction the train was roaring through Slough Station with the glorious disregard of an express. The woman in the crochet hat, who sat next to Mrs Shannon, cunningly offered her some magazines, and for a while there was peace.

Mary was only half aware of what went on in the carriage. She was used to her mother's restlessness, and she was busy looking out of the window and thrilling herself inside with the thought that nothing now short of a train accident—she touched the wood of the door quickly—could stop her going to Charbury. She could still almost cry when she thought of that dreadful time last holidays when she had got measles, a week before the end of term. She had held out desperately with a temperature of a hundred and three, with watering eyes and a head that felt six times its normal size, until she had finally fainted during the geography lesson, and not all the glory that this, and being taken home wrapped in blankets in a taxi, had given her among her school-fellows, could make up for one minute of the time that she missed at Charbury.

Then there had been the time when her other grandparents, Mrs Shannon's mother and father, who lived in damp defeat in a half-shut-up house in Dulwich, had wrecked the Easter holidays. Grandfather had elected to have a stroke on the very day before they were supposed to be going to Somerset. All the cases were packed, and the fortnight's supply of birdseed for the love-birds bought for Uncle Geoffrey, who otherwise could not be trusted to spend money on them, but they had to stay in London. Grandfather had taken a week to die, and afterwards there were countless arrangements to make and Mrs Shannon had had to go and stay down at Clarice Hill, Dulwich, trying vainly to make her mother abandon the melancholy house. There had been nobody to take Mary down to Charbury, for all the cousins and aunts had already gone. She had been furious, and had cried herself dry and kicked the furniture, and said a lot of bitter outrageous things to Mrs Duckett, the daily woman, who, although deaf, provided the satisfaction of an audience that no amount of solitary storming could give.

Mary was inclined to take every disappointment as a personal affront, a sort of, 'Why should this happen to *me*?' attitude, to which Uncle Geoffrey's infuriating answer was: 'Why not?'

All that was in the past, and grandfather's death ancient history by now, and this time they really were off. Mary sat with her comic paper unopened in her lap and watched the dolls' houses of the suburbs give place to the green, the thrilling green of the real country, with the changing shapes of the fields, and the cows that stared as Mary rushed by like a queen on the way to her kingdom. A cindery bank rose abruptly between her and the view, and, growing incongruously on the sooty cutting, there were primroses! Starry clusters of them, inviting her to linger there and smell their faint clean fragrance, but the train cared nothing for such glimpses, and rocked importantly on towards the magnet of the West Country.

Now the bank dropped sharply away and revealed the beginning of a town, where before there had been fields. Row upon row of grey slate roofs, parallel lines of wheeling perspective, heralded the approach of a station, but the engine, with its eye on a further goal, seemed to increase, rather than slacken speed, as signal-boxes, trucks, the eyeless walls of brick sheds loomed into view, roared at the train and fell behind. The slope and level of the platform ran alongside, and pale, gaping faces, mackintoshes, the moon-face of a clock had one ephemeral moment of existence as the train rushed through, trailing its scream behind it like a banner. More roofs whisked by, with a glimpse of a stout, aproned figure or a flaunting line of washing, and then there was a huddle of factories, and three gasholders with the morning sun glinting on their curving tops. The bank rose up, spangled again with the primroses, and when it sank, Mary knew she could settle down to an hour or more's scarcely interrupted greenness. She sat with her dangling legs not quite reaching the floor, her elbow on the arm-rest, occasionally leaning her forehead against the smutty window-pane, drugged with the train's thumping rhythm and the endless succession of delights that raced past her eyes. Each field, each little copse and half-concealed farmhouse looked like a place in which you could quite happily spend the rest of your days. The telegraph wires soared into the air, to be pulled down regularly by each pole, only to rise again in their endless, futile endeavour to climb out of sight before the next pole. Behind her, Mary was vaguely conscious of the noises in the carriage; the ripple and rumble of talk between her mother and the old gentleman, and the occasional crackle as the woman in the crochet hat turned a page of her newspaper, clearing her throat each time with a short, dry sound, as if she were stating an uninteresting fact.

Mary knew the landmarks all the way down. Here came a familiar bank with giant letters marked mysteriously on it in stones. It was a very long cutting, but just as she thought, as always, that it would never end, they plunged with a shriek and rush into the clattering gloom of a tunnel, and someone was treading on her feet, trying to shut the window. She knew the exact length of this tunnel, and she knew what she would see the moment they were out of it. You had to look quickly or you would miss it, and she kept rubbing her window so that it could not steam over. The ghost of a light appeared on the wall of the tunnel, grew, brightened, became day-lit brick for a moment, and then, with a sudden lifting of the concentrated noise, and a dazzle of sunlight, they were out—and there it was! The standing white horse, the Westbury horse, that stood on the hillside so close to the train that you got a distorted, elongated view of it as you squinted upward. Mary liked it far better than the other white horse nearer London, that trotted away by itself in a detached manner, miles and miles from the railway. It was friendly of this one to be so near, and it was a landmark that meant only three-quarters of an hour to Taunton.

Presently the train began to slow down. 'Frome,' said the younger man in the carriage—the first thing he'd said since Paddington. Fancy not knowing that it was pronounced Froome, thought Mary pityingly, especially as he seemed to be getting out there. He and his wife began to pull suitcases and umbrellas down from the rack on to people's heads, and the old gentleman was evidently getting out too, for he fished out a hold-all from under the seat between his legs. At Frome, Mrs Shannon kept him standing on the platform, while she thought of a few more things to say to him, and then they exchanged cards, and, by the time the train drew out, they had promised each other a reunion, undeterred by the distance between West Kensington and Somerset.

Now Mary was able to put her feet up on the opposite seat, for her dangling legs were getting fidgety, and it seemed hardly any time at all before her mother was saying: 'Better be putting your hat on, darling,' and beginning to make the commotion of departure. Mary saw with a thrill the first outlying houses of the town go flying by as she smoothed out the creases in her cartwheel hat on which she seemed to have been sitting. She jammed it on to the back of her head, with the elastic under her chin, and put on her fawn woolly gloves. Then she felt politely dressed, and sat demurely with her hands in her lap, and her inside tense with excitement.

The train began to slacken speed gradually, gradually, until it finally hissed to a standstill alongside the unsophisticated activity of the down platform at Taunton. Mrs Shannon was still dusting herself off and pulling and poking her short hair into place under the brim of her round felt hat, so Mary opened the door and hopped on to the platform, her legs feeling almost as stiff and unfamiliar as they did when she got down from her pony. She stood waiting for her mother, sniffing the sweet, clean country air like a little dog, rejoicing to hear again the soft Somerset bur of an old porter's: 'Mind yewer backs!' Everything moved at a much slower tempo here. Even the train had lost the impatience that had sent it snorting out of Paddington right on time, and seemed content to linger here while things were unhurriedly put in and out of the gaping holes in its side. Mary and her mother went along to see that their luggage was taken off, for once it had been amiably left to go all by itself to Penzance. To Mary's secret relief, Mrs Shannon did not discover that she had left her gloves in the carriage until after the train had gone, so Mary could not be asked to go back and face an unhelpful carriage in search of them.

There was nearly an hour before the little single-line train would start for Yarde, so they always had lunch in the station buffet while they waited. Mrs Shannon had, at one time or another, hopefully tried all the food on the counter and had reached the conclusion that biscuits and milk chocolate and a cup of tea were the most harmless. Mary always had a large sausage roll, a ham sandwich, two doughnuts, and a stone bottle of warm ginger-beer, which came back afterwards down her nose. It was fun, this lunch. Mary had a passion for tradition, and for keeping time-honoured customs year after year. Her mother used to laugh at her, and say she was 'a regular old die-hard, just like Granpa,' because her birthday and Christmas treats always had to be the same, and things like getting into bed a particular way, and walking to school on the same side of the road, were sacred. As grown-ups went, Mary found her mother the most entertaining company. Mrs Shannon knew nothing about the bright patronage that some people use on children; she said to them, as she did to grown-ups, whatever came into her head and, as a comedian, she was a wild success. Her mimicry always tickled Mary, and sometimes at the flat she and Uncle Geoffrey would roll hysterically about on the floor when her mother was being funny.

'Excited, Puss-cat?' she asked, as Mary came back to the table with her second bottle of ginger-beer. 'I wonder if Denys is down yet,' she added casually. 'Aunt Mavis said she wasn't certain whether they were going this week or next.'

Mary blushed, as she always did if anyone caught her unawares with Denys' name, and took a long and gassy draught to recover her poise. Denys was her cousin, two years older than herself, who could do everything, not only miles better than she could, but quite marvellously. He and Mary were engaged.

Although Mary had not confided in her, the romance had not passed Mrs Shannon by, and she could not resist a little occasional covert probing.

'He's going to Eton the term after next, you know. Bates says he'll eat his hat if he doesn't get into the cricket team,' said Mary, looking over the top of her glass with awe, for the words of Bates, the head gardener, who had once been twelfth man for Somerset, fell from his lips as pearls.

'Then you'll be able to go to Lord's in a fluffy dress and a big, floppy hat, and watch him play in the Eton and Harrow match. But not,' added Mrs Shannon, while Mary was contemplating this pleasing picture, 'not with a large black smut on the side of your nose.' She fished in her bag for her handkerchief and licked a corner of it. 'Here, hold still while I clean you up,' she said, the tip of her tongue protruding ever so slightly as she applied herself with concentrated delicacy to her child's nose. Mary was struck anew by the problem of why other people's spit smelt different to one's own. It was one of the great unsolved mysteries of life that no grown-up seemed able to explain; like why water running out of a basin should always swirl the same way.

When they had finished their lunch, they wandered out on to the almost empty platform and walked along in the sun to the end, where it sloped down to the cinders of the track, and before they turned back, Mary put out a foot, pretending, for the benefit of the man at the points, that she was going to brave the forbidden territory. The air was full of pleasant, lazy sounds: the leisurely rhythm of their footsteps on the stone, birds singing in the elm trees at the other side of the line, a dog barking from a cottage, and the desultory clang of milk churns as a man lined up the empties for the Yarde train. Mrs Shannon sat down on a bench that said: 'Pattison's, *the* Sheep Dip,' and lit a cigarette, and Mary climbed into the neat little cattle-pen and pretended she was a horse, which meant standing quite still and feeling like a horse inside, without any outward pantomime.

When the little Yarde train pottered in with its engine at the back, she got in at once, although it would not go for a quarter of an hour, or even longer, if the driver felt like holding it up for a friend. There were only two carriages, with seats along the sides, like in the Tube, and the passengers that truckled in were very different from those on the London train. There was a farmer with a beard and leggings and a waistcoat hanging open over his collarless shirt; country women in best black straw hats with roses; a man in a tweed suit and cap, with a lovely black-and-white spaniel with sad eyes.

'Funny,' said Mrs Shannon, squirming to look out of the window, 'there's generally someone we know on this train.' As she spoke, Mrs Cotterell heaved aboard in magnifying tweeds and a hard felt hat with a pheasant's feather. Mrs Cotterell lived in a red house on a hill above Yarde, and she sometimes came over to Charbury to tea, bringing her little boy for 'a romp with the children.' He was called 'Bubbles,' and he wore corduroy knickers and silk shirts, and had to be allowed to do what he wanted, and always be given the best tricycle, otherwise he cried and ran to the grown-ups.

Mrs Cotterell came and sat beside them and said: 'And how is Margaret?' to Mary, and then began to tell a long story of how she had been into Taunton to interview a *cook*, 'because my wonderful Mrs Ellis has turned out to be a *snake in the grass*. When I tell you,' Mrs Cotterell lowered her voice, scandalized, 'of the intrigue that went on at the back door; conspiring with the tradesmen to cheat me on the bills——' With a creak and a lurch, the train began to move out of the station, and Mary knelt on the seat to look out of the window, while outraged fragments of Mrs Cotterell's story reached her from time to time—'Goodness *knows* how long this has been going on'—encouraged by sympathetic noises from Mrs Shannon.

Yarde was only about fourteen miles from Taunton, but the 'Umpty train,' as it was called in the family, took more than half an hour over it, winding its unflustered way through fields and over high-banked lanes, adapting itself to the contours of the countryside, making detours round little hills, instead of cutting its way ruthlessly through them, as the main line would have done. Mary knew every yard of the way; each halt they stopped at, with the Somerset voices sounding very clear in the sudden silence, was a milestone. As they got nearer Yarde, the scenery was more than just familiar to her because she had seen it so often from the train. There were places where she had actually been herself, and would go again. She had often ridden as far as that hill with the clump of trees on top—there was a glimpse of the road which you took if you went to Taunton by car—here a wood where they had stood for hours and hours and seen the sun come up, when Uncle Tim had taken her and Denys cub-hunting. The excitement that had been mounting in her all the way down from London was intensified almost to bursting-point as the train idled into Yarde Station, and jumping out, she saw the same red geraniums in the stationmaster's garden, the old porter Jacob, with three dead ducks in one hand and a dog-basket in the other, and, crowning joy of all, Linney, large and square and smiling, waiting by the weighing machine for them in his dark green uniform, a grin like a slice of melon cutting his face in half. She rushed at him and he staved off her exuberance with his hands in the big brown leather gauntlets, with half an eye on Mrs Shannon descending from the train.

'Well, Miss Mary, aren't you ever going to grow tall?' he asked, as he always did, and she made the stock joke, which never failed to amuse: 'Not till you grow thin!'

'You're a terror, you are,' he said, shaking his head and grinning more broadly than ever as she skipped along beside him to the luggage van, peppering him with questions about the dogs, the horses, her mustard-and-cress garden, and his wife's swollen feet.

Mrs Shannon and Mrs Cotterell at last tore themselves loose from each other in the station yard. Mrs Cotterell drove away top-heavily in a governess cart, and Linney put Mary and her mother and the luggage and a drum of artificial manure that had come on the train into the old green Lancia that was used for the station.

'I left Mrs Ritchie in the town, 'm,' said Linney, as he stuffed his bulk into the front seat. 'We've to pick her up at the Lib'ry.'

'All right,' said Mrs Shannon. 'Denys *is* down, then,' she said unnecessarily to Mary, smiling to see her grinning away to herself in the corner of the car.

Mavis Ritchie was waiting outside 'Stationers, J. G. Ingledew, Newsagents,' standing on the pavement by the revolving postcard stand, whose pictures of trains and views and fat-legged toddlers saying: 'I'se missin' 'oo,' had not been changed within memory. She was always ready and waiting too early. Ever since her husband had forgotten her at a wedding and taken the car home without her, she was always expecting to be forgotten, even by people who could not conceivably have had too much champagne. She was Mary's father's sister, the eldest of the Shannon family, a tall, pigeon-breasted woman, of whom in her late thirties people said, not 'What a good-looking woman,' but 'She must have been very pretty as a girl.' A little rice-powder was all she would put on her face, and she lay awake at nights wondering whether she dared have her hair bobbed. She strove earnestly with life, but was constantly perplexed by it. One of her favourite remarks was: 'Thank goodness I've got a sense of humour.'

'Hullo, Lily my dear! And Mary—you haven't cut her hair yet, I see.' Linney stowed her into the car, and she leant over to give Mary a damp, breathy kiss.

'How long have you been down?' asked Mrs Shannon, as Linney turned in the main street and started off down the hill.

'Oh, only a few days. Such a nuisance having to change my library book already, but the girl had given me one that she said was very amusing, and, my dear, it was not at all—*you* know. Very . . .' Mary, looking across to see what on earth she was talking about, saw her screw up her face as if she smelt something bad.

'Oh dear,' said Mrs Shannon, 'what was it called?'

'Something about Youth. *Morning Youth*, or some name like that.'

'Oh, *Noontide Youth*, you mean,' said Mrs Shannon, refraining from mentioning that she had read and enjoyed it. Mavis would blind herself to the beauty of the Song of Solomon because it was 'Not Quite.' 'Tell me the news,' she went on. 'Who's at Charbury? Anyone besides the family? How are they all, and are the daffs out yet? I met that appalling Cotterell woman in the train. There's not a thing I don't know about her domestic arrangements or the tickle in little "Bubbles'" throat. How's Mother?'

'She seems quite well *in herself*, you know, but I don't like the sound of that cough of hers,' said Mavis, sitting well forward and hanging on to the strap at the side of the car. 'I get very worried about her.'

'But she's had that cough for ages, hasn't she, poor darling?'

'That's just it. Dr Munroe says it's chronic, but that's only another way of saying he doesn't know how to cure it. It's too hard, you know.

22

If it were loose, one wouldn't attach any importance to it, but it breaks my heart to see her sitting there cough, cough, cough, and she's so good about everything.' She sighed. 'I don't know what Father would do without her, but I often wonder if it won't be a merciful release when she——'

'She's very happy,' said Mrs Shannon shortly, and changed the subject. 'Is Winifred there?'

'Poor Winifred. Yes, she's back again. That trip she took wasn't a success. She and that friend of hers seem to have had a quarrel, and they came home separately, but she wouldn't say much about it. She ought never to have gone, of course.'

'Who else is down?'

'Well, all my young people, of course. Ivy came by car this morning. Tim's at sea, as you know. Lionel and Grace with their two——'

'Three, you mean.' Mrs Shannon laughed, and Aunt Mavis puckered her mouth and said, '*Pas devant les autres*,' and frowned, first at Linney's broad unconscious back, and then towards Mary.

Mary was singing to herself the song that the children always sang on the road between Yarde and Charbury. It went to the tune of 'The Keel Row,' repeated over and over again, as each stage of the journey was greeted with a monotonous chant of 'Here comes the *tar* road the tar road the tar road, there goes the *tar* road, te dum te dum te dum. Here comes the ruin house, the ruin house, the ruin house, here comes the corner where mademoiselle was sick.' A relic of the thrilling day when a French governess that Denys and Sarah had, had cried: 'Stop the car! Stop the car! *Il faut—il faut*——' and fled, handkerchief to mouth, into the hedge. On went the car, swishing between the high hedges over the lanes still wet from yesterday's rain, and on went the song, past the honeysuckle hedge, the chicken farm, the cross-roads where Linney slowed down and always gave two methodical hoots. 'Here comes the steep hill, the steep hill, the steep hill,' and at the bottom was the ford, which went by the exciting name of Red Flood, and through which, when there were no grown-ups in the car, Linney would not crawl, but would go with a fine splash that doused the windscreen and made the children shriek.

At last Mary got to: 'Here comes the *Av*'nue that leads to Charbury House,' and the car, with her mother and Aunt Mavis still chatting as if nothing exciting were happening, turned up past the triangular bank, where the weather-streaked noticeboard, at the foot of the little knot of fir trees, said 'Charbury House. Private.' Linney had to change down, for though the gradient was slight, the Lancia was old, and they hummed up between the bramble hedges and the elms which roofed the avenue thinly here and there. Beyond the hedge on the right Mary could see the pale lime trees and the darker shapes of oaks and chestnuts, standing among the folds and little hollows of the park. At the top of the hill they turned through grey, stone gateposts with iron gates standing open, and there, at last, was the house. It was long and low, with twisting chimneys and irregular gables, and pale grey walls smudged by massing creepers. The drive ran short and straight to the front porch, and Mary had barely time to get a rapturous glimpse of the daffodils on the bank beyond the bordering lawn, before Linney had crunched round to a stop on the gravel space before the front door, and she was out of the car and running, running—round in circles on the lawn, anywhere—she just knew, like a puppy, that she had to run.

'Mary! Mary! The grass is wet!' called Aunt Mavis, and even her mother said: 'Hi! You come back and change your clothes before I let you loose!' Mary came back, panting, and followed them through the front door and into the warm, sweet welcome of the Charbury Smell.

The hall at Charbury was the most lived-in room of the house. You came into it through the narrow lobby where the hats and coats and walking-sticks were, and the big oak chest, stuffy and camphor-smelling inside and crammed with rugs, cushions, croquet mallets, broken rackets and anything anyone cared to put there. Beyond the heavy inner door, which was propped open by a stump of fir-trunk with a brass ring in the top, the hall spread out square on either side, with the wide, shallow staircase opposite. In the middle of the room a round oak table held a great bowl of flowers, rearranged each day by the plump hand of Mrs Wilcox, the housekeeper. A small tree burned in the wide, stone fireplace, and before it there was a cushioned fender on which short-skirted women perching displayed a great deal of leg. There was a window-seat too, looking out on to the drive, and a careless gathering of sofas and armchairs, whose springs were at the perfect stage of comfort—half-way between newness and decadence.

On one of these sofas in front of the fire Mary's grandfather lay fast asleep, the swell of his stomach rising and falling, the broad folds of his face puffing in and out to his gentle snores.

'Ssh! Don't wake him suddenly!' said Aunt Mavis in a piercing whisper that made her father wake with a start, sitting up with his mouth open and the grey fringe of hair round his bald crown standing on end. 'Wha—what?' he stammered, still lost for a moment in the vacuum between sleep and waking. 'Why, Lily, my dear!' he said, blinking, 'you quite startled me. I had an extra glass of port at lunch, so I stole a little nap to sleep it off.' He kissed his daughter-in-law and stood up, short and fat—not gross, but comfortably egg-shaped—the compromise between plus-fours and knickerbockers that he favoured for country wear making his legs look even shorter than they were.

'Well, well, well, and how's my Poppet?' he said, his smile deepening the creases of his face as he bent to kiss Mary. Although he was clean-shaven, a hoary patch of stubble where his cut-throat razor had failed to negotiate a furrow gritted into her chin as she hugged him. She loved him exceedingly. He was the sort of person you could confide in; he was safe, and friendly and cheerful, and laboriously and unsarcastically witty. He always smelt so nice and clean, of Palmolive soap and the lavender stuff he rubbed into his head to make the hair grow.

'Run up and change, Mary,' said her mother, 'and then you can go out. Here's Violet coming to take your case up for you.'

Mary always had the same room, on the top floor of the house, up a little extra flight of stairs that had a door at the bottom of them. Her room was called 'The Cabin,' because it was so small that the furniture had had to be built in round the walls, and the bed had drawers underneath it like a bunk. It was right under the window, and she could sit up in the morning and see the sparkling greenness of the terraced lawns that stretched away from the side of the house as far as the park, with the clipped yew hedges on one side, and the beginning of the beechwood on the other. Sometimes, if she woke in the middle of the night with the cool, dark air blowing on her face, she would sit up and see the lawns lying stone-clear in the moonlight, and hear the frogs croaking from the water garden in the wood. Everything in her room was white, and there was a blue rug on the floor, and over the dressing-table a picture of a cornfield, with a bright yellow, solid-looking wedge of standing corn that was being cut by two horses, one brown and the other white as the clouds that raced over the blue sky above him.

It was good to be back and see the bed made up ready with crisp, clean sheets, and the room so neat and tidy, although it would be a shambles before long, for there was always so much to do outside that there was no time for putting things away. Whenever she came into her room in the daytime, it was only to rush in to fetch a jersey, or to dab hastily at her hair with a brush before lunch, before she rushed out again, determined not to waste time, terrified that something would start without her. She scrambled into her country clothes—a blue shirt, grey flannel shorts, held up by a boy's snake-buckle belt, gym shoes, and an ancient scarlet prep-school blazer with a stag's head on the pocket, that Denys had bequeathed to her. She flipped her long hair free of the collar with the back of her hand, and ran along the passage and down the little staircase, but instead of going down by way of the hall, she went down the backstairs, and landed with a jump and a clatter on the red stone passage outside the kitchen door.

'Well, I never!' said Mrs Linney, teetering out on her swollen feet, her hands huge with a coating of dough. 'Here she is, turned up again

25

like a bad penny. Do 'ee want a scone, then, lovey?' With the floury
scone, hot from the oven, crammed into her mouth all at once, Mary
went along the flagged passage, out of the back door, and stood for a
moment, munching, irresolute. Where would we find him? There were
so many places he might be: the stables, the pine-wood, the kitchen
garden, the cricket-field, the Play House—where should she look first?
She decided to try the stables, for even if they were not there, Tom
might know where her cousins were. She turned to the left, and going
up the hill to the stable yard, found Tom in a loose-box, gravely pulling
hairs out of the tail of Chuck, the big brown hunter. Her grandfather
kept three horses, two to ride and one to drive in the dog-cart, and
there were three hairy ponies for the children running loose in the
Park.

'If yew're looking for Master Denys,' said Tom, accompanying each
word with a tweak at the tail of the wincing Chuck, ' 'e come up here
'bout half an hour ago, botherin' me for a bit o' rope—going to 'ang
someone, 'e said. I dunno where 'e's to now.'

'Oh, thanks awfully,' said Mary, and flew back down the stable hill.
If there was a hanging going on, it was probably where most tortures
or capital punishments were staged, in the Play House, the big bare
wooden shed with the sand-pit, that Granpa had built in the beechwood, so that the children could make all the noise and mess they
wanted, well away from the house. At the bottom of the hill, where it
joined the gravel drive coming round from the front of the house, she
branched off into the corner of the wood, along the hard, beaten track,
where clumps of moss like velvet clung to the foot of the trees. As she
came into the clearing where the Play House stood, she heard a shrill
feminine shriek and a shout of triumph in a boy's husky, breaking
voice. Denys!

Had Mavis Ritchie been able to see the sight that met Mary's eyes
as she clicked up the latch of the door, she would have fainted dead
away. Her daughter Sarah was being hanged. She was a heavy girl, the
same age, but twice the size of Mary, with vacant brown eyes like a
cow, and a stolid, but untrustworthy nature. She would read people's
diaries and sneak to the nurses without the smallest compunction. At
the moment she was standing with her feet straddled over the open
trap-door that was used for sweeping away sand into the hollow space
under the floor of the hut, and round her neck was a looped rope, the
other end of which was slung over a beam in the roof. Hanging onto
the end of the rope, a sack over his head with a hole cut in the front,
out of which his little robin's eyes sparkled with excitement, was
Michael Shannon, the eight-year-old son of Mary's Uncle Lionel. His
elder sister Margaret, who, with her sticking-out teeth and tin spectacles
and damp, clumsy hands, was always relegated to the duller rôles of

26

any game, was earnestly holding up a volume of the *Children's Encyclopædia*, out of which Denys, with his shirt hanging out over his trousers, was reading the burial service.

Mary entered casually, almost as if she had only stepped outside for a moment, and was immediately absorbed, just as casually and naturally into the game.

'Hullo, Maria!' said Denys. 'Come on, you can be hangman. Take that sack off, young Michael, and let Mary have a go. You can be a sorrowing relation. Here, take my hanky.' He chucked a dirty, crumpled rag over to the little boy, who was struggling out of the sack, resentful, but obedient, because Denys' word was law in everything. It was a good game. It consisted in a gloating denunciation of the prisoner's crimes, a short prayer from Denys in a very good imitation of the Yarde parson, and then, after a final gabble of 'Ashes to ashes and dust to dust, so you shall be hanged by the neck until you are *dead*——' the long-suffering Sarah had to drop down through the trap-door making gurgling noises, while Mary kept the rope tight enough so that, although Sarah's feet were on the ground, she was almost hanging.

The Ritchie nurse, coming to fetch the children for tea, arrived on the fourth repetition of the scene and gave a shriek which made Mary loosen her hold on the rope, causing Sarah, suddenly unsupported, to fall on to her knees, striking her chin hard on the edge of the hole. Her suety face contorted, and she began to cry, climbing out of the trap-door howling unintelligible words of complaint. The others stood about, dashed. It had spoilt the whole thing.

'There now, you see,' said Nurse triumphantly, 'that sort of naughtiness always ends in crying.' She was an old-fashioned Nanny, shaped like a cottage loaf, with a grey moustache and a mole with three long hairs growing out of it, and she was a mine of all the stock nursery sayings like: 'Curiosity killed the cat,' 'Don't care was made to care,' and 'There's no such word as can't.'

'Come along in to tea the lot of you and mind you wash your hands,' she said, starting back to the house leading Sarah, who was still wailing dismally.

'Come on, Maria, let's go round by the back path,' said Denys, tucking his shirt back into his shorts.

'I'll come too!' said Michael brightly. 'No you jolly well won't,' said Denys, 'you go back with Margaret. Go on, buzz off.'

He bundled him down the steps outside the hut and, with a smack on his behind, sent him trotting angrily off after the dawdling figure of his sister, turning back every few steps to shake a puny fist, for he was a tough, peppery little boy.

Denys laughed. The adoration of his cousins and his superiority as their eldest had made him sublimely arrogant. He was vice-captain of

27

his preparatory school, captain of cricket and boxing, and the hero of the small fry. Grown-ups suffered his bumptiousness by saying to each other: 'Well, never mind, he'll have it knocked out of him in his first term at Public School,' making no attempt to prepare him for the shock that was in store for him. Mary, unwittingly made it worse, for she bolstered up his conceit by her blind devotion. She thought he was God, and didn't care how he treated her, and was delirious with gratitude when, strictly in private, he was nice to her, and allowed her to be engaged to him.

He was an exceptionally good-looking boy—a younger, softer edition of his father. He had the same dark eyes with innocently long, curling lashes that should have been inherited by Sarah; the same infectious smile and the eagerness to laugh at anything for the sake of laughing, and the same combination of naturally brown skin and very white teeth. His black hair grew in a widow's peak like his father's, though as yet not so pronounced. Guy Ritchie was a man who radiated charm as naturally as perspiration from every pore, and his son Denys looked like growing into the same 'Damn good chap' to men and 'My dear, who *is* that attractive man?' to women at parties.

Denys grabbed hold of Mary's hand, and together they jumped out of the hut and raced round the back away from the others, along a path that brought them out on to the lower of the three terraced lawns. Mary stopped, looking towards the ha-ha wall that dropped the smooth clipped lawn into the long uneven grass of the Park.

'Shall we go and see the ponies?' she suggested, yearning particularly to see the little grey 'Mouse,' who was as good as her own, because no one else ever rode him.

'No,' said the boy, tugging her the other way. 'Who wants to see the old ponies? I rode this morning. I jumped, by the way—a tree trunk—at least that high.' He held his hand flat at a distance from the ground that indicated a larger tree than any in England. 'Tom said I sat down to it like a good 'un. You must try tomorrow. Tell you what——' he said, suddenly struck by an idea, 'I dare you to jump off the ha-ha! We'll go and see the ponies before tea if you do,' he added magnanimously. 'Come on,' he pulled her to the edge of the wall, 'I dare you, Maria!'

The drop was about fifteen feet, and the usual method of descending to the park was by stepping-stones which stuck out of the wall at intervals. None of the children except Denys had ever jumped it, and he had only done it last holidays because his father had made him. The mere thought of it made Mary feel sick and dizzy. She stood at the top of the wall, staring with widening eyes at the park below, a green abyss of thistles and stones and cow-pats. A dare was a dare, especially if it came from Denys.

She turned to him pleadingly. 'You go first, then I'll do it.'

'All right,' he poised himself on the edge, rolling up his sleeves for no better reason that that the effective gesture gave him confidence, and jumped springily like a cat, landing on all fours, cursing at a thistle that pricked his hand. Mary took a deep breath. It didn't make the jump any easier now that he had gone—it merely gave it a despairing inevitability. She shut her eyes, heard Denys' voice below beginning to chant, 'Cowardly, cowardly custard,' and launched herself into space. Her inside rushed upwards as her body dropped down and then, with a jar that stung the soles of her feet, she landed, lost her balance, lurched forward and fell at full length. When she sat up, she was dazed by the mortifying, enraging pain of the smack in the face.

'Are you all right?' Denys was squatting beside her. 'Oh, Maria,' he said aghast, and she saw his face go quite white, 'you're bleeding!' She put up her hand and stared at the sticky red smear on the palm when she lowered it. 'Where is it?' she asked. 'I can't feel a particular place hurting.'

'You've gashed your forehead,' said Denys, peering at her with a horrified fascination. 'It's colossally deep. It's sort of white inside—I say! I think you've cut yourself to the bone!' Mary felt sick, but rather thrilled. It was pretty important to cut yourself to the bone. She could not feel any acute pain yet—only the bruised ache where her whole face had hit the ground, and it was gratifying to have something to show for that. Denys rose sublimely to the occasion. Mary's heart nearly burst with loving him as, with his dark eyes troubled and serious, he tore a strip off the bottom of his shirt and bound it untidily round her head. He looked at her.

'The blood's coming through——' He sounded rather scared. 'We'd better get back.' He stood up and squared his shoulders. 'Shall I carry you?'

'No,' said Mary, to his relief, 'I'm all right.' He helped her up, and then went before her up the steps in the wall, turning to give her a hand. They walked up to the house, she leaning on his arm, pushing up the bandage as it kept slipping over her eyes. She was beginning to feel a more localized pain in her forehead now, a sharp, cold ache, as if someone were holding a block of ice there.

'Grown-ups or nurses?' asked Denys as they reached the drive, with Mary struggling to keep back the tears that were rising with the growing pain.

'Nurses,' they said unanimously, as being the lesser of the two hysterias, and they stepped on to the little stone terrace, and went through the French windows into the nursery.

They were all at tea. Nanny Ritchie opened her mouth to say: 'All behind like the cow's tail,' but at the sight of Mary, with tears and blood running together down her face, she gave a faint scream in which were mingled shock, solicitude and automatic reproof, and bustled towards her.

'Mary's cut herself to the bone,' said Denys, and Sarah and Michael and Margaret stared, thrilled, and Denys' baby sister, Julia, began to make an infuriated commotion in her high chair. Margaret and Michael's nurse joined Nanny, as she unwound the blood-soaked strip of shirt, and together they tut-tutted and argued as to what should be done.

'Let me take her up straight away, it's really a nasty cut,' said the younger nurse, but although Nanny had been told over and over again by Mary's mother that she could take responsibility for the child as if she were one of her own charges, she was far too righteous for that.

'No, Nurse,' she said, making a buttonhole of her lips, 'that's not *right*. It's our duty to take her to her mother, so straight to her mother she shall go, just as she is. Come along, my lamb.' Mary was weeping freely now, with uncontrollable sobs as much of fright as of pain, and Nanny took her by the arm and led her through into the hall, with Denys running ahead.

He burst in on the circle of chairs and sofas round the fire, where the grown-ups were having tea, crying excitedly: 'Mary's cut herself to the bone! Mary's cut herself to the bone!'

He got his effect. The commotion which sprang up was turned by the sight of Mary into pandemonium. She was dimly aware of female figures rushing at her, examining, exclaiming, and the startled face of her mother, before Uncle Guy picked her up in his arms and carried her howling up the stairs. As they went, she heard, through the din behind her, Uncle Lionel say: 'It's deep, but it's nowhere near the bone, you silly young idiot,' and the anguished disappointment of Denys: 'But I saw the bone—I saw it, I tell you!'

Doctor Munroe put a couple of stitches in Mary's forehead and promised her no more than a tiny scar—'That's very important to young ladies, I know. Ha, ha!' and as far as she was concerned, apart from a certain amount of pain and one or two agonizing nights when her mother had had to sing to her and give her aspirin, the accident hardly affected her. She was soon allowed to career about and ride and play cricket and do anything she liked, with a large cross of sticking plaster sitting drunkenly over her left eye. Denys' chivalrous behaviour had added to his glory, as well as to the charm of her wound. She was undyingly grateful to him for having been there when she did it.

Among the grown-ups, however, life was not so simple. Although she was unaware of it at the time, Mary learned afterwards that there had been a first-class row between her mother and Aunt Mavis, as to whose child's fault it was. It was only one of the periodic eruptions of the unacknowledged antipathy that had simmered between them ever since Lily, a dressmaker's daughter, had presumed to hook Mavis' brother George at the unguarded age of twenty-two. Lily was not averse to a good row occasionally. It was an outlet for her energy, and it kept her from stagnating, she said. She had once waged a six months' feud with a butcher in Kensington High Street, which had been conducted entirely on postcards, like some people play chess, and there was a permanent vendetta between her and the Postmaster-General, who had the unfair advantage of not having to pay for his stamps.

When things got too dull at Charbury she would deliberately bait Mavis, or her brother-in-law Lionel. There was the time when she said: 'Women and children first!' as she stood aside to let Lionel's wife precede her ponderously through the dining-room door, and shocked Lionel to the depths of his spinsterish soul. Mary's mother, retailing all this to her years later, had put forward the theory that whenever one of the children was about to be born, Lionel spent the hours of Grace's labour looking under every gooseberry bush in the fruit cage. To Mary, at the age of eleven, her Uncle Lionel was just rather a bore. In later years, she discovered that he was a crashing bore.

Like Guy, he was in the family business—'Shannon's Restaurant,' in Northumberland Avenue. He divided his life into compartments, office, home, holidays, social. He pursued with a German thoroughness any sport that was offered at Charbury, and would never discuss business down there. He was an uxorious husband and a conscientious father, but any parental jacosity he may have had in the home withered like an autumn leaf as he approached the office above the banqueting-rooms of the restaurant in Trafalgar Square.

He had a narrow head and a thin, pale nose on which he wore pince-nez, attached to one ear by a silver chain. His body was small-boned, like a chicken, and already, at thirty-six, he had a dry, used-up look, as if he had never been young. His wife, Grace, was small and plump and comfortably domestic. She would far rather darn socks than read a book, and seemed to take a delight in being so stupid that she had to refer to her husband in everything. She worshipped Lionel with an almost unwholesome devotion.

Margaret had inherited this sticky trait from her mother, but did not confine it to her father. She was always flinging herself on people, clinging round their necks with limp reptilian arms, and saying, 'Auntay' or 'Un-kerl, I want to speak chyou. D'you like me?' If she got a snub, she would creep away and commune with her conscience, which was more than life-size. When she had no sins of her own to fret over, she would fret over somebody else's. She would be a 'good woman' when she grew up, you could see it coming miles away.

One Saturday afternoon the five children were all up in the Swing Tree, a huge old elm in the park, which had, above the branch that held the swing, any amount of convenient and fascinating angles to perch in. Margaret always had to be hauled up the lowest stretch before the branches began, though all the others, even little Michael, could shin up it alone. They each had their special seats. Denys sat at the top, of course, so high up that he swore he could see the spire of Exeter Cathedral. Occasionally he would gasp, 'Gosh, I nearly fell then!' to remind the others lower down how dangerous it was up there. Underneath him, with his gym shoe dangling almost in her eye, Mary sat on a smoothly curving branch, with her back against the tree trunk. From here, she looked out through the bright green, early summer leaves, right over the park to the farm across the Avenue, and over the sweeping ploughed field beyond, and the green folds and hidden valleys beyond that, as far as the cement works' chimney and the glimpse of roofs that was Yarde. Below her, to the left, she could see the broad back of the grazing Mouse.

She had ridden him that morning, all the way to Lymchurch, with Tom on Buck, and Denys on the old polo pony, Warrior, who 'pulled like a train' as Tom said, so that even Denys could not always hold him. She and Denys had had a race and Mouse had galloped really fast—like a racehorse—with his little legs thudding away in an ecstatic rhythm of speed, and his grey shoulder moving strongly below her, darkening with sweat. It had been glorious, exhilarating, and when they pulled up, she and Denys had waited with shining eyes and scarlet cheeks, for the long-legged Buck to come cantering leisurely up behind them.

'Fair terrors to go, yew are,' said Tom. The sun had been shining, and the larks singing, high up, and she and Denys had sung as they trotted along the road for home, radiant in the intimacy of a shared joy. Then she had been enormously hungry for lunch, and there had been roast mutton and treacle tart.

Life was perfect. She was more than just content up here in the moving green of the Swing Tree, with the idle chatter, and feeble, excruciating jokes passing up and down among the branches—she was actively happy.

Tomorrow was Sunday and it was the custom at Charbury on this day for one of the children to lunch in the dining-room; a treat that was coveted more for the food than the company.

'It's my turn to lunch in the dining-room tomorrow,' Mary announced.

'No,' Margaret's voice came floating up from a safe, uncomfortable seat lower down, 'it's mine.'

32

'Oh, dash you,' said Mary. 'Is it really her turn, Denys?'

The oracle considered, 'Must be,' he said judicially. 'She comes after Michael, and he was there last week, weren't you, young Mike?'

'Yes, I was. We had chocolate soufflé and I had two c'lossal helpings and an extra go of cream when no one was looking.'

'Mrs Linney told me they're having creamed spinach tomorrow, too,' moaned Mary. 'You are a lucky old sow, Maggie.'

Margaret, like Joan of Arc, suddenly heard the Voices. She looked upward, her spectacles glinting through the leaves. 'I'll let you have my turn, if you really want it, Mary,' she said exaltedly.

'Gosh no, you can't do that,' said Mary, 'it's your *turn*.'

'I don't care,' said Margaret, hanging on to a branch for fear she should be transported straight to heaven, 'I wish you to go in my place. If you don't go, I shan't either—there!'

'Well—all right,' said Mary ungraciously. 'I don't mind.' She knew Margaret adored lunching in the dining-room as much as the others did. There was something sickening and shaming about her blatant, uncalled-for sacrifice that tainted the prospect of going in her stead. When Margaret grew up, she cast herself passionately and indiscriminately into good works, so overpoweringly charitable that everything she did was plastered all over with the label, 'Charity.'

Mary forgot about it a moment later, when she spied two figures and a pram on the path below. 'Look—Nurses!' she said, tweaking Denys' foot. 'Oh, cheers!' he said, 'let's let 'em have it.'

Letting them have it was the screamingly funny game of hurling insults from the safety of the tree on to the two bonneted heads as they passed beneath.

'Margaret's nurse has a mousta-ache,' chanted Denys. 'And when she bends, the bones in her cor-sets creak,' replied Mary in the tones of the Anthem. 'Don't be so ridiculous, don't, says Nanny,' came from Sarah, and Michael shouted excitedly, nearly falling out of the tree: 'And she has a mole on her face—a mole, a mole, an ol' mole!' The tree shook with giggles, but the nurses knew that as they couldn't climb trees, the only thing to do was to ignore the children—until later.

'It's not *right*,' said Nanny to Nurse Shannon, as they passed out of sight, pursued by cries of: 'Nanny says "didn't ought," and she didn't ought to say "didn't ought." ' 'It's not right that I shouldn't report this—for the children's own sakes.'

It was Granny who spoke to them about it in the end. Every night before they went to bed, the children went in turn to say good night to their grandmother, and she would give them each a chocolate from the inexhaustible tin beside her bed. Sarah had once saved her chocolates up, night by night, and when she had hoarded enough to have an orgy, she found they had all gone stale.

When she had had her hot milk and biscuits in the nursery, and before her mother came up in evening dress to tuck her into bed, Mary went down the little staircase in her blue dressing-gown and slippers and along the soft-carpeted passage to her grandmother's room. She put her ear to the door to see if there was anyone there, for Granny liked to see them alone, but there was no sound except Granny's cough. Mary knocked, and entering on the gentle 'Come in!' went straight up to the big bed under the window.

Mrs Shannon had not walked for twenty-six years. Just before her last child was born, she had stumbled over her little pet dog, and had fallen heavily, breaking her hip. The child, Winifred, was born prematurely, with a slight affection of the brain, and later, tuberculosis had developed in the mother's hip and spread. Mary accepted it naturally that her grandmother lived in bed, or in the wheel-chair, or in the wicker armchair with a high back like a Punch and Judy show, that stood in the hall in winter, and was taken into the summer-house if it was hot. Granny had no legs, she thought, and boasted of it to the girls at school.

On the foot of the bed lay a Skye terrier, a descendant of one that had caused her mistress's fall, for though at the time, Herbert Shannon had wanted to have the dog destroyed, his wife had said, 'No, no, it wasn't Sukie's fault,' and loved the dog all the more.

'Well, my darling,' she said, as Mary sat down on the chair by the bed, 'tell me about your day. I didn't see you at tea-time, because Taggie wouldn't let me come down, the ogre.' She made a grimace. Taggie was Nurse MacTaggart, who looked after her, and carried her about in her brawny arms like a baby.

Mary told her all about the ride, reliving it in her enthusiasm. She loved telling things to her grandmother, and hearing her say, 'Yes, yes, I can see it!' when she managed to describe something as it really had been. Granny was always so quick to understand—not like most grown-ups who seemed deliberately to get hold of the wrong end of the stick. She would interrupt sometimes with, 'And then, I suppose, he said——' and would make some apt remark that showed that she grasped the point exactly. When Mary had finished about the ride, instead of saying, as even grandfather had done: 'We'll have to get you a bigger pony soon, young woman,' Granny said: 'What a wonderful pony Mouse must be. I'll get Taggy to push me down to the park tomorrow, if it's fine, and you shall show him off to me.'

After they had compared notes about their respective lunches, Granny said casually, looking down and flicking something off her bedjacket: 'And then, I suppose, you—er—sat in the Swing Tree, did you?'

'Yes, we all did, and Margaret was awfully soppy, like she is, you

34

know, and then the nurses came under with Julia, and we——' She stopped herself, prudently, just in time.

'Never mind,' said Granny, 'I saw you with my telescope and heard you with my magic ear-trumpet. Darling,' she said, taking Mary's hand, 'it was rather a rude thing to do, wasn't it; surely you knew that?'

'Well, in a way, I suppose it was, Granny, but it's so jolly funny.' Mary looked up, hopefully; Granny was generally on the side of a joke.

'Wouldn't it have been funnier still if it had been a joke everyone could have laughed at—the nurses, too? Remember what Queen Victoria said when the courtier was impertinent?'

'We are not amused.'

'There you are. Nanny wasn't amused either. She and Queen Victoria, they both knew that to be well-mannered is one of the most important things in the world. That's why Victoria was such a great lady and so many people loved her—because she was gracious. Be gracious, my Mary. You're such a dear little shrimp, I want everyone to love you.... And they will.' She pulled Mary towards her. 'Now, then, first a hug, and then a choc, and then you're off to bed!'

Chapter Three

THE cab drew up with a squeak, and Mary and her mother fell out on to the pavement, stiff and weary after a journey that had seemed longer and dirtier and more tiring because it was the journey home. As she entered the 'Flats 20—40' door of Clifford Court, Olympia, Mary was greeted by a smell that was as familiar as the Charbury Smell, but instead of inhaling it gladly, she wrinkled her nose. It was a mixture of the porter's cigarettes, the electricity smell of the slow, clanging lift, and the announcement, that drifted through the letter-box of the ground floor flat on the right, that its occupants existed solely on brussels sprouts.

The spotty young porter put down his paper-backed copy of *Her Pride was her Barrier*, and rose sulkily from his chair to take them up to the fourth floor. Uncle Geoffrey opened the door of No. 37, and said at once: '*Well!* It's good to have you back. I've been lonely as Hell.' He was wearing his Paisley dressing-gown over an old shirt and trousers, and was smoothing back his sleek hair in that familiar gesture of his, as if he were determined to make the top of his head even flatter than it already was. It was nice to have someone to welcome you, thought Mary, but once she got over the first pleasure of greeting him and the love-birds, and feeling that all her possessions were to hand, she felt flat and miserable and suddenly desolate.

'Supper's ready as soon as you are,' Uncle Geoffrey told them, 'so buck up and wash, Little Tich, because I'm off to the theatre in half an hour.' Mary didn't feel hungry. She stayed by the love-birds' cage in the window, running her nail along the bars, her underlip trembling, as she thought that this time yesterday she and Denys had been crouching in the damp warm cave under a laurel bush, hiding from Nanny, who was calling them through the dusk to come and have their baths.

'Go along, darling,' said Mrs Shannon rearranging ornaments and photographs on the mantelpiece. 'I do wish you wouldn't dawdle so.' Mary slouched out of the sitting-room and went across the passage to her own room on the right of the front door. It was stuffy and cold at the same time from disuse, and did not look as though it cared whether she were back or not. To anyone who had not known the charm of The Cabin, it was a nice enough little room. There was a chest-of-drawers, a wardrobe, a bookcase on the bedside table and a lot of pictures on the walls, framed or stuck up with drawing-pins. The woolly rug on the floor was rather thin, and only covered a small area of the brown linoleum, but there was a cheerful, multi-coloured striped counterpane and curtains to match, that had been bought by the yard at Pontings' sale. Mrs Duckett had evidently given the room 'a good turn out,' which Uncle Geoffrey said reminded him of Cascara, for Mary's collection of dolls and woolly animals had been put away in a drawer, and most of the books in the bookcase were upside down.

She went over to the window and looked despondently out at the darkening view, which consisted of the grey brick of the flats across the courtyard well, and mostly bathroom or kitchen windows, with here and there a milk bottle on the sill or a dishcloth hanging out. She took off her hat and coat and hung them in the cupboard, where her blue alpaca school dress reminded her smugly that the day after tomorrow was the beginning of term.

Her mother called her, and, at the second call, she went along to the dining-room without washing any of the train grime off her hands. She felt dead tired. Uncle Geoffrey and her mother were having macaroni cheese and bottled beer, and for Mary, there was cocoa, a boiled egg, and bread and butter. It was rather chilly in the dining-room. At Charbury now, she would be sitting on a stool in front of the high nursery fire-guard, with both hands round a mug of hot, sugary milk, and a plate of *petit beurre* and squashed fly biscuits on her knee. Mary took a sip of cocoa, and put down the cup, as she had a sudden vision of Granny's room as it would look if she were going to say good night. She saw the peacock pattern of the drawn curtains, the log fire, the flowers everywhere, and the wide expanse of green carpet that you sank into as you crossed it to get to the bed where Granny lay in a nest of pillows in her little quilted bedjacket that matched the eiderdown.

When she broke the top off her egg in the neat, clever way that Uncle Geoffrey had taught her, the egg ran out, watery and underdone, just how she didn't like it. The other two were chatting away nineteen to the dozen, and they didn't notice Mary begin to cry, and sit dabbing blindly at the egg with her spoon, big tears rolling down her face on to the plate.

Her mother glanced her way. 'Mary! Why didn't you wash your hands? They've got half the train on them. Oh, darling, what's the matter now?' she cried as Mary's tears burst forth, and she dropped her spoon and buried her face in her grimy hands.

'Overtired,' said Mrs Shannon to her brother, as she rose and came round the table to Mary, and he said: 'The West Kensington Blues. Too much Charbury methinks.'

'Come on now,' said Mrs Shannon, helping Mary out of her chair, 'let's get you to bed. You can skip your supper for tonight. Come along, you'll feel like a queen in the morning.'

Sure enough, when she was tucked up in bed, with the teddy bear that went everywhere with her, she felt better, and when she woke after a twelve hours' sleep, she felt better still. She soon settled quite happily into the London routine, and was too busy looking forward to the summer holidays to come, to look back and mourn the holiday that was past.

Mary was to have one more year at Manton House, the unambitious school in Cromwell Road, and then, if she could pass the entrance examination, she was going to a big public day school in Kensington. Her grandfather was going to pay the fees, although she didn't know this at the time. All she knew was that her mother had looked up one day from her end-of-term reports from Manton House, and said: 'No, darling, you're not the sort that gets scholarships, I'm afraid. If you're going to St Martin's—and I would like you to—we'll just have to pocket our pride.'

Mary didn't mind at all about not being clever. Some of the girls at Manton House were, as Mrs Linney said of Aunt Winifred, 'not quite the thing,' and Cicely Barnard couldn't even write her own name and was not allowed to lock the door of the lavatory. Mary had read, however, in the prospectus of St Martin's, about the 'extensive curriculum of sport,' and had seen pictures of girls with legs like sausages hurling themselves about with lacrosse sticks, and this made her a little apprehensive. The games at Manton House consisted of hockey or

37

cricket according to season, twice a week in Kensington Gardens, in charge of a red-faced, ginger-haired young woman with a pea-whistle, called Miss Treadwell. Mary was captain of cricket—the only distinction she ever gained. It was played with a soft ball, and Mary, who had had hours of coaching from Denys and Bates in the nets on the cricket field at Charbury, might have been playing a different game to the others, who mostly favoured the one-handed, governess style of futile swiping. She could even bowl Miss Treadwell out, and then everyone would hop about on one leg and cry, 'Well *played*, Mary! I *say*!' The education at Manton House was spasmodic, for some of the mistresses were qualified teachers, and others were fitted only for raffia work and lampshade painting, and were quite out of their depth when confronted with questions that were not answerable from text-books. By great good luck the English mistress happened to be an inspired old lady with snow-white hair and a gold chain pencil that snapped on and off her taffeta bosom on a coiled spring. She managed to infect the children with some of her own enthusiasm for the poems and books she taught them, and instead of setting them essays to write about 'What I did in the holidays,' or 'My pets,' encouraged them to write adventure or fairy-stories, or anything they liked. Mary got so intrigued by this that she bought penny note-books and began to fill them, out of school hours, with stories of blood and crime and reckless passion, that never got finished, but were tremendously exciting to start.

Her birthday treat that summer was to go to a matinée of Uncle Geoffrey's new play—*Young Gentlemen of Oxford*. She sat with her mother in the front row of the dress circle, on tenterhooks lest Uncle Geoffrey should forget his words or make a fool of himself, and at the same time, thrilling with pride to think that it was *her uncle* upon the stage, that everyone was laughing at and enjoying, and in the intervals she talked about him loudly, so that people should know. The heroine was called Renée Aimée, and Mary thought she was beautiful. She sang and danced and said things like: 'Darling, I loved you the very first moment I saw you,' and was kissed by nearly all the young gentlemen, including Uncle Geoffrey, and altogether had such a romantic time that she put an idea into Mary's head. She would write a play that she and her cousins could act at Charbury in the holidays, and the grown-ups would come and watch it. She never doubted that.

After the play, when he had changed and taken off his make-up, Uncle Geoffrey joined them at tea at the Criterion. Mary was almost shy of him at first, remembering him as Lord Footle, the rich young nincompoop, but it was soon clear that he was no one but Uncle Geoffrey, with nicotiny fingers and a passion for anchovy sandwiches. At tea, Mary was moved by happiness, excitement, and a quantity of chocolate éclairs to confide her great idea to them.

'By Jove,' said Uncle Geoffrey, who had played the same sort of part for so long that he sometimes lapsed into his stage language, 'what a topping idea. What's the plot?'

'Oh—er,' said Mary, who had not actually got further than visualizing herself as the starry-eyed heroine called Chloë, 'it's going to be about a princess—and a prince—and they fall in love, and get thwarted, and come together in the end, of course. There'll be some killings, too——' she broke off as ideas began to form deliciously in her imagination.

On the evenings when she had no homework, and at the week-ends, Mary wrote her play. Uncle Geoffrey turned out to be a great help. She had not let him have a look in at first, but once or twice, when she had been stuck and had appealed to him for help, he had responded brilliantly.

One hot Saturday in July, Mrs Shannon, striking and chic in a white linen dress with red buttons, with a white turban on her short glossy hair, went off to a river picnic organized by Uncle Guy. Uncle Geoffrey had been invited as well, but he had said, lying on the sofa and fanning himself with a newspaper: 'Too something hot. Count me out, Lil,' and added: 'Honestly, your rich relations scare me. I always feel they want me to go home and change my tie.' He was resting in the theatrical as well as the physical sense, for the 'Young Gentlemen of Oxford' had finished their pranks, and unemployment always made him more inert than ever.

Mrs Duckett went home after lunch, so Mary got tea for both of them, and had a heart-breaking time trying to cut wafer-thin bread and butter with a blunt knife and a crumbly loaf. In the end they had door-steps and black treacle and got sticky about the chin. When, feeling very domesticated, she had cleared away and done a little sketchy washing-up, she fetched her limp red note-book out of her under-clothes drawer, and went back to the sitting-room, where Uncle Geoffrey, in khaki linen trousers and a striped sports shirt, was trying to master the ukelele from a self-tutor. He could already play the Swanee Whistle, but though that was enough for the lady in the next door flat, it was apparently not enough for him. Mary sat at the table by the window in her short-sleeved cotton frock, with the window open at the bottom, letting in any air that was to be had, and the stray noises of the Hammersmith Road. For a while, the only sounds in the room were the slow, plaintive strains of Uncle Geoffrey trying to master 'Ukelele Lady' and Mary's deep sighs as she sucked her pencil, bit her nails, tucked imaginary wisps of hair behind her ears, and wound her legs round the rungs of her chair. She was having trouble with her abduction scene.

'Look here, Uncle Geoff,' she said eventually, 'he's got her in the castle.'

'Who—the prince? Are they married yet? You can't have them together in the castle if they're not. Think of your Aunt Mavis. . . . *May*-be she'll cry. . . .'

'No silly, not the prince. Sir Egbert of Corsica. He's kidnapped her, you know, and he's pressing her for her hand, under pain of death, while all the time she knows Prince Frederico is galloping to her rescue.'

'I see. So she's playing for time. Good situation, that. How far've you got? What's the villain said to her—anything outrageous?'

'Not much yet. They've had dinner—we'll have to have real food, I think, don't you?—and then the butler (that'll be Margaret, of course) comes in with the port, and Sir Egbert says : "Will you wine with me?" Shall I read you as far as I've got from there?'

'Rather.' He began to strum softly.

Sir Egbert : 'Will you wine with me?'

Chloë : 'Charmed.'

Sir Egbert : 'This is the rarest vintage of Oporto, red as your tempting lips.'

Chloë : 'This is a new lipstick I have on—Houbigant.'

Sir Egbert (*softly*) : 'So much beauty!' ('I got that out of a book, Uncle Geoff, but I don't think it matters, do you?')

'Not a bit. You're not the first one to do that. Go on, it's stunning.'

'Well, that's as far as I've got. I can't make Frederico arrive yet, because he's got a hundred miles to come, and he didn't start till just before dinner. He sneaked out of the house while his father and mother were dressing for dinner. They don't approve of the match, you see.'

'Oh.' Uncle Geoffrey pondered. 'What was the last line again?'

'So much beauty.'

'Oh, yes. Well, obviously, her reply to that is : "Ah, flatterer." '

'Oh, that's lovely, and then he says : "Not flattery, but the naked truth." ' She began to write furiously.

'No, just "the truth" will do.' Uncle Geoffrey struck a chord. 'I turn faint,' he said suddenly, in a high falsetto, 'the wine! the port wine! You have drugged me!' (Clasps hand to throat.) 'Listen,' he sat up excitedly, to look over his shoulder at Mary, who sat with pencil poised. 'Here's the idea. He's drugged her, and while she's unconscious, he'll get the clergyman to come in and marry them, so that when she wakes up, she's his wife, willy-nilly—those are his very words, in a soliloquy.'

'Yes, but if she's unconscious, she wouldn't be able to say "I do." '

'Sir Egbert is a ventriloquist, of course. I say, this is good. She swoons, you see, and as she falls, the handkerchief flutters out of the

40

window—you'll have to throw it, of course—and catches on to a bit of ivy——'

'And Frederico sees it,' gabbled Mary, 'and climbs up the wall and comes in at the window with the handkerchief between his teeth.' She could already see Denys doing it. 'It's marvellous. Don't tell me any more, I don't want it to be all by you.' She began to scribble rapidly. 'How do you spell nuptials?'

At six o'clock, Uncle Geoffrey yawned, dropped his ukelele on the floor, stretched his arms above his head, and said: 'I think I'll just go across the road for a quick one. My thirst in this heat is phenomenal.'

Mary waved a hand at him without looking up from her writing, and by the time he got back, she was sitting flushed, dishevelled and triumphant, leaning backwards in her chair and blowing out her cheeks. 'I've finished!' she called out, as soon as she heard the front door slam. 'I've finished the whole play. Look, here's the last line: "Darling, I loved you the very first moment I saw you." Curtain.' She looked up at him searchingly, to see whether he recognized the crib from *Young Gentlemen of Oxford*, but if he did he gave no sign.

'Well done, you clever little Tich! By Jove, that's marvellous! And what do you think's happened to your old uncle?' He waved an envelope at her. 'Here's a letter from my agent to say I start rehearsals next week in——' He struck an attitude—'*Monte Carlo Nights!*'

'I say, don't you think this calls for a celebration? How about you and me going on the razzle? Come on, I'll take you up to the West End and give you the biggest dinner you've ever had in your life. Mummy won't mind. Wait a sec,' as Mary got down from her chair and began to do a solemn little excited dance on the hearthrug, 'let's see if I've got enough money.' He dived into his pockets and actually pulled out some notes. 'Hooray, look at this! I'd forgotten Roddy paid me what he owed me, bless his heart. We'll go in a taxi. Don't bother to put on anything fancy—get a coat, and I don't even think you need wash as it's a celebration. You'd better brush your hair though, you look like Lilian Gish.' Mary shot off to her room, and emerged a few seconds later sleek, with her blue school coat over her cotton dress. Uncle Geoffrey was in the bathroom, putting more sticky stuff on his hair, and sagging at the knees to see himself in the glass while he smarmed it down. Then he added an orange tie to his sports shirt, a blue tweed jacket over that, and they were off.

Mary wished it had not been the porter's day off, so that he could have seen them hailing a taxi.

'Where are we going, Uncle Geoff?' she asked, perching well forward to watch the streets go by.

'Where would you like to go?'

41

'The Ritz,' ventured Mary, and was not quite sure after she had said it whether it was a restaurant or a theatre.

Behind her, Uncle Geoffrey laughed. 'That comes of having a grandfather in the restaurant business. And we won't go to Shannon's, either,' he added, 'even though we might get something off the bill there, because it's not the place for the likes of us. It's for blokes who don't care what they pay so long as they know they're eating the best, or who don't care what they eat so long as they're paying a snob price. No, I'll tell you where we'll go—the Café Royal. Ever been there?' Mary shook her head, wide-eyed. 'Good spot. Bound to be someone there I know, too,' he added with a hint of optimism. Mary hoped not. It was much more fun being on their own; with Uncle Geoffrey's friends, you never knew whether they were laughing at you or not.

It was not yet dark by the time they reached Piccadilly, but already the electric signs were brilliant in the waning light.

'Look, a Tom Mix film!' called out Mary, on her knees by this time, on the prickly mat. '*Could* we, after dinner perhaps—not if you don't want to, of course—but could we . . .?'

'You bet we could. We'll have our blow-out first, and then I'll take you to the flickers and hold your hand when the lights go down. How's that?' The cab swung round to the door of the Café Royal and Mary jumped out eagerly under the arm of the huge commissionaire. Inside, she felt smaller than usual, and would have liked to take Uncle Geoffrey's arm, but refrained. She had not been to many restaurants in her life, except Shannon's, which was different, because she always went with Granpa who belonged there, and Lyons' Corner House, which was different, too, because it was so full of people that there was no chance of being noticed. She followed Uncle Geoffrey as he walked into the restaurant with elaborate nonchalance. It was hotter than ever in here, and the air was thick with talk and clatter and smoke, and a glorious smell of food. They had to walk right through the room to get to their table, and Mary felt as if everyone's eyes were going through her like rivets. She wished she had worn her best coat. Once Uncle Geoffrey stopped to speak to a man who was eating spaghetti, and Mary was left hovering behind him, trying to look as though she was not there. It gave her an uncomfortable, itchy feeling to be standing when everyone else was sitting down. At last they reached the haven of a red-plush sofa, the table was pushed in over their knees, and Mary could view the room with more equanimity. The waiter did some impressive flourishing with table napkins, and a final flourish conjured a menu before them, on which there seemed to be printed every dish in the world.

'What've you got?' Uncle Geoffrey screwed in his monocle and looked up at the waiter, his underlip non-existent.

'What would you like, sir?' said the waiter, putting the finger-tips of one hand on the table and leaning back with a faint air of ennui.

'What would you like, Tich?' He turned to Mary and flipped the back of his hand down the long page, 'it's all yours.'

'Tomato soup,' said Mary, putting her finger on it. 'Oh——' She looked at him doubtfully, and whispered: 'It's a shilling. Is that too much?'

He laughed at her. 'I told you—we're dining out regardless tonight. But tomato soup in this weather——'

'Oh, yes, please. It's cooling really.'

'O.K. You're going to eat it. One tomato soup then, to start with, and I'll toy with hors d'œuvres.' They took a long time to choose the rest of the meal, but finally, after a great deal of struggle, and changing of Mary's mind, they fixed on salmon mayonnaise, braised kidneys with peas and mashed potatoes, and the expectation of an ice to follow. It was difficult to know quite where to fix in sardines on toast. 'Perhaps at the end,' said the waiter, raised his eyebrows, bowed, and withdrew.

Uncle Geoffrey took out a bandana handkerchief and mopped his face. 'That's got that settled, thank God. The smallest effort this weather makes me sweat like a pig.' He put in his eyeglass again into the other eye and turned to Mary.

'Will you wine with me, Princess Chloë?' She thought he was excruciating.

'I don't know, Sir Egbert,' she said through her giggles.

'Champagne, Burgundy, Rum Punch, Apollinaris—ask and you shall receive.'

'C-could I have cider, d'you think?'

'Why not? You'll probably get drunk as a lord on it in this heat.' He had a long, frosted glass of golden beer, lowered it at one draught, and promptly ordered another. 'Ah, that's better,' he said, setting down the half-empty glass, and looking about him with revived interest. 'Look at that stunning woman over there,' he said, as Mary lowered her spoon into the creamy depths of her soup. 'She's got everything.' He sighed and gazed dreamily across the room, with a sardine drooping from his lifted fork. Mary looked, but couldn't see that the woman had anything special except scarlet lips in a dead white face, and a huge hat with a veil, so she went back to her soup.

'I'll tell you something, Tich,' said Uncle Geoffrey beginning on his Russian salad, 'if I wasn't so darn lazy I believe I'd get married. But is it worth the effort, one asks oneself.'

'Have you got a best girl, then, Uncle Geoff?'

'Hundreds—but not one, that's the trouble. These things need concentration. Maybe I'll marry you.'

'Oh, I'm so sorry.' Mary looked up at him and smiled. 'I'm already engaged.'

'Well, well, well! These bright young things. . . . Get on with your food,' he said suddenly, 'and don't talk tripe.'

Mary ploughed her way happily through the dinner and drank two glasses of cider that produced a faint buzzing in her head. 'Anything more?' said Uncle Geoffrey rather apprehensively, as she chased the last fragment of ice round the cup with her spoon.

'No, *thanks*,' she sighed contentedly. 'I'm F.U.T.B.T.'

'What on earth's that?'

'Full up to back teeth, of course. Are we going to the cinema?'

He called for his bill, winced slightly when he saw it, but slapped down a couple of notes as if it were not more than a bus fare. Mary was horrified. 'One pound ten! Did it really cost that?' He snapped his fingers airily. 'A mere bagatelle. Now if I'd taken you to the Ritz——'

'You are decent, Uncle Geoff. Thanks awfully. Shall we go to the cinema now?' She let out a reef in the belt of her dress and put on her coat. As they were walking through the tables at the other end of the room where the starched tablecloths gave place to marble tops and the company deteriorated accordingly, there was a shout of 'Percy!' from somewhere on their right. Uncle Geoffrey, surprisingly, spun round. A fat man with little eyes in a white flabby face was waving at him. 'Come on over and have a drink, old boy!' Mary followed Uncle Geoffrey over to the table where the fat man was sitting with two girls, a man with a semi-circular fringe of beard, and a lot of bottles.

'My, my!' said the fat man, as they came up. 'Who's the girl friend? Catching 'em young, Percy?' Everyone laughed, and Uncle Geoffrey said: 'Keep it clean, Uncle, for God's sake. This is my sister's kid. Mary, meet Uncle Joe, and this is Babs, and this is Raymond with the face fungus, and this exceptionally beautiful lady in the red hat goes by the name of Wanda. Chaps, this is Mary. She's just turned out to be an infant prodigy, so we're celebrating.'

They all, especially the girl called Wanda, who had short, bright yellow hair slicked forward into a curl on each cheek, and a heavily powdered snub nose, were very friendly and paid a lot of attention to Mary at first. They sat her down between Uncle Geoffrey and Raymond, and gave her some ginger ale to drink, and asked her questions about her play and said: 'But, my dear, I think that's too marvellous!' They wouldn't believe she was more than eight years old, and *what* was she doing with an uncle like Percy? Mary felt quite a success, partly due to the fact that the cider was still buzzing in her head, but after a bit they began to talk among themselves, unintelligible stuff about people with names like Dezzy and Marge, and forgot her existence.

44

She pulled at Uncle Geoffrey's sleeve. 'What about the cinema?' she whispered.

'What? Oh, yes—yes, all right, Tich. In a sec.' He turned away from her again. He was drinking whisky and soda, and talking earnestly to Wanda on his other side. Mary could not hear what he was saying, but once Wanda said, 'Why, Percy!' and slapped him lightly on the hand. Mary drummed her heels on the chair, sighed, took a drink of ginger ale and after a few minutes tried again. He didn't hear her this time, and she didn't like to try any more. 'You're rather a darling, aren't you?' he was saying to Wanda, his front teeth nearly coming out of his head. Mary turned to Raymond, who was holding a glass of beer up to his chin and thoughtfully wetting his beard, while he listened to Babs, who wore a green beret tipped over her haggard face, and talked with a fluctuating American accent.

'So when I got there,' she was saying. 'I said to him: "Well, Mr Hammerstein, you can take it or leave it," I said. "Either I say all my lines, or I don't say one." And I turned on my heel, and did that!—to him,' she clicked her fingers under Uncle's blob of a nose.

'You *didn't*, Babs?' said Raymond, raising his head, his beard crested with foam. 'No——' she suddenly laughed. 'What the hell d'you take me for? But wouldn't it have been swell if I had? Hullo, honey,' she said, suddenly seeing Mary watching them. 'Bored?'

'No, not at all, thank you. Could you tell me the time, please?'

'Half-past nine,' said Raymond, shooting a hairy wrist out of his pea-green jacket. 'Your bed-time, huh?' said Babs, and Uncle said: 'And Percy's too, by the look of it,' and shook all over with wheezy laughter.

'Shut up, Uncle,' said Babs. 'Hey!' she threw the cap of a beer bottle across the table, 'come up for air, you love-birds, and do something about your offspring.'

'It's all right, really, thank you——' Mary was saying. She would rather be disappointed about the cinema than have everyone making a thing of it. Uncle Geoffrey turned round to her, and Wanda leaned across him and gushed a little.

'Oh, Lord, I'd forgotten—I promised to take the kid to the flickers,' he said. Wanda pouted and sat back. 'Tell you what,' said Uncle Geoffrey, his face brightening, 'you're a big girl, how about going by yourself? Here's ten bob, then you can take a taxi home afterwards. I feel like making a night of it myself. What about it?'

'Well, for heaven's sake, Percy,' began Babs, but Mary took the ten shillings enchanted. She had never been to a cinema, and hardly ever in a cab by herself. Here was adventure. She shook off the sleepiness that had been threatening her ever since dinner, and began to get up.

'Thanks, awfully, Uncle Geoff, that'll do marvellously. Can I go now?'

'We'll take her along, shall we, Geoffrey?' said Wanda, wetting a finger and arranging bits of her face in a minute mirror. She got her feet back into her shoes, collected a large patent-leather handbag and a pair of tasselled gloves and stood up. 'Come along, then, Ducky,' she said. 'I'll take your hand.'

Mary drew away, so Wanda gave the hand to Uncle Geoffrey instead. The other three said good-bye to Mary, and 'don't do anything I wouldn't do,' and 'write a part for me in your next play,' and she giggled and stood on one leg.

'Hop it,' said Uncle Geoffrey, and the three of them went out together. Outside, it was a hot, breathless night, with the first stars riding high in a greenish sky. It was good to be in the open air again.

'Thank you for a lovely dinner,' said Mary politely, as they waited on an island in the middle of the road. 'Aren't you a lucky girl,' said Wanda, on Geoffrey's other arm, 'to have an uncle who takes you out? No one ever did that to me when *I* was a little girl.' She laughed like a neighing horse.

'Sweetheart, you're only a little girl now, aren't you?' replied Uncle Geoffrey, and looking at his face, glistening with perspiration in the light of the lamp above, Mary thought he looked very silly.

They walked the few yards to the cinema, and Mary was eager to leave them and go into the brightly-lit, exciting foyer. Uncle Geoffrey was seized with a last-minute anxiety as he saw that besides the Tom Mix film there was Leatrice Joy in *Eve's Leaves*.

He studied the photographs with deep interest, changing his monocle from eye to eye. '*Eve's Leaves*,' he said wistfully, turning to Wanda. 'Look here, don't you think we ought to go in with her?'

'Oh, no,' pouted Wanda, who was as keen to get away as Mary was for them to go.

'Well, look here, Tich,' said Uncle Geoffrey, 'if you see anything you think you shouldn't, go under the seat. Sure you'll be all right?' He hovered on the pavement, with Wanda clinging to him like a growth. 'Give the commissionaire a tanner to get you a taxi afterwards, and for God's sake see you're home before your mother. She said she'd be late. Got your key?'

'Yes, yes, to everything. Good-bye-ee!' Mary aimed a kiss at him before she turned to go, and then Wanda aimed a kiss at her that smelt of the lavender cachous that Mrs Duckett took for her breath. At last she was inside and walking importantly up to the pay-box.

Leatrice Joy was half-way through her cloche hat vamping act when Mary wriggled into her seat past furious knees, and she made no

46

attempt to follow or understand the film; it was soppy, anyway. Figures mouthed and did hurried things in a permanent rainstorm, and Mary just sat back and felt emancipated.

At last it was Tom Mix, and Mary perched forward, tense, with her seat half tipping up. Although she was hardly aware of the presences that peopled the mysterious, breathing darkness all round, the thrill of being on her own among them intensified the spell of the screen. There was no one to recall her to earth by reading the sub-titles, or explaining in a penetrating whisper something that she already understood. No one to whom she had to turn dutifully and say: 'I *am* enjoying it, aren't you?' She was one with the dashing, miraculous cowboy. When he rode on his white horse, Tony, she rode with him on Mouse. Together they bent low to avoid the noiseless shots of the pursuers, together they thundered up to the wooden saloon, vaulted from the saddle and swaggered in among the bad men with spurs clinking. The rain that had fallen on Leatrice Joy fell also on Arizona, but Mary did not even notice it.

When it was over, she stood through 'God Save the King' in a trance, sighed deeply and went out into the night. She had never been out so late before. She stood on the pavement and watched the cars and taxis, and the crowds of happy, noisy people going by, some arm-in-arm, a party of men singing an inane, raucous song. It must be rather fun, after all, to be a grown-up. She didn't feel a bit tired. If she were grown-up, she would probably be going to dance at a night-club. The thought conjured up unnameable, fascinating visions of debauchery. She yawned, and stepped quickly backwards as a large, unsteady man knocked into her and said: '*Look* where you're bleeding well going!' She suddenly decided what she would do: she would put off the moment of getting home, and also save money, by going home in the Underground. Her mother was always talking about economy, and how pleased Uncle Geoffrey would be when she handed him back his ten shillings all but half a crown and fourpence!

She felt complacently virtuous as she stood in the lift, watching the ridges of the shaft slide upwards as she descended into the bowels of the earth. She knew which way to go, and where she had to change, for she had often travelled this way after a shopping expedition or a treat. A few people looked at her, and some smiled, and one or two said something disapproving to their companions, but she felt completely self-possessed. She had a feeling of calmness, almost of dignity, that she had never had when she was not alone. With other people one was only an unconsidered fragment of the company; alone, one was a complete entity by oneself. She sat and looked at her dim, flattering reflection in the opposite window, with the lights and wires of the tunnel rushing by behind it, and tried sleepily to remember Tony's tricks that she contemplated teaching to Mouse. 'Earl's Cou-urt!' bawled a voice, and Mary shot to her feet and struggled to slide open the heavy doors, in a sudden panic that the train would go on before she could get out. She might be whirled away to some unknown, sinister destination, like the awful story of the girl who got locked in a carriage, and had to go round and round the Inner Circle, passing and repassing the station where she wanted to get out, until they finally found her, stark, staring mad, with all her hair torn out by the roots.

She had to wait a long time for her next train, and she sat down on a bench and thought of her bed, and how good she was not to have taken that taxi home. She could hear Uncle Geoffrey's, 'By Jove, some niece!' when she proudly handed him his money. She yawned again, vastly, and listened to the measured beat of a man's footsteps walking up and down, up and down, in the unreal silence of the platform. The clock showed her it was nearly midnight. At last, far away, a faint murmur grew, swelled to a roar, and became a rattling, banging dragon that rocked out of the darkness with blue sparks flying from the live rail, and stopped with a jarring shriek. Mary got into the train as it was beginning to make the high, juggle-juggle-juggle noise that it always made at Earl's Court, and after a senseless wait it started at last. At Addison Road, she stumbled on to the platform, handed her ticket to a collector who looked as if he thought people were mad to be out of their beds at this hour from choice, and climbed the steps into the street more dead than alive. She had only a little way to walk, and she could see the vast barrack of Clifford Court brooding before her, unwelcoming, but welcome. She hoped her mother would be in already to greet her. She could visualize her surprise at seeing her come home alone, her praise, and her eagerness to hear about the evening and to discuss her own, for they both knew that half the piquancy of enjoyment lay in the retailing of it afterwards.

The front door of the flats was still open, but the porter was not there and neither was the lift, nor did it answer to Mary's finger on the button. Wearily, she climbed the four flights, hauling herself up by the banister, and stuck out her tongue as she passed the lift, slumbering on the third floor, too late to be any help. Had she had gloves when she started out? She certainly hadn't now, but if they were lost, they were lost, she thought, fiddling her key into the lock.

Before she had time to get inside the door, a whirlwind bore down and engulfed her, inarticulate, gabbling—crying! Her mother was crying—kneeling down in her dressing-gown on the oilcloth of the passage, hugging and holding Mary, and saying things like: 'Oh, darling, I thought——Where have you *been*? How *could* you, darling —you don't know what I've been through—oh, my Mary, my baby!' Mary was stunned. Evidently she had somehow not done the right thing after all. She began to cry, too, from exhaustion and disappointment, and her mother recovered in order to comfort her.

'Now,' she said, when Mary had dried up to a snivel, '*where* were you?'

'Uncle Geoffrey took me out to dinner.'

'That's what I thought when I first came home, but then, when it got so late, I got worried, and I rang up that Teddy's club that he goes to sometimes, and they told me he'd just left with a party of people. "Any sign of you?" I said, but no. So I was frantic, I kept seeing pictures of all the things that might happen to you; I even went and hunted round the street. Then I rang up the police, twice I've been on to them, they're probably combing the underworld for you at this moment——' She gabbled it all off, excited, incoherent in her relief, exaggerating and even enjoying what she had been through now that it was over. Mary's head began to go round.

'I'm sorry, Mummy,' she began, but before she could explain, Mrs Shannon cut in with: 'But what *happened*? Did you get lost? How could Geoffrey take you out and lose you? He might at least have left a note—where have you been? Why didn't you ring up or something? I don't understand——'

'I went to the cinema.' Mary went into her bedroom, her mother following behind, ejaculating. 'Uncle Geoffrey didn't want to come, so I went alone. It was——' she was going to say how marvellous it had been, but suddenly found that she could not bother to describe it. She was too tired, and it was such a long time ago, anyway. 'I remember now,' she went on, 'Uncle Geoff told me to be sure and be home before you and he gave me some money for a taxi, but I came home by train instead, because I—because I——' a salty tear dropped off her cheek into her drooping mouth.

'You should have taken the taxi, but it wasn't your fault, really. That stupid Geoffrey—just like him to do a ridiculous thing like that. I'll be so angry with him, when I see him—my lord, I'll be angry. . . .' Mrs Shannon stormed away while she helped Mary to get to bed. Mary tried half-heartedly to explain that it had not been Uncle Geoffrey's fault at all, but the effort was too great, and she was already half-asleep. She would put it right in the morning, and save herself from Uncle Geoffrey's contempt, or he would never take her out again.

What actually happened the next day was that Uncle Geoffrey, who had not come home till 5.30 a.m., lay in bed a senseless log until half-way through the afternoon, when he woke, moaning, and called weakly for a cup of tea. Mary took it in to him, asked brightly if he was ill, and delivered the joyful news that Wanda had telephoned twice while he was asleep, and had left a message the second time to say she was coming round to see him at four. Uncle Geoffrey struggled to a sitting position, the front of his hair in his eyes, the back standing on end, stiff with grease. His face looked yellow-white, like wax, with a dirty shadow of beard round his chin.

'To see me?' he said stupidly, goggling, 'today?'

'Yes,' said Mary, 'and Mummy says to tell you that if you want to give her tea here she'll have to put up with bread and butter and honey, because she's blowed if she's going to go out and buy cakes.'

'For the love of Mike!' Uncle Geoffrey was fully awake now. 'She can't come here. Oh—it begins to come back to me—oh, my God!' he groaned and fell back again limply, shutting his eyes. 'Came the dawn. . . . Why didn't you warn her off?'

'But, Uncle Geoff, I thought you liked her. Last night——'

'Please, Mary,' he winced. 'Last night I was a young boy; today I am a very old man. Leave me, I would weep.'

Mary went away puzzled, and was relieved to find that her mother seemed to have forgotten about her coming home alone. Mrs Shannon went into her brother's room, and when she came out she was chuckling and raised her eyes to heaven. Uncle Geoffrey followed her out tying the cord of his dressing-gown. 'If you let her in, Lily, I'll murder you—and you too, brat,' he said catching sight of Mary hovering inquisitively in the passage. 'Anyone got any Eno's?' he shuffled into the bathroom.

He was still in there when the front-door bell rang, and as her mother was busy in the kitchen, Mary went to answer it. There stood Wanda, wearing a very short black coat and skirt, a shovel hat, and an extra layer of powder over last night's.

'Hello, darling!' she stepped inside before Mary could stop her, and Mary ducked away from her lavender-charged kiss. 'If that's that woman,' came Uncle Geoffrey's voice clearly from the bathroom, 'keep her out of here, for God's sake.' He looked out into the passage, smoothing his hair. 'Struth!' he said, catching sight of Wanda, and retreated. Mary didn't know what to do. Wanda looked blank. 'Well!' she said. 'I never was so insulted in all my life!' then her face crumpled, and Mary was terrified she was going to cry. To her intense relief, her mother appeared round the corner from the kitchen and dealt with the situation.

'I'm *so* sorry, Miss—er——' she said smoothly, 'but I'm afraid my brother is not at all well. He really can't see anyone.' Somehow, Wanda, too dazed to do more than protest feebly, found herself manœuvred to the door, looking as if she had been struck by a brick.

'You can come out, rat!' Mrs Shannon thumped on the bathroom door.

'Gone?' said Uncle Geoffrey, looking nervously out, like a rabbit. 'I say, thanks awfully, Lil.'

'Don't thank me,' she said, folding her arms and frowning at him. 'I didn't get rid of her for your sake. Poor girl, I thought she was better off without you than with you, that's all. All the same,' she looked up at him mischievously, the tip of her tongue in the corner of her mouth, 'from the look in her eye, I should say you *had* asked her to marry you. She'll probably sue you for breach of promise.' She dusted her hands off lightly, one against the other, and went back to the kitchen.

'Oh, God,' said Uncle Geoffrey, 'I'm going back to bed. If I don't wake up by morning, you can bring the hearse.' His bedroom door slammed, and Mary was alone in the passage, mystified and intrigued, but with a presentiment that, however many questions she asked, nobody would ever explain exactly what it was all about.

Manton House did not run to a speech day or prize-giving, but at the end of the summer term there was a school concert, at which Mary, in a flowered tussore dress and with an expression of acute anguish, played Schubert's 'Marche Militaire,' and parents in the audience nodded and hummed, as much as to say: 'Haven't I heard that tune somewhere before?' Mrs Shannon was able to attend, as her college had already broken up, and she promised her half a crown if she played it well. As she had hardly practised at all, she played it very badly, but her mother gave her the money all the same, under the feeble pretext that 'it was a good try.'

After the concert, good conduct medals were presented. Mary, who had never yet got one, felt entitled to it this term because she had several times sharpened pencils for the Mathematics mistress, and had once even brought Miss Carson a potted fern.

She did not get a medal—it was not fair. 'What a swizz,' she whispered bitterly to her mother as Cicely Barnard's name was called. 'She simply doesn't know enough to be bad.'

End-of-term reports and cups of tea and pink shortbread fingers were then handed out to the parents, and that was the end of school for two whole months. Going home, Mary ran ahead of her mother, swinging her boot-bag, touching lamp-posts and pillar-boxes, and then running back again. Mrs Shannon was walking slowly, reading Mary's report as she went, a faint smile twitching the corners of her mouth.

'Let me see? What does it say? Oh, *let* me read it!' clamoured Mary, hopping round her, pulling at her arm.

'Wait till I've finished. You shall see it; can't you wait a sec? It's not so bright, anyway, chicken.'

'Oh, buck up.' Mary hit her mother gently on the behind with the swinging boot-bag, and shot ahead, supercharged with excitement and high spirits. Charbury, Charbury, Charbury soon; school life was miles behind already, and she had lost half her interest in the report by the time her mother spun it across the table for her to read at tea.

'Fair; could do better; satisfactory; lacks concentration; carelessness spoils good work . . .' she read down the list of subjects, it was much the same as usual. 'Games: Mary plays a topping game of cricket, but is a rather unenterprising captain,' declared Miss Treadwell in a breezy ingenuous hand. Drawing was good and so was English: 'Shows a keen interest, especially in poetry. Handwriting and spelling lamentable, but essays show originality and imagination. Good progress.' Mary's gratification was duly damped by: 'Position in class: 7th. No. of girls in class: 10.' She looked up and caught her mother watching her, smiled deprecatingly and returned to 'General Remarks.'

'Mary is a dear little girl,' it began, in the chatty, unscholastic style favoured by Miss Carson, 'but we find a tendency in her to resent authority to the point of resistance. Although she is popular with her fellow pupils, I am afraid she is a bad mixer, being at the same time intolerable and unconfident of others and disinclined to enter into the life of the community. But her heart is right, and we feel sure that when she has overcome the difficulties of a rather reserved nature, she will mature into a fine woman.'

'God forbid!' said Uncle Geoffrey when he read it. 'Sounds like Clara Butt as Britannia. These school-marms give me the pip. Why can't they just say: at the moment, she's a blister, but there's hope?'

The first thing Mary did when she got to Charbury that August was to hold a meeting in the Swing Tree, to tell the others about the play. Margaret and Michael were keen, Sarah unmoved, and Denys torn between enthusiasm for the idea and the fact that it wasn't his. 'Who's going to produce it?' he asked doubtfully.

'Well——' Mary had thought she would, but she said instead: 'You can, of course, if you like.'

'Bit of a fag,' he said, 'but—all right. When shall we start?'

During the next few weeks rehearsals were begun with a great deal of giggling, strife, and even physical violence, and were generally ended by someone saying: 'I'm sick of this—let's go and catch water-beetles in the lily pond!' or, 'They're haymaking in the big meadow, let's go and help!' The Play House was to be the theatre, with curtains half-way across, said Denys, to divide the stage from the auditorium.

'Curtains?' said Mrs Wilcox, rising stout and stolid from a crowd of excited, clamouring children. 'I suppose I'm to conjure them out of the air, am I? Don't hustle me, will you?'

52

'But, Wilkie, darling, you must!' shrieked Mary, while Michael tried frantically to stand upside down on his head. 'The play's tomorrow, you know.'

'Well now—how would dust-sheets do you? There's enough and to spare in the west attic, but you must——' Michael came right side up again and they rushed away before she could finish, out of the servants' hall, scampering down the stone passage like a lot of uproarious mice.

'Mary and I'll go up to the attic—you others cut along up to the stables and get heaps of string and a hammer and nails!' shouted Denys. 'Whoops! Come on, Maria—race you to the attic!' He bounced up the back stairs and Mary hurled herself after his flying bare legs. All day the air had been sultry with thunder, charged with an expectant electricity that had got into the children and made them out of control, the despair of the nurses at lunch-time, and working up to a mad excitement as the afternoon darkened before the coming storm. Following Denys along the low passage at the top of the house, Mary felt that she would burst out of her skin with the tingling exuberance that possessed her. She knew Denys felt as crazy as she did, and when they had jumped round the last dark corner and up the three steps into the attic, he began to pull dust-sheets wildly down from the big pile under the sloping beams, laughing and shouting and hurling himself down among them, twisting them around him and kicking his legs. 'Dust-sheets! Dust-sheets!' It seemed a colossal joke. Mary rolled on the floor and yelled with him, dizzy with the stifling smell of camphor. Then without any warning at all, he suddenly clutched hold of her and kissed her. For a second she felt the softness of his lips on hers, and his rumpled hair brushing her forehead, and then they were sitting apart, sobered, staring at each other, Denys' eyes very big and dark, with a strange wild look.

'Hullo, Maria,' he said, and laughed uneasily. 'I feel—Gosh, I don't know——' he got up, stretching his arms above his head. 'I feel all sort of mad inside, don't you? Something's going to happen, I think.' He went over to the window in the gable end. 'My hat, it's getting dark. I say, look at the sky!' She suddenly realized that all the light had gone. She could only just see Denys' white shirt where he stood at the other end of the attic. She went and joined him and together they peered out, awed.

Under the oppressive sky, everything in the garden stood out strangely clear and still. Although it was so dark, you could almost see each individual blade of dry summer grass, waiting. . . . The first huge drops of rain fell weightily, one by one, gathered force, and then: 'Here it comes!' shouted Denys, and the storm broke, with thunder, lightning, and sheets of rain all together.

It was a queer feeling to be watching the storm up here with Denys.

They might have been alone in the house. They held hands, and stood quite close, the blue shirt-sleeve against the white, bare forearms touching, neither admitting to fear even when the lightning slit the black sky with a jagged white streak, or the thunder crashed right overhead with a noise like a million falling planks.

'Where in the world have you been?' demanded Nanny, when they came down after the storm had passed, still a little lightheaded, their arms full of dust-sheets, their eyes on the tea-table.

'Watching the storm from the west attic,' said Denys airily. 'Wasn't it a super one?'

'I'm glad you think so,' said Nanny, taking off the tea cosy and pouring herself another cup of tea, sniffily. 'Here's Margaret been half out of her mind with fear. Such a circus as we've had with her, haven't we, Nurse?'

'We have indeed,' said Nurse. 'Thank you, Nanny, just one more cup, then, if I'm not greedy,' and Margaret looked up from her Swiss roll proudly, hoping she looked pale. 'Silly cow,' said Denys, 'where's the currant bread and butter?'

'It's been finished, and there's going to be no more cut,' said Nanny. 'Those who come late must go without. Mary, put those dust-sheets tidily in the corner before you sit down. You can do what you like in your mother's house, I daresay, but make my nursery into a pigsty you shall not.'

'When are we going to put them up?' asked Michael, coming out of his mug with a white moustache.

'After tea,' said Denys, and Nanny added automatically: 'You'll put on mackintoshes and Wellingtons, before you go out in this rain.'

> *'We start manœuvres after tea,*
> *Dust-sheets numbering twenty-three,'*

said Mary with a sudden flash of inspiration, and she said it again, she liked it so much. Phrases that rhymed always fascinated her. She loved:

> *'Maisonette*
> *To be let,'*

on House Agents' boards, and almost the only history she knew was:

> *'Sixteen hundred and sixty-six*
> *London was burnt to rotten sticks.'*

And

> *'In forty-four a foreign host*
> *From Gaul assailed our southern coast.'*

54

After tea, Aunt Winifred came into the nursery to borrow a book. She was peculiar; she read their picture books and comic papers, and once Mary had missed a golliwog for days, and had found it in the pocket of Aunt Winifred's Burberry. The servants and the nurses talked about her in whispers, clicking their teeth, and the grown-ups told the children that they must always be especially kind to Aunt Winifred, and never, never laugh at her. It had not occurred to them to do so; they accepted her quite incuriously as a sort of hybrid—neither a grown-up nor a child—who was often sulky and taciturn and didn't bother anyone. She was just Aunt Winifred, who wore colourless, shapeless clothes on her heavy body, and had a large pasty face that somehow looked wrong, as if all the features had slipped a little, and made it not quite a face after all. She had moods sometimes when no one must speak to her, and she would go tramping off by herself for hours and come back with her brogues and woollen stockings clogged with mud, and her dry, dun-coloured hair escaping in wisps from the coil over each ear.

'Are you coming to our play, Aunt Winifred?' Sarah asked her, as she searched in the glass-fronted bookcase for a book. She spun round.

'Oh, yes, if I may. Have you asked me?'

'Course,' said Denys, 'everyone's coming.' Aunt Winifred seemed pleased. A large smile spread over her heavy face as she turned back to the bookcase. 'I love seeing plays,' she said. 'What's it called?'

'*Love's Golden Ending*,' said Mary, and Aunt Winifred turned round with *The Golliwogs at the Seaside* clasped to her breast.

'Oh, that's lovely, that's beautiful,' she said. '*Love's Golden Ending*. . . .' Her mouth was slack, her eyes staring rapt at the opposite wall.

'Well, actually,' said Mary, 'it was Mrs Linney's brother's idea. I couldn't think of a good title, and he was here one day when I was talking to Mrs Linney about it. He has a paper shop, you know, in Taunton, so he knows about books and things, and he said straight off: "Why not call it *Love's Golden Ending*?" Wasn't it marvellously clever? I've dedicated the play to him. Well, good-bye, we've got to go now.' They were all putting on their Wellingtons and mackintoshes, and Nurse was tying under Michael's chin the strings of an oilskin sou'wester, which he would take off the minute he was out of her sight. Aunt Winifred didn't want them to go. Sometimes she didn't come near the children for days at a time, and at others she seemed to cling to them almost humbly, as if she had lost something and thought they could help her to find it. They galloped off into the rain, shouting: 'We start manœuvres after tea, dust-sheets numbering twenty-three,' jumping off the terrace into a puddle on the drive, squelching through sodden leaves into the pattering damp of the beechwood. Mary, looking back for a moment, saw Aunt Winifred standing in the french windows looking after them, the book still clasped in front of her, the driving rain bouncing off the stone terrace into troops of little marching men at her feet.

Apart from the fact that the actors, having about three different parts each, kept confusing their lines, that Michael extemporized doggedly all through, and that Sarah, as the Queen-Mother, lost her knickers half-way through the first act, the play was a smash hit. All the grown-ups came and sat on the assortment of chairs and stools and packing-cases, with Granny in her bath-chair in the middle. Mrs Cotterell brought Bubbles, who was so furious at not being in the play that he threatened to have a fit and had to be taken home half-way through.

The nurses grudgingly entrusted Julia and the new baby, John, to the care of Mrs Wilcox, who said she didn't trouble about theatricals, and 'kept themselves *to* themselves' on a bench at the side, and some of the servants hung about against the backwall as if they were trying to obliterate themselves right through it.

The audience laughed in all the right places and not too many of the wrong ones, and Margaret, as the butler, brought down the house by shaking up the decanter of Jeyes' Fluid, which was supposed to be port.

'Don't shake the *port!*' A simultaneous roar came from Grandpa and Uncle Guy and Uncle Tim, and the bewildered Margaret stood blinking behind the thick lenses of her glasses, looking helplessly towards her mother. 'It's all right, dear,' hissed Aunt Grace, looking up from her crochet, 'very nice, indeed. Go on, dear.' Mary put out a leg behind her chair and kicked Margaret on the ankle, and Denys, waiting impatiently outside the window for his entrance was heard to say: 'Get on with it, you feeble ass.'

Before the last act, he stepped out in front of the curtain in his velvet, cottonwool-trimmed cloak that had come out of the dressing-up box in the attic, and made a speech, which they had decided, from long experience of their parents, would be essential.

'Ladies and Gentlemen, during the execution scene in the next act, mothers' (with a glance at his own) 'are requested to keep their seats, and *not* rush on to the stage, because it's really not as dangerous as it looks.' With this alarming announcement, the dust-sheet folded over the string behind him slid jerkily aside, revealing a hanging noose. Aunt Mavis gave a slight scream, Granny said, 'Oh, dear,' and Taggie behind her said, 'Will you look at that?' and the black furry caterpillars that were her eyebrows shot up into her hair. 'A trifle macabre. Almost Tchekov, one might say,' murmured Uncle Guy, as he crossed his long legs and leaned back, preparing to enjoy himself. Needless to say, when Sarah, as Sir Egbert of Corsica, in Denys' riding breeches and boots with a green satin blouse of her mother's, dropped through the trap-door and was hanged, mothers and aunts rushed on to the stage as one protesting woman. The play came to an abrupt end, cutting off Denys' 'Darling, I loved you the very first moment I saw you,' and the final kiss.

'But I *told* you——' he protested through the uproar. 'Oh, these women!' He shrugged his shoulders and walked off the stage to join the men. Mary was so excited by the play's success, that she was not upset by its untimely end, although she was disappointed to miss even a theatrical embrace from Denys. The most chagrined person was Michael, who, in the executioner's bransack, was all ready to play 'God Save the King' on his mouth-organ, and now nobody wanted to hear.

Afterwards they all had tea in the summer-house, still wearing their costumes. Mary sat on her grandfather's knee in the evening dress that had been short-skirted on her mother, but trailed about her feet, and they shared a slab of chocolate cake, while he told her how clever she was. Even Uncle Lionel praised the play, although he showed the same tedious inclination to hold post-mortems that made people loth to play bridge with him.

Granny argued mildly with him. 'You can't improve on a master-piece, Li,' she said from her high-backed basket chair. 'Give me another cup of tea, will you, Mavis dear? My silly throat's so dry again.' She began to cough, holding up her little lace-edged handkerchief that always smelt faintly of lavender.

'You should rest your voice, you know, Mother,' said Mavis. 'You oughtn't to talk at all when you're tired.' Grandpa put Mary off his knee and went over to his wife, bending over her, patting her jerking shoulders. 'I'll get you your lozenges, shall I, dearest?'

'No, let one of the children go. Margaret—off you go! Quick sharp!' said Uncle Lionel in the martial tone which he used for giving orders to his children. 'Of course, Daddy,' said Margaret, and was off across the lawn, with her spidery legs going in all directions.

'Now then, Denys,' said Aunt Mavis. 'You shouldn't sit back and let a girl run about. Where are your manners?'

'She likes it,' he said. 'Anyway, I promised to go and have an hour at the nets with Bates before the light goes. Excuse me, everybody.' He got up, and began to stroll off, feinting a swish at the head of a rose with his wooden sword as he went.

'No, Denys——' said Granny anxiously.

'Aha!' he twirled round suddenly. 'I wasn't going to! I'll split thy guts, foul knave!' He lunged at her, his dark eyes dancing, and she

57

laughed with him, captivated. 'Begone!' she said, beginning to cough again, and Denys left them, his swaggering back view showing that he thought all eyes were upon him.

He was particularly glorious that summer, Mary thought. The long, outdoor holidays put a deeper tan on his brown skin, and when they went over in the old Lancia to bathe at Lyme Regis, he dug a trench in the sand as deep as himself, and afterwards swam right out to sea, while Mary paddled like a dog in the shallows, with one foot on the bottom. At Taunton Gymkhana, he won the children's jumping competition on Warrior, stiff-jointed but ardent, and Uncle Tom, who was home on leave, introduced him to the glorious red-faced Master of Hounds, who said he was a likely youngster and he would blood him next season. The fact that he was going to Public School in a month—three weeks—a fortnight's time, haloed him with an extra glamour. Mary was almost afraid of him. When he left for London, she made her farewell to him as casual as his to her, and afterwards she went up to the West Attic, and stood on the spot where he had, incredibly, kissed her, and said out loud in the dusty silence: 'God make him enjoy himself, and make him be Captain of cricket as soon as possible, and please let him still like me when he comes back.'

Chapter Four

IN spite of the fact that she paraphrased 'Much have I travelled in the realms of gold' as 'I have made several expeditions to the gold-mine district,' and had to write a French essay on trees without knowing the word for leaf, Mary passed the entrance examination for St Martin's High School.

She cried when she left Manton House, not because she minded, but because it was the thing to do. Miss Cardew kissed her in the hot-house temperature of the study and told her always to remember the School motto: 'Faint not nor fear,' to which Mary only just stopped herself from replying automatically: 'Half-time is near, then comes the biscuits and ginger beer.'

Carrying a new cardboard suitcase that looked like leather and wearing a cumbersome navy blue coat and a velour hat of unbelievable hardness and ugliness, Mary approached the imposing edifice of St Martin's. Under the coat, she wore a dark blue serge tunic with a red and white shield embroidered on the bosom, and a white shirt slightly too large to allow for shrinking. At thirteen, she was still very small for her age, with her hair still uncut but worn now over her ears, and showing a distinct tendency to wave, that sent Mrs Shannon into ecstasies.

Those first few days at St Martin's showed Mary why people hang themselves with a dressing-gown cord behind their bedroom door. Out of the two hundred and fifty odd girls, nobody spoke to her. She did not know where the lavatories were, and she hid at lunch-time because she did not know where to sit. She sat dumbly through lessons, avoided the playing-field and walked round the playground an outcast, her head splitting with loneliness. She had never minded being alone before, it had often been desirable, but here it was despicable and conspicuous. The herd were happy, the pariahs were wretched, and she saw no hope of ever joining the herd. Not that they seemed particularly attractive, but their very lack of charm made all the more galling their reluctance to receive her. There was one girl that she kept seeing—a tall, radiant creature, with a real grown-up bosom covered with medals, who was always dashing about somewhere, as if she had all the things in the world to do. Every time she flashed by, Mary, who never had anything to do, would blush scarlet and gaze after her with breathless awe.

All the time she was at St Martin's, even when she was in the thick of everything, and herself one of the goddesses who turned new girls to stone, there was never a time when she could say to herself: 'I am part of this place; I am one of the things that make it.' She never got rid of the idea that it belonged to the other people and that she was only there on sufferance.

There were three other new girls in her class, but two of them were friendly already and went about glued to each other, eyeing everyone else suspiciously. The other, a girl called Angela Shaw, was mad. She was so eccentric and made such disconcerting remarks that people would look at her, bewildered, and say: 'I say, Shaw, are you *ill* or what?' After a time, she turned out to be quite normal and eventually became Mary's best friend.

'When I came here,' she explained to Mary, 'nobody took any notice of me, so I thought, "Well, I'll jolly well make them notice me; I'll be mad." So I was, and they did.'

This filled Mary with admiration; her own first term at St Martin's was taken up with trying to be exactly like other people, and trying to cope with the work, which was far beyond the wildest efforts of Manton House. She had hours of homework to do after tea, and it was a pathetic sight to see Mary with rumpled hair escaped from its slide and falling over her shoulders, ink-stains on her fingers and nose; her mother sitting beside her with puckered brows trying to cast her mind back to the days of the Dulwich High School, and Uncle Geoffrey breathing down the back of Mary's neck, out of his depth but willing to have a good guess, all tearing themselves to bits over an Algebra problem.

'If a tank is filled by three taps in $97\frac{3}{4}$ hours——' he would say, with the air of Archimedes pondering in his bath. 'And the tank is $9\frac{7}{8}$ by 14 by $131\frac{1}{4}$ yards in vol.' said Mary, sucking her pencil gloomily.

'What's this?' put in Mrs Shannon, 'something about water pressure——'

'No,' said Mary irritably, 'you're looking at the next sum. Oh, I'll never do it and Miss Whitworth is terribly mean, you know. She says I could do the work if I would give my mind to it. If she could see me——'

'Let x equal the volume of water,' hazarded Mrs Shannon. 'No, that won't do; the answer's got to be in hours. What on earth do they mean by that?'

'If a tank——' said Uncle Geoffrey, whose policy was, when in doubt, always go back to the beginning.

'Mummy,' said Mary, 'I suppose when I leave school, all this'll be of some use? I mean—well, why does one learn things, I often wonder.'

'Oh, well, darling, if you want to have a job when you're grown-up——'

'Oh, no, I shan't do that, I'm going to be married and have twenty-six children with names going all through the alphabet, like Arthur, Barbara, Chloë, Egbert, Felicity, George, Harriet, Ipheginia——'

'All right,' said her mother, 'I can guess the rest. But even if you don't have a job, you have to be educated in order to take your place among people, to be able to hold your own in conversation.'

'Well, you can't do Algebra, and you seem to get on all right.'

Uncle Geoffrey snorted, and Mrs Shannon said: 'Get on with your homework. You're getting ideas beyond your age. Now, let x equal the rate of filling——'

'If a tank,' mused Uncle Geoffrey doggedly.

There was so much to learn at St Martin's besides the actual work. You had to know all sorts of subtleties, like using people's surnames and calling food 'grub.' Mary was struck over the head by a giantess in her first game of lacrosse, and bumped on the nose at netball. Drill was called gym, and besides plaiting her hair and exposing herself in her blue serge knickers with elastic at waist and knee, she had to hang by one hand from a bar right up in the ceiling, or struggle incapably on the end of a swinging rope, taking all the skin off her feet and hands in her desperate attempts to go upwards.

Not having yet learned that the first person who speaks to you on a cruise invariably turns out to be the ship's bore, Mary was caught unawares when a girl with a lumpy skin and fuzzy hair that hung in a thick pigtail down her skinny back, made overtures to her in the play-ground. It took her nearly two months to throw off what proved to be the oppressive attachment of Muriel Hopkins.

Muriel was like those undergraduates whose political and religious convictions are as obtrusive as their Adam's apples, and who, despair-ing of converting their seasoned contemporaries, tackle every freshman in the first bloom of his gullibility. Her opening gambit according to comparisons that Mary made later with Angela Shaw, never varied.

Mary was walking aimlessly round the playground during break, solitary among the shouting, ball-throwing, gregarious horde, when Muriel materialized from the mêlée, and fell into step beside her, saying: 'Your name's Mary Shannon, isn't it?' She was a close-range talker, and as they walked, she peered sideways, thrusting her face close to Mary's. 'You're a new girl,' she said, 'aren't you?'

'Yes,' said Mary, gratified at being addressed by anyone.

'Where d'you live?'

'Near Olympia. In a flat.'

'I live at Sheen. My father's a doctor there, you know.' Mary thought it was a pity he didn't do something about his daughter's breath. Muriel was saying: 'What does your father do?'

'He's dead.'

'Oh, dear, that's sad, isn't it?' She had an insistent way of stressing every remark with a question, as if she were determined that the other person should reply. When all the personal details had been elicited, diffidently from Mary, and spontaneously from Muriel, she suddenly said, bringing her face so close to Mary's that her prominent blue eyes became one: 'Will you be my best friend?'

'Well'—It was rather staggering, but it meant salvation from solitude and from ignominy when a mistress said: 'Take partners all!' so Mary said hesitatingly, 'Yes, if you like.'

Muriel breathed a sigh of relief and mercifully withdrew her face a fraction. 'Let's try and change our desks so that we can sit next in form, shall we?' she said happily.

It was Muriel who said to Mary, in front of several others, 'You think Avril Goss is an angel, don't you?' In spite of the fact that she had no idea who Avril Goss was, it was clearly expected of her to say heartily, 'Of course!' and thus Mary was saddled with her first and only 'Crush.'

Avril Goss turned out to be the girl who had dazzled Mary on her first day. Once having committed herself to a deathless passion, there was no backing out, and although the system was entirely new to her, she gradually gathered what her emotions were supposed to be. Stimulated by the power of suggestion and the fanatical example of Muriel and half the Lower Fourth, she rapidly got to the state of turning giddy whenever Avril passed, and when the goddess, who was Lacrosse Captain, was knocked over the hand by the bestial goalkeeper from all Saints', Ruislip, Mary and Muriel came giggling to school with two fingers on the left hand bandaged.

When she plunged into her other world in the holidays, Mary told Denys about everything at St Martin's, except Avril Goss. Although he talked a lot about a hero called the Elder Thompson, she was afraid he would think her silly and perhaps disloyal. It might be difficult to make him understand that the affaire Goss was only something to add a spice to school life, and did not affect in any way her love for him.

Most of her second term was spent hiding in doorways or round corners, either to see Avril go by, or to avoid Muriel. Her best friend's conversation was turning out to be almost exclusively confined to stories of the District Railway, such as how she had forgotten her season or got carried on to Richmond: 'Wasn't it a shriek? Wasn't it, Mary?' Spring seemed to be doing her breath no good.

Mary took a long time to shake her off. Once, on a rash impulse, she had taken her home to tea. Mrs Shannon was not yet back from the College, and Uncle Geoffrey had taken one look at Muriel and had to go out and see a man about the back legs of a horse. The two girls were left together with the tea that Mrs Duckett had laid before she 'loved them and left them' and went home to Fulham. Muriel ate everything she could lay hands on, and said: 'Are those your birds? Was that your Uncle? Fancy not having more pictures on the walls. At Sheen, we've got a grand piano in the drawing-room.' Mary noticed for the first time how dirty her neck was; it was not so conspicuous, somehow, at school.

'What would you like to do?' she said after tea. She felt fidgety. Muriel was out of place, she didn't belong here. Nobody belonged in her home, she realized, except the people who looked as natural in it as the furniture.

'I don't mind,' said Muriel, shaking her pigtail over her shoulder and back again in a way she had. 'I know,' she giggled, 'let's write a letter to Avril, shall we, and put it in her locker tomorrow. She'll never know who wrote it. Shall we?'

'No,' said Mary, 'don't let's.' Avril did not belong here any more than Muriel. They ought both to be immured for life within the walls of St Martin's. 'We really ought to do our homework, I suppose,' she said, 'there's all that geometry for tomorrow.' She began to clear the table. Beyond saying: 'Oh, do you clear the table yourself? At Sheen——' Muriel made no effort to help. They spread their books and papers and pencil-boxes over the table by the window. Muriel had a superior pencil-box with her initials stamped on the lid and every sort and colour of pen and pencil inside. She also had a leather folder containing enough geometrical instruments to elevate St Paul's, and a black fountain pen clipped into the top of her tunic. Mary, who had never before wanted to have more than one pencil chewed to ribbons, one relief pen ditto, one ink-stained ruler and a pair of compasses without a screw, was irritated. And she could not work out her theorem.

'Can you do the first one?' she asked Muriel.

'Oh yes, I've done it ages ago. It's ever so easy. I'm on number three now.'

'Be an angel and tell me how to do it.'

'Oh, I can't, that'd be cheating.'

'Well, you might at least give me a hint,' said Mary bitterly, remembering all the times she had seen Muriel peering over the shoulder of Felicity Peters, who sat in front of them in form.

'All right, I suppose I can. You have to draw a line at right angles to the base of the triangle; that's all I'm going to tell you.'

'It doesn't help at all,' said Mary crossly, and hurled her note-book across the room. 'I'm not going to do the rotten thing.'

'You'll get a report,' said Muriel, writing Q.E.D. at the bottom of a page and ruling two perfectly symmetrical ink-lines underneath it with immense satisfaction. Mary blinked back tears of anger. Muriel took out her history book and began to copy down a list of dates; she seemed to have settled in for the night. How did one get rid of guests? Her mother would know; Mary wished she would come home.

Mrs Shannon arrived tired, but with an idea that she must be nice to Mary's friends, whatever they looked like, so she detained Muriel with conversation and even suggested a game of rummy. Muriel, who had never played before, was very slow and dense, could not shuffle, always had to be told when it was her turn to play, and ended up by winning.

By sheer overpowering persistence, she forced Mary down to Sheen, a visit that Mary described afterwards to her mother as solid purgatory. They had milk, not tea, two sorts of cake, rivals in dullness, and scones with not enough butter on them, at a huge mahogany table in the dining-room, which had still-life pictures on the walls and smelt of Sunday lunch.

There was Dr Hopkins, who evidently had a way with children and talked to Mary with untiring coyness all through tea; Muriel's younger brother, who wore football boots and showed all the food in his mouth when he laughed; Muriel's baby sister, with an immense white bow in her hair, who must have been at least six but followed the successful policy of behaving like a precocious three or four, and Mrs Hopkins, a fatter edition of Muriel, who called the children 'people,' and was intent on drawing Mary into the simple happiness of their family life.

Afterwards they played snakes and ladders, at which Muriel's brother and sister both cheated, and then Muriel took Mary up to her room and took her through six photograph albums and a packet of postcards collected from the bleaker seaside resorts all over England. They sat on the bed and Mary kicked something underneath that went ping, which made her shudder as much as the sight of the hairs trailing through Muriel's brush and comb on the dressing-table.

Soon after this, Mary and Angela Shaw discovered that they liked each other, and so, having no longer any need for Muriel's company, Mary weaned her with more determination and brutality. After a while, Muriel stopped following her about saying: 'Sit *next*?' and 'We are friends, aren't we?' and, with the well-known gleam in her eye, attacked the batch of new girls who arrived at the beginning of the summer term.

Angela Shaw was the first girl that Mary had ever wholeheartedly liked. She was much taller than Mary, with legs that looked endless in her black school stockings, and tunic that was always shorter than anybody else's. She had a face like a boy's, freckled and snub-nosed, with soft, light eyebrows and lashes, but an entirely feminine crop of curly red-gold hair, that fell over one eye in an artless, endearing fore-lock. Mistresses, according to the degree of authority that they commanded, described her manners as unfortunate, defiant, unsporting or 'downright rude.' Mary could be as sullen or rebellious as anyone on occasion, but she never achieved the glorious abandon with which Angela simply went her own way, uncaring. She managed to avoid complete censure, because she was clever and could toss off an Ovid translation, or an essay on the causes and results of the Reformation with as much ease as she tossed an inkwell out of the window on to the Eton-cropped head of the hockey mistress.

That summer, Mary asked if she might invite her to Charbury, and Granny wrote back to say: 'Of course, darling, bring the whole school if you like.' She invited her during a cricket match, while they were waiting for their turn to go out and bat for their form against the demon round-arm bowler of the Lower Fifth. As she did so, remembering Muriel Hopkins, she had a momentary qualm. Would Angela realize that she was going to paradise?

Angela, who had heard enough about Charbury to sicken a less enthusiastic character, reacted gratifyingly. She was thrilled, 'But I shall be scared stiff,' she said. 'Isn't it all frightfully super, with people going huntin' and shootin' all the time and butlers called Death handing round the Boar's Head on solid gold plate?' Mary laughed and told her about the nursery, where all the children except Denys had their meals in growing disregard of the nurses; the tea parties in the servants' hall, with fortune-telling by the under-housemaid, who was reputed to have been left in the hedge as a baby by gipsies; and what Uncle Guy had looked like when, in front of everybody, he fell off Buck into a heap of manure when the hounds met at Charbury.

'Shaw, Shaw! Wake up there!' Miss Simmons was blowing a whistle and waving frantically from the cricket pitch.

'Oh curse, is somebody out? It's me to go in, then. 'Bye, and thanks awfully—I'll be back in a sec—I always am.' She pranced off to the wicket swinging her bat and proceeded to swipe blindly at every ball within reach, connecting sometimes, to her own vast surprise and the disapproval of Miss Simmons, whose motto was Style before Boundaries.

Once she was satisfied that Angela would appreciate it, Mary looked forward to showing off Charbury to her; she was as proud of it as if it were her own. Angela herself lived with casual affluence in a large house in Regent's Park. Mary used to lunch there sometimes on Sundays, and she was always reduced to paralysis by the black sea of dining-table with its lonely little islands of lace mats and cutlery and glasses, and the aristocratic anæmia of Mrs Shaw, who had to have special pernickety food in a separate silver entrée dish, and who looked as though her feet were not made for walking, nor her hands for doing anything more than each colouring the other's nails a delicate shell pink. She used to embarrass Mary by stroking her long hair and saying she was charmingly old-fashioned and looked like Reynolds' 'Age of Innocence.' It was funny to think that she was the mother of Angela, who treated her awe-inspiring surroundings as if they had been a one-roomed shack, and thought nothing of crawling under the table if she felt inclined, or bursting into laughter through her ginger ale, and misting the polished table with spray.

'Gently, dear, gently,' her mother would say vaguely, while Mary sat silently wondering how to eat her asparagus. She always felt more at ease when Mr Shaw was there, for, although he could not be trusted not to slap you on the back when your mouth was full of food, he was reassuringly genial. He was a great hippopotamus of a man, with flat feet and a roaring laugh, who worshipped his only child to the verge of imbecility, and any friend of Angela's was automatically swept into the hurricane of his affection.

'Herbert Shannon's grand-daughter, eh?' he had said, embracing Mary at their first meeting. 'I must be one of his best customers. Well, young woman, you can tell your grandfather from me that his *Filet de Sole Maison* is simply——' He kissed his fingers to the air, and brought them down to chuck Mary neatly under the chin. Sometimes he played

c

tennis with them on the hard court in the garden. Angela was very good and Mary was very bad, and Mr Shaw, who had been a champion in the vanished days of his boyish figure, wallowed about on the other side of the net, turning to liquid before their eyes, his white flannels refusing to come higher than half-way up his stomach. He was not always there, however, for even on Sundays he was often too busy making money in what Angela dismissed as 'something to do with advertising.' When he was not out somewhere in his long black Chrysler, he would be shut in his study with a tray of beer and sandwiches, and going past the door the girls would hear him telephoning at full blast.

There were also dread Sabbaths when Mrs Shannon took Mary to lunch with her grandparents at Dulwich. When he could not think of a plausible excuse, Uncle Geoffrey had to come too.

'My life in two continents,' he said to Mary, as they sat despondently on the bus one morning with Mrs Shannon chattering from the seat behind. 'Or "From Regent's Park to the Crystal Palace," by Mary Shannon.' 'Last Sunday,' said Mary dreamily, 'they had a sort of Lobster Mousse, and then Chicken Salad and Chocolate Ice.'

'This Sunday,' he said, 'I can promise you boiled mutton with gree-ee-eens,' he pronounced the word with venom, 'underdone potatoes, cold gravy, and—if you're a very lucky girl—a scrumptious spotted dog to follow. Just the thing for a hot day.'

'Don't, Geoffrey,' said his sister, 'she's naughty enough about going to Mother's as it is, without you encouraging her.'

'Ha!' he said, and subsided into a sulky schoolboy silence. As they walked up the hill from the bus stop, Mrs Shannon said, as she always did: 'D'you remember how tired we used to get walking up here from school, Geoff? I'm not sure it wasn't cruelty to children. Our poor little legs——' They toiled on, past the large, sad houses of Clarice Hill, where it seemed impossible to think that anybody young had ever lived, and turned in at the gate you couldn't miss, for the plaster on the posts was the dirtiest in the road.

'Shades of my boyhood,' remarked Uncle Geoffrey, as they rounded the semi-circle of laurels to the front door. 'Shades of the prison house begin to close——' he added, as broken-down Annie opened the door to them and they passed into the long dark hall-way of 'Laureldene.'

Mary always connected places inseparably with their smells: the Charbury smell, the Clifford Court smell, the smell of hot girls in the dressing-room of St Martin's, the clean paint and the heady scent of too exotic flowers in the spacious hall at the Shaws'. The smell that haunted the hall of her grandmother's house was among the nastiest in her collection. It was a mixture of fusty clothes and meals. Not meals to come—the appetizing savour, perhaps, of a roast, as you came ravenously in at the front door, but the lurking shade of meals that had been; the stale story of bygone cabbage soup, or the deathless reek of stew that had drifted and settled there from kitchen and dining-room.

Mrs Payne received them in the drawing-room. Although it was needlessly large, she had refused to shut it up, and as Annie, with equal stubbornness, refused to dust unnecessarily, they had compromised by draping the back half of the room in dust-sheets and newspapers and only using the front half. Whether or not Annie was taking advantage of Gran's failing perception, it seemed to Mary that every time she saw the room the uncovered half was slightly smaller, as if the dust-sheets, like an encroaching tide, were seeping imperceptibly over everything, until finally, even the shabby old lady in the tapestry chair would be just another ghostly, cotton-covered mound.

Gran's house always gave her eerie thoughts, and Gran herself was not too comfortable a presence; Mary had been terrified of her when she was very young. Once, when she had been put to sleep in Gran's bedroom after lunch, she had been woken by the yellowing, blear-eyed face that always twitched a little, bending over her. Mary had got such a fright, that she had gone completely over the top, and had cried and screamed for hours and had to be given bromide, and taken home in a stupor. Nobody ever knew what Gran thought about this insult. As she hardly ever spoke her mind, you never knew whether a thing had passed her by, or whether she were storing it up to produce triumphantly at some inconvenient time like the Last Judgment. She was only a year or two older than her other grandmother, but to Mary they might have been two different generations. Granny Shannon was ageless in the sense of seeming eternally young, whereas Gran Payne was ageless because the years of her decreptitude were uncountable.

She was helped downstairs by her son and daughter, with Mary following behind carrying her footstool, and it was as Uncle Geoffrey had predicted—boiled mutton. Mary looked at him as Gran said: 'Will you carve the mutton, Geoffrey, on the sideboard?' and he winked at her with both eyes in turn, for he did not wear his monocle at Dulwich. Mrs Shannon said brightly: 'Oh, how nice, Mother, I always like a joint,' and frowned at her brother. Annie handed round the vegetables with a take-it-or-leave-it air that made the brussels sprout tops look more lank, the potatoes more exhausted, and the meal proceeded to the exhilarating accompaniment of a glass of tonic wine apiece, watered down for Mary.

It was said at St Martin's that if you could eat the school lunches you could eat anything, but Mary found Gran's food difficult to stomach. Mrs Payne had a good appetite, but very little sense of taste, and Annie, trading on this, probably had some commission system with the tradesmen, whereby they unloaded on 'Laureldene' all the food that nobody else would have. The mutton today had obviously been the bell-wether of the flock. Afterwards came, not spotted Dick, but bread-and-butter pudding, with a few deceptive currants on top and none underneath. 'Cream today as a special treat,' said Gran, but it turned out to be only the top of the milk, slightly gone off.

As Mrs Payne lived the life of a complete recluse, and would not even read the papers, because they were unsettling, nor any book more modern than Mrs Humphry Ward, she had nothing to talk about except the trials that beset her. Mary could remember that her husband had been a very complaining man, too; he was always shaking one leg and saying that his big toe was tingling, or demanding that someone should feel how cold his hands were. In the intervals of champing noisily at her food, Gran delivered a few creaking observations on the state of her sciatica, and the itching in her scalp, and told how a nip in the air had presumed to catch her unawares without her spencer. Her daughter Lily made gallant efforts to entertain her with outside news, but she had been out of the world so long that it had little interest for her. Uncle Geoffrey hardly spoke at all except to ask if there was any cheese, when he saw the bread-and-butter pudding.

When she was neither talking nor eating, Gran had a disconcerting habit of watching. Mary, looking up once from her pale pink drink, caught the eyes under the hooding lids fixed on her intently as though Gran were reading every thought in her brain. Mary smiled nervously, and Gran said, without removing her gaze, 'The flies this summer seem to be worse than ever.'

It was uncanny not to know whether she said this on purpose to camouflage what she had been thinking, or whether she had not really been looking at Mary at all. Later on, when Mary thought she was watching Uncle Geoffrey, she suddenly said: 'I hear Mary's head girl of her school,' which was an obvious invention to cover her real thoughts, for she could not possibly have heard anything of the sort. Nanny would have called her a parcel of deceit, and Mary even doubted at times whether she was really her mother's mother. She had a theory, inspired by the origin of the Charbury housemaid, that Mrs Payne had found Lily in a basket on her doorstep, and characteristically concealed the facts.

After lunch, they had to stay until it was time for the old lady to take her rest. 'Not that I ever sleep,' she said, though Mary had more than once heard her snores revervebating through the house, before they had even time to put on their hats and coats. Up in the drawing-room, Mrs Shannon and Uncle Geoffrey smoked, while their mother flapped her hand in front of her face and coughed ostentatiously. The same collection of infantile books that had been appearing since she was six was brought out from the bottom shelf of the bookcase for Mary. She sat on the floor and looked idly at the unpleasant pictures in *Struwelplter* which she knew by heart, and wondered how old Gran thought she was.

At last Annie appeared at the door with a stone hot bottle, saying, 'Time for your lay down,' and when Mary had suffered the agony of the good-bye kiss, she was free. Free to hustle her mother and uncle into their outdoor clothes and out of the house, free to scrabble past the laurels, bolt out of the gate and hare down Clarice Hill, bowling imaginary balls, working the infection of old age out of her young limbs.

The end of the summer term saw the introduction, at Speech Day, of Mary's mother and Angela's father, and they took to each other so well that old Smithie, the Geography Mistress, had to shush them into silence during the Head Mistress's Speech about minor epidemics, clement weather, and Scholarships at Girton. It also saw the extinction of the last flicker of Mary's attachment to Avril Goss, who appeared on the last day wearing a choker of pink pearls and shiny silk stockings that revealed the true nature of her legs.

On the day after Bank Holiday, Mrs Shannon, Mary and Angela went down to Charbury. Uncle Lionel and his family were not there that summer, for they had departed, with all the trappings of sea-sick nurses, Humanized Trufood and folding prams, for the Golf Hotel, Digues-sur-mer, Belgium. Aunt Mavis wrote to say that the drains were a scandal and that Margaret and John were both down with foot-and-mouth disease.

With everyone at Charbury, Angela was an immediate success. She arrived with a wardrobe of expensive clothes that her mother considered suitable for a country-house visit, and spent the whole time in a pair of Denys' old blue football shorts and any shirt that she could find in the bathroom airing cupboard. Granny and Granpa said she was a sweet child; Uncle Guy said she was sex-appeal in embryo, to which Aunt Mavis replied, 'I don't know what you mean.' Mrs Linney said she was a real cup of tea; Bates said she would never make a cricketer; Tom said she would take a cab-horse round Aintree if she'd a mind to it. Nanny said: 'I'm glad I didn't have the bringing of you up'; Julia said, 'Pretty Angela, tell Ju-ju story'; and Denys said she and Mary were the only two girls he'd spend five minutes with. Mary had been terrified at first that he would not like Angela, and then she was terrified that he liked her too much.

He was just sixteen, almost as tall as his father, with the glory of being Captain of the Second Eleven and twelfth man for the first, and the middle-weight boxing champion of the school. Since that first soft boy's kiss in the attic his feelings towards Mary had been entirely undemonstrative. This seemed right to her, for kissing she knew was both unpleasant and unhealthy. Once, the lift-boy at Clifford Court, who was shortly afterwards convicted for assaulting a little girl on Barnes Common, had tried to slobber all over her in the lift. She vowed that she would never kiss anyone, even Denys, as long as she lived.

She never went with him when he went rabbit shooting, because she hated it when a rabbit was killed, and he said it was a wet blanket to have somebody around who said, 'Good,' every time he missed, so he took Angela instead. One day, they were away nearly four hours, while Mary moped about in the garden in an agony of half-ashamed jealousy. When tea-time had come and gone, she was already composing brave little speeches that she would say to Denys: 'Don't think of me; I'm glad you love her,' and 'I hope you'll always let me be your friend.' She was almost in tears by the time Angela's shining head appeared over the top of the ha-ha. Seeing Mary on the distant terrace, she hailed her and galloped up the three levels of the lawn, waving a rabbit by its hind-legs.

'Look what I did!' she shouted. 'Wasn't it ghastly of me? I felt awful about being bucked when I hit him. It was quite by mistake, too, I can't aim for toffee. Look at his lovely fur and all,' she stroked the stiffening body regretfully. 'Oh, sorry, I forgot. You don't like it, do you?' She plumped down on the stone seat beside Mary, with her long brown legs stretched out in front of her, and they watched Denys following slowly up the lawn, carrying three more rabbits and looking very manly, with the gun over his shoulder.

'I'm glad you had fun,' said Mary nobly, hoping she was not going to cry.

'I wish you'd been with us, though,' said Angela. 'And so did Denys; he said so. I wish I had a cousin like that. Mine all treat me worse than if I was their sister. You are a lucky beggar; and having this super place to come to whenever you want. The nearest my family ever get to the country is Sunningdale.'

Denys swung on to the terrace and dropped the rabbits at Mary's feet. 'What d'you think of the bag?' he said with casual pride, and as she beamed up at him, a last burst of evening sunshine flung his long fantastic shadow across the terrace and flooded everything with a glorious amber light.

In the winter of 1931, when Mary was sixteen, five things happened.

The first was that she began to grow. From having been the smallest in her form, she was moved up and up in the line at gym; bus-conductors no longer addressed her as 'Tuppence,' and all her clothes had to be bought with inches to let down at the hem. Her reports from St Martin's mentioned that: 'While still lacking in any high degree of team spirit, Mary Shannon is beginning to take a more prominent part in the school activities, and we hope that her comparatively high position in the school will give her the sense of responsibility which is essential to every useful member of society.'

Angela's reports still read: 'Shows all too clearly her contempt for authority,' or, 'High spirits lead her to regrettable insubordination.'

Mary thought she was grown up. Her chief theme at home was: 'Mummy, when can I cut my hair?'

'Wait till you leave school and see what you look like with it up,' Mrs Shannon would say.

'When can I leave school, then?'

'When you've passed your Matric.'

'That's as good as saying never. Mummy, am I—*am* I to waste the best years of my life playing hockey and cricket in that nunnery? You should see what it's like when a man comes in. All the mistresses go sort of mottled and flushed up their necks and their mouths quiver. I'll get warped.'

'Darling, don't be silly. You're only sixteen, after all. No one leaves school before that.'

'Indian girls marry when they're twelve—and have babies. Mummy, Angela goes to dances and things. She went to a night club once. *And* she uses lipstick, why can't I?'

'You don't need it, Puss. Why all this rushing on to get to another age? Why not try enjoying the age you are for a bit? You don't really need powder, either, you've got a lovely skin.'

'Oh, Mummy, I do! I shine like a beacon. At school, we have to powder in the lav. Once they found a compact floating in one of the pans, but no one owned up to say it was theirs, so all the upper school had to miss swimming for a week. Wasn't it futile?'

Mrs Shannon's faith in St Martin's was shaken, but she didn't admit it.

Mary yearned after the shoddy sophistication of frocks in the small dress shops of Kensington High Street, and scoffed at the simplicity of the clever little dresses that her mother made for her. Once, she saved up her tiny allowance and bought what she thought was the smartest red hat ever seen. When she entered the flat in it, humming with affected unconcern, Mrs Shannon screamed and fell back on to the sofa with her eyes closed, and Uncle Geoffrey looked up and said, 'My God, a tart,' and went back to his crossword puzzle.

The second thing that happened was that the mother of one of Mrs Shannon's pupils, who had more money than experience, offered her the job of managing a dress shop that she had just taken over in South

Molton Street. She would get a larger salary than at the College, and, said Mrs Wilkes Armitage, a percentage of the profits if she cared to put money into the business. Mrs Shannon had no money to put, but she accepted the position with alacrity, shook the hated dust of the Domestic Science College from her tiny court shoes and 'went all Mayfair' as Uncle Geoffrey said in the time-honoured accents of the stage peer.

The third thing was that the tide of Uncle Geoffrey's career, which had for some time been at ebb among the backwash of *démodé* farces and seaside tours, was turned to a rising hope by the offer of a contract from a visiting Hollywood agent.

'It's marvellous, it's terrific,' he said, announcing the news to his sister and niece with unprecedented animation and the beginnings already of an American accent. 'I thought farce was dead, but it seems, my children, that in Hollywood it still flourishes, and—whoopee! I flourish with it.'

'I'm so pleased for you, Geoffrey,' said Lily. 'We shall miss you desperately, of course, but—oh, it really is marvellous! Just imagine Mary and I sitting in a cinema and suddenly seeing your ugly mug flash on to the screen. Darling,' she hugged him, knocking him backwards on to the sofa, 'I hope you make a million.'

Mary was thrilled. It was far better to have an uncle on the films than on the stage. 'You must get me everybody's autograph,' she said, perching on his knee and flipping out his tie. '*Everybody's,* and two of Douglas Fairbanks—one for Angela. Gosh, I suppose you'll meet them all, you are a lucky beggar. Why do they—well, I know you're frightfully good and all that, but what made them—I mean, why specially——'

'What in God's name made them pick on me, you mean? Search me. When the old Oik mentioned it over a couple of whiskys in the lounge of the Piccadilly, I nearly passed out, but apparently I'm Zaccariah Stinkenbaum's conception of the typical English Milord, and—well, who was I to disillusion him? Let me up, Tich, I have to go round and break it to the blonde at the "Murray Arms" that she's about to lose her best customer.'

It was not until he was actually leaving them that Mary realized how attached she was to him. He might be aggravating, unreliable, messy, disgustingly lazy, but he was an awful dear. He was always doing sweet, improvident things, like arriving home with a bottle of champagne and a chicken whenever he could think of an excuse for a celebration, and once he had gone quite mad and taken a box for the first night of a musical comedy, with the tailor on his very doormat presenting the Final Demand. He had been the man of the house for so many years that life was suddenly unimaginable without him. On the morning of his departure, she threatened to weep over the monstrous checks of his new overcoat.

'Hey, hey, be a man, Tich,' he said. 'Tell you what, if it's good pickings there, I'll send you a telegram, and you can come straight out and be a star.' Mary saw dazzling and entirely credible visions. 'And you can keep that red-headed girl friend of yours on ice for me,' he went on. 'You once turned me down, I remember, but I don't think she'll be so sniffy about Giorgio Pimento, the Casanova of the screen.'

'I'm coming to see you off,' said Mary suddenly.

'You can't, Puss,' said her mother, 'you're late for school as it is. Goodness, it *is* late! I've got to fly myself. Geoff, I must go, I daren't get in the old trout's bad books at this stage.' She tore herself away, and departed in a flurry to South Molton Street and Uncle Geoffrey said good-bye to the widowed old lovebird, gave the porter a tip unheard of in those parts, and drove away with his variegated luggage, and Mary, feeling guilty but determined, at his side.

At the station, he was very debonair and sophisticated about everything, and while he was lounging about in the weighing-hall, prodding at things with his stick, Mary rushed away and returned with a carnation. 'I couldn't get a red one,' she panted. 'Will pink do?'

'Pansy, eh?' he said, as she fixed it into his buttonhole. He wore his monocle, and kept eyeing women who passed, and wondering if they were going on his boat. Leaning out of the carriage window, while Mary stood on the platform below, pulling up her stockings and feeling suddenly shy of him, he said: 'Sweet of you to come, Squib, but don't stay. It's torture seeing a train off—standing about saying: "Send me a card," and "If you can't get it off with petrol try benzine." '

'No, no, I must see the train out.' She was so late for school already that she might as well be a little later. 'Don't forget about the autographs,' she said for the sixth time.

Just before the train left, four or five of the boys and girls came squealing and jabbering down the platform, and Uncle Geoffrey had to get out again to be slapped on the back and shouted at and chaffed by everyone at once. The train began to move.

'Now then,' said a porter, 'anyone goin' of this little lot?' Uncle Geoffrey dived between the boys and girls to kiss Mary standing uncertainly in the background, hurled himself into the carriage, begging the pardon of a furious woman with violets on her hat and corsage, and then, as the train gathered speed, he was gone—dear silly, amusing Uncle Geoffrey. Mary, left forlornly behind, was unable to cry, because of the boys and girls.

'Didn't we meet once before?' asked one of them, as they all turned to go, and Mary recognized Uncle, the fat man at the Café Royal. He was fatter than ever and considerably shabbier but no less exuberant.

73

'Well, well, well,' he said, pumping her hand, 'this is a treat. Old Percy's niece—and all grown-up too.' He put her hand through his arm. 'How about it? Are they open yet? Come on, little Miss What's-your-name, come and drink the health of your Uncle Perce.'

'Oh no, really,' said Mary. 'I've got to——' She had taken off her school hat, and with a reefer coat buttoned up to her neck, they could not have seen her uniform. 'I've got to get somewhere.'

'Oh, come on, be matey. Or aren't you allowed in pubs yet?'

'Of course I am, it's not that. But honestly——'

'Come on then.' They went to a big place just outside the station, and sat on a leather settee in the lounge, where last night's cigarette butts strewed the floor.

'On me,' said Uncle. 'What's it going to be?' Mary copied one of the other girls and said sherry, and when it came, drank it down quickly because she knew she didn't like the taste. Then she sat fidgeting and wondering how soon she could get away without seeming rude. The others were ordering a second round and had apparently settled in for the day.

She stood up, holding her school hat behind her and feeling slightly drunk. 'I really must go, thank you ever so much, it was lovely.' She edged away from their amiable protests, backed into a little table, upset a small port, and fled. Outside, she had to wait nearly ten minutes at the terminus for her bus, and she thought how silly she would look if the boys and girls came out and found her there. After a hiccough or two, she felt better.

All the way along in the bus, she watched clocks anxiously. By the time she alighted, it was nearly twelve o'clock, and she darted across the main road to the fury of a bus driver and two men in a swerving car. Twelve o'clock—at this moment the sixth form would be settling down with much sighing and banging of desk lids, to Miss Langford's history lesson. She was Mary's form mistress, so she would know when she arrived that this was her first appearance. What would she say— what should she say to that paralysing lizard-like stare? One sherry was not enough to fortify her against the apprehension that grew with every running step that brought her nearer to St Martin's. In the cloakroom, she wrenched off her coat and tore upstairs without stopping to change her shoes—a crime in itself. It felt strange to be the only person about; there was a hush of foreboding along the deserted corridors. Miss Everard, the Lacrosse mistress, coming from the staffroom passage as she passed, looked at her suspiciously, but only said, 'Walking, Shannon, walking,' as if she were a horse.

Through the glass top of her form door, Mary saw the scene of which she herself had so often been a part. Heads bent, bodies sprawled in boredom, or alert with pious attention, and Miss Langford looking smoother and more inhuman than ever. She stood up to write something on the blackboard, turning her back to the room, and Mary took a deep breath and slipped in, shutting the door quietly. She walked past the whispers and titters, slapped someone's tweaking hand, and stood by the desk on the platform.

'Yes, what is it?' Miss Langford turned round, chalk in hand. 'Oh—good *evening*, Shannon.' Mary noticed with satisfaction that no one, not even Muriel Hopkins, laughed. 'Have you a written excuse for being late?'

'No,' said Mary, 'I'm afraid not. I was seeing my uncle off at the station—er, he's going to America.'

'Your uncle—hm.' Miss Langford dismissed the Casonova of the screen with a slight lowering of her lids. 'You should have asked permission yesterday. I really can't allow—why, Shannon!' She leaned closer. 'You've been drinking!'

Behind her, Mary could hear the stirrings of scandalized delight, the loathsome glee of the virtuous. Before her, Miss Langford, with meticulous features, waited triumphantly for the explanation or denial that she was already prepared to disbelieve.

Something that Mary had no idea was in her rose suddenly up in a red-hot gush of Bolshevist madness. Before she could stop herself, she had burst out: 'It's no business of yours what I do outside school. You're only paid to boss me here!' The flaring lunacy that had produced the words died as soon as they were spoken. Mary was aghast. Had she really said that? She couldn't have said that. A chilling fear crept over her, and in the silence that hung on the suspended breath of the stricken room, she could hear her heart beating in her head. A lump in Miss Langford's smooth, reptilian throat rose, bulged and settled again.

'You may go and sit down,' she said.

For a whole day, Mary walked about with the uncertainty of her fate hanging over her. No one, not even Angela, could fully understand or relieve the agony of her apprehension. She kept telling herself that it was absurd to feel like this at sixteen, that she had not committed murder, and that in a few months' time the whole thing would seem ridiculous, but it was no good. She was terrified. The narrow world of St Martin's might have been the Universe. She was terrified.

It was almost a relief when the suspense was broken. She was slouching in the playground alone at Break, scraping her toes along the asphalt, when a very small girl with a pigtail sticking straight out on either side of her head, accosted her. 'I say, are you Mary Shannon, or some potty name like that?'

'Yes,' said Mary, too wretched to remonstrate.

'You've got to go to Old Strawberry's Study,' said the brat. 'At once,' she said with added relish, and stood watching with goggling eyes as Mary turned away to her doom.

Old Strawberry was the Head Mistress, Miss Gertrude Strawbridge, M.A. (Cantab.), F.R.C.T., who was as sexless, omnipotent, and terrifying as God. As she trailed down the playground steps, through the swing door, up the stairs, and down the passage that led to the tabernacle, Mary was thinking that nothing that could happen to her in her whole life, nothing could ever be as bad as this. It was like the end of the world. Years afterwards, marvelling at her distorted sense of proportion, she could remember exactly the feeling of fatality—like a doomed man walking to the gallows. She knocked on the study door, and in a moment's pause before she went in, she made a vow. When she came out again, ten minutes later, the vow was strengthened: 'If I ever have daughters, I shall never, never make them go to school.'

It was not the punishment, though it was severe enough, that she minded, but the humiliation of the refinement of contempt meted out to her by one old, desiccated machine of cultured joylessness. Was it jealousy of youth that ravaged the uncaressed bosom of old Strawberry? Did she resent the blossoming in others of the chance that she herself had lost for ever? In years to come, Mary saw that perhaps it was not hatred she should have felt, but pity.

The fourth thing that happened was between Mary and Denys. That year, Mary had a long white chiffon evening dress for the Christmas dinner at Charbury.

'Are you *sure* it doesn't look like a nightdress, Granny?' she insisted, posturing and pouting in the middle of her grandmother's bedroom before she went down to dinner.

'It looks more like something out of Sylphides, if you know what that is,' said Granny, smiling from the bed. 'It's lovely, darling. Just right for——' She broke off as a quick little rhythm of knocks sounded on the door. 'There's Timmy! I knew he'd get here. Come in!' The effort of raising her voice started her muffled cough again, and Uncle Tim came in and strode quickly over to the bed, taking his mother's hand and looking down at her with an anxious pucker on his round red face, redder than ever now from the cold of driving.

'Better now,' said Granny, and he kissed her.

'Happy Christmas, darling. I managed to wangle it all right, you see. Got a couple of nights' leave as a matter of fact. I got here from Plymouth in two and a half hours. What d'you think of that?'

'That's too fast, Timmy. You ought to be more careful. Run along now and change, there's a good boy, or you'll be late for dinner. Look at Mary, doesn't she look sweet?'

'Mm—not bad!' He paused on his way to the door to inspect her at arms' length, his hand on her shoulders. 'You'll have to come down to the ship one day and let some of the young chaps in the Wardroom have a look at you.'

Mary blushed at this intriguing but rather terrifying prospect, remembering what had happened to the heroine of one of Uncle Geoffrey's plays—*The Saucy Sub-Lieutenant*.

When Uncle Tim had gone, Mary went over to the bed. Granny's little hand lay on the eiderdown like a scrap of parchment, and Mary took it up, playing with the big ruby and diamond ring that slipped round so easily on the finger it once had fitted. 'I wish you were coming down to dinner, Granny,' she said. It was more than two years now since Granny had suddenly, mysteriously 'taken a bad turn' as the maids said, discussing it in whispers. Since then, she had not been allowed to come downstairs any more; the bath-chair had been put away in the coach-house, but the wicker chair like a Punch-and-Judy show still stood in the niche between the fireplace and the window-seat in the hall, as if it had not given up hope of her coming.

'Taggie's going to settle me early,' she said to Mary. 'I'm a drowsy old woman tonight. Oh, you haven't had your chocolate.' She reached for the tin. 'It'll spoil your dinner, but never mind. Here you are—the last one. Ask Willie to order me some more tomorrow, will you, darling? Don't forget, it would never do to run out.'

'No, it wouldn't,' said Mary. 'You can't break traditions. Good night, Granny. I'd better be going down now.' Bending down, she kissed her, and went to the door feeling light and excited in the airy, floating dress, treading the soft carpet in her thin evening slippers as if she were bare-foot. Looking back as she opened the door, she saw that Granny was watching her, her head turned sideways among the pillows, smiling.

'Good night,' said Mary again.

'Good night. Enjoy yourself, my heart.'

When dinner was nearly over, and everyone was cracking nuts or peeling tangerines, and the port had gone round and Aunt Grace had secured a bowl of fondants to herself, the electric lights were turned out in favour of the candles. The big Christmas tree in the window blossomed with a hundred little circles of yellow light, and all down the table the tall silver candlesticks were glowing islands in a room full of shadows. Talk broke up into groups and chairs were turned more intimately. Mary leaned back happily, twiddling the stem of the wine-glass in which, with great strength of mind, she was keeping a drop of divine, nose-tickling champagne for the Toast. Her gaze wandered round the table, seeing the familiar faces unfamiliarly mysterious in the flattering candle light.

Granpa was at the top, in his usual place opposite the windows, and facing him at the other end of the table, Uncle Lionel sat with the Christmas tree glittering behind his narrow head. Granpa's white shirt front was bulging out over his waistcoat, deep shadows creasing his smiling face above the collar that looked too tight, as he told a laborious funny story to Mary's mother. He had already been ten minutes over it, and did not seem to be approaching the end, but Lily's appreciative attention was unflagging. She was prepared to laugh uproariously at the end whether she saw the point or not. Granpa was not one of those fiendish old men who paralysed your polite laughter by saying, 'And what was the point of that story, my dear?'

Mary thought her mother looked particularly smooth tonight. Her little black shingled head turned like a bird's, neatly, this way and that, on the neck that rose white and bare out of an extremely smart evening gown from South Molton Street, about which Aunt Mavis had not yet made up her mind. Mavis herself sat on Granpa's other side, wearing wine-coloured velvet, gathered bunchily in all the places already accentuated by middle-aged spread. Next to her was Michael, in his cadet's uniform. He had only been at Dartmouth for one term, but he already behaved as though the entire British Navy were incorporated in his short stocky body. He and Uncle Tim had talked across Mary all through dinner, like a couple of bearded old seamen. When Uncle Tim leaned forward, Mary could see, behind his broad back, Sarah, large in blue satin, sitting next to Uncle Lionel. She was more developed than Mary and had short hair—someone had been at it with the tongs tonight—but, though she might look older, Mary knew she was not nearly so grown up. She was at boarding-school and, to Mary's eternal scorn, she adored it, and lived only for the end of the holidays. She was always talking about a Miss Soper, whose picture she kept in her handkerchief drawer, and to whom she wrote long, verbose letters that she read aloud to Mary and then had not the courage to post. She and Uncle Lionel were getting on stickily, in spite of the fact that he was so determined to have the Christmas spirit that he had insisted on pulling a cracker at the beginning of dinner and wearing a foolish mauve paper hat all through the meal. Aunt Grace, on his other side, wore one too— a bonnet, that suited her round face and saucer eyes. She was wearing flowered georgette with a velvet coatee embroidered by her own hand with woollen *motifs*. Her clothes never let you forget that she was 'good with her needle.' She took immense trouble over them, but it would have been so much better if she had not. Uncle Guy sat between her and Margaret, sticking out his underlip and looking rather bored. Mary wondered whether he had had a more exciting invitation in London. He was always going to parties. Once, Angela had met him at a reception to which her parents had taken her and he had danced with her and given her a champagne cocktail. 'He's a super dancer,' she told Mary the next day, 'but rather a dirty old man.'

Beyond Margaret, who wore yellow with a dingy hair-ribbon to match, was Denys. Now that he was grown up people commented more than ever on his likeness to his father, but Mary thought that he was far better-looking than Uncle Guy could ever have been. In his dinner-jacket, with his dark hair smooth and shining, he looked so handsome that she could hardly bear it. He was like a picture that she had seen of Rupert Brooke, with those dark eyes and soft, dreaming mouth. Next year he was going to Oxford, and already he shaved and smoked a pipe. She watched the glowing lights and steep shadows that the candlelight threw on his face as he leaned forward to be nice to his mother. Mary wondered whether he liked her white dress; it was wasted, otherwise, in this entirely family gathering.

When she had come down the staircase before dinner he had looked up and seen her, but he had not said anything, or smiled, just looked at her very intently, and then looked away and gone on filling the glasses on the tray from the cocktail-shaker.

Ever since she was seven or eight Mary had been allowed to sit up for Christmas dinner, and it had always been just the same, hardly ever one of the family missing. This year Aunt Winifred was away; she had gone on a walking tour in Scotland with her friend, Kathleen Perron, the daughter of the Vicar at Yarde. It was better, really; she didn't enjoy parties, and last year she had cried, suddenly, in the middle of the Christmas pudding course, and everyone had been very embarrassed and had had to behave as if nothing had happened.

Mary loved Christmas for always being the same, year after year; the dining-room filled with the sharp, sweet scent of the Christmas tree that came from their own pine woods, and all round and above them the moving, friendly, fire-lit house, safe and old, and glad that they were all there.

Granpa stood up, pushing back his chair with a little scraping sound that caught everyone's attention. 'I give you a toast,' he said. They all stood up, and raised their glasses, and Michael, knowing his cue, nipped from his place to open the dining-room door.

'My wife,' said Granpa with a funny, stiff little bow, and as they clinked glasses everyone cheered. There was a tiny, listening pause, and then, from far away, came the faint tinkling of Granny's handbell to show that she heard, and thanked them, and was drinking their health in barley water.

Although he himself had given up riding, Granpa still kept two horses in the stable, and from the back of a perky little bay mare called

Joy, Mary was initiated by Denys into the delirious thrill of an occasional day's hunting.

'But, Mary,' Margaret, with troubled eyes, had tackled her about it, 'how *can* you? It's so cruel. I know you don't like seeing things killed, either, because I remember that time you were sick when Michael wrung the chicken's neck.'

'Don't remind me of it,' said Mary. 'Of course I hate seeing things killed, you ass, who doesn't? I go for the riding, not the sport. I always pray the fox'll get away. Denys says it's "Hunting to ride instead of riding to hunt," and in the Shires I should be blackballed, whatever that is.'

'But that makes it even worse,' said Margaret, clutching her arm earnestly. She could never talk to anyone without touching them. 'You're encouraging cruelty; all those dogs and people after one poor little fox——'

'Honestly, Maggie, I don't see that it makes any difference to the fox whether I'm there or not.'

'But the poor, pretty little things with their lovely bushy tails,' drivelled Margaret, her eyes beginning to swim.

'You wouldn't be so keen on them if you'd ever smelt one,' retorted Mary with the callousness to which Margaret often roused her.

This year the Boxing Day Meet was at Coombe St George, about six or seven miles away, so Mary and Denys breakfasted hugely off porridge and sausages, and started out before most of the family were up. Mary had wanted to go and show her grandmother what she looked like in her new bowler hat, with her long hair looped neatly in a chignon at the back, but Taggie had stopped her at the door. 'You can't go in to her now,' she said. 'She's sleeping. She'd a bad night, poor lady,' so Mary had to be content with the acclamations of Mrs Linney.

'Proper little swanker, ain't she? Turn around, lovey. Eh, dear, what it is to be a lady!' Although this was one of her favourite remarks, Mary had never yet discovered who was supposed to be the lady—she or Mrs Linney.

'Here's your sandwiches, and this is Master Denys', and don't 'ee ask me for ginger nuts, because us hasn't got any, nor shan't have till goodness knows when.' She followed Mary to the back door. 'Bring us back a rabbit for the stock-pot!' she called, as Mary went up to the stable hill, pleased with the firm, tramping sound of her boots.

Denys was already swinging up on to Buck, and Tom led out Joy, who struck the cobbles and snorted, twitching her ears back and forwards, as if she knew why her saddle and bridle were spotless and shining, her mane plaited, and her hoofs oiled.

'Mind now what I said about not letting her rush her jumps, Miss Mary,' said Tom, giving Joy a little slap on her taut behind as they turned out of the yard. They jogged along the back drive below the pine wood, and turned out through the gate by Bates' cottage, on to the flinty, sunken road. It was a lovely crisp day, with clouds furling like sails, in the pale blue winter sky, a day to make you acutely conscious of life. Mary's skin was tingling with it, and she kept putting her hand on to Joy's firm, clipped neck, to feel the warmth and vitality as she caught at the bit and did a little dancing step to show she would rather trot than walk. Denys and Mary discussed last night's party in snatches, but mostly they jogged along without talking, enjoying the morning and the excitement of what lay ahead. Mary was always firmly convinced every time she went hunting that she would be brought home on a hurdle, and whenever she approached a jump she had a quick vision of herself lying in a crumpled heap on the other side, which made it all the more rapturous when Joy landed on all fours and galloped away with Mary still in the saddle.

The cross-roads of Coombe village were jammed with people and horses and cars, for everyone turned out for the Boxing Day Meet. Denys seemed to know a good many of them and kept raising his hat to people Mary had never seen before. 'There's Major Wiley over there,' he said, pointing with his whip to a whiskered veteran in a pink coat on the other side of the crowd. 'I've got to go and give him a message from the old man. You'd better wait here, Maria, they'll be moving off this way. They'll draw Chuffey Wood first.'

Mary had no idea how he knew these mysterious things, but he was always right. The science of hunting was non-existent as far as she was concerned, but Denys always knew which way the fox would run, and where he was making for, and which small boy had headed him on the road. She manœuvred Joy up a little bank, well in the background, where there was no danger of kicking a hound, or of getting in the way of one of the loud-voiced pink coats and black moustaches, or the terrifying, side-saddle women in top-hats, who pushed their way about through the crowd on tall, thin-legged horses. The most terrifying of all was the Master's wife, Mrs ffrench-Burrowes, who strode about on the ground with a yellow fur coat thrown over her habit, calling everybody—gentry, peasantry, and hounds—by their Christian names. Under her straight-set top-hat, her weathered face was like an axe, her profile a succession of razor-edges. Her equally terrifying horse, a black giant with a red ribbon on its tail and a yellow gleam in its eye, was being stampeded from a horse-box with a great deal of swearing and clattering, a small Irish groom swinging in the air from his tossing head. He snatched at the bit and showed the whites of his eyes, sidling away as the groom gave Mrs ffrench-Burrowes a leg-up. As her thin seat-bones hit the saddle, Mary heard her say: 'Damn you, Charlie!' and wondered whether she meant the groom or the horse.

81

Everyone seemed to know everybody else, and Mary was quite gratified to be hailed from the road below, even when it turned out to be only Mrs Cotterell. Mrs Cotterell had given up hunting long ago, owing to fatty degeneration of the heart, but she was looking very sporting in a tweed fishing hat, white mackintosh, and Newmarket boots. She had also a shooting-stick, on whose inadequate seat she planted herself with widespread legs, wherever a horse or a car or a pack of hounds wanted to go by.

'Hullo, there, Margaret,' she said, scrutinizing Mary from below. 'Not a bad little mare you have there. How does she go? Can she leap?'

'Oh, marvellously, thanks,' said Mary.

'Bubbles is out today,' said Mrs Cotterell, pointing to where a boy in a jockey cap and corduroy breeches was sitting paralysed with fear on a small shaggy pony, with a groom firmly attached to its mild head.

'Only his second time out,' boomed the proud mother. 'He's only going to follow to the first covert or so, of course. We have to be *extremely* careful of his health, you know. The doctors say his brain is too great a tax on his body.' A hooting car bore down on her, and she had to flounder up the bank for safety, clutching her seat behind her, ready to plant it in a new place. Joy decided that she liked the look of the grass on the other side of the road, and carried Mary away. She let her put her head down and eat grass, glad that she was standing quietly.

'Shouldn't let him do that, Miss,' said an officious groom, holding a very smart horse in a crested rug, 'I seen 'em get the Staggers——'

'Thank you,' said Mary coldly, and jerked up Joy's head.

'Let me tighten your curb for you, Miss, you don't want to get taken charge of.' Mary had to let him, though she wished he would go away and look after his own beastly horse. She was sure he knew that she was wearing second-hand boots.

'Hounds, please!' The crowd on the road parted, and through them, following the Whip, came the joyful, stern-waving black and white and brown tide, jostling and pattering about the legs of the Master's horse. Mrs ffrench-Burrowes rode behind, flicking with her whip at the hounds that paused even for a moment to investigate a smell, reviling them harshly with: '*Git* along there, Dainty! Ah, now, Ransome, would you? Git forrard. Forrard, Boxer!' Denys came along with the cavalcade, and Mary kicked Joy into line beside him. He introduced her to a vacuous youth in a top-hat, who was lounging beside him on a yellow horse. 'Good morning,' said Mary, trying to get her whip and reins straightened out.

'Mor',' said the young man, and dropped his jaw again as if the effort had exhausted him.

'I saw Mrs Cotterell,' Mary told Denys, as they jogged along in the middle of the bumping, clattering crowd. 'Bubbles is out, the brave little man.'

'Is he? I hope I jump on him, then,' said Denys. They turned off the road through a gate, and the field spread out, cantering up a broad, sloping meadow. Joy, delighted to stretch her legs on the turf, gave a series of little bucks, which made Mary clutch at her mane. 'You can't gallop yet,' she panted, holding her in. 'I'll tell you when.'

In front of them, Mrs ffrench-Burrowes' horse was doing some impressive rodeo business, standing alternately on front and hind legs, with its rider perched on top as unshakeably as a feeding mosquito, swearing at everyone she knocked into.

'This way, Maria,' said Denys, cantering past, looking as if he and Buck had been together all their lives, and she followed him over to the corner of the wood. Sure enough, after ten minutes of waiting and listening to the thrilling horn notes and calls, and whimperings from inside the wood, it was at this corner that the hounds came struggling and leaping out to stream away up the hill in full cry, with Mrs ffrench-Burrowes crashing after them over a high hedge, almost on top of Mary. She and Joy were carried along by the charging crowd, squashed in a gateway, squeezed through, and before Mary had time to think, Joy had hurled herself over a post-and-rails, stumbled, recovered herself, and galloped on.

Mary's exhilaration grew as they raced across a huge grass field, and hopped neatly over a little ditch at the end. It was going to be a run, and she was well up at the front. A high black hedge rose up in front, and people were dividing, to follow one another over the only two jumpable places. 'Follow me,' called Denys over his shoulder, and streaked for the right-hand gap, going neatly over with Buck's heels flashing together in the sun.

Mary was close behind him, riding Joy at the jump, when, to her fury, a fat man on a wild-looking, foam-flecked horse pushed past her, and she had to hold back while he charged at the hedge, working his elbows, spattering her with mud. Joy was too close to the hedge to jump it now, and she slid to a standstill on the muddy take-off, nearly shooting Mary over her head. 'Get out of the way!' people were shouting from behind, and Mary, flustered and seething with rage, had to pull out and take her place at the end of the line. By the time everyone before her had gone, there was hardly any hedge left, but she and Joy were both unnerved; they flounced up to it half-heartedly, and for the second time Mary nearly jumped without her horse.

'Give 'im the whip!' yelled a yokel standing by, as Mary jerked away to try again. 'Come on, Joy, you must, you must,' she said through clenched teeth, giving her a whack on the ribs that sent her bounding forward.

'Oh, you must!' she shrieked desperately, as Joy slowed up again, sticking in her toes, but suddenly there was a noise like a traction-engine coming up behind. 'Gerr-r-rout of it, yer——' roared the yokel, brandishing a small thorn bush, and the startled Joy found herself on the other side of the hedge, with Mary clinging round her neck.

They pounded across a clogging ploughed field. They had lost the hunt. Fifty people on horseback, a pack of hounds, and a fox had disappeared from the face of the earth. Mary was distraught. The only people in sight were a few runners, floundering doggedly over the plough, a bearded farmer on a cart horse, and an old lady with a back view as vast as her horse's, lollopping through the mud with a serene smile on her face and a large bunch of violets in her coat, as unhurriedly as if it were Sunday morning in Rotten Row.

Now they were over a small bank, and on to a grass field with a ridge and furrow across which Joy lurched and plunged like a tramp in a rough sea. They caught up with the farmer.

'Follow me, Missy,' he said, 'we'll soon catch 'em,' and he turned his cart horse in a wide sweep like a battleship, and made for a gate in the corner. With a dubious glance at the old lady, who was keeping happily on her course, with a rocking-horse motion, Mary followed him out on to a tarred road.

She was thankful that Tom was not there to see Joy's legs pounding along the tarmac. They turned down a slippery chalk hill, through a gate at the bottom, and sure enough, there was the whole field, standing about at the corner of a wood, in a crowd of steaming, blowing horses.

Mary found Denys, and he lent her his handkerchief to wipe the mud off her face, and then, for an hour or two, nothing much happened. They trotted about from covert to covert, to little copses and even turnip fields, finding nothing. It was very pleasant; the sun was surprisingly warm, and in the clear air you could see the country for miles, looking bright and fresh, and as if it had been made especially to ride over. Mary and Denys ate their sandwiches. 'Oh, Golly,' said Mary in the middle of a bite, 'I forgot to ask Wilkie to order some more chocs. for Gran. She asked me to, specially.' Julia and John were still babies enough to be disappointed when they went in to say good night. There would probably be tears. In any case, it would be the first time, as far as Mary could remember, that the supply had failed. How awful of her to break the tradition. She worried for a little, but not for long, because the day was too glorious, and she could never worry as intensely in the open air as she did indoors.

Mrs ffrench-Burrowes had collected a boy friend—a man with a face like a bloodhound and an unbrushed top-hat on the back of his head, who looked as if he had a hang-over from Christmas. They were talking very loudly and sharing a flask, without wiping the top between drinks. To facilitate the process, Mrs ffrench-Burrowes had lifted her veil, resting it on the tip of her sharp nose. Presently her husband rode crossly out of the osier bed that he had been drawing for half an hour. 'Not a hope in hell,' he said. 'That fool Martin hasn't been stopping the earths.'

'I always said he was a bastard,' said his wife calmly.

Mary listened entranced.

'Where the hell are the second horses, anyway, Jumbo?' she went on. 'This brute's cut his fetlock.'

'God knows,' said Jumbo. 'I'm going on to Withy Wood.' Putting the horn to his lips, he rode away, calling to the hounds, who came tumbling out of the osier bed, plastered with mud, their tongues lolling, and loped amiably after him.

The field moved off, jostling through the narrow hunting gate. A foolhardy girl let her horse nibble the black horse's tail, and even though his lashing kick did not break her leg, the stream of abuse from his rider broke her spirit, and she slunk away, crimson to the brim of her ill-fitting bowler hat.

While they were waiting outside Withy Wood, Mrs Cotterell, who had been following in a car, turned up complete with shooting-stick, and planted herself down to tell Mary and Denys that Bubbles had jumped a ditch, and sank into the mud up to the hilt.

With the going down of the sun, a chill crept over the afternoon. 'I wish something would happen,' Mary said to Denys, and at that moment a blood-curdling scream and a 'Gone awa-aa-ay!' galvanized everybody into action. A solitary horseman on a hill away to the right was waving his cap against the skyline, and in the cavalry charge that followed, Mrs Cotterell had to climb a fence to save her life. Mary found herself well in the front. Before her, the chorusing hounds streamed over the grass, close together like a flock of birds, Mrs ffrench-Burrowes, who had evidently found her second horseman, rushed by her, fighting a pulling horse, and all round, in front, and behind was the thrilling, thick drumming of galloping hooves.

It was glorious. Joy flew over fences without checking her stride, and Mary, as she galloped, felt a delirium growing in her. She was a goddess, riding Pegasus; nothing could stop her. She charged recklessly at a blackthorn hedge, without choosing her place. It was too high for Joy, but she rose at it, caught a hind leg in the top, and landed on her nose. Mary rolled off, lost her reins, and stood up with her head spinning to see Joy preparing to follow the hounds on her own. Before she had time to burst into tears of frustration, Denys, darling Denys, was trotting back, leading Joy, wild-eyed, with swinging stirrups.

'All right?' he asked. Mary nodded. 'Hop on then,' he said, his eyes dancing with excitement. 'We shan't lose them, they've checked at the corner down there. Isn't it terrific?'

'Absolute heaven,' gasped Mary, as Joy started off while she was still scrambling into the saddle. It was the best run she had ever had. The hounds ran on and on, never checking for long, and Joy seemed tireless. Where she could not jump, she scrambled and hopped, or forced her way through with her little square chest. They were always up at the front. Mary could have sung with joy and the excitement of it. Once she and Mrs ffrench-Burrowes rushed at a jump together, and went over it with their stirrups clashing, her skirt brushing the knee of Mary's breeches, and Mary was exalted enough to yell: 'Keep out of my way, can't you!' before the other woman could open her mouth to damn her.

The run lasted for more than an hour, and ended up in a grass-grown gravel pit, where the fox went to ground. Mary noticed with satisfaction that several people had dropped out; the rest were standing about in a cloud of steam, while the hounds scrabbled at the earth and whined impatiently. She slid to the ground, tired and triumphant, and Joy stood with her legs planted apart, nostrils blown out squarely, her sides going in and out like bellows. She was dripping wet, with a bead of sweat on each bristly black eyelash. While Mary patted her and told her how marvellous she was, she butted her in the chest and tried to rub the chalky foam off her head on to Mary's coat.

To her secret delight the fox refused to be either dug, smoked, or chivvied out by a squeaking wire-haired terrier. 'Damn shame,' said the vacuous youth, coming up with Denys, his feet dangling out of the stirrups, and a cigarette on his lower lip. 'They oughter got him.'

'Oh, yes,' lied Mary fervently.

'Toppin' run, though. Nigh'.' With a vast effort he summoned the strength to raise his hat, and rode away, his reins flopping on the neck of the weary yellow horse.

'We'd better be pushing off,' said Denys, 'we've got miles to go.'

'Have we?' said Mary. 'I've no idea where we are; I hadn't thought about it. Oh, wasn't it gorgeous, Denys? I wouldn't have missed it for anything. Let's go, shall we?' She climbed stiffly into the saddle. 'Golly, my behind! You don't notice it till you get off.'

'I'm pretty raw myself,' he said, 'but it's worth it. I haven't had such a day for years. You and Joy went jolly well, by the way.'

Mary glowed. 'Wasn't she marvellous? You know, that time she fell it was my fault completely. All the other jumps she simply flew over, honestly. You should have seen the width of the place where we jumped that stream, under a willow, too, and all muddy——'

'Bet it wasn't as wide as where I took it. You could hardly see the other side—like a damn great river. How did you manage with that stile where you couldn't see the ditch till you were up to your neck in it?'

'Oh, that was nothing to us. Denys, I jumped a gate—five-barred—or no, perhaps on second thoughts it was only four.' They jogged happily down the road into the gathering dusk, boasting, chattering, reliving every moment, tired and relaxed and utterly happy.

'Did you see me bump into Mrs ffrench-Burrowes?' asked Mary. 'I believe I actually swore at her, I hope I did. Isn't she ghastly? She's a far better argument against being a hunting woman than any Maggie ever produces.'

'She's a bitch,' said Denys. He was always using words like this now, with a casual air that impressed Mary and outraged Aunt Mavis.

They passed through a village as darkness was falling, and Mary said, with a yawn: 'Could we—wouldn't it be heaven to have some tea? Would it hurt the horses to stand for a moment? I'm famished and parched and a bit cold, aren't you?'

'Good idea,' he said. 'There's quite a decent little pub. here, I believe; the nags would probably like a drink, too.'

They rode into the tiny, littered yard of the 'Red Lion,' and a man came out of the house, wiping bare arms on an apron, and showed them a shed where they could leave the horses. 'Can you manage?' he asked, glancing furtively back at the patch of light from the open back door. 'I'm doin' a bit of a job for the wife, and you know how 'tis if you look like knockin' off. There you are,' he said, with a kind of uneasy pride, as a screech of 'Willy!' reached their ears, 'proper old tartar, ain't she?' They laughed in the darkness of the shed when he had gone, feeling along the broken-down manger for rings to tie the horses to. 'What d'you suppose she's making him do,' giggled Mary, 'wash-up?'

'Wash the babies nappies, probably. Blast—there's a wheelbarrow or something here.'

'Oh, Denys, have you hurt yourself?'

'Only broken my leg.' He struck a match. 'There you are; what did I say? A pram. Look here, Mary, we can't leave them here, there's all sorts of junk about. One of them would have a pitchfork through the leg by the time we came out, and they oughtn't really to stand without their rugs. D'you mind awfully if you don't get your tea?'

'No, of course not, but I'd just got Joy nicely tied up.'

'Well, untie her, then. Let's sneak out before Willy comes back.'

'I can't. I knotted her reins so tight I can't undo them.'

'Here, I'll do it.' Denys felt his way over to her, dragging Buck after him. 'What on earth sort of a knot is this?' he said, fumbling with Joy's reins.

'Let me undo the buckle.' Mary bent close to him. She had taken off her hat, and her loose, untidy hair swung against his face.

'Blast this knot,' he said, 'I can't——' He broke off. 'How lovely your hair smells,' he said suddenly in a funny, breathless sort of voice, and before she could say anything, he had twisted it round the side of her neck and pulled her close to him. 'Mary—let me kiss you.' His face was vague above hers in the darkness.

'Oh, no, you mustn't,' she stammered. She could feel her heart beating madly against his coat, half with excitement, half with fright, and sudden shyness. Her romantic imaginings about him had always faded out before the final close-up. She tried to turn her head away, but he was holding her hair too tightly. 'Oh no, you mustn't,' she said again, as he began to kiss her eagerly and inexpertly all over her face. 'Oh, Denys——'

Behind him Buck shifted restlessly and stamped on the hard earth floor. Denys lifted his head and jerked at the reins. 'Quiet you!' He stared at Mary through the gloom. 'Gosh, darling, I've been wanting to do this ever since last night. When I saw you in that white thing, it was like a sort of seeing you for the first time. I suddenly realized you weren't a kid any more. You know, I'd always thought of you running round in shorts——' He held her against him. The tiepin of his white stock was pressing into her forehead as she hid her face against him and mumbled:

'But you kissed me that time in the attic—don't you remember?'

'Oh, that!' He kissed her hair. 'That was only fooling. We must have been a sloppy pair of kids. Mary, d'you love me?'

'I always did.' She twisted a button on his coat, whispering.

'No, silly,' he brushed it aside. 'I don't mean that. I mean now.'

'Yes.'

'I love you, Mary. Isn't it fun to say? Here——' He forced her chin up with his hand and began to kiss her again. Mary shut her eyes. He loved her; he wanted to kiss her; she let him.

'Anything wrong?' They broke apart, guiltily, at the sound of Willy's voice from the doorway. 'The wife sent me out to say *if* you're wanting tea are you comin' in for it or ain't you? You don't know the wife. Once she's got the tea-leaves in the pot, drink it you've got to, whether you want it or no.'

'Well, we're awfully sorry,' began Mary and Denys together, and laughed. He squeezed her arm. 'I'm afraid we can't stop, after all. We thought—er, it's really later than we thought, you see, and we've got to get back. If half a crown would be any compensation——' He went

88

to the door, feeling in his pocket, and Mary marvelled at his sophistication. 'I love him,' she whispered to Joy, leaning her cheek against the horse's warm neck, and Joy blew hot, wet breaths into her hand. When Denys had untied her, they led the horses out, with Willy watching and muttering from the back-door step, wondering whether he would get better value for the half-crown as a peace-offering for the wife or beer for himself.

Once out of the village they trotted steadily along the road, their coat-collars turned up against the cold. Mary kept peering at Denys through the deepening violet of nightfall, and loving what she saw. Occasionally, he leaned across and kissed her, and when she thought about him saying, 'I love you,' she was so happy that she could not keep her mouth from stretching into a grin of its own accord. She could remember everything that he had said.

He had said they were sloppy kids. Well, it must have been sloppy of her then to have been in love with him and fancied that they were engaged all that time ago. Were they engaged now? she wondered; he hadn't said anything, but it was all right. He loved her; soon he would propose, and it would all be desperately romantic. She would never tell him all the things she had thought when she was a child; she had been a sloppy kid. Fancy not knowing the difference between that and the real grown-up thing. He thought her grown-up. She would cut her hair without her mother's consent, if necessary, and be more grown-up still, and then he would propose to her.

The darkness and the steady clip-clop of hooves on the road lulled her thoughts as she rose and fell, rose and fell to the rhythm of Joy's trotting feet. Beside her, Buck moved half-unseen, with his longer, swinging stride, and she had only to put out her hand and there was Denys', squeezing it, lifting it up to nibble her fingers through the string glove. It was quite dark by the time they turned into the back drive, and a square of light was shining on to the road from the Bates' window. Between the undrawn lace curtains they had a glimpse of a tea-table, and Mrs. Bates in a flowered apron cutting bread. Mary swore she could see tinned salmon.

'Gosh, I'm hungry,' she sighed. 'I hope they've kept us some tea. There might be muffins—and scones.'

'I could do with an egg or two myself.'

'Oh, so could I; and won't a bath be heaven? With about half a ton of those bath salts my mother gave yours for Christmas.'

'I don't suppose Ma uses them, anyway.'

As they rode into the yard, welcoming light was streaming out from the stable door. Tom was inside, forking down the horses' beds, and he came to the doorway, rake in hand, and took hold of Joy's bridle, as Mary slid stiffly to the ground.

'Well,' he said, 'fancy givin' 'em such a day of it, and they only half fit.'

'But, Tom!' Mary followed him, as he led Joy into her stall. 'She didn't seem to get a bit tired, and we had the most marvellous run, for miles and miles, and she jumped everything—and I fell off once—and we finished up right over by Ilfracary. That's why we're so late back.' She wanted to tell him all about it. He was always interested to hear about their day, but all he said was: 'Proper tucked up, the mare is,' running his hand over Joy's ribs. 'You'd ought to know better than to give them such a doin'.'

'What's up, Tom?' Denys came in at the door with Buck, blinking in the unshaded electric light.

'Oh, you don't know, of course,' muttered Tom, his head under the saddle flap, tugging at Joy's girths. 'Your grandmother—— She—she died, 'sarternoon.'

That was the fifth thing that happened in that winter.

Chapter Five

'MARY,' said Mrs Shannon, looking distastefully out of the window at the mackintoshed crowds being sucked into the 'Ideal Home Exhibition' across the road, 'this place gives me the pip. What would you say to not renewing our lease in the autumn and getting a wee house somewhere? I would like to have my own front door, and really, you know, I doubt whether one can live in West Kensington these days—it's almost a music-hall joke. I'd like to be nearer the shop, too—*my* shop.' With the money that Granny had left her she had bought herself into a partnership with Mrs Wilkes Armitage, who, being a woman of whims, was already tiring of her latest, and was only too thankful to halve the responsibility.

'How would you like that, chicken?' she went on, turning back into the room. 'You and I in a cute little house with geraniums in tubs and check curtains in the kitchen?'

'Mm,' said Mary, without looking up from the history book that she was trying to study while she ate her tea. The Matriculation Examination was only four weeks away, and she was feverishly stuffing her head with facts until it felt as if it would burst. She was trying to make up for the time she had wasted after she heard that Granpa was going to sell Charbury and live permanently in the Berkeley Square flat which had formerly been only his *pied-à-terre*. Everything seemed so hopeless then that she had abandoned all thought of work. Nothing had seemed to matter any more, and Denys didn't answer her letters, except once to send a postcard of the cricket pavilion, saying: 'Cheer up. Frantically busy. No more now. Love, D.'

They had met in the holidays, those gloomy Easter holidays when London had never seemed so ugly and so undesirable, but there had been nothing to do except to go to the cinema, or walk in the park, which he didn't like. Once, she had gone to tea at his house when all his family were out, and they had sat on cushions in front of the drawing-room fire, and for half an hour it had all been perfect, as it was before. Then Sarah came in and snapped on all the lights, and said: 'What on earth are you sitting in the dark for? How *weak*.'

The examination lasted three days, and took place in the school hall, fitted up with chairs and folding desks at such wide intervals that not even Muriel Hopkins, the expert at the sideways glance, could cheat. The eagle-eyes of a mistress on the platform raked the room continuously, and when Beryl Massey wanted to go and be sick, she was accompanied to and from the basin by a prefect, to see that she did not look up the date of the Battle of the Boyne while *in extremis*.

At each question paper put before her Mary's spirits sank a notch lower. They were impossible, they were unfair, they were things she had never even heard of. In the middle of trying to wrest a meaning out of an untranslatable Latin ode, which had not even the grace to have a verb in the first four lines, she suddenly thought of Charbury, and cried surreptitiously on to her folded arms for ten minutes of the precious time. She was so unnerved when it came to the French Oral that she could hardly say more than 'Oui' and 'non' and 'Oh, natur*elle*ment,' which made the examiner go 'Tt-tt-tt,' and so far forgo etiquette as to say: 'Oh no, no, no. Next please.'

When the results came out, Angela had passed with honours and Mary had failed. Angela was going to Switzerland in the autumn, and Mary might have been allowed to go with her, but now she was to stay on at St Martin's and take the examination again next spring. Nobody was ever quite able to say why it was so important; it was just something that Mary's mother and grandfather had got into their heads, and no amount of furniture-kicking from Mary could get it out. The only bright star on her horizon was that she was going to see Denys play in the Eton and Harrow match at Lord's. He was captain. Could greater glory be achieved on this earth? Aunt Mavis was going to take her, and Mrs Shannon was having a yellow muslin dress with a hat to match made for her at the shop.

'But, Mummy, I *must*, I simply *must* cut my hair. I've tried putting it up, but it simply won't stay. I look like Aunt Winifred, and pins keep falling out all the time. I can't go with it down my back; I don't look grown-up.' Denys would not want to show a schoolgirl off to his friends.

'Darling, you promised you'd wait till you left school. It's not often I put my foot down, but this time I really do. This lovely hair——' She lifted it up and let it fall, and Mary wriggled. 'Don't mess me about,' she said sourly, and went away to brood.

When she had decided on the shop, she walked up and down outside for five minutes before she dared go in.

'I want to have my hair bobbed, please,' she said in scarcely more than a whisper, to the girl who sat behind the desk, manicuring long talons that sent shivers down your spine.

'Hev you an appointment?' asked the girl, still filing.

'Er—no.'

'Och.' She flipped through the ledger, scraping her nails on the pages. 'Mr Pee-aire can do you in half an hour,' she admitted, so Mary went away and had a cup of tea and a rock cake in the tea-room of a High Street store, but the waiting was nerve-racking. The more she thought about it, the more lovely was the heaviness of her hair, and the snugness of it at the back of her neck, and the feel of the brush swooping through it at night. All round her women were eating ham teas and Devonshire teas, and all the peculiar things like egg-mayonnaise and fried fillet of plaice to which shopping seems to stimulate the appetite. They nearly all had short hair. She wondered whether they had gone through these pangs before they bobbed it, or whether their husbands had laughingly clapped a basin over their heads one fine Putney day and run a pair of shears round as casually as they would trim the garden hedge. Then she thought of Denys, and rose, left twopence under the plate, paid her bill, and walked determinedly back to the shop.

As the great chunks fell to the floor from the skilful scissors of Mr Pee-aire, whose accent was more Cockney than continental, the pale face that stared back at Mary from the mirror became more and more scared. She looked naked, she looked almost bald.

'Haven't you cut it rather short?' she asked timidly, fingering the bare, bristly nape of her neck with horror.

'Oh no, 's a lovely bob,' said Mr Pee-aire, whisking a brush over her shoulders. 'What are you going to do with the residue?' He kicked the sea of hair at his feet. 'Stuff a sofa?' When he had gone out, Mary picked up the curliest bit she could see and put it into her bag. Perhaps Denys would like to have it. He had said, 'How lovely your hair smells.'

When she put on her hat she found that she looked like an egg, so she took it off again and walked home bareheaded, shaking her head and trying to feel a joyous wind-blown freedom, but finding only an uncomfortable draught. To her relief, her mother was not yet home. Mary went out again and bought some sausages and a cauliflower, which she made into a cauliflower cheese for supper. She laid the dining-room table; she changed her school tunic for her brown dress with the big white bow, and had just decided to nip round the corner and buy some flowers, when she heard her mother's key in the lock. She arranged herself hurriedly on a sofa and, with a pounding heart, pretended to be reading a book. It was the first time Mary had ever seen her mother struck dumb. She just stood in the middle of the room, with her bright, little black eyes nearly coming out of her head, and a slow blush crept up Mary's face, as she tried to stare her out.

'Let me tell you one thing,' said Mrs Shannon, when at last she spoke. 'Don't ever become a mother.'

Mary and Aunt Mavis arrived at Lord's just in time to see Denys finish a glorious innings of fifty-three—and be bowled out by what Granpa and his clique in the Pavilion declared was a No Ball.

'What on earth have you done to yourself?' were Denys' first words to Mary. 'Oh, you chump, you've cut your hair.'

'Don't you like it?'

'Of course, I like everything about you. Come on, let's walk up this way and see who's here.' Mary was wildly happy and proud to be seen with him. He looked so splendid in his white flannels and pale blue blazer, with his white opened-necked shirt making him look more like Rupert Brooke than ever. Everyone looked at them as they strolled along, and Mary heard people say, 'That's the captain—the boy who made fifty.' Small boys in top-hats nearly had a stroke when he passed, and dug their relations in the ribs and said hoarsely, 'Look, Mater—or Pater—or Uncle Benjamin—that's Ritchie!'

'Oh, *what* a good-looking boy,' said mothers dreamily, and put up lorgnettes.

After lunch, when he went out to field, Mary sat with Granpa, who sat with his top-hat tipped over his eyes, knees apart, hands resting on the top of his stick, and followed every ball every inch of the way on or off the bat. Poor Granpa, everybody said he was being wonderful and 'picking up in a remarkable way,' but Mary didn't think he looked wonderful at all. He was quite different; the lines of his face had taken on a lost, worried look, like a dog, and when he had made his little jokes it was as if he had to, calling them up from somewhere with an effort because they did not come of their own accord. He went to the office every day now, instead of only occasionally, but he had confided to Mary's mother that even his beloved restaurant did not seem to want him any more. It was the child of his creation, and now it was slipping away from him. Thanks to Lionel and Guy, there was no longer anything for him to do, and they fobbed him off with unimportant things to keep him busy.

'How's "Shannon's"?' Mary said, for she knew he liked to be asked.

'Flourishing, thank you, my Poppet. You must come and have lunch with me soon and I'll educate your palate; I don't suppose you know much about food and wines, do you? You know, I laid down some port for your father when he was born, like I did for the other boys. It ought to be yours really. Shall I give it to you when you marry? If you marry a man with the sense to appreciate good stuff, that is.'

'Oh, yes, please.' Denys loved port. 'And I'd love to come to lunch, Granpa—one Saturday, could I, perhaps?'

'Whenever you like, I'm not busy. And you can see your Uncle Guy's latest monstrosity, too,' he added rather bitterly.

'What's that?'

'A cocktail bar, of all things—trying to Americanize the place. All done up in that shiny, what d'you call it stuff.'

Mary had been going to say 'How lovely,' for she had always thought 'Shannon's' too old-fashioned, but she checked herself.

'You shouldn't allow it, Granpa, if you don't want it,' she said, her eyes on Denys, streaking along the boundary to intercept the ball.

'I've no say in the matter; I only own the place. Oh, well fielded, sir! Jove, that's a good lad! See that, Tomlinson?' He turned round to a man behind them, who had a nose like an over-ripe strawberry.

'Lovely bit of work,' said Tomlinson, 'never saw such a smart lot of lads in the field. Oh, well bowled, sir! Middle stump——'

'Clean out of the ground. Good man, good man!' Granpa was thumping his stick on the boards enthusiastically. 'Now we've got 'em. Even if the light holds——' he turned round to Tomlinson again. He seemed to have forgotten his grievance about the cocktail bar. Mary thought how pathetic it was how little old people needed to make them happy. If only life could be a perpetual cricket match for Granpa, then, perhaps he would never feel lonely or unwanted. She took his hand and squeezed it, but he was watching someone doing his best to get run out, and patted her knee absently.

After the match she went back to dinner at Aunt Mavis's, where she was very shy because there were a lot of rather smart people there whom she didn't know, and another boy who had played in the match, who was a baronet, and called everyone 'My dear old thing.'

When it was time for Mary to go, Denys saw her out, and said she was a sweet child and kissed her in the hall, somewhat perfunctorily, because he said he ought to get back to the guests.

'When'll I see you again?' asked Mary.

'Oh, pretty soon—the end of term. I don't know, though, we're biffing off to France then, and after that I'm going to stay with Cape's people in Scotland. Tell you what, you must come up to Oxford next term, darling. I'll show you round and we'll have a good time.'

94

'I'll still be at school,' she said, pouting, 'I've got to stay two more terms.'

'You can't possibly. Tell 'em I said so. Look, I must go back. We don't want people to guess about us.' He kissed her again.

'I don't care——' Mary was reckless in her love, and she thought that she would not see him for so long. Everyone would have to know eventually, anyway.

'Good Lord, Ma would have ten fits if she knew, and Pa would say it was incest. Look, sweet, there's your taxi, you'd better go. There!' He kissed the end of her nose, and pushed her gently out of the door. 'Good-bye, darling.'

'Good-bye, Denys darling.' She turned back half-way down the steps. 'Denys, what's incest?' but the front door was already shut, and she went on down the steps, puzzled, in her yellow muslin dress that was wilting and crumpled now, like a dead daffodil.

In August Mrs Shannon, who was tired and overworked, took advantage of her growing influence over Mrs Wilkes Armitage to insist on three weeks' holiday, which she spent with Mary on a Mediterranean cruise. Her henna-headed partner, querulous at being chained to London in the silly season, was left wringing her hands among bales of tweeds to be made into sporting suitings 'for the moors.'

Mrs Shannon bought every variety of hat, handbag, and trinket at Gibraltar, Marseilles, Genoa, Palermo, Algiers, Tangier, Madeira and Lisbon, and then got discouraged with them in the atmosphere of the English Channel, and pressed them all on the stewardess as they passed the Needles. Mary played ping-pong and table tennis with a crowd of jolly young people in flowered beach pyjamas, and was kissed on the boat-deck by a wireless operator from Glasgow. A background of moonlit Tangier, rising white and mysterious out of the bay, made this feel pleasantly like Tropical Romance, until he sent her below in a panic by asking her to be his 'wee lassie' just for one night.

Her mother played bridge all day and all night, with a long cigarette-holder clenched between her teeth. She picked up a bone specialist with a ginger moustache, called Gerald Rigley, whose wife spent most of the trip enjoying ill-health in her cabin. Mrs Shannon made him laugh, and he followed her about looking like a whimsical Airedale, repeating *bons mots*.

But it was not Charbury.

When they came back Mary went to stay with the Shaws in a house they had taken in the Isle of Wight, and discovered the ecstasy of sailing. Mrs Shaw lay in a hammock on the lawn in exquisite white dresses, sipping orange juice, and Mr Shaw came down at week-ends and was very Yoho. He wore a small yachting cap on the back of his head and made more noise than ever, especially when he talked to the fishermen and the boatmen, whom he almost addressed as My Hearties. The house seemed to be always full of bronzed young men, and girls who had the knack of making Mary feel untidy. Even Angela's growing *savoir-faire* and attractive appearance made her feel shyer than ever.

'You're very silent,' Mr Shaw would boom at her at meal-times. 'I bet you're in love. Are you? Come on, now!' She blushed furiously and let it pass undenied. Anything to provide an excuse for being unable to keep up with the lightning exchange of topical jokes and the deflating vivacity of the others. She was happiest when they went sailing—Angela generally dragging her along to make the third with some young man: 'My dear, you must come. I simply couldn't bear to be alone with him.' Once Mary had got past the stage of pulling the wrong rope and being struck over the head by the boom, Angela and the young man were only too happy to allow her to steer the little boat unaided, while they joked and scrapped on the tiny forward deck. Mary would sit blissfully in the well of the stern, in a yellow bathing dress that sea-water had shrunk and faded, diligently keeping the boat's head to the wind, glorying in the smooth tug from the tiller and rope that made sailing like riding a horse, and the feel of the wind on her cheek as they slipped along with the sun dancing on and off the tops of the little Solent waves. When she wanted to execute a smart tacking movement she would shout excitedly, 'Look out, I'm going to turn!' and she would do hazardous things with the sail and the tiller which, when she didn't becalm them, nearly tipped the other two into the sea. All very dangerous, as Uncle Tim pointed out when he heard about it afterwards, but highly exhilarating.

But it was not Charbury.

Angela went excitedly off to Switzerland with a lot of new clothes, and Mary trailed sulkily back to a St Martin's that was bleaker than ever without her and held nothing but work and lacrosse. As Mary hated lacrosse, there was only work. She and her mother now lived in a state of semi-installation in a tiny house in Marguerite Street, off Sloane Square. The only thing that seemed to get painted was the scarlet front door, which had no fewer than three coats 'because the painter so enjoys doing it, probably an out-of-work artist, poor man,' said Mrs Shannon. 'More likely because red's the most expensive colour,' said Mary. Mrs Shannon had quite a time alternately giving cups of tea or pieces of her mind to carpenters, furniture removers, gas fitters, and the man who kept calling to ask if they were troubled with rats.

Mary passed her examination in the spring, and left St Martin's at the age of nearly eighteen, feeling as old as the hills, and as if she never wanted to do another stroke in her life.

'Well now,' said Mrs Shannon one evening for the hundredth time, rubbing cold cream briskly into her face. 'What are you going to *do*? Have you thought any more about it?' She worked her jaw about, contemplating herself critically in the dressing-table mirror.

'Oh, Mummy, don't keep on so, I've only just left school. Don't I get a minute's breathing space? I got your rotten Matric, what more d'you want?'

'Well, now you've got it, you'll be able to get a job or start training for something.' Her mother wiped off the cream and began to apply astringent lotion to her face with vindictive slaps.

'Oh, secretarial or something. No fear. Wearing my finger-nails down to the quick and writing up to *Home Chat* every week to ask if the boss means anything by taking me to dinner at the "Strand Palace" and telling me his wife doesn't understand him,' said Mary scornfully. 'Why must I be anything? Couldn't I do something at the shop—a mannequin or a—or a mannequin or something?'

'There's nothing much for you to do. Old Wilkie always cluttering up the place with inane débutantes as it is.'

'Well, if you'd only let me go to the Dramatic College with Angela——'

'Oh, darling, must we have all this again?' Mrs Shannon spoke quite crossly, but her face leapt into a high, artificial smile to enable her to rub on her rouge in the right place.

'How d'you know I wouldn't be a success? You don't seem to think much of your own daughter.' Mary was wandering round the bedroom, fiddling. She picked up a bottle and dropped it, spilling some of the lotion on her mother's new pale green carpet.

'Oh, Mary, I wish you'd leave things alone. Go and get a cloth before it leaves a mark.'

'Because you see,' continued Mary, coming back with a face towel, 'it's in the family after all. Look at Uncle Geoff: he was marvellous in that film, and it was only his first.'

'He was good, wasn't he?' said her mother, through a cloud of powder. 'D'you remember the bit where he tripped over the mat as he was going out of the door! I thought I'd die. Or maybe I'm prejudiced, but I don't know—when he met the fat policeman in the park——' she pattered on, and Mary had to wait until she paused for a moment to apply lipstick, to bring her back to the point.

'Yes, that's all very well,' said her mother, 'I give you an expensive stage training, and then ten to one you go and get married.'

'It's not expensive, it's quite a sordid place. Besides——'

'Besides what?' mumbled Mrs Shannon, out of the distorted mouth that accompanied the application of Mascara to her eyelashes.

'Oh, nothing.' Mary had been going to say: 'Denys and I couldn't get married for ages, if he's going to the Bar,' but her mother did not know that she was going to marry Denys. Nor did Mary herself in her heart of hearts. That was the chief reason why she wanted to do something exciting, like training for the stage, that would take her mind off the tiny, nagging doubt that she would not acknowledge, even to herself.

Mrs Shannon rose and struggled into a tight, black dinner dress, settling it into place with satisfied dabs at her unmatronly figure. 'Earrings or no ear-rings?'

'I don't care,' said Mary, sitting on the bed, swinging her feet against the valance and picking out the threads of the counterpane. 'I don't approve of your going out with a married man, anyway.'

'Oh, darling!' her mother chuckled, screwing in the diamond pendants that her husband had given her nearly twenty years ago, 'don't pose. In any case, I don't call a woman a wife who won't have children and who's practically bedridden for nothing at all as far as I can see. If she won't come up to town with her husband, well—she can't expect him to go out with the chaps *every* night.'

'Gerald only comes to London to see you.'

'Don't talk rubbish,' said her mother, pleased. 'He has to come up every month for those lectures.'

Mary sniffed. 'Well, anyway, leaving me all alone——'

'Oh, darling, I'm so sorry. Do you mind?' Her mother turned round swiftly, comb in hand. 'No, of course you don't,' she said, turning back to the mirror. 'You're only sulking, you love being alone. Mabel's left you a lovely supper, and I thought you told me you were going to the cinema afterwards with that messy girl—Toots, Boots, whatever you call her.'

'Her name's Poo, and she's not messy. Even if she is—so would you be if you lived with four brothers and sisters and a consumptive mother and a father, who slaves his guts out doing something—I forget what, but something pretty foul—so that they can have a joint on Sundays, in a ghastly flat over a draper's shop, where every time they go in or out, they have to step over piles of suspenders and dress preservers and——'

'All right, all right, there's no need to get Red about it, but you might ring up a cab for me, there's a good girl.'

Mary came to the front door, as her mother was going out in a faint aura of perfume, her velvet cape gathered round her shoulders. 'For the last time,' she said, opening the door—'Can I go to the Dramatic College?'

'For the last time—*no*,' said Mrs Shannon, going down the two steps and crossing the pavement to the taxi.

98

Dearest Tich (wrote Uncle Geoffrey from Hollywood, in green ink on wafer-thin paper),—*Thanks for your letter. No, I'm not married yet or divorced, though there is a very cute little Momma from Springfield, Ill., who has caused stirrings in my girlish heart, or maybe it's the spring. Glad you liked the picture. You ought to be seeing the next pretty soon, unless they decide to haul it in and remake it again. They've remade it so often, once more wouldn't hurt.*

Well, well, so you're thinking of following in Uncle's footsteps. I wish you luck, and more skill than I ever had, but why a Dramatic School? In my day, I don't think there were such things, but times have changed, of course, and far be it from me, etc. Maybe some day you and I'll put on our own show on Broadway. A year and a half of this have made me long for the boards, but—dough is dough.

Yors til deth

Uncle Geoff

PS.—Maybe this is none of my business, but have you ever thought about getting a job where there would be more chance of you helping your mother out a bit in the money line? She says she's doing fine, but that's the way she always is. Forget I said this—I'm not one to talk, anyway.

Mary's course at the Dramatic School did not start until the autumn, so she spent an idle summer doing nothing much except getting rather fat.

'You grew late, now you're getting your puppy-fat late,' said her mother, stitching away at a skirt that she was letting out for her. 'You used to be such a skinny little thing, but you'll fine down. You'll have to fine down before you get your name in lights.'

'I hope to goodness I do,' said Mary, finishing the last square of a bar of chocolate, and getting up to fetch a banana from the dining-room.

The peak towards which all her hopes and dreams and excitement were rising was the 'Commem.' ball at Denys' college, to which he had asked her.

She had only been up to Oxford once, with Linney and Granpa in the Daimler, and they had had tea and buttered buns in Denys' rooms, and afterwards they had gone all round the colleges, with Granpa reminiscing every yard of the way, and dragging them into detours to find elusive corners where he used to climb into college after hours, or where old Sickert—'He's a High Court Judge now'—had shinned up a lamp-post with a policeman's helmet.

'We did it all on beer, too. None of those poisonous spirits that you boys seem able to afford. Beer was beer, too, in those days—not gassy stuff in bottles. My Scout used to bring it up in great bedroom jugs, I remember.' Denys winked at Mary behind his back, and then Granpa had told them his story about Entwhistle: 'Divinity student—you know the sort, all God and no guts—got a First in his Finals, and wanted to celebrate. So what does he do? He gets about ten chaps up to his room and then he locks the door on 'em. "Now then, you devils," he says, producing one bottle of claret from behind his back, "not one of you leaves this room until every drop of this is finished." '

They had seen the New College lawns, Magdalen tower, and the Martyrs' Memorial, with its tradition that one member in each generation of a certain family must climb to the top and hang something rude on the highest spire. Mary, wearing high heels, had got very tired, and was discouraged by a whole afternoon of being with Denys and yet not with him. She was rather awed by his impressive status as an inhabitant of this essentially masculine world, his carefully slovenly clothes, with a strip of ragged black cloth called a Gown hanging from one shoulder, and his new air of nonchalance that made her feel very school-girlish.

However, now she was a schoolgirl no longer. She had discovered how to manage her hair, had been to one or two parties and a night club, and laid on lipstick with the idea that each layer was a layer of sophistication.

Mrs Shannon was inclined to be dubious about letting her share a room at a hotel with an unknown girl called Greta Daniel, and going to the ball under the vague chaperonage of someone called 'Old Nick's Aunt.' However, the constant defeat of her good nature by Mary's stubbornness was sapping her morale, so she only protested feebly as a matter of form, shrugged her shoulders, and said, 'Oh, well, I suppose times have changed since my day.' The knowledge that Aunt Mavis was furious because Denys had asked Mary to the dance instead of Sarah strengthened her approval.

Mary and Greta Daniel were to travel up to Oxford together. Meeting at the bookstall at Paddington, carrying a newspaper for identification, they loathed one another at sight.

Greta was stupendously smug, with nothing at all to be smug about. She was insignificant-looking, with fat legs, a face that was quite pretty in a niggling way, and a badly set permanent wave. She had been to Oxford many times before. She knew the platform, she knew which part of the train to get into; she almost had a season ticket. Denys' friend, George Gurney, was, it appeared, her fiancé, and she showed Mary a rather common little cluster of amethysts on the third finger of her left hand.

Mary wished she had a ring from Denys to display. Oh, it would be nice to be sure of him! murmured the voice inside her to which she never listened.

'What year's your cousin?' asked Greta.

'First.'

'Oh, yes, of course. George is in his second.'

Conversation on the way up was sticky. Since they had got to spend a night in the same room—ghastly thought—Mary thought they might as well make an attempt to get on together, but it was impossible. Greta was clad in an impenetrable armour of self-satisfaction. Mary, watching her apply an almost colourless lip-salve as they neared their destination, made her own mouth more scarlet than ever, defiantly. She prayed that it would not be a double bed.

Denys and George Gurney met them at the station. Greta took over George with a quiet proprietorship from the moment their hands met and remained clasped, and if that was her fiancé, thought Mary, she had less to be smug about than ever. He was very tall, strong enough, doubtless, but unwieldy, and broad all the way down from his shoulders. He had straight, thick, red hair and a face like a box, with horn-rimmed spectacles, and he talked a great deal and very earnestly in a surprisingly high, shrill voice. 'He's a Buchmanite,' said Denys in an explanatory aside to Mary as they left the station.

They parted at the college, and Denys took Mary to have tea in his rooms. 'Darling,' she said, 'do you live on buttered buns?' Someone called Fat came in in a pair of straining flannel trousers and a canary-yellow cardigan, ate most of the buns and stayed quite a long time, lounging on the ancient sofa. Mary wished he would go away. She didn't want to hear his rude limericks; she wanted to be alone with Denys. She could hardly take her eyes off him; she was so acutely conscious of him when they were in the same room that she could never be natural. Fat thought she was a bore, she could see that, and after a while he heaved himself to his feet and loafed off, yawning. Denys and Mary sat on the sofa and he kissed her. His kisses were different, much more exciting, but—strangely different. So this was one of the things that Oxford taught people.

A clock chimed somewhere in the collage. 'Mary, darling,' said Denys, 'I could stay here all night with you, but if we're going to this show, we really ought to go and change. We're dining in Nick's rooms at half-past seven and we can't be too late.' Mary wished for a moment that there were going to be no dance, that it was going to be just her and Denys alone all evening. When they were together with other people, she was always terrified that he was comparing her with the others, unfavourably, thinking that she was not as clever, not as smart and pretty, noticing that she was shy.

'I'll take you along to the hotel,' he said, pulling her to her feet. She looked round for a mirror. 'You can fix yourself in my bedroom, if you like,' he said, and she went through into the other room, prying about when the door was shut, looking fondly at things that he wore, things that he used every day. There were photographs of his father and mother, with Aunt Mavis looking all chest, and holiday snapshots of Julia and Sarah, with Sarah in a bathing dress also looking all chest. He ought to have one of me, thought Mary, I'll send him one with that lock of hair I kept.

While she was combing her hair in front of the mirror, he came in and put his arms round her from behind, digging his chin into her shoulder, rubbing his cheek against hers. She looked at his face in the glass. He was so marvellous looking: how wonderful it was to be in love with someone you could be proud of. It would be so shaming to have to produce George Gurney as one's fiancé, and yet he *was* Greta's fiancé, whereas Denys—but it was all right. It was just that men took things for granted; they didn't always have to put things into words as women did.

'What's the tragedy?' asked Denys, smiling at her serious reflection.

'Nothing.' She turned to him, and he kissed her, holding her close. 'There now,' he said, 'you'll have to powder your nose again. Buck up, we really ought to be going.'

It was fun to walk along the crowded High with him, skipping across the road among the buses and the droves of bicycles, with the evening sky pale above the fantastically old buildings. Denys seemed as usual to know everybody. He kept greeting other undergraduates, wearing the grey flannels and sports jacket that were almost a uniform, some callow, some quite exciting-looking, a lot of them with girls attached. Mary put her hand through Denys' arm and felt as possessive as Greta Daniel.

Greta was already in the bedroom when Mary went up, washing her face vigorously with soap and water, wearing a green kimono and velvet slippers with stupid rosettes on the toes. There were two beds. Greta's evening dress—pale green taffeta—was laid out on the larger, more comfortable one, near the window. Mary said nothing, but sighed pointedly as she dumped her suitcase on to the smaller bed.

'You'll have quite a rush,' said Greta, emerging red-faced from the towel.

'Who cares?' said Mary. 'Any chance of getting a bath?' She began to throw off her clothes. Greta turned her back. She herself went through a complicated process of dressing without removing the kimono and emerged miraculously in a very decent locknit petti-coat.

When Mary came back from her bath, Greta was sitting in the bad

102

light at the dressing-table, doing her face with the aid of a tiny sample tube of vanishing cream and a solid powder compact. She applied her pale lipstick carefully to her small mouth and then as carefully rubbed it all off again with the tip of her little finger; then she put on a hair-net before getting into her dress.

'What a pretty frock,' said Mary politely, wandering round the room scantily clad to annoy her.

'It is rather, isn't it?' said Greta, smiling at her reflection in the long mirror. 'I always say green's a difficult colour to wear, but if you can wear it, you should.' She put on a pair of boat-shaped silver shoes with low heels.

'Why don't you wear high heels?' said Mary, taking a hand-mirror over to the window to do complicated things to her eyelashes. 'You'd be a better size to dance with your fiancé then. I always do, and you're even shorter than me.'

'Oh,' said Greta, 'I'm afraid I'm not very keen on high heels.' She combed out the woolly ridges of her permanent wave, puffed out the sleeves of the ingenuous taffeta dress, and said: 'Well, I think I'll be running along. George is waiting for me downstairs. *Isn't* this fun?'

When she had gone, Mary put on her dress and tried to see herself in the mirror with Denys' eyes. She had saved up her allowance and bought a white dress, because he had liked her in white that Christmas, more than a year ago. It was very lovely, but rather tight at the waist, and if she breathed too hard or laughed, the side fastening would go pop-pop and reveal a little slit of bare skin. I wish I was a bit thinner, she thought. I really ought to diet. Still, men like curves.

In her hair, she fastened a paste clip that she had had as a bridesmaid's present at Uncle Tim's wedding last winter. Uncle Tim had married a girl called Annabelle, who came from Southsea, and was not nearly as glamorous as her name. Mary learned afterwards that she had been hanging around the Navy for years, and was commonly known as the Portsmouth Hack. However, after several gins, Uncle Tim's growing itch for domesticity had got the better of him and landed him up under an archway of swords, very red in the face, with Annabelle like a triumphant horse at his side. In the photographs, it was Uncle Tim, not the bride, who looked sacrificial.

When Mary went downstairs, Denys was in the hall, finishing a drink. 'Can I have one?' asked Mary, to prolong the time in which they would be alone together. He ordered two cocktails and then they each had another, and by the time Mary pushed through the revolving doors into the street, she felt very lighthearted; and as if her cheekbones were higher than usual, and she must smile.

When they arrived at the rooms where they were to dine, the party was already seated at a long table. There were nine people, including

103

Old Nick's Aunt, who had evidently been dug up from some obscurity for the occasion, and was having difficulty in making her hair stay up. Mary had to stand and be introduced all round, and the other girls eyed her like hostile dogs, furious because Denys was so much better-looking than anything they had got. Greta, eating grapefruit with little finger well cocked, was still perfectly satisfied with George, and said, 'Oh, Mary and I are *old* friends,' when it was her turn to be introduced.

Some of the other girls were terrifyingly *soignée* and looked much older than the men, one or two of whom looked like little boys dressed up in their white ties and tails. Next to Denys sat a blonde girl, with an incredible white skin and a large orchid in her hair. He seemed to know her. Mary was horrified to hear her address him as 'Denys, darling,' and hoped that she called every man that. She drank a glass of champagne quickly and felt better. Next to her was Old Nick himself, undersized, like a comic little monkey. He and Mary got on quite well while Denys was talking to the blonde girl, and Mary felt like Madame du Barry, no less, when Denys turned round and said, 'Now then, Nick, no flirting with my girl.'

After dinner, the Aunt, still fumbling about with hairpins, led the girls downstairs to powder their noses. They passed through a quadrangle and Mary saw that the college garden had been turned into a fairyland of coloured lights and Chinese lanterns, with sitting-out places suggestively arranged in the shadows.

In a small dim room, a crowd of women struggled to get at two fly-blown mirrors, and there was more suspicious eyeing. Mary saw the blonde girl putting blue on her eyelids and made a mental note to get some herself tomorrow.

'Your dress is undone at the side,' said Greta, passing by. Mary was delighted to see that champagne brought out a rash on the back of her neck.

Then they went out, and Mary danced with Denys in the marquee that was so big you couldn't hear the band at one end of it. All round the sides sat ancient specimens, male and female, of Oxford's past, telling each other that 'it does the heart good to see the young ones enjoying themselves.' Every time the music stopped Mary clapped vigorously and prayed that it would start again. She never wanted to stop dancing. Champagne and love were making her head sing with happiness. Just by tilting her eyes upwards she could see the line of Denys' cheek. He held her very tightly and they danced without speaking. After this, he would take her out on to the lawn and say lovely things to her in the darkness. She moved her fingers on his sleeve, caressingly. With a roll of drums and a clash of cymbals, the band announced that this time they had finished with 'Little White Lies' for good.

'My God,' said Denys, 'I need a drink. Come on.' Mary stood feeling rather lost, while he fought his way to the bar, and came back with champagne for them both. They drank it, wedged into the talking, laughing, shouting crowd. Denys kept hailing people. The blonde girl with the orchid in her hair came wriggling through the crowd with Nick, and they all had another drink together. The blonde was very witty and disparaging about everybody in sight, and Mary felt dull, but she consoled herself with one of her stock phrases: 'Men don't like catty women.'

In the distance, the band could be heard drifting into the rhythm of an old-fashioned waltz. 'Oh, Lord,' said Nick, 'one of the things I can't do, Anne.'

'Oh, but I love to waltz,' said Anne, pulling down her moist red mouth. Before Mary could say, 'So do I,' the blonde had somehow spirited Denys away in the direction of the dance floor.

'Come and sit outside,' said Nick, and they went and sat on two uncomfortable chairs behind a bush, and Mary felt happier because Nick was amusing, and flirted with her mildly.

'I suppose you'd scream for help if I kissed you?' he said.

'Yes,' she said, and wondered if she really would. Although the night was young, everybody seemed to be kissing everybody already. On their way to find somewhere to sit, they had passed countless huddled shapes, and the air was full of heavy breathing. It felt almost silly to be sitting out here and not kissing.

'We ought to go back,' said Mary, getting up and looking anxiously to see if the garden chair had marked the back of her white dress. 'I promised I'd dance the next with Denys.'

It was horrid when she could not find him anywhere, and eventually she got rid of Nick by going into the ladies' cloakroom, where she found Greta having a frill of her taffeta dress sewn on by a down-trodden woman in a black alpaca dress.

'There, that's the best I can do,' she said, breaking off the thread with a sigh. 'It would take more than I can do to make a proper job of it.' She stuck the needle back among the crop of pins in her bosom.

'George tore it,' Greta told Mary with satisfaction. 'Wasn't it naughty of him?'

Mary was revolted. 'What would Dr Buchman say?' she asked witheringly.

'Well, you see,' Greta followed her over to the mirror, 'if you get guided to do a thing, you have to do it. George is guided to be madly in love with me. Shall I tell you what he said to me?'

'No thanks,' said Mary. 'I'm not a member of the Group.'

The old Greta had been bad enough, but this new, confiding one was far worse. Apparently there was nothing, not even sex, that she could

105

not be smug about. Mary hurried out, lost her way among the cloisters and, to her relief, discovered her way to the bar, where she found Denys, slightly dishevelled, drinking and laughing with a crowd of people.

'Darling!' he greeted her, 'where have you been? I thought you were being raped by Nick. Come and dance.' He missed his step once or twice and whirled her round faster and faster, excited, laughing, with a lock of hair falling over his forehead. She thought of that crazy time in the attic at Charbury, when he and she had been drunk with the electricity of a thunderstorm. After the dance, he took her out on to the lawn, but there was something about him kissing her there that she didn't like. It made them one of the huddled shapes over which people stumbled and giggled on their way to find somewhere to become a huddled shape themselves.

'Darling, couldn't we go back to your rooms?' she said, but they couldn't because it wasn't allowed and also it was supper-time.

At supper there was more champagne and variegated, rather messy food that people seemed more inclined to throw about than to eat. So Mary threw it, too, because it was the gay thing to do. Denys kissed her on the lips right in front of everybody, which she hated. 'Don't,' she said furiously, but he only laughed, and took her away to dance. While they were dancing, the buoyancy that the champagne had given her left her all at once, and she slumped and felt suddenly tired and miserable about all the things that Denys should have said and done and hadn't. At the end of the dance there was one awful moment when she was bored. She didn't want to go and be kissed in the garden, she didn't want to drink any more, Denys was in no mood for conversation; what was there to do? She was bored. It was a terrible, treacherous thought to feel like that when you were with someone you loved.

They ran into a crowd of Denys' friends, and Mary made herself be bright and say silly, amusing things. Wit was beyond her, but it was not necessary. One of the men, a square, sporting buffoon with a fluffy moustache, asked her if she would 'tread a measure' with him. 'D'you mind, Denys?' She was suddenly wise, and realized that she would be better away from him for a while—a very short while. With his hair falling over his forehead, he was sweeter to look at than ever.

'Of course not, darling,' he said, waving a vague hand at her. 'Keep the next one for me, though!' he called after her, as she went away with her partner, whose name was Tuppy.

Tuppy did not dance very well. He pushed her steadily round the room, ignoring the waltz time, and she wondered whether she could tell him it was a waltz and perhaps count, '*One*, two, three—*one*, two, three,' like in a dancing class. But he seemed quite happy, sweating profusely, and trundling her round as if she were a milk churn. After-wards, they sat on a sofa under some stairs and she was more bored than ever. Tuppy did not even want to kiss her. He talked about cars while her jaw ached with trying not to yawn. The lovely effects of champagne were quite gone and only the nasty ones were left: the taste in the mouth, the splitting ache in the brow and the impotence of not being able to clarify one's thoughts.

To her relief they heard the music start again, and Mary got up, doing up the side fastenings of her dress for the hundredth time.

'Thank you so much, it was lovely,' she said. 'I must go and find Denys now.'

'Oh, I say,' stammered Tuppy, surprisingly. 'You will have another with me, won't you? You know, I think you're a damn nice girl, honestly. Brains, too,' he tapped his practically non-existent forehead. 'That's what I like.' Mary shook him off in the crowd round the entrance to the marquee.

How did people go on and on being so gay? she wondered, watching the couples whirl with undiminished vitality. It was nearly three o'clock. So this was the grown-up fun that had been the goal of her school-girl ambition. She wanted Denys badly, and he would be looking for her. 'Keep the next for me,' he had said, sounding quite anxious. It was a nice thought to think of two people looking for each other and coming together in the middle of this jumbled mob. But where was he? She wandered about looking in the bar, the cloisters, all the sitting-out rooms. He must be in the garden. Perhaps he was stuck with a girl he could not shake off. She walked out on to the lawn, passing couple after couple, the only one alone. An extra bright Japanese lantern made visible a horrid scene on a bench. That green taffeta frock, that red hair; it could be nobody but Greta and George locked in the most uncouth of passionate embraces. They would have to be under a lantern, too. The unattractive people were always the most shameless. She passed on, thinking of pungent things to say to Greta in the privacy of their bedroom, which she knew would never get said.

She went back to the cloisters, searching everywhere, down every passage, returning every now and then to the marquee to see if he were there. Oh, Denys! She began to hunt frantically, pushing people aside who were in doorways through which she wanted to go, hurrying everywhere as if she were on some desperate mission. She even opened the doors of one or two rooms off staircases. In one of them a man was in bed and swore at her. In another, she clicked on the light and revealed no less than three couples, blinking furiously from various pieces of furniture. She thought of asking some man to go and look in the Gents' for her, and went down again to the cloisters. Three men, coming singing round a corner, knocked into her. 'Whoa!' said the middle one, reeling, 'mind the pretty lady!' One of the others was Nick.

'Oh, Nick,' she caught his arm. 'Have you seen Denys? I've been looking for him for hours and I can't find him anywhere.'

'Denys?' said the reeling one. 'You couldn't mean Denys Ritchie, by any chance?'

'Yes, have you seen him?'

'Shertainly. Denys Ritchie, last seen embracing a blonde on the shofa in *my* room. My room, mark you!' He wagged a finger under her nose.

'Shut up, Arthur,' said Nick uneasily. 'Come on, Mary, I'll take you to have a drink.' He tried to take her arm, but she shook him off. 'No,' she said, trying to be flippant, with her stomach feeling as if it were dropping out of her body. 'One likes to know these little things. I suppose it really was Denys you saw?' she persisted to Arthur.

'O-oh, yes.' He chuckled, his mouth loose and inane.

'And the girl, she—er, she had an orchid in her hair, did she?'

'Lady,' said Arthur, swaying towards her, with a blast of alcoholic fumes, 'she may have had 'norchid in her hair when she went *in* to my room, but when *I* saw her'—he put out a hand to steady himself against a pillar—'she was distinctly—what's the ruddy word?—*derangée*.' He brought out the word with pride.

'Oh,' said Mary faintly, and then turned and fled, ignoring Nick's: 'Just a sec—Mary, wait!'

She felt quick sick. She must go somewhere, anywhere to be alone. She passed the door of the cloakroom and went in without thinking.

'Ow,' said the down-trodden woman. 'You do look bad. Feeling poorly?'

'A bit,' Mary turned away and pretended to be doing things to her face in the mirror.

'I'm sure I don't know what I can do for you,' said the woman defeatedly.

'It's all right,' muttered Mary crossly, and rushed out again. She was going to cry. She ran into the dark garden. People, people everywhere; was there nowhere she could be alone and dissolve in self-pity about this thing that Denys had done to her? She made blindly for the shadow of one of the buildings, and as she passed a doorway a man stepped on to the path. It was Denys.

'Hullo,' he said quite naturally, 'where are you off to in such a hurry?'

'Oh, Denys.' She looked at him in the light of the doorway; he had lipstick on his face. Mary burst into tears.

108

'What the——? Here, control yourself, for God's sake.' He pulled her into the shadow and began to walk along the path.

'Oh, how could you—how *could* you——' she stumbled beside him, searching vainly for a handkerchief, trying to wipe her eyes on her skirt. 'To kiss me and pretend you loved me—and then go straight to another girl!' she wailed.

'Oh, for God's sake,' he said furiously, kicking at the gravel, 'you talk as if you owned me.'

'But I thought, I thought——' If only he would stop walking and give her a chance. All the doubts that she had been forcing to the back of her mind for so long, came tumbling forward into miserable certainty. She hardly knew what she was saying. 'But I thought we were engaged!' she blurted out.

'We were *what*?' He stopped at last and faced her, and she could see that he was livid with anger. Oh, fool, fool, that she was to have said a thing like that. She pressed her hands to her cheeks, with her fingers under her eyes, sobbing against the palms, staring at him, stricken. He suddenly laughed, absurdly, trying to make a joke of it. 'You've got it wrong somewhere,' he said, putting his hands in his pockets and looking down at her, his face very white. 'He travels fastest who travels alone, that's my motto.'

'But at Charbury——' she put out a hand to touch him, but he stepped back irritably. 'Oh, Charbury. Why bring that up? What the hell's that got to do with it?'

'But that time coming back from hunting——'

'Oh, that.' He began to walk on again, and she had to run after him, breathless with sobbing.

'But you said you loved me, you said it—in that shed——'

'D'you have to throw every word I ever said back in my face?' he flashed. They had reached the end of the path and he turned back, walking along under the building again, muttering. 'Every bloody word—— Can't you understand, Mary? Look here—you're making me say this—it's pretty lousy, but can't you understand that it was different then? I mean, I wasn't even grown up, I hadn't met any other women. After all, we are cousins——' His voice was almost ashamed, but she was crying so much she hardly heard what he said. 'Oh, look here,' he stopped again and faced her in desperation. 'Stop crying, Mary, for the love of Mike. You make me feel the world's biggest cad. Here—take my hanky.' He thrust it at her. 'God, I feel terrible,' he said, putting a hand to his forehead. 'Look here, am I drunk or are you?'

She was hysterical by now. She crushed his handkerchief in her hand without putting it to her eyes. 'You beast, you beast, I hate you. All I want to know is,' she gasped, 'do you love me or don't you? If you don't, say so. Well, go on, say it!' she almost shrieked as he stood helplessly, saying nothing. 'Say it—go on!'

'Well, all right, you asked for it.' His face was terrifying in his sudden blaze of anger. 'You asked for it—No!' He hurled the word at her and then was suddenly gone. She heard the scrape of his feet as he ran up the stone steps into the building, a thudding on wooden boards and then a door slammed and she was alone in the silence and darkness. Somewhere a man's voice shouted, jubilantly, unsteadily, and there was a burst of laughter and then a silence again, in which she could hear the far-away, tuneless throb of the band.

She sat down on the steps in her lovely white dress, and dabbed at her eyes with his handkerchief. She couldn't cry any more. After a while, she got up listlessly and trailed across the lawn to the cloak-room. She averted her face while the peering woman gave her her coat and bag, and then walked away by herself to the entrance of the college, with the coat hanging over her shoulders. She didn't even bother to powder her nose.

'Taxi, Miss?' said the porter in a surprised voice.

'No, thank you.'

'Aren't you going to stay for the photo, Miss? Oh, what a shame!' She slumped down the steps and began to walk along the street. Her legs felt shaky and she had a blinding headache. When she got to the cross-roads, she looked down the street and saw a pale streak of light in the eastern sky. The darkness was already lessening imperceptibly. Morning was coming; tomorrow, and another tomorrow, and another and another after that. Days and days of regrets with nothing to think about except what a fool she had been.

She could not bring herself to look at her face when she got to her room. She simply threw off her clothes and hunched herself in bed, with the curtains drawn against the coming light. The lovely white dress was a formless glimmer, crumpled up half on a chair and half on the floor. Mary's eyes ached and the lids were swollen and throbbing, but she could not sleep. She dreaded Greta's return. Her head spun round and round. It felt so heavy and seemed to press deeper and deeper into the pillow, as if she was sinking . . . sinking . . . dropping into oblivion, then—click! The electric light snapped on in an agonizing blaze, and there was Greta, complacently dishevelled, her face glistening like a pine-apple chunk. She had not even bothered to pull her dress up from half-way down her shoulder. She was all ready to discuss every detail of George's pseudo-religious sex urges, but Mary slumped over on to her side and pretended to be asleep, refusing to answer Greta's openings of: 'Well, I must say—I hope you enjoyed yourself as much as I did,' and: 'George said he loved me in this frock, but he would like me even better without it. Isn't he *dreadful*?'

110

Greta was awake bright and early, ordering sausages, and Mary struggled unwillingly to consciousness, out of the thick mists of a drugged sleep, into the dull misery that was waiting for her with the first return of memory.

'I don't feel well,' she told Greta. 'I'm going to take an earlier train than I meant to. We'd better go home separately.'

'Oh, no,' said Greta, hopping out of bed in mauve pyjamas with short narrow legs. 'I can't let you go alone if you're not feeling quite the thing. George will have to do without his walk along the river.'

'No, don't,' said Mary, goaded. 'I'd rather be alone, really.' She began to stuff things into her suitcase.

'Aha!' said Greta, going back to her sausage, 'the morning after the night before, eh? I know what you need—a big glass of Eno's!'

'Don't make me sick!' muttered Mary, stuffing her slippers into the case so forcibly that the soles cracked.

Greta crunched toast noisily. Mary picked up her lovely white dress and began to fold it haphazardly. Underneath it, on the chair, lay the crumpled white ball of Denys' handkerchief. Tears pricked the back of her eyes, and she quickly stuffed the handkerchief down beside the slippers and bundled her dress in on top.

Even when she had done her face, it still looked puffy and hideous.

'Yes, you do look seedy,' said Greta, who was fiddling round the room in the green kimono, 'I wish I had a thermometer with me, I'd take your temp.'

'I'm all *right*,' said Mary, jamming on her hat. 'Good-bye.' She picked up her case and held out her hand. 'I must fly or I'll miss the train.'

'Good-bye, my dear. I do hope we'll meet again soon. You shall come to our wedding.'

When she was paying her bill downstairs, the clerk handed her an envelope. 'Gentleman left this for you this morning, Miss.'

It was Denys' writing. If she had been a girl in a film, she would have thrown it away unopened, and it would turn out in the end that it had been a letter proposing to her and making everything all right after all. But she was not a girl in a film, so she opened the letter in the train, and it said:

Mary dear,

    What can I say except that I'm sorry and I hope we'll always be friends. I'll understand if you'd rather we didn't meet again.

                                                     D.

With the beginnings of a new determination, she tore the letter up into very small pieces, and watched them flutter backwards out of the window as the train gathered speed.

She kept his handkerchief at the back of the drawer in her desk for a long time.

Chapter Six

'Now, girls, we're going to register Despair, Fear, Anger, Courage, Hope, Ecstasy, in six simple movements. On the knees, all! Start with the head dropped, raising it by degrees to end with the head thrown back for *Ec*-stasy!' Miss Dallas flung back her head with an abandon that nearly broke her neck.

It's a bit too much to ask at nine-thirty in the morning, thought Mary, dropping on to her knees like a sulky camel and flopping her head forward so that her smooth dark hair fell over her face. These Movement Classes were almost the worst of the many tortures that had revealed themselves in two and a half terms at the Rockingham College of Dramatic Art, especially if you were not one of the stars. To crown the degradation, they had to be attended in green tights and brief green tussore tunics with V-necks and elbow sleeves.

'Despair,' intoned Miss Dallas, and Mary, glancing sideways under her curtain of hair, saw Myrtle Drew practically writhing on the ground in a passion of realism. 'Fear!' All fifteen girls raised their heads slightly, turned up their eyes and cringed. Myrtle went one better by raising the back of her hand to her mouth. 'Anger,' growled Miss Dallas, and the heads rose a little, eyes rolling, fists clenched. Mary shook back her hair and wondered whether she looked as big a fool as she felt. 'Courage!' Everyone tried to look like Sybil Thorndike as Saint Joan. 'Hope!' said Miss Dallas on an indrawn breath, and the heads began the backward tilt, eyes heavenwards and mouths hanging slightly open. '*Ec*-stasy!' She made the word onomatopœic, and those like Myrtle Drew strained to achieve delirium, while those like Mary hung their heads backwards, raised their arms and hoped for the best.

'So!' cried Miss Dallas, jumping to her feet with a little skipping movement, her tunic—slightly longer than the students'—with a pearl bar brooch at the neck—fluttering about her green cotton thighs.

'Now let's take that through quickly—— One continued, swift play of expression from Despair to Ecstasy, shall we?' Her brightness met with small response, except from Myrtle who, with clasped hands and bated breath, awaited a further opportunity to display her genius.

'Drop heads—commence!' Miss Dallas jollied them along, clapping her hands briskly to mark each change of emotion, a brave smile fixed in the small space between her nose and chin, undaunted by the maniac scene before her. They went through this frenzied performance several times more, with a pause between each for Miss Dallas to say: 'Middleton, I don't like your Fear. Beautiful Hope, Drew. Just show the others, will you? Girls, turn round and watch Drew's Hope. Put more into it, Shannon, dear, I can't tell the difference between your Fear and your Anger.'

Then they scrambled to their feet, with the knees of their tights wrinkled and dusty, and had to march round the room for ten minutes with bean bags on their heads. This was easy enough and you could talk out of the side of your mouth to the person in front or behind, under cover of Miss Dallas's shrill exhortations.

'This is what we pay twenty guineas a term for,' muttered Mary to Angela, who was pacing in front of her on her beautiful long straight legs. 'Little did we know, when we were so keen to come here.'

'Still, it's worth it, if it's going to get us on to the stage.'

'Yes, *if*. I'm beginning to get discouraged; these tights are enough to kill anyone's ambition. Besides, I can't even act, much less register ecstasy directly after breakfast. It's different for you, you're good.'

'Oh, I'm not, I'm terrible——'

'Now, now, now, Shaw! You're here to work, not to chatter. How do you expect to act if you don't know how to walk across a stage?' Miss Dallas clapped her hands, gave a little skip which brought her feet into the fifth position and said: 'Into line now, for Individual Miming!' This was the worst part of all. The students stood in a whispering line against the wall, and each in turn had to step into the middle of the room and render in dumb show whatever Miss Dallas' whimsical fancy conceived.

The first girl, a strange creature called Muriel Willoughby, with wild hair and spindly legs, was told to be the Spirit of Spring. As an impersonation of Nervo and Knox, it was brilliant. One could not laugh; it was all so sad and embarrassing and too painfully suggestive of what one probably looked like oneself.

Myrtle Drew made a great hit as a shepherdess gazing into a still pool at sunset. Miss Dallas clapped and said, 'Splendid,' and Myrtle saw her name in lights.

As her turn drew near, Mary began to grow cold with apprehension. She watched Angela, with her shining coppery hair in little curls all over her head, saunter into the middle of the room, discover a dead body, and collapse from shock. There was no doubt about it, thought Mary enviously, she was good.

113

'Now, Shannon,' said Miss Dallas, who did not think much of Mary, but was paid to be impartially enthusiastic about everybody, 'let's see what you can do with "Puck." '

Oh, it was too much. Why couldn't she give it to someone else who knew how to do whimsical things with their arms and legs? All Mary could think of was to poke her outspread fingers at the air in the traditional pantomime manner, and mince about on tiptoe, pausing occasionally to strike a sort of 'hark' attitude. She felt herself going crimson, suffused with waves of heat as from an oven door, and finished her act as soon as she dared.

She returned to the wall, casting baleful glances at Miss Dallas, who only said, 'So!' with undiminished jauntiness and passed on to the pleasure of seeing Lola Stubbs shoot off a bow-and-arrow with thrown-out chest and flashing teeth.

At half-past ten the girls all trooped out of the big bare room, dropping a perfunctory, stumbling or sweeping curtsey to Miss Dallas *en route*. They had to put top coats over their shoulders on the way to the cloakroom in case the male students saw them in their tights.

The cloakroom smelt of grease paint, shoes, and wet mackintoshes. Mary changed into her blouse and skirt, amid a jumble of bodies, and was unwillingly aware that Margaret O'Gorman's underwear needed the twelve-minute Rinso soak.

'What's next, Angel?' she asked, as Angela's lovely pointed face struggled through the neck of her dress.

'Recitation.'

'Not with Rocky?'

'Mm. That's why I'm putting on more lipstick.'

'Fat lot of good that'll do you. He only likes boys.'

Everyone insulted, disparaged and ridiculed Julius Rockingham behind his back, because in his presence they were paralysed with fear. He was nearly seventy, very thin and tall, with a lined ascetic face and a commanding nose that must have spoiled his otherwise successful profile in the days before he abandoned the stage to teach.

By a sadistic process known as 'knocking off the corners,' he reduced his pupils, particularly the girls, to a state of pulpy shame. When they had reached the required level of self-abasement, he proceeded to build them earnestly up to his own conceptions, until, three years after they had brought their spontaneity and ambition through the doors of his college, they staggered out, carrying their disillusion, and a tendency to take themselves deathly seriously. In about half of them, fortunately, the call of the stage was stilled for ever. Of the other half, those who were Rocky's favourites sometimes managed, with or without his influence, to get into Repertory or Touring Companies. The rest battered out their youth against the doors of agents, did crowd work for the films or sacrificed their so-called innocence for a walking-on part or a chance in Cabaret. All this was dawning on Mary by degrees. She was beginning to realize that Uncle Geoffrey had been right; this was no place for her, but as it had been her idea she could not possibly admit it. She had discovered quite early on that she would never be an actress, but she struggled along in the wake of Angela, who had both talent and beauty, and in between the moments of terror and degradation, the College was amusing enough.

It had helped her to get over Denys; she could now be almost natural in his presence, and her heart no longer gave quite such a sickening lurch if she met him suddenly. At first she had thought that her heart was dead. She told herself that she had been through a searing experience which had left her as a woman set apart from love—a tragic figure. This sustaining vision had tided her over the misery of the end of last summer, until the excitement and newness of the Dramatic College had given her something else to think about. She had not told her mother about Denys, but she had a suspicion that Mrs Shannon knew all about it nevertheless. It was unlike her not to want to satisfy her curiosity when she came upon her daughter sobbing in various parts of the house. She had asked no questions; she had simply donned the rôle of the heavily understanding mother, and had done a lot of shoulder-patting and given Mary an expensive evening dress from the shop. Mary had no idea how she knew, but was certain that if she had not known she would never have rested until she did.

Besides Julius Rockingham, there were four or five teachers of elocution, stage technique and production at the College, also Miss Dallas and Miss Yvonne E. Bullock, who taught Greek dancing twice a week in a grubby toga, with a snood worn very low on the forehead. There was also Count Borchens, who taught fencing, and who had escaped from the revolution with practically nothing but a sensuous Russian eye and roving hands.

The students were divided into two groups, according to year, and most of the classes were mixed, but there were no American collegiate boy-and-girl affairs flourishing in corners. A mutual dislike and jealousy flourished between the sexes, fostered by Rocky's delight in belittling one in front of the other. In any case, the men were either the dregs of humanity, or like Robert Darwin, the king of the second year, who was tall and willowy, with soft brown hair and a profile that was never off his mind.

Rocky's recitation classes were held in the College's little theatre, which boasted of a complicated and dangerous lighting plant, but hardly any scenery. Economy and dramatic simplicity were combined by long green curtains, which hung all round the three sides of the stage, with openings here and there for exits and entrances.

115

'Follow your spirit,' Henry the Fifth would cry, brandishing his tinfoil sword, 'and upon this charge, cry: "God for Harry, England and Saint George!" ' He would stride from the stage, with arm farthest from the audience raised, and knees slightly bent à la Gielgud, only to find that he had to pound frantically along the curtains looking for the way out.

The stage furniture was adequate and friendly with repeated use. There was a block of steps that had been everything from a bank 'whereon the wild Thyme blows,' or the moonlight slept so sweetly, to the ascent to the guillotine in the *Tale of Two Cities*. The high-backed armchair of carved oak, when it was not being used for a throne, or a judge's seat, stood in the middle of the front row of the stalls, and from it Rocky conducted his recitation classes.

It was terrifying. Each week you were given a poem to learn, and you had to mount the stage alone in alphabetical order and give of your best to Rocky, who was determined from the start that your best would never be good enough for him.

Mary and Angela sat in the third row of wooden chairs, and after a glance at her note-book Mary shut it, telling herself that there was no need to panic. She loved learning poetry and never had any difficulty in memorizing it, and this week she dared to hope that she could say her poem fairly well. She had locked herself in her bedroom and declaimed it over and over again, striving to get the utmost meaning and effect out of each phrase, with her mother clamouring at the door to know whether she felt all right. She had wailed, she had shouted, altered stresses and inflections a hundred times until the sound of her own voice meant nothing to her, and the final result, as she had said it through in her bath last night, had seemed quite pleasing. She loathed and despised Rocky, of course, but it would be marvellous if he said, 'Good.'

When Julius Rockingham came into the theatre, it was like a Judge coming into Court. The murmur of voices died to a respectful hush and all the students stood up as the door at the back opened, and he stalked in, wearing the dark trousers and alpaca coat that made him look like a hungry crow. He passed through them with a brief acknowledgment, sat down, and opened the register with the air of one who wishes to get an unpleasant task over as soon as possible. He had an extraordinary power to create terror before he even opened his mouth. His movements and the expression on his face were redolent of doom, and when he spoke the first name, it was like a knell.

'Armstrong.'

Armstrong was a poor little short-legged, round-shouldered youth, whose trousers were too short and narrow, and whose hair wanted cutting and thinning and brilliantining. He looked and was rather dirty.

He handed his note-book to Rocky, and going up the steps at the side of the stage, stood at the centre front with his arms clamped straight down at his sides.

'Last night, ah, yesternight between her lips and mine——' It was one of Rocky's forms of torture to give people poems that were as unsuitable as possible.

'Come, Armstrong,' he interrupted, after the fourth line, ' "Passion" is the word you have just said. I suppose you know what that means?'

'Yes,' said Armstrong, who did not know but had read books.

'Put some of it into your voice then.'

Armstrong swallowed and started again, and Rocky's toneless interruption at the same place, of, 'Begin again, please,' was more disheartening than any criticism. Armstrong gave a harassed sigh, and mustering all his manhood, lunged forward with one foot, stretched out large, useless-looking hands and poured out his soul. With a final flourish of his hands, he ended up : 'I have been faithful to thee, Cynara! in my fashion,' and stood waiting, panting a little.

'Must you burlesque a lovely poem?' asked Rocky. 'Here, let me show you.' He strode on to the stage and pushing the cringing Armstrong out of the way, he spoke the poem—you had to admit it—quite beautifully. There was a depth and resonance in his voice, an old-fashioned, almost melodramatic quality that was intensely moving. An echo of the voice in which Forbes-Robertson spoke 'Hamlet' and Irving cast a spell over vast audiences in *The Bells*.

Armstrong felt like a crumb of humanity and never wanted to recite again.

'See?' said Rocky, pacified by the sound of his own voice. 'Let me hear it again next week.'

Back in his chair, he summoned Edna Barrow, a pretty skittish blonde, who trickled through a passage from 'L'Allegro' without Rocky doing more than mimic her from time to time without comment.

Mary wished her name did not begin with S. It was so much worse to have to wait one's turn, with one's confidence ebbing away with every minute. She could not enjoy listening to the others. If they were good, she was envious; if they were bad, their discomfiture was a hint of what her own might be.

Four or five girls followed each other on to the stage, were virtually stripped naked, and retired to nurse their shame. An objectionable youth called Davy Morgan then bounced on to the stage and proceeded to recite in a voice like the breath of the wind over the Welsh mountains:

> *'Now when we two have been apart so long*
> *And you draw near, I make you mine with song.*
> *Waiting you in my thoughts' high, lonely tower,*
> *That looks on starlit, hushed, impenetrable gloom,*
> *I know your advent certain as the flower*
> *Of daybreak that on breathless vales shall bloom.*
> *Ah, never hurry now, for time's all sweet,*
> *And you are clad in the garment of my dreams.*
> *Led by my heart's enchanted cry, your feet*
> *Move with the murmur of forest-wandering streams*
> *Through earth's adoring darkness, to discover*
> *The paradise of your imperfect lover.'*

When he had finished, there was a little hush, and then Rocky cleared his throat and the spell was broken. Mary sighed, and thought about love. One must have it; one must have the paradise of an imperfect lover, and she was as far away from finding it as she had ever been. She had thought that Denys was the answer to everything, and when she had found that he wasn't she had been left alone with no one on whom to pin her burden of romantic devotion.

Davy received Rocky's praise with a smirk. Being one of his favourites, he always got the best poems to say, not like poor solid Margaret O'Gorman, who had to blush through an appalling bit of whimsey about china ornaments on a mantelpiece. Mary stopped thinking about love, for her turn was imminent; her mouth was beginning to go dry and the pit of her stomach was shrinking.

'Shannon,' said Mr Rockingham without relish, and she plunged on to the stage, tucking her yellow blouse in at the back of her skirt.

'For God's sake don't fiddle with your clothes!' came the voice from below, doing nothing to make her feel more at ease. She took a deep breath, clasped her hands behind her, and began quickly:

> *'With blackest moss the flower-pots*
> *Were thickly crusted, one and all——'*

'Title?' snapped Rocky.

'Oh, sorry. Er—"Mariana." '

'Author?' he said, before she had a chance to say Tennyson.

Thoroughly unnerved by now, the beginning of the poem came out quite differently from the satisfactory rendering in the bath, but after a while the words began to waft her into their rhythm. He let her get as far as:

> '*Hard by a poplar shook alway,*
> *All silver-green with gnarled bark:*
> *For leagues no other tree did mark*
> *The level waste, the rounding gray.*'

Rocky held up his hand. 'Why do you stand with your toes turned in? You're not deformed, are you?'

'Oh, no.' She shifted them quickly, hating him. Why couldn't he let her get on with the poem? It was typical of him to interrupt just as one was getting into one's stride. She stuck out her lower lip and went on. Not even Rocky could spoil the poem's sad spell of beauty.

> '*But most she loathed the hour*
> *When the thick-moted sunbeam lay*
> *Athwart the chambers, and the day*
> *Was sloping towards his western bower.*
> *Then said she, "I am very dreary,*
> *He will not come," she said:*
> *She wept, "I am aweary, aweary,*
> *Oh, God, that I were dead!"*' '

Because he let her say the poem through without criticism, and because he had neither dropped his head into his hands with a groan, nor clutched his hair, raised his eyes to heaven and said, 'Oh, God!' through clenched teeth, she thought she had got away with it. She waited, watching him like a dog that hopes to be taken for a walk.

'Er—Shannon, dear,' he said, using the epithet for patronage rather than affection, 'you said that poem as if you like it.' Mary's heart leaped. Rocky studied his finger-nails and went on in a bored voice: 'Tell me now, d'you think he came back, the man that she was waiting for?'

'Er—no, I don't think he did,' said Mary surprised.

'Really? That's very interesting. May one ask why?'

One might ask, thought Mary, but one would not necessarily get a coherent explanation. She was not prepared for this; she had not thought that there was any question of the man coming back, the whole tone of the poem was desolation. Was this one of Rocky's traps? She tried to find words, but with that predatory eye fixed on her, it was difficult not to stammer and lapse into 'sort of' and 'well, you see——'

'You see, you see, you see!' said Rocky, jerking his crossed legs irritably as if someone were testing his reflex. 'I don't see, and it's quite clear you don't either. Come down here. No, girl——' as Mary started to obey by the quickest method of jumping off the platform, 'by the steps. For God's sake try to move like a woman instead of an elephant.'

119

Mary was furious. She was not as fat as all that. How dared he? She advanced to the throne in silence, feeling a chilly gap between her blouse and skirt, but not daring to do anything about it.

'Do you ever think about anything?' asked Rocky coolly, leaning back with his elbows on the arms of the chair, and tapping the tips of his long fingers together.

'Why, yes, of course, I——'

'There you are!' He pounced triumphantly. 'That's what's the matter with you, Cannon—Shannon—whatever your name is. All over you is written, in flaming letters of fire, the one word "I." You're so ut-terly wrapped up in yourself that you have no interests outside your own egotism. You've obviously been accustomed to having your own way all your life—someone to do this and that for you, to listen to your complaints and pander to your moods——'

Mary thought back tears of rage as she stood looking at a crack between the boards of the floor, biting her lips and seething. Even if what he said was true, why should he be allowed to get away with being so damnably rude, just because he had the reputation of being a 'Character'? She had said the poem well enough, too, for her, and he had probably not even listened. He had been so busy thinking up something to take her down a peg. When he had finished attacking her, he dismissed her with: 'You may go and sit down. It's girls like you who waste my time.'

'Swine,' muttered Angela, as Mary slumped into the chair beside her.

'Utter, utter swine,' repeated Mary, blowing her nose, and looking up, stuck out her tongue at Davy Morgan, who was leering at her over the back of his chair, with what he fancied was a quizzical look.

Angela hopped on to the stage when her turn came, looking so attractive with the light shining on her casual-looking curls, in her cheeky little check dress that had probably been absurdly expensive, that even Rocky must have seen hopes for her future. In spite of this, or perhaps because of it, he stopped her half-way through the opening of 'Endymion' to say: 'Please don't come to my classes wearing bangles—it's unsuitable.' Angela clutched the three gold bracelets that 'a divine man called David' had given her for her birthday.

'I'm sorry,' she said, smiling.

'Go on, go on,' said Rocky, but her mind had wandered and she lost her place and got hopelessly mixed up, while Rocky waited, tapping a long-suffering foot.

'Can I start again at the beginning, Mr Rockingham?'

'No,' he said wearily, 'say it again next week.'

The last on the list was poor Muriel Willoughby, who always looked as if she had a cold. Standing in the middle of the stage, as if it was a pillory, she made her mouth into a genteel shape suitable for reciting, and said drearily:

'Thaey caeme, yew knoew, ander told me yew weyer daeid.' She never got beyond the first line, because, by the time Rocky had made her repeat it five times, giving a cruelly exact imitation of her accent each time, the clock struck twelve, and he rose and delivered his parting shot: 'Is that a spot on your face?' Muriel had probably been trying to disguise it for hours. 'Can't have spots, bad for make-up,' said Rocky, and took himself off, muttering.

The summer term trickled away in the same routine of petty spites and jealousies, uncharitable gossip, rare enthusiasms, and more frequently, moments of terror, embarrassment or fury. Mary never bothered about where, if anywhere, her dramatic training was leading. The news that Uncle Geoffrey was coming home to work with an English film company strengthened her resolve to stick to it.

Mrs Shannon was in a fever. She was doing up the spare room, which for so long had been nothing but a dump for trunks and old curtains and cardboard dress boxes. 'Which d'you think he'd like, this one—this one—this one?' she kept asking Mary, displaying patterns of distemper, curtains or gas fires. When it was all finished, she suddenly stopped in the middle of the road one day. 'Oh,' she said, horror-struck.

'What's up?' said Mary, pulling her on to a refuge, just in time, as a bus bore down on them.

'Supposing he doesn't mean to live with us after all? He's got more money now, he'd probably rather have a flat of his own, or something. Oh, I never thought——'

'Oh, no, darling, I'm sure he'll want it to be like it was before.' Mary took her arm and steered her across to the opposite pavement. She was always rather an anxiety in traffic, because she would not concentrate. 'He always was a homey old bird, and when he sees the way you've done his room——' But her mother refused to be reassured. She sent off a panicky cable, and continued to fret until she got an answer, going up to the spare room from time to time, standing dismayed in the middle of its masculine perfection, saying: 'Oh, if only I'd thought——'

When the cable came, saying: 'WHAT DO YOU MEAN A FLAT STOP YOU DON'T GET RID OF ME THAT WAY STOP YORS TIL DETH GEOFF,' she said: 'There you are, I knew he'd want to live with us!' popped on her perkiest Paris hat and went trilling off to South Molton Street.

Mary never trilled on her way to Rockingham College, for the annual examination was looming on her horizon like an ever-blackening cloud. It was the great occasion of the year. Every student was given a chance in a scene from a play, which was performed to an audience of proud parents and fidgeting friends, and judged by any theatrical personages whom Rocky could persuade or blackmail into attending.

Miss Gould chose the plays for the third-year students and allotted the parts, and being a fanatical disciple of Rocky, she took the same delight in incompatible casting. Mary, who, on the stage, was transformed into something only slightly more animate than a stick, was given the part of Margaret Dearth, the dream daughter in *Dear Brutus*. Everyone told her how lucky she was, but she knew that it was not her line. What exactly was her line, neither she nor anyone else had yet discovered, but it was certainly not flitting about among imaginary trees, delivering lines that Barrie has poised on the knife-edge between charm and whimsey, leaving it to the actress to decide on which side they fall.

As there were fewer men than girls at the College, many of the men had to play in more than one scene, irrespective of what year they were in.

'So bad for them,' said Angela to Mary, over Camp coffee and nut milk chocolate in the cloakroom, 'makes them feel so necessary.'

'Well, men are necessary when you think of it,' said Mary gloomily.

'Not these ones, thank God. Darling, did I tell you about that heavenly man I met last night? Greying, my dear, at the temples, like in a magazine story. Quite old, of course, but they say he's a devil with women——'

'Yes, you told me—twice.'

'Oh, did I? Sorry. What's the matter with you? You're sour.'

'Well, you'd be sour if you'd heard what I've just heard.' Mary sighed. It was the fashion at the Rockingham College to have a grievance about something, but this time life was really black.

'On top of having to play that impossible part,' she went on, '*who* d'you think is going to play opposite me?'

'Armstrong?'

'Worse.'

'Oh, darling, not Stringy Henshaw?' said Angela with real concern. Stringy was lank and limp and pale as a length of spaghetti, repellent to look at and slimy to the touch.

'Worse still. None other than Robert Pansy Darwin.'

'Oh,' said Angela, sitting back relieved, 'I don't call that so bad. He is at least clean.'

'Only compared with the others. He can't act for nuts. All he can do is display that profile, and I can't act either and I haven't even got a profile to display, so we ought to be a riot. He won't try, either, because he knows Rocky'll bribe the judges to give him a good mark. I shall be bottom. Still you'll be top, that's something,' she added with faint enthusiasm.

'Oh, I shan't, you idiot,' said Angela delightedly. 'I'm fearful. Miss Gould says I am the worst Sydney it has ever been her lot to witness. Come on, we'll be late for fencing. I must mend that hole in my tights before the Count sees me.'

As well as being rehearsed by Miss Gould in square tweed suits and brogues, the students were supposed to rehearse their examination scenes on their own, between class hours. Bob Darwin was not disposed to waste much of his time on Mary, so by the time the examination date approached, and Rocky himself began to rehearse the scenes, *Dear Brutus* had not made much progress.

Mary dreaded the weekly rehearsals with Rocky. He sharpened his wits on her; she was getting a persecution mania.

'Now I'll take the *Dear Brutus* scene,' he would say with quiet menace, and Mary and Bob would go up to the stage from opposite sides of the hall, Bob bored, and Mary with a sinking dread. They met in the wings, he acknowledging her sometimes by a patronizing glance, sometimes by a mutter of 'For God's sake give me right cues this time,' or 'You'd better not muff that bit where you put your hair up today. The old man's in a hell of a temper.'

'Curtain up!' snapped Rocky, which meant 'begin' for the curtain was not down. Mary, with the despairing courage with which she had once launched herself off the ha-ha wall at Denys' command, burst through the opening in the curtains and ran on to the stage with her hands feeling very much *de trop*, crying in a voice that, she realized too late, she had pitched too high:

'Daddy, Daddy. I have won. Here is the place. Crack-in-the-eye-Tommy!' Bob never entered immediately on his cue, because he had got used to Rocky interrupting wearily at this point: 'How many times have I told you, my *dear* girl, that you won't sound quite so silly if you say: "Crack-in-*me*-eye, Tommy!" '

'Crack-in-me-eye-Tommy,' repeated Mary, dispiritedly, and Bob entered, carrying a camp stool and an imaginary easel, which they had to erect with elaborate pretence, Mary finding it very difficult to follow the stage directions and get in the way of an easel which wasn't there. Presumably they would be allowed to have a real one, on the day.

Mary had only exaggerated slightly when she said Bob couldn't act for nuts. His appearance and pleasant voice carried him through juvenile leads, but he could not be anything more than barely adequate in a part like Will Dearth, the run-to-seed artist, who gets a glimpse of what he might have been in the mysterious wood on Midsummer's Eve. Between them, he and Mary managed to rob the scene of all its original enchantment. The faults in his acting were negative rather than

123

positive ones, and his discrepancies were not so glaring as hers. He had only to sit on a stool and make the motions of painting, delivering Gerald du Maurier lines with a pipe in the corner of his mouth, while Mary, with the whole of the rest of the stage to herself, had to be incessantly on the gambol. Rocky's criticisms were directed almost exclusively at her, and, with all the rest of the College looking on, knitting, doing their nails, and making disparaging comments, self-consciousness crept over her in paralysing waves.

When they reached the part where the girl, Margaret, puts up her hair with a forest pool as her mirror, Mary invariably found that she had forgotten to put the combs in her pocket, and even when she had remembered, her hair was too short to be able to manage properly. If only she still had her long hair. For the first time, she regretted the work of Mr. Pee-aire. She imagined that to have had hair that was right for the part would have given her a confidence that would have altered her whole performance.

'No, no, no,' Rocky would moan, hiding his face with a convulsive hand. 'This isn't pantomime. You can't make a guy of yourself like that. Why don't you practise pinning it up?'

'I have, but——' began Mary, coming down to the footlights with one side of her hair scragged on top of her head and the other escaping down her neck in wisps.

'Well, get your nanny to show you how,' sighed Rocky, who would harp on the myth that Mary was surrounded by a horde of pampering attendants. 'I'll have to cut that bit otherwise, and if I cut any more of this scene it won't be worth doing at all. Not that it really is now,' he added audibly to himself. 'Go on, go on,' he waved her back with the book in his hand. 'We haven't got all day. Shake your hair down and go on from there.'

Mary looked blankly towards the prompt corner. She had forgotten her lines.

'You are thinking what a handful she is going to be,' prompted Myrtle Drew in an unnecessarily loud, clear voice. Mary struggled on, her discomfort rising to sweating point when she had to do things like clutching Bob round the legs and saying, 'Oh, how you love me, Daddikins.'

'Yes, I do rather,' answered Bob, with a beautiful smile on his lips and a look of distaste in his eyes, and then the limelight was mercifully removed from Mary by the entrance of Muriel Willoughby as the vagrant woman—a short but incredibly dreary performance, enlivened by a mocking running commentary from Rocky in his seat below.

After Bob's exit, singing a French song in an accent more French than the French, Mary had to run about from tree to imaginary tree, her stumbling movements belying the fact that she was supposed to be a wraith returning to the dream-world. 'Daddy, come back,' she panted, 'I don't want to be a Might-have-been!' As there was no curtain-fall at rehearsals, she was left standing uncertainly on the stage, while Rocky told her she sounded like a banshee, that she ought to take dancing lessons, and that he himself was a criminal for letting one of the loveliest scenes that Barrie ever wrote be so mutilated.

When he had finished with her, Mary flounced off the stage, knocked into Bob on purpose, and walked from him without a word, to fall into her seat beside Angela, biting her nails with vicious fury.

When Uncle Geoffrey arrived in London, Mary and her mother met him at the station, Mrs Shannon twittering with excitement, and saying: 'There he is!' indiscriminately as she spotted perfect strangers in the distance.

'There he is—it really is!' She began to run forward.

'No, it's not,' said Mary automatically, but it was. Darling Uncle Geoffrey, looking slightly debauched, as if every night on the *Queen Mary* had been a thick one. He looked exactly the same, yet subtly different. He wore his monocle, a green pork pie hat, a just-possible suit, and co-respondent shoes, but it was as if he wore them not because he was Uncle Geoffrey, but because he was trying to look like Uncle Geoffrey. You felt that even his teeth protruded because it was in his contract that they should, and his speech was a mixture of dutiful haw-haw and involuntary Americanisms.

'Cheerio!' he said to one acquaintance, and to another: 'Call me up some time, honey.'

He was gratifyingly thrilled to find Mary grown up, and looked her up and down with the eyes of a connoisseur and said: 'Why didn't someone warn me what a gorgeous niece I'd got? And as for my sister—where the hell did you get that hat, Lil?'

'Oh, I *am* glad you like it,' said Mrs Shannon, taking his arm. 'Come on, let's walk home, there's such lots to talk about. We can put your luggage on to a taxi.'

Mary took his other arm, and together they turned out of the station and walked down Victoria Embankment with the evening sun in their faces, pestering him with questions which they didn't give him a chance to answer. Mary was as talkative as her mother. She was anxious to keep the conversation off the Dramatic College as long as possible, because she knew from Uncle Geoffrey's letters that he was going to be disparaging, and she didn't dare let him enquire too far into the progress of her theatrical career, because there was too much to disparage.

'Well, Tich,' he said, as they turned up Elizabeth Street, 'not engaged yet?'

125

'Oh, no.' She turned the conversation hastily away from herself. 'What about you?'

'My dear, I'm far too old for games like that.'

'What about the blonde from Springfield, Ill.?'

'Oh, that's a sad story. It turned out she had a Daddy already back in Salt Lake City.'

'Geoff, you fool,' said his sister, 'stop talking like an old man. Don't forget you're my younger brother.'

'Well, I feel old today, sister,' he said. 'Too many bars on that damned boat. But I want to hear about Mary.' He was not to be deterred. 'Aren't you even walking out with some nice upstanding young Englishman?'

'No, I'm not actually.'

'Oh, Mary's always going out,' said her mother proudly. 'She's got lots of boy friends, haven't you, darling?'

'Oh, no, I haven't, Mummy, and they're all pretty mothy, anyway,' she mumbled. Through going out with Angela she had picked up one or two stray attachments, most of whom bored her to tears, but one had to go out whenever one was asked, for the sake of going out. She never stopped to think why, she just thought that it was so. Also, there was always the chance that she might meet Denys somewhere, and it would be satisfying to show him that she had got another man, even if it was only Frank Baxter, who was always pressing his visiting cards on people who didn't want them, or Freddie Gordon, with a stammer and a ragged moustache, whom waiters conspired to ignore.

'And what about the——' went on Uncle Geoffrey, but Mary interrupted him. 'Look round this corner and then you can see it. That's our house with the red front door. Isn't it adorable! Aren't the window-boxes divine? I did them. Come on.' She dragged him across the street. 'I'm longing for you to see it all. Wait till you see your room.' She kept him off the subject of the Rockingham College successfully until dinner-time, but it was bound to come out.

They had chicken salad and champagne in the dining-room which looked on to the tiny strip of back garden, and outside the wide open window birds were singing in the soft evening light. It was very pleasant to be together again. Now that Uncle Geoffrey was back, Mary realized how much they had missed him. She loved her mother very much, but their temperaments were so dissimilar and Mary found it increasingly easy to be irritated these days. Three people in a house was safer than two, especially when life was a little grim, as it was for her at the moment.

'Well, Sarah Bern-what's-her-name,' said Uncle Geoffrey at length, 'what about it? How's the drama?'

'Oh, fine, thanks,' said Mary airily.

'Got any offers yet?'

'Oh no, of course not. I'm only in my first year. It's a two-year course.'

'Great Scott, what a helluva waste of time,' murmured Uncle Geoffrey, bringing out a packet of Lucky Strikes and flipping out a cigarette adroitly.

'Not a bit.' Mary was prepared to defend the College to her last gasp. 'The idea nowadays is to learn something about acting before you appear in public,' she said crushingly.

'My, my, you don't say. Cigarette, Lil? I hope you like these; they're the only sort I smoke now. Does Garbo smoke?' He held the packet out to her. 'Thank you,' said Mary with dignity, and he flipped one up for her.

'To get back to your art,' he went on. 'I hate to seem inquisitive, but you can't blame me for being interested. I mean, my future leading-lady's got to be *good*.'

'Oh, I think it's all right, Geoffrey dear,' broke in Mrs Shannon, scenting an antagonism without knowing the reason for it. 'They do lots of acting. Plays, you know, and Shakespeare and things; and Mary's got a big part in a Barrie play at the end of the term.'

'Yeah, but even Shakespeare ought to have an audience. How can you tell how bad you are if there's nobody to throw a tomato? Don't you ever give shows or anything?'

'Of course we do,' said Mary rashly. 'Crowds of people come to watch the Exams at the end of this term; big bugs and relations and friends and——' She stopped suddenly, horrified, as Uncle Geoffrey pounced on her remark: 'They do? Oh, that's marvellous. Your mother and I'll be in the front row, rooting for you like mad, won't we, Lil?'

'Oh, no,' Mary said faintly. 'I wish you wouldn't——'

'Why not? Nothing could keep me away.'

'Of course we'll come and clap,' said Mrs Shannon. 'You never told me we were allowed to. What is it, the Barrie play?'

'Yes. *Dear Brutus*,' grunted Mary.

'Never heard of it,' said Uncle Geoffrey. 'What's your part?'

'Well, I'm Margaret—a sort of dream daughter.' It sounded idiotic, but she was too miserable to explain further. It was bad enough having to give her inept performance before strangers, but the thought of anybody she knew witnessing her shame was almost more than she could bear. She had been purposely keeping it from her mother. She knew she would never hear the last of it from Uncle Geoffrey. She could already hear his delighted imitations afterwards of 'Crack-in-me-eye-Tommy' and 'Daddy, I don't want to be a Might-have-been.'

He continued to pump her about the College at odd moments, and she continued to stand up for it with stubborn pride, though she was

127

liking it less and less. Uncle Geoffrey was very busy for the first few days, looking up old friends and doing mysterious things called 'contacting people' in the environs of Wardour Street, but on Sunday morning he and Mary went for a walk in the park. Leaning on the Row railings, they watched the cavalcade of old men shaking up their livers and young girls shaking up their bosoms, and Uncle Geoffrey said casually, with his eyes on a yellow-shirted chorus girl, who was maintaining her balance by the reins alone: 'Anything wrong, by the way?'

'No, of course not,' said Mary quickly, for she had been brooding on her grievances. 'Why?'

'Oh, nothing much. It suddenly occurred to me—stop me if you've heard this one—that you don't laugh as much as you used.'

'I laugh when there's anything to laugh at. You don't expect me to go shrieking inanely about the place—the loud laugh that speaks the vacant mind, or whatever it is.'

'Hell no, you know I don't mean that, but——' He drew patterns in the Row with his stick, his chin sucked in under his teeth. 'For God's sake don't take life too seriously, whatever happens. You've got to get a kick out of every minute of it; you'll see why, when you're too old to enjoy it in the same way. Here—I'm talking like the aged parent. You can't let me do that. Let's stagger along and lend our ears to the band for a bit. Coming?' He gave her one of his speciality five-dollars-extra-a-day grins, and began to saunter along the path swinging his stick. Mary took his arm, turning her head away from him, for the oncoming people were misty before her eyes. He meant so well; he always had done, but neither he nor anyone understood the extent of her troubles. She hung on to his arm and stumbled over a small terrier, her vision blurred by unshed tears of self-pity.

By dint of accosting Bob Darwin at every possible opportunity, planting herself squarely and demandingly before him and saying bitterly: '*What* about going through our scene?' Mary managed to make him rehearse with her once or twice.

Their scene was one which demanded special co-operation between the two players. The audience must feel the affinity between father and daughter, and between Bob and Mary the only affinity was their mutual dislike. At each rehearsal she got more and more discouraged. Bob did not consider it necessary to do more than say his lines with the maximum speed and the minimum expression, sketching his movements as superficially as he sketched the moon on his imaginary easel. Mary wondered that he was not more concerned with perfecting his performance for the examination. Did he think he was so good, or what? It was not that he was disinterested. She knew he was keen for success on the stage, and even though his ambition visualized the fans and the good luck telegrams and the parties rather than the acting, it was still ambition.

Mary wished she dared ask him why he didn't try, but in spite of herself she was faintly intimidated by his acknowledged status at the College, and the fact that if he did not like a question he just refrained from answering. She was enlightened, however, one day, as they made their way down one of the dark, dusty passages, looking for an empty practice room. She asked him whether he knew who the judges were going to be.

'Don't know them all,' he said, sloping along in front of her in his pale suede shoes. 'Mervyn Garstein is one, though. Friend of my Pop's. I was talking to him at a party the other night, and purely *entre nous*,' he said, slowing down and speaking directly at her for once, 'he's sending *Cat's Whiskers* on tour in the autumn, and he's promised to try me for a part when I've left this dump.'

'You're lucky,' said Mary coolly, refusing to be dazzled by this bit of news, but furiously jealous.

'Yes,' said Robert languidly. 'He's a coming man, Garstein. He'll be a really big name before long, you wait.' How could it be otherwise, he implied, since he was to be the discoverer of Robert Darwin, the idol of the wooden camp stools?

On the morning of the examination, Mary woke feeling as heavy as lead, and as she dressed she began to feel sick. It was all she could do to drink a cup of coffee at breakfast, and she was thankful that Uncle Geoffrey, who had not yet started work at the studios, was still in bed, and could not remark on her pale, despairing silence. Her mother was absorbed in a new batch of fashion magazines and only said, as Mary kissed the top of her head on the way out: 'Good luck, my pet. I can't wait to see you; I know you'll be marvellous.'

With masochistic gloom, Mary put on a hat that didn't suit her, grimaced at herself in the glass, and then the front door banged behind her and she was being drawn by the inevitable thread of Fate nearer and nearer to the fulfilment of her dread.

In the morning, Rocky held a sketchy dress rehearsal of all the scenes. 'A simple, becoming linen frock,' Miss Gould had prescribed for Mary, calling up visions of Anne Hathaway teas with dainty slices of sand cake and not enough hot water. Mrs Shannon, raising her eyebrows, had run Mary up a short girlish affair in a blue linen that Mary had bought without discovering that it creased if you looked at it. She fixed a small bow in her hair and presented herself unhopefully before Rocky, who asked her if she thought she was the Kenwigs prodigy or what.

'And if I may be allowed a suggestion,' he added, with a heavy

E

politeness which meant he was tired and worried and particularly disposed to be unflattering, 'what about rubber soles on the feet? The effect of your entrance might be a little less, shall we say, deafening.'

'Gym shoes?' asked Mary.

'Yes, yes, I said rubber soles, didn't I? What more do you want? Have I got to tell you what underclothes to wear, how to put on your make-up, comb your hair——' He worked himself up and ended with a testy 'Pfwah!' that brought on his catarrh.

'Get on. Get on with the scene,' he said through his coughing.

Bob was looking infuriatingly handsome in flannels, a dark-blue blazer and an open-necked blue shirt that displayed to the full his beautifully modelled throat. This afternoon he would have to make-up as an older man and dust a little grey into his chestnut hair, but for the moment he looked like the boy Byron, and Rocky, feasting his eyes on him, allowed Mary's performance to run without criticism.

'What was I like, Angel?' asked Mary afterwards, anxiously.

'You were jolly good,' said Angela stoutly, but it was no good. Mary had no illusions and she still felt sick.

The afternoon approached, blackly, like a thunder-cloud.

There was an atmosphere of nervous excitability everywhere. All the staff were in a 'don't bother me' mood, and rushed about doing so many things that they got nothing done. The men students, even Armstrong, who would reel on a glass of lemonade, were talking about 'going out and getting tight as a lord when this show's over,' and the girls were behaving as if it was a matter of life and death to find a reel of black cotton.

The food in the little restaurant seemed to Mary more fly-blown than usual and she hardly ate anything at lunch-time. She had three cups of black coffee as a dramatic sort of 'living on your nerves' gesture. Then she and Angela went to the cloakroom and fought for a place at one of the make-up benches under the long, harshly lit mirrors. Mary saw from the list on the wall that the *Dear Brutus* scene was almost the last. She had at least hoped to be able to get it over early and be able to wash her face and slip into the back of the hall to watch other people making fools of themselves. The judges would be tired and sour by the time her turn came; she herself would be completely demoralized by the hours of nervous waiting, and Bob, exhausted by a passionate performance in *Romeo and Juliet*, would act with the indifference of anti-climax.

Angela's scene was third on the list, so Mary left the disordered scene of girls clamouring for a stick of No. 8 or for someone to do them up at the back, and dodged into the back of the theatre, evading the dreamy eye of Miss Yule, the elocution mistress, posted at the door to prevent this very thing.

After the first scene was over—Edna Barrow and others loosing genteel emotion in *A Month in the Country*—Mary looked round for her mother and Uncle Geoffrey, but they did not seem to have come yet. If only she could have got through her scene before they arrived. She saw Mr and Mrs Shaw, he spreading himself over an inadequate chair in the second row, and she with a lace handkerchief held delicately to her mouth as if she thought there were germs about. A familiar voice was heard outside the door and Mary hid behind the broad back of a father as her mother came in, in case she should hail her. Mrs Shannon was looking particularly smart, Mary was glad to see, and Uncle Geoffrey wore quite a modest tie and a carnation in his buttonhole. Mary hoped people might have seen his films and would recognize him. Although his parts had been small, they had been spectacular. She had had quite a success boasting of him at the Dramatic College—her only success, in fact.

There was a slight commotion as Mr Shaw spied Mrs Shannon and indicated obtrusively that she must come and sit with them. Rocky turned round and glared, and Mary was reminded of Speech Day at St Martin's. Uncle Geoffrey sat down next to Mrs Shaw, who continued to hold up her handkerchief.

As the curtain went up on Angela's scene, Mary was at first nervous, then admiring, and finally, frankly envious. She looked so fascinating; she was genuinely touching and spontaneously gay, even though her young man was only Jordan Holmes, with a thin black moustache and a slight squint. At the end, there was a lot of applause, which could not have been for Jordan, who had looked and acted like a shop-walker, nor for Connie Rogers, who had failed to convince a soul that she was anyone's maiden aunt. Mary saw the three heads of the judges in the front row bent over the table on which they recorded their verdicts. The one on the right, who had curly black hair, and was presumably Mervyn Garstein, said something to the middle one, who nodded vigorously and bent to write again. Rocky sat beside them, rather aloofly, as if offering his students with a take-it-or-leave-it air. He had probably told them over a good lunch beforehand, who was good and who was not. Mary stayed to see Bob Darwin in black tights, and Mona Ray, one of the star girls in the third year, give a rather saccharine performance of the balcony scene, and then she left the hall and went down to the cloakroom, more depressed than ever by the six or seven scenes she had watched. Nobody, not even the worst, was as bad as she was. She had hoped that someone before her would disgrace themselves, so as to lessen the effect when she did, but so far no one had been more than faintly ridiculous.

With a heavy heart, she plastered make-up on her face with an even heavier hand, and hoped that the result would look like wide-eyed innocence from the other side of the footlights. She put on her gym

131

shoes, remembered to put the combs in her pocket, and went up to the wings to reconnoitre and to look for Angela. She needed comfort.

'Shannon,' whispered Miss Gould hoarsely, stealing up behind her on her stout crêpe soles, 'you know perfectly well you shouldn't be up here unless your scene is on. Get below and wait your turn. Mary had been able to glimpse that *Escape Me Never*, with Myrtle Drew's legs having the chance of a lifetime in Austrian shorts, was nearly over. Only one more to go. She walked about the dark, rambling passages, saying her part through to herself, trying to still the growing panic that made her unable to stand still. Running feet came looking for her. Gladys Hoover, beside herself with importance, told her that she must hurry, that she was wanted on the stage.

'All *right*,' said Mary, 'there's lots of time,' but when Gladys had sped away to agitate somebody else, Mary ran breathlessly back to the theatre, only to find them still removing furniture from the last scene. As she crossed the stage behind the menacing dropped curtain, she suddenly had a wild, crazy thought. 'Supposing I'm good. Supposing when I'm on the stage with the lights and the audience and everything, I act like one inspired.' This forlorn hope occupied her mind during the deathly moments of waiting in the wings with Bob, greying gracefully at the temples, with a tan make-up and one or two becoming wrinkle lines. Just at the end, when the stage was clear, and she could see Miss Gould across the stage, with her hand on the wheel that raised the curtain, Mary suddenly thought, 'I can't do it—I can't go on,' and then before she could think again, the curtain had swished up, rather sideways as usual, and she had run on to the stage in her gym shoes, and caught sight, even as she said her first line, of the popping eyes of her mother and Uncle Geoffrey.

They say that when you are on the stage you are oblivious of the audience as individuals and can pour out the deeps of your being without self-consciousness into the darkling vaults of the upper circle. Mary was acting to a small, insufficiently darkened hall, painfully conscious of the familiar faces of fellow-students next to their surprising parents. Mr Shaw enjoying himself hugely, her mother perched anxiously forward on her chair, and Uncle Geoffrey screwing in his monocle as if he could not believe his eyes. In the front row, there was Rocky, frowning, shaking his head and pushing out his mobile lips, and three men in armchairs—one young Jew, one fat man yawning, and one lean scowling face that Mary recognized, with a horrified thrill, as a well-known actor that she had always admired intensely.

The self-consciousness that she had felt during sessions with Rocky was as nothing to the burning, blushing agony that possessed her now. She heard every sentence that she spoke as if someone else were saying it, and every movement that she made felt grotesque. Bob, amazingly, was playing up. He had fallen into a careless ease that was exactly right. Strangely enough, as he became more and more natural, Mary became more and more sticky, as if she sensed how the audience must be contrasting them.

There was a terrible moment when she shook her head to make her pinned-up hair fall down again, and found that she had pinned it so successfully that it would not fall, and when she finally put up her hands to pull out the combs, she saw that Uncle Geoffrey's face was one huge grin. The beast, the utter, utter swine. She gave up looking at the audience after that, and most of her remarks to Muriel Willoughby were probably inaudible. She finished the scene very near tears, and her 'Daddy, come back! I don't want to be a Might-have-been,' came out with a break in her voice that must have made it the only convincing line in her performance.

The curtain thudded down, and she turned away without looking at anyone and went down to the cloakroom, knowing that she had just been through the biggest ordeal of her life. She could not think about it yet, but a glorious feeling of relief was stealing over her at the thought that she would never have to go through that again.

In the cloakroom everyone was distributing lavish praise to everyone else, in the hope of getting some back. Mary began to grease and wipe her face, and Angela came up to her, dazzlingly pretty with her bright make-up still on. 'I've been sitting with our families,' she said. 'Your Uncle Geoffrey is a scream; he's been trying to get off with my mother. Darling, you were jolly good. I told you you would be.'

'Don't even speak of it,' said Mary, shuddering. 'I'd like to forget it ever happened, but *you*, Angel, you were simply——'

She was interrupted by Miss Gould bellowing from the door: 'On the stage, people. Come *along*.'

Mary hastily dabbed powder over her greasy face, and still in her girlish dress went up on to the stage with the rest, where they stood whispering and pushing, waiting to hear the judges' verdict. It was read by the actor, Ralph O'Connor, saturnine, brutally virile, fascinatingly ugly, as his matinée audiences thought of him. He got lazily to his feet with a long white paper in his hand, and dealt with the students alphabetically, giving a percentage mark and a brief criticism of each. His voice was modulated and unemotional, and he had an effective way of pausing occasionally after a name, and looking up with a steady glance at the stage. 'Ambrose . . . Argyll . . . Armstrong . . .' At 'Darwin; 92. Romeo was adequate, but the other was an extraordinarily good rendering of a difficult part.' There was a stir of excitement, which was redoubled when he came to 'Shaw; 92,' and raised his chiselled head once more to look calmly before him. Mary squeezed Angela's arm as if in a dream, for she was listening to the words that still rang in her head: 'Shannon; 20. Should study move-ment. A rather flat performance, probably insufficiently rehearsed.' Mary bit her lip, as he read smoothly to the end, as if unconscious that he held their fears and ambitions in his hand. Insufficiently rehearsed! And this was the man whom she had often paid money to see and applaud. She vowed never to go near one of his plays again. Twenty out of a hundred; nobody else had got less than twenty-five, except Muriel Willoughby, who didn't count. Mary was glad that she was in the back row, where she could not see how her mother and Uncle Geoffrey were taking her disgrace. She dreaded facing them tonight. What would happen? They would not ridicule or rage; they would be pitying, and it would be unbearable.

Ralph O'Connor sat down again at the end of the list, without having announced the winner of the coveted cup. Bob and Angela had both got the highest marks, and everyone was speculating as to which would be chosen. Angela had gone deathly pale, and held Mary's arm in a pinching grip, which Mary scarcely felt. The three judges and Rocky were in conference, and Mary saw her mother and Uncle Geoffrey get up and prepare to leave, though Angela's parents, with Mrs Shaw looking distinctly faint, were waiting to hear the result.

Mrs Shannon caught sight of Mary and waved to her, mouthing, 'We're going,' and she and her brother left the theatre, causing a slight disturbance at the door, where she was apparently insisting that she had left her gloves behind. Uncle Geoffrey, however, settled the matter by refusing to go back for them and bundled her out, with a parting grin for Miss Yule, which nearly knocked her backwards.

At that moment, Ralph O'Connor rose again, with his knees to-gether, a little wearily. 'Ladies and Gentlemen,' he announced, 'the judges have decided that Miss Shaw and Mr Darwin shall each play their scene a second time to decide who shall win the cup.' Chattering whispers broke out among the fifty-odd students on the stage, and Rocky stood up, feeling that it was about time his voice was heard. 'Clear the stage, please. No talking,' he said, parading his authority.

Mary pushed her way off with the rest in a fever of anxiety. Which scene would Bob have to play—*Romeo and Juliet* or *Dear Brutus*? It *couldn't* be that she had got to undergo that ordeal again—things like that simply didn't happen in life. Angela flew excitedly down to the cloakroom to renew her make-up, and most of the others crowded down the passage to go round and sit in the audience. Mary hung about until Miss Gould bore down on her like a trampling bull.

'Hurry up, there, Shannon,' she boomed. 'You're in Darwin's scene, aren't you?'

'Yes, but isn't he going to do "Romeo"?' asked Mary imploringly.

'No, no. Mr Rockingham says he's to do *Dear Brutus*. She boosted

134

Mary towards the cloakroom. 'Go and get on your make-up. The other scene comes first.' Mary went down, kicking the stairs. So that was it. She knew why they had chosen her scene; because it would be fairer on Angela, as Jordan Holmes was so bad. She and Bob should have the equal disadvantage of acting with a dud. Mary and Jordan Holmes—what was Uncle Geoffrey's word?—the stooges.

Angela was putting the finishing touches to her make-up, brushing the thin curve of her eyebrows, pushing her bright curls into careful disorder, her eyes luminous with excitement. 'Oh, Mary—I'm terrified. Oh, wish me luck. Don't let Bob be too good in your scene. Can't you put him off his stroke or something? Oh, there's the ghoul yelling——'

'Good luck!' called Mary, 'I know you'll win,' as Angela rushed off to the stage and she was alone amid the litter of cast-off clothing, spilt powder and dirty little bits of cotton wool. She put on her make-up carelessly, sullenly, enlarging the miserable droop of her lower lip.

'Daddy, come back! I don't want to be a Might-have-been,' she mouthed insultingly at her reflection, grinning a ghastly, gargoyle grin. Then suddenly an idea came to her, so fantastic that she put it out of her mind at once. She was not mad yet, only being slowly driven so.

She tweaked and patted her linen dress, in a vain attempt to remove some of the creases, retied her gym shoes and dragged herself up to the wings of the theatre. Angela's scene was nearly finished, and Mary watched, peering through a crack in the curtains. Oh, but she was *good*. She did deserve to win. It must be lovely to be able to act like that.

The thought of what she was about to go through lay like lead on her heart.

When the scene was over, Mary, crossing to her entrance corner, found that Bob did not look nearly so handsome, when his features were small with anxiety.

'Now, for God's sake——' he began, but Mary was at the end of her tether. 'Shut up,' she snapped, suddenly infuriated, and stood seething, while people dealt inefficiently with a sofa on the stage. Butchered to make a Roman holiday, that was her; bullied and patronized by a pansy, and the laughing-stock of rows of silly gaping faces. She was still fuming when the curtain went up, and a push from Bob propelled her on to the stage, calling out her opening line automatically. Some of the visitors, having had about three hours of it, had gone home, but the theatre was full of disparaging students, and in the front row the fat bald man was nearly asleep, and the other two were bored and weary.

Bob made his entrance, and, as she was fumbling through the business of erecting the still non-existent easel, the lunatic thought that had come to Mary in the cloakroom assailed her again, and her simmering resentment suddenly boiled over. Once before in her life, at St Martin's, she had been taken possession of by a blinding madness

135

that made words burst out of her before she could stop them, and now, as then, she suddenly went crazy. She began to burlesque.

What happened to her afterwards she could never quite explain, but she was conscious only of a feeling of exaltation, a kind of glory, as she let go everywhere and worked the rancour out of her system. As she leaped about the stage in a frenzy of archness, working herself up to a spluttering pitch of hysteria, she caught glimpses of the transfixed faces of the audience, Rocky's bewildered fury, the beginning of a smile broadening on Ralph O'Connor's swarthy features, and Mervyn Garstein leaning back in his chair helpless with laughter. She felt completely, hilariously drunk, and began to deliver some of her lines in a French accent. Bob had gone to pieces long ago, muttered and swore and clutched at her as she tripped by him, and had to be prompted for nearly every line.

It was not until the audience's incredulous giggles became titters, then roars of laughter, that Miss Gould took the situation in hand and wound down the curtain. Mary came to with a shock, and stood still, swaying dizzily as if she were coming out of a trance. The realization of what she had done brought with it a miraculous lightness of heart. She was free. She would get the sack and she was glad. Why had she allowed the needless oppression to weigh her down for so long? She felt like a religious convert who has suddenly seen the light, and then outraged people were rushing at her from all sides, and the next thing she knew was that she was in Rocky's office, facing him across the big shabby desk, and snapping her fingers mentally at his withering monologue.

'Out!' she heard him say. 'Out of this place within five minutes, and if you so much as show your face inside the door again——'

'Good-bye,' said Mary, smiling sweetly and holding out her hand. 'Thank you for all you have taught me.' She left him quickly, before the old fear of his presence could re-establish itself and baulk her of her dignified exit. Outside in the passage, Miss Yule was waiting, wringing her hands and thoroughly upset. The events had been more than her anæmia could stand.

'I have taken all your things to the front door,' she said, turning watery eyes on Mary.

'Oh, but I must go down to the cloakroom and say good-bye. People will think it so odd.' She wanted to see Angela.

'No,' said Miss Yule, taking her limply by the arm and beginning to pilot her down the passage. 'You are not to see anyone. Mr Rockingham is, I think, afraid of your influence——' Mary began to giggle. At the corner of the stairs they met Myrtle Drew, who flattened herself against the wall, drawing her skirts aside to avoid contamination. Mary thought it was very funny. She wished Angela could have been there to share it. She put her coat on over her skimpy blue dress, while Miss Yule messed about among her possessions, cramming them into Mary's arms, dropping her shoes and sighing distractedly.

'Well,' she said, opening the front door, 'good-bye, Shannon, I'm sure I don't know——'

'Oh, that's all right,' said Mary, 'good-bye, Miss Yule,' and, loaded to the chin, she staggered out into the street and looked about for a taxi, to relieve her of the toppling burden of tights, dancing shoes, tunic, and all the despised articles that she visualized rising in smoke from a bonfire in the back garden to-morrow.

On the way home, her cheerfulness was tinged with apprehension. How would they take it? Would her mother be cross at the waste of her thirty pounds? What would Uncle Geoffrey say? How should she tell the story? She wished she had not had to take a taxi so that she could have more time to collect her thoughts. She let herself into the house quietly, and dropped her clothes on the floor of the hall. She took off her hat, found a comb, and tidied her hair in the hall mirror. She still had her stage make-up on, but at least she could look nice if there was going to be a scene.

'Mary?' came her mother's voice from the drawing-room.

'Hullo,' said Mary brightly, and made a face as Uncle Geoffrey's drawl floated out to her: 'Daddy, Daddy, I don't want to be a Might-have-been!'

She heard her mother say, 'Shut up, Geoff,' and something like, 'It's not fair,' and then she called again, 'Come in, darling. Gerald's here.' Mary was thankful. Now there wouldn't be a row; her mother would never make such a mistake in front of an admirer. Mary opened the drawing-room door, and stood in the doorway, grinning sheepishly at the three of them; Gerald Rigley standing on the hearth-rug, her mother perched on the arm of a chair, and Uncle Geoffrey shaking cocktails, with a cigarette drooping sideways under his front teeth. 'Hullo, Might-have-been,' he began, but Mary held up her hand. 'Don't say it. It's too true. I'm not even a "Might-have-been," I'm an am-definitely-not. Mummy, do you mind awfully? I've got the sack.'

'Whatever for?' and 'Well, thank God for that,' said her mother and Uncle simultaneously, and Gerald roared with laughter, as he always did when he was uncertain how to take anything.

Mary began to tell the story, looking anxiously at their faces, and to her delight she saw that it was a success with them.

'Oh, lordy, lordy,' said Uncle Geoffrey, downing his cocktail at one gulp. 'Ain't laughed so much since father died. Tell us about it again, Tich. You mean to say you got up there and gave them burlesque? I'd have given anything to be there. I bet old Garstein signs you up for a comedy lead in his next show.'

'I hope he doesn't,' said Mrs Shannon. 'I can't tell you how glad I am, darling, that you're out of the place.'

'You mean you really don't mind? What about your thirty pounds?'

'Oh, that,' she snapped her fingers. 'I'd have paid double that to get you cured of wanting to go on the stage. One in the family's enough, goodness knows, and you were never really fitted for it——'

'I *was* bad, wasn't I?'

'No, dear, you were really quite promising,' said Mrs Shannon without conviction. 'Crack-in-my-eye-Tommy,' murmured Uncle Geoffrey, pensively.

'Never mind, Mary,' said Gerald, giving her one of his sideways smiles. 'I bet you were jolly good. Let's all go out to dinner somewhere and think of something for Mary to be. What d'you say, Lily?'

How nice people were, thought Mary, going upstairs to change her dress, and how churlish she had been to them in her preoccupation with her own exaggerated troubles.

She turned on the gramophone and sang as she moved about her bedroom. She was so happy; if only she had Denys now, everything would be perfect. Denys, or—somebody. The mythical man about whom she made stories in bed. But if she couldn't have Denys, who could she have? Where was this somebody that was supposed to exist for everybody? She was nineteen and it felt wrong not to be in love.

Chapter Seven

ON the strength of having won the Dramatic College cup, Angela was taken on in a summer repertory company at Penzance, which performed Greek tragedies and *Prometheus Unbound* to people who would have preferred a concert party but turned up nevertheless to show that they were as cultured as the next man.

Mary went down once to see Angela act, and fell in love with a young man in the company who had sweeping blond hair and eyelashes. Martin O'Dwyer was engagingly vague amd beautifully romantic. He took Mary out on the cliffs in the moonlight and flung throbbing lines of poetry far out to sea.

'Just to have you near me, all my life,' he said to her. 'I'd ask nothing more.'

When he came back to London, he took her out quite often, and he still managed to be fairly romantic in Lyons' Corner House, the two-and-sixpennies at the cinema, or the gusty echoing passages of the Tube. The evening before he was due to sail for Ireland to see his 'lovely little mother,' he discovered that he had forgotten to cash a cheque and would not have time to go to the bank in the morning. Mrs Shannon willingly lent him five pounds, and so vague was he that he faded away like a beautiful dream and was never heard of again.

Mary mourned him for a while, partly because her pride was hurt, partly because it was good for her figure. After leaving the College, she had determined to get herself thin without waiting for the fining down that her mother promised her. By drastic dieting and strenuous undignified exercises, she was achieving satisfactory results, and Aunt Mavis or Aunt Grace rang her mother up nearly every other day to say that the child would injure her health and looks, and to cite cases of terrifying feminine diseases contracted through banting. Even Gerald told her that she was a silly young chump, but she didn't care.

She didn't like him when he became paternal. She often wondered whether he contemplated getting a divorce and marrying her mother, and she wanted to tell him that if he did, he might as well think again. He and her mother seemed to be very good friends, but he was much too slow for her, and often had to have jokes explained to him, which was amusing at first, but tiresome in the long run. Her mother would never marry him. It was obvious, too, that she put the shop before everything else these days.

Mrs Wilkes Armitage, no longer able to resist the call of the Riviera which had been irking her for some time, gave Mrs Shannon the option of buying her out, and nipped off to Antibes to snap up an actress's villa that had just come into the market. Mrs Shannon bought her out on the instalment system, against the advice of Uncle Lionel, the family oracle on money matters, who said, with a face like an adding machine, that it would be a millstone round her neck until she paid it off.

However, business was good and she was confident. She changed the name of the shop from 'Nell Gwyn'—another of Mrs Wilkes Armitage's whims, to match her hair—to 'Lilianne' and redecorated it in white and gold and dark crimson brocade.

'Now, darling, if you still want to,' she said to Mary, 'I'd love to have you working with me. Would you like to?'

Mary was thinking. 'Of course, I'd love to work there,' she said, doubtfully. 'But what could I be, exactly? I mean I don't know anything about it, I wouldn't be much help.'

'That's where my idea comes in. I thought you might go to Paris and study dress designing. I've always wanted you to do something with your drawing. There's a marvellous school there, and if you were good at it, you'd be a tremendous help to me. I haven't got anyone with ideas. Oh, damn that telephone—it never stops ringing. What d'you say,

139

Puss? Think it over while I—Hallo?' She picked up the receiver. 'Oh, hallo, Mavis.' She made a suffering face at Mary. 'Yes, my dear, yes, quite well. And you? . . . Oh, I'm sorry to hear that. Why's that? . . . *No*, my dear, what has she been up to? . . . She *what*? . . . Yes, you must be. What does Guy say about it?' Mary waited impatiently. There was something interesting going on. She could hear the voice at the other end quacking like a duck, and her mother's eyes were dancing in a way that Aunt Mavis's telephone conversation never inspired.

'Cigarette,' mouthed her mother, slipping from the arm to the seat of the chair, and settling in for a long session.

'Well,' she said, when at last she rang off, '*what* do you think?'

'I haven't the slightest idea. What?'

'It's very funny really, after what we were talking about before. Mavis wanted to know if I'd give Sarah some work at the shop, to distract her mind.'

'What from, for heaven's sake? Mummy, do *tell* me.'

'She wants to get married, to a penniless school-teacher on the Gold Coast. He only gets leave every five years, and this is one of the times, and she met him in the reading-room of the Marylebone Public Library and came home with her eyes fastened on space. Poor Mavis, she presents her at Court, drags her to all the deb. dances and gets her lined up to marry a rich duke, and now she wants to go and live in Uganda with a man with a name like Roebuck, and have about twenty children, some black, some white——'

Mary giggled. 'It's really awfully funny. Poor Aunt Mavis. She's the sort of woman who's destined never to get what she wants.'

'As you can imagine, she's gone off the deep end completely, and she says Guy's in a white-hot rage and throws ornaments about,' said her mother. 'I said no about the shop, of course, and Mavis was furious. But apart from the fact that I don't need her, specially if I'm going to have you, why shouldn't Sarah marry Roebuck, if he loves her? God knows he's about the only man who ever will. Well, Puss,' she hopped back to the previous subject. 'What about Paris? Have you decided?'

'Yes,' said Mary. 'I'd love it. Paris . . . Mummy, is it true that it's got quite a different smell from anywhere else?'

She found that it was true. It was more a quality of the air than a definite scent, as enchanting as the Charbury smell, but much more intangible, more difficult to define. The Paris smell was an exciting, elusive mixture of spring flowers in the Bois, pavements in the sunshine, Dubonnet, the hot, metallic tang of the Metro, and the lightness and clearness of the air itself. You could never imagine a fog in Paris. Indeed, to be there in springtime was to be unable to imagine it at any other season.

Mary lived in Passy, with a family called Robeau, in a high narrow house, with high, narrow green shutters to every window. This was an economical *au pair* arrangement, for the eldest Robeau daughter, who wanted to study in London, had gone to live with Mary's mother and Uncle Geoffrey in Marguerite Street. Mary wondered how they were getting on with Lucienne. She had arrived in London before Mary had left—large and soft-bodied, with a small pink mouth and a flat, unresponsive face. She looked the sort of girl who would be as easy to get on with as she was unexciting, but she was probably boring Uncle Geoffrey to tears by now.

Mme Robeau was widowed '*il y a ne me demandez pas combien d'années,*' and though not well off, she behaved as if they were paupers. She never bought a new dress. She was ever picking old ones to pieces, and making them up again a new shape, with odd bits added here and there, and she had been known to take two hats apart and fit the crown of one to the brim of the other and vice versa. Mary did not mind that the food was not lavish. She was still watching her figure anxiously, and in any case, on the way to the dressmaking school there was an irresistible *pâtisserie* that nearly always saw her pushing through the tinkling swing door into the hot, sugary interior that made you feel like the jam inside a doughnut.

Mme Robeau had two daughters besides Lucienne. Jeanne, who was sweet and docile and taught in a kindergarten, had a pink-and-white young man called Albert, who was going to marry her in the dim future of *quand j'aurai succès avec mes affaires.* Didi, the youngest, was rather common, and wore very uplift brassières and patent-leather shoes with heels like stilts, and taught Mary a lot of French words, for some of which she did not even know the English equivalent. Mary had taken an intensive course in French before she came over to Paris, and although the Robeaus could speak a certain amount of English, she preferred to practise her French on them, and gradually she found that it was becoming easier to understand what was going on at the dressmaking school.

She loved the work there, but she was astonished to find how long it took to produce any garment in the authentic Flambert manner. First you designed it under the small black eye of M. Flambert, who took the drawing classes. He was fat and paunchy, with a mouth that opened and shut flatly, like a toad's, and a habit of pinching the nape of your neck while he bent over to look at your work. Not until your picture was a work of art were you allowed to transform it into a paper pattern. This was a complicated process involving more geometry than Mary's French could cope with. Then, from the paper pattern, you made a canvas *toile*, which was pinned together and fitted on you by Mme Flambert, who sat like a concierge in a tiny stuffy office, on a carpet of pins and press studs. Finally, under the excitable direction of Mlle Sylvie, you were allowed to cut out the stuff that you had bought half price at the Galeries Lafayette, and make it up in the room where the sewing machines whirred all day long like baritone canaries.

Mary was happy. She enjoyed the work at the school, especially the drawing part, and she thought she was going to be quite good at it. The other girls were pleasant, the Robeaus were bearable, and she adored Paris. She saw none of the things Granpa had told her to see, but she went up the Eiffel Tower with Jeanne and was pinched by a sailor in the lift, and Didi sometimes took her to seedy night spots with her cheerfully common friends. Best of all, Mary liked to sit in the huge cafés on the Champs Élysées or the Boulevards, drinking coffee and *Dubonnet Cassis* alternately, and watching the people for hours at a time. Madame was always telling her that it was not *comme il faut* to sit alone at the cafés.

'My girls,' she said, 'would never do such a thing.' She did not know about some of the places that Didi went to at night nor, being deaf, what time she came in.

Mary always said: 'Oh, it's all right. In London, one goes everywhere alone. I like to be alone. If men speak to me, I say I'm on my way to meet my fiancé, who is *boxeur*. That always works.'

She would come out of the school in the late afternoon, and instead of turning to the right and going along the embankment to Passy, she would cross the Place d'Iéna, and walk along the river to the Place de la Concorde. From there, it was only a question of whether to go straight on to the Boulevard des Italiens, or turn up the Champs Élysées. Having chosen her café, she would sit at one of the tables on the pavement in the light balmy air, and watch the fascinating, endless processions that passed between her and the darting, strident cars.

To and fro went the inhumanly chic, expensive women with dogs; bent old women with black hair, black clothes, black lives; lads of the village with tilted hats and immense overcoats that hung straight to the ground from shoulders padded as if the coat hanger were still inside; tourists—the Germans hideous, most of the English hideous, too, and talking their own language even more loudly; fascinating, sinister men with tight lips, carrying briefcases and bound obviously on some secret diplomatic mission; old women in taut black satin; young women—typists and shopgirls, smarter than the smartest deb. in London; children in preposterous clothes—little boys in plus fours, long black stockings and boots, and girls like miniature fashion plates; a soldier or two, with his box-like cap on one side, his blue cape swinging. She would sit and watch them all, entranced, until the light began to fade, and it was time to go back to Passy for the juggled remains of lunch that was supper. She loved to be alone like this in a crowd, yet

142

feeling part of the life. Paris had a knack of making you feel at home.

At first, she used to go to cinemas alone, but she gave it up after a man's hand had materialized once out of the darkness, groping, assured. She stuck to the cafés.

It was thus that she met Pierre.

She was sitting in the Colisée one golden evening after a day of rain, when the air had the damp freshness of the violets that a small boy in a black overall was selling among the tables. Mary felt that, for once, her clothes were worthy of Paris. She was wearing the first finished product of the École Flambert, a dark blue dress with a little fitted jacket, trimmed with white piping that had taken years off her life, but was worth it. Her money from her mother had come that morning, so on her head was a large blue sailor hat, subtly Parisian, with a white ribbon hanging down at the back over her dark curls.

Usually, if anyone spoke to her, she would ignore them, and if they were persistent, get up and go somewhere else. But this evening, when a voice behind her said quietly, '*Bon soir, mademoiselle*,' she rashly turned round. It had not sounded the sort of voice that usually spoke in one's ear on the streets of Paris, accompanied by a shifty eye and a pitted skin. When she turned round, she saw a very clean-looking young man, dark, with a smooth skin and a charming smile that was faintly suggestive of Maurice Chevalier.

'*Bon soir*,' she said, and smiled back, wondering whether this was what people called making yourself cheap; but how could one ignore anything quite so nice-looking? He was sitting just behind her, and he got up immediately and stepped forward to her little round iron table.

'*Vous permettez?*' he said, with his hand on the back of the other chair, heels together, bowing slightly. He was very polite, but the smile was still there, roguish, promising. Mary shrugged her shoulders in what she hoped was a sophisticated, Gallic gesture. '*Comme vous voulez*,' she said, pursing her lips.

'Ah,' he sat down at once. 'You're American?' That must be because she had her hat on the back of her head.

'Oh, no,' she said. 'I'm English.'

'But that's marvellous!' He leaned forward. 'I hope you don't think it's very rude of me to speak to you—I know in England, one doesn't—but I had been watching you for a long time, and I was alone too, so I thought it would be more—fun, to be together.' He spoke English almost perfectly, with only just enough accent to be attractive. Mary, not knowing quite what to say, commented on this, looking down shyly, fiddling with her glass of coffee.

'I was at Cambridge,' he said, 'and I am always with English people. My father is director of the Paris branch of an English bank. Look,' he

143

handed her a card, 'this is me. So you see I'm not a ruffian from the gutter who you must be afraid of.' His name was Pierre Mathieu. When she told him her name, he said: 'But that's perfect for you. Mary . . . that's just right, you know, because you look *vierge*.'

Mary blushed. No Englishman had ever said that on five minutes' acquaintance, and even Didi's strange boy friends had been rather wary of her because she was English, and because she was much quieter than Didi or Riette, or any of the others.

'Please have a drink,' said Pierre. 'Let's drink to our meeting. What will you have?'

'*Dubonnet Cassis*,' said Mary, because it was the only French drink she knew.

'Jolly good,' said Pierre, who was full of schoolboy Anglicisms. 'So will I. *Garçon!*'

His self-assurance was exciting and his admiring interest stimulating. Aunt Mavis would have called him 'a most personable-looking young man.' Mary wished that someone she knew could see her. The waiter swooped towards them with a tray of bottles balanced on one hand, and set two large goblets before them. '*Dubonnet Cassis pour Madame?*' A wineglassful of Dubonnet, a dexterous dash of Cassis, clink—he dropped in the ice, and filled the glass up with soda, till the creamy mauve froth rose over the top.

By the time they had started on their second drink, Mary was feeling less nervous. Under the influence of the smile which Pierre kept turning on her, she told him a lot about herself, her own family and the Robeaus.

'I must go,' she said at last. 'I shall be late for supper and I'm supposed to be going to see *Rasputin* afterwards with Jeanne.'

He frowned, sticking out his lower lip. Could it be that he copied Maurice Chevalier on purpose, and spent anxious hours practising before his mirror? No, it was just a very fortunate resemblance.

'No,' he said decisively. 'You're dining with me. Give them a *coup de telephone*, and say you're not coming back.'

'Oh, Madame would be horrified. She's always warning me about strange men.'

'Well, say you've met a friend from England—anything,' said Pierre, impatiently. 'Come,' he smiled at her devastatingly. 'I'll take you to telephone. Then we'll go and have fun, eh, Mary?'

How could she say no? In any case, she didn't want to. How different this was from England, she thought excitedly, threading her way after him among the little tables. Englishmen would hardly ask you to 'stagger round the floor' with them at private dances unless they had been introduced, but this Frenchman just came along, was in your life from one moment to the next, and told you you were dining with him, just when you were wondering rather anxiously whether you would ever see him again.

He came into the telephone box with her and put his hand over hers when she raised it to put in the money, and then held the hand and kissed the fingers softly one by one, while she lied to a sweetly complaisant Jeanne. When she pulled her hand away and whispered, 'No, you mustn't,' he began to breathe gently in her ear. She told herself she would have to be careful of him. Thrills ran up and down her spine.

When they went out to Pierre's car, Mary, who had been suspecting that he might be rich, was sure of it. The car was very long and black and shiny, with an array of badges on the radiator, and smelt expensively of new leather inside.

'It is a new one?' she asked, as they turned into the Champs Élysées.

'Yes, rather. I change every year. It's better. So you don't know Paris, eh?' he said after a moment, dropping his hand lightly on to her knee.

'Oh yes, quite well. I've been here nearly two months.'

'Oh, you've seen the sights, of course. I don't mean that. What about Paris at night—Montmartre, Montparnasse?'

'I've been to *boîtes* with Didi,' said Mary proudly, and named one or two.

'Oh,' he stuck out his underlip again, and put on his brakes with a jerk as a gendarme suddenly went mad in front of them on a pedestrian crossing, doing frantic things with his whistle and baton. 'Filthy holes. You can't go there. What about "*Schéherezade*"?' She shook her head. ' "*Florence*"?' he went on. ' "*Bœuf sur le Toît*," "*Chez les Nudistes*"? "*Casanova*"? Oh, I've got a lot to show you. Come on, this is going to be fun.'

The gendarme's whistle shrilled again and they roared ahead, rounded the Arc de Triomphe at speed, and began to go back the way they had come.

'Where are we going?' asked Mary.

'Harry's Bar. First, we'll have a drink and I'll tell you why I like you.' He turned on the wireless on the dashboard. A man was singing '*En parlant un peu de Paris*' in a smooth, caressing voice. A line that Mary had read somewhere came into her head. '*Pour connaître le vrai Paris, il faut être amoureux*.'

Afterwards, Mary could never remember the sequence of that dizzy, joyous evening. It seemed that in Paris, unlike London, where you booked a table in a restaurant and were there for the evening whether you liked it or not, you went from place to place as the fancy took you. Mary could not remember where they had dinner, though she had a distinct recollection of *Poulet à la King* somewhere, and the nonchalant humour of the waiter who served it, and through the whole evening

145

there had flowed a golden, sparkling stream of inexhaustible champagne.

At *Schéherezade* there had been a velvet-eyed Russian singing lonely little songs that turned you to water, and in another place, luscious girls had displayed various bits of themselves to the accompaniment of gleeful, jaunty choruses. At *Casanova*, which was just a little room with a bar and a fat pianist and a few very smart people who all knew each other, Mary had found herself standing by the piano singing 'Night and Day' in English for them, with incredible success.

She had never enjoyed herself so much. Pierre was an exhilarating companion and kept saying deliciously outrageous, flattering things to her. They danced cheek to cheek and he held her very close, and she discovered that, miraculously, with him she could dance the tango. In the brown velvet darkness of *Schéherezade*, he kissed her on the corner of her mouth, and whispered, 'Turn your lips to me.'

She drew away. 'Pierre, I really ought to be going home, it's awfully late,' she said doubtfully, and to her surprise, he agreed at once and called for his bill. Mary went worriedly to the cloakroom. Had she annoyed him? Was he bored with her? He ought not to want to go home; she didn't want to. In the car, he put an arm round her and drove with one hand, and she put her head on his shoulder, wondering muzzily what was going to happen.

'How old are you, Mary?' he asked suddenly.

'Nearly twenty.'

'Baby,' he said, and she could tell from his voice that he was smiling his impudent smile.

'How old are you then?'

'Twenty-five.'

'Well, that's not so old——'

'Not for an Englishman, but I'm French, remember.' Mary smiled to herself. His complete self-assurance was one of the things that she found the most attractive about him, because she lacked it herself.

'Pierre!' She sat up abruptly. 'Where are we going? This isn't the way home.'

'Yes it is. All good little English girls take a drive through the Bois on their way home, didn't you know?'

'Oh.'

When at last she was in bed, curled up between the chilly sheets with her make-up still on and her hair unbrushed and the grey light of dawn brightening the gap between the curtains, she thought again how different this was from England.

Englishmen in cars or taxis either put the unforgivable question, 'May I kiss you?' or else breathed heavily, made a clumsy dive, and looked extremely foolish when they missed their mark. But Pierre; oh,

146

Pierre was different—marvellous, unlike anything she had ever known. She closed her eyes and began to drift into sleep, thinking of things that he had said to her out in the Bois, when the only other sounds were the ticking of the clock inside the car and the dark rustle of the trees outside. Tomorrow—today—was Sunday, and he was going to drive her out to the country. She must sleep. She must look beautiful for him.

Mary's interest in the École Flambert waned. She still went there every day, but more to fill in the time while Pierre was working at the bank, until they could be together again. He used to come and fetch her sometimes, and Mary was proud to see the stir he created among the other girls. She had a wonderful time with him. He took her everywhere and showed her a Paris that without him she would never have found. They went to every sort of night club—select, turbulent or frankly indecent; superb restaurants, where Pierre gave her food that she had never even dreamed existed, and tiny intimate places on the heights of Montmartre, where the proprietor treated them like his own children. They rode in the Bois in the daytime and drank Porto Blanc and danced in the fairy-lit cafés among the trees at night. They went to the races at Auteuil, the first night of a Sacha Guitry play, and to Lunar Park, where Pierre kissed her open mouth on the switchback. He took her to dinner at an inn at Melun, where his brother was doing his military service, and they drank red wine and sang 'C'est la Béguine' with a crowd of riotous, unshaven soldiers. He took her to his home, too, and she met his mother and father, and sometimes she had to go to dinner parties there, which frightened her so much that she could never speak a word of French, and Pierre would laugh at her and call her Baby on the way home.

The Mathieus were very rich indeed. Even to talk about them put a sparkle into Mme Robeau's eye, and her opinion of Mary had soared. They lived at what Mme Robeau called 'une élite addresse,' in a grand, square house, with wrought-iron gates and an inner court with a fountain. Pierre's mother was no more than a cold, unemotional peg on which to hang diamonds; black-haired and bony-nosed, like a raven decked out in its stolen jewels. Mary much preferred M. Mathieu. He was a kind little man, who was always beautifully clean, like Pierre, with spotless shirts and collars, and a face that looked as if it was either shaved three times a day or never had to be shaved at all.

They also had a country house just outside Paris—a hunting lodge, Pierre called it, which raised Mary's hopes until she discovered he meant shooting. He drove Mary out there on Sunday, and they had spent the day there, eating a messy, glorious lunch in the kitchen, straight out of the frying-pan. After lunch, Mary wanted to go for a walk. There were hills and little woods and inviting, unfenced fields, but Pierre stuck out his underlip and persuaded her to stay in the house. They had made a fire in the big sitting-room that was decorated and furnished with fabulous rusticity, and that was where he wanted to be with her. She was disappointed at first. French people never seemed to have that feeling in the country that you must be in the open air every possible minute. She consoled herself with the thought that an Englishman would probably have gone tramping off over the hills with a gun and a dog and a pipe and forgotten her existence.

It was there, in the room with the stags' heads and sporting prints on the walls, on the bearskin rug that no Mathieu had ever shot, that the struggle between Mary and Pierre began. It broke out again nearly every time they met, whenever they were alone together, and often Mary came near to giving in, but always her stubborn instinct asserted itself in time. Pierre tried everything: persuasion, promise, abuse, and even scorn.

'We are in love, aren't we?' he would argue. 'Well, what's all the fuss about then?'

He would storm at her. 'Oh, you don't know anything about love,' or 'You're just a silly prim little English Miss. What a schoolgirl you are!' Mary used to cry, if not with him, when she got home, lying on top of her bed with her dress on, distraught and emotional. She knew that she was right; she didn't even have to think about it, but apart from that, even if she disregarded her instinct, she was frightened. How could she say that to Pierre? It sounded so young.

One evening, she dined at his home in the Avenue Henri Martin. There were only two other guests, a business friend of M. Mathieu's and his wife, who was *soignée* to the last hair, witty and vivacious, with an eye that glittered as hardly as the emeralds at her throat. She made Mary feel like a deaf mute in sackcloth. She had had an argument with Pierre the evening before, and she was pale and tired after a troubled night. She wore a plain black dinner dress with Pierre's gardenias, and she wondered whether, perhaps, she would have felt better and been more of an asset to the party in red sequins with an ostrich feather in her hair. Pierre, sitting opposite, looked at her often, but he hardly spoke to her, for he was too busy laughing and joking with the exquisite specimen at his side, comparing the two of them, probably, thought Mary, resisting M. Mathieu's kindly efforts to draw her out.

After dinner, however, when Pierre's mother suggested Bridge, he announced that he was going to take Mary out to dance, and so they shook hands politely all round, and left the others already seated, with Mme Mathieu's diamond-encrusted fingers shuffling cards at an impossible speed.

If Pierre had been anyone but Pierre, Mary would have suggested going home and having the first long sleep she had had for nights and nights, but he was always full of boundless vitality at the end of the day and had never heard of such a thing as an early evening. A footman with calves that looked silly enough to be padded brought her her coat in the pillared hall, and bowed them both out into the warm May night. Mary would have liked to walk a little in the quiet, absorbed streets, but the car was standing under the porch outside the door, so to save arguments she got into it and Pierre drove off with a swish of the gravel and an arrogant arpeggio on the horn as he turned into the road.

'Where are we going?' asked Mary, and thought, as she said it, how many times in the last weeks she must have asked this question. It was always Pierre who decided. He knew everything there was to know about Paris at night, and everything there was to know about taking a woman out. There were never any of those depressing moments that Mary had experienced once or twice in London, when, having secured a taxi after the theatre, usually through her initiative, her escort would turn to her, fingering his tie, and say uncertainly, 'Where would you like to go?' How could one choose when one didn't even know how much money he had? Sometimes it ended up by the man lurching forward and enquiring through the front window of the taxi driver, who invariably advised a place with no other merit than that the doorman was his pal.

Tonight, as usual, Pierre knew where they were going. 'I'm going to take you somewhere where you've never been before,' he said. 'It's not exciting, it's not chic, but I'd like to take you there to-night.'

'All right,' said Mary, and leaned back, watching his square well-manicured hands spinning the wheel of the high-geared, American steering, as they rounded the Étoile. He seemed quieter than usual. He generally chattered and laughed and teased her or made love to her, as they drove through the glitter and glare of the town at night. It was not like him to be thoughtful. Soon they were climbing, through narrow streets that turned and twisted, always upward. When Pierre stopped the car, they got out into a little cobbled square, with dark, irregular houses all round. From somewhere came the faint throb of an accordion.

'Are we somewhere near the Sacré Cœur?' asked Mary, looking about her.

'Yes. We're at the top of Paris.' Pierre took her arm. 'This way.'

'Lovely how new the air feels when you're above a town,' she said, turning her head to feel the slight breeze as they crossed the square. They were making for a little café, quite a dingy place, more like a shop, with no tables or awning outside, and a dim light showing through its steamy windows. 'In here?' said Mary, surprised.

149

'I'll go first,' he said, and she followed him through the swinging half doors into a sort of public bar, where one or two large, dirty men were lounging over tiny drinks, thickening the atmosphere with foul pipes and yellow cigarettes. They glanced incuriously at Pierre and Mary, but the fat man behind the bar, who had a huge white head with strands of oily hair plastered across the top, greeted Pierre delightedly, and squeezing himself through the flap in the bar, led the way out of the room through a bead-curtained doorway. They were suddenly in the open air again, on a little terrace, which was dark until the *patron* switched on two dim pools of light. Mary crossed quickly to the low wall opposite, and looked over with a gasp of delight. There, beyond the roofs of the houses immediately beneath her, was Paris, looking like the intensified reflection of a starry winter sky. Here and there were bright concentrations of light—floodlit buildings and the dazzling Citroen sign that made a lighthouse of the Eiffel Tower.

'Like it?' said Pierre behind her, putting his arm round her waist.

'It's perfect. I've never seen anything like it. What's it called here?'

'Café Bellevue, of course, what else could it be?'

'*Parfaitement. Café Bellevue, Ma'mselle,*' echoed the *patron*, who was hovering eagerly round them. They sat down at one of the tables by the parapet, and Mary leant her elbows on the edge and gazed over, fascinated, forgetting everything but the enchanted infinity below.

'Hi!' Pierre's voice broke into her absorption. 'Are you with me or with Paris?'

'I'm sorry.' She turned back, smiling, to meet his smile. The fat man had gone away, and there were a bottle and glasses on the check tablecloth.

'What's this?' she asked suspiciously, as Pierre filled her glass with a yellowish green liqueur.

'*Specialité de la maison.* You have to drink it here whether you like it or not. I believe old Jo-Jo would throw you over the edge if you didn't.' He raised his glass, his face suddenly serious.

'You're very beautiful,' he said. 'I love you.'

He had never said it quite like that before, quietly and simply. He had said: 'I love you,' '*Je t'adore,*' '*Tu est mon amour,*' and a hundred other things that had burst out of him from passion or exuberance, but this time it was as if he had suddenly discovered, to his astonishment, that he meant it.

Mary too had said, 'I love you,' thinking it was true, but this time she didn't say it, because she had suddenly discovered, to her astonishment, that perhaps she did not mean it.

'Thank you, Pierre.' She looked down and began to trace the squares of the tablecloth with her finger.

150

'I think you'd better marry me,' he was saying, and she went on drawing her finger along the rough cotton thread where the red square met the white square, trying to collect her startled thoughts.

'Well—look at me, Mary—will you?'

'Oh, Pierre,' she looked up, and her heart sank, because he was so attractive and it would be so easy to say yes. 'I don't know, darling. I don't know what to say.' How could one make a decision, taken unawares like this? She must have time; time to think, calmly and alone, without that infectious smile urging her from the other side of the table. She looked out again over the roofs of Paris, but the bright tracks of the streets led to no answer.

'Am I awfully silly?' she said, turning back to him. 'Can I have time to think about it? You know I'm going over to England in a few days' time. Could I think about it then, when we're not together, and tell you when I come back?'

'I suppose it's because I'm French and you're English, is that it?' said Pierre, moodily, his smile dropped to the beginnings of a scowl.

'Well—yes, it is, in a way.' The consideration had not entered her head, but she welcomed it. It was the safest, least unkind reason.

'All right, Baby,' he said, 'have your think. But it doesn't make any difference, you know—our nationalities. I'm a man and you're a woman, it doesn't alter that. A man and a woman, Mary. You can't go against what's meant to be. You've got to belong to me, you know that——' The intensity of his voice frightened her.

'Don't, Pierre, please,' she said breathlessly. 'You said you'd give me time to decide. Let's go, shall we?' She got up, pushing back her chair, and shook out the long skirt of her black dress. 'Let's go,' she repeated, as he still sat, looking up at her. 'It's getting a bit cold, and——' She laughed uncertainly. 'I don't like that drink much. It—it tastes of boot polish.'

Mary and Lucienne Robeau were changing places to spend the long Whitsun week-end with their own families. Half-way across the Channel, Mary saw the boat in the opposite direction, to Calais. 'There goes Lucienne,' she thought, 'in a new summer hat from Selfridge's bargain basement, wondering whether I have spilt ink on the counterpane or broken the pin tray in her bedroom, and here go I, in a questionable hat of my own and Mme Sylvie's making, wondering how lavishly she has helped herself to the scent I left behind, and whether she has fiddled with the hands of my china-plate clock.' But chiefly she was wondering, as she had been continuously for the last three days, what to do about Pierre. She remembered something that Granny had once said to her, years ago, when she had been telling Mary the story of the three men who had wanted to marry her. Von

Zalpius, the German, who had flung himself on one knee before her in the middle of a cotillion, declaring, 'You are my queen!' George Vallery, who was kind, and ardent, but made the mistake of introducing her to Granpa, and Granpa himself, who had proposed to her in a punt at Henley.

'Poor George,' Mary had said. 'It must be awful having to say no to anyone. It would sound so, sort of—rude. And, anyway, how does one know whether to say yes or no?' She remembered Granny's answer.

'The smallest doubt in your mind,' she had said, 'must be enough to show you it's not the right man. That doubt won't disappear after you're married; it will grow until it becomes first an annoyance, and finally, perhaps, even a hatred.'

But surely there was nobody about whom one would not have doubts? No two people were identical. Nobody could ever be so completely oneself that nothing about them was discordant.

She leaned over the rail and watched the first wave scooping away from the side of the boat like dark-green jelly. That blur on the horizon ahead was England. Three days more, and she would be looking at a blur on the horizon ahead that was France, and by then she would have to have made up her mind. Did she love Pierre enough that the little things that she noticed about him, indulgently now, would never irritate her, and even, as Granny had said, turn to hatred? They were only things that he did because he was French, and therefore they did not matter, but did the fact that she had noticed them now mean that one day they would matter very much? They were only little things, but they had to be faced.

He wore a pearl tie-pin, and frequently a double-breasted waistcoat, and a bowler hat at peculiar times of day. He powdered his face with talcum powder after shaving, and there was the possibility that he wore a hair-net while dressing, as she knew many Frenchmen did. He wore a watch-chain hanging out of his trouser pocket. He had an unhealthy partiality for cream cakes. The country was to him a hobby, not a necessity. He always wanted to know whether people were *bonne famille*, and he spoke of his English friends by their titles, if any. He said things were 'jolly fine' and 'topping,' and never tired of displaying his familiarity with the adverb 'rather.'

She did not mind any of these things. After all, they were only part of the romantic fact that he was a Frenchman—a Parisian, and knew how to make love as did no Englishman of her acquaintance.

Although the blur on the horizon was only just beginning to materialize as cliffs, Mary could already hear behind her the agitation of British travellers preparing to disembark. Perhaps she had better fight her way down to the ladies' room to tidy her hair and rearrange

152

the angle of the questionable hat. She turned away from the rail, thinking that it was petty of her even to have noticed those things about Pierre. He was attractive and clean and honest and gay and alive, sure of himself and of how to treat her. That was what counted. And yet, as she made her way over and round muffled, prostrate bodies, hat-boxes, golf clubs, and men in tweed caps discussing Baldwin, she could not put Granny's voice out of her head: 'The smallest doubt in your mind . . .'

As soon as Mary saw England, she knew that she could never live anywhere else. If she married Pierre, he would have to get transferred to the English branch of the Bank, that was all.

If Paris had a feeling of its own in the air, so had England, but you only noticed it when you had been away. It was a feeling of damp, fresh security. Everything looked so right and so comfortably unexotic, like a cabbage. It seemed that even the breezes blew there because they knew that England was the only possible country in which to blow. Mary had never been away for so long before, and she stepped down the gangway with the joyful feeling that she was returning to where she belonged.

The train sped through the fields of Kent, and their greenness was an almost unbearable joy. How strange that in two countries that were once one, separated now by a bare twenty miles of water, the colour of the grass could be quite different. The meadows of France were grey-green, like the field uniforms of her soldiers, but here, in England, the meadows that for centuries had known only peace shone with the brightest, greenest green of early summer. Mary had never been particularly fond of Kent, but she took it to her heart now, and stared out of the window, oblivious of the carriage behind her, as once she had done in the train that took her to Charbury.

She had hoped that there might be someone to meet her at Victoria, but there was nobody belonging to her among the embracing, chattering crowd. At Marguerite Street she banged in at the front door with a shout of, 'Hullo, somebody, it's me!' but the only person who answered her call was Mabel, the sciatic daily maid, who came creaking up from the little basement to say, 'Welcome 'ome, I'm sure,' as if she were not sure at all.

'Hullo, Mabel, how are your legs?' asked Mary automatically. 'Where's my mother, and Mr Payne?'

'*She* don't come home from the shop these days till close on seven, working herself like a black she is, and didn't ought to do it. I told her so, straight. "You're wearing yourself to a shadow, 'M," I said. It's never been my way to beat about the bush, as you know, Miss M. I speak as I find——'

'Yes,' said Mary wearily, going into the drawing-room and hunting about for a cigarette. 'And my uncle's down at Denham, I suppose?'

153

'That's right. Still set on the films, 'e is, but you oughter seen 'is last. I went all the way up to the West End to see it, and talk about dull! That may be all right at the "Capitol," but they'll never stand for it at the Putney Palace. I told him so, straight. And that French girl. Talk about jabber! I couldn't make head nor tail of what she said. She and your Ma, at it hammer and tongs—oui oui oui, oh la la—as I said to Wilkins only the other night, "give me English," I said. Not that I've anything against Miss Rowbow, mind; she's clean about the house, and gives you your name very civil, but it's just that I've never had to do with foreign ladies and gentlemen.' She pulled down her mouth.

'Yes, Mabel,' said Mary, hunting vainly in the corner cupboard for the cocktail bottles that usually lived there. 'Isn't there any gin or anything? I'm terribly tired, I think I need a drink.'

'No more gin this week, *she* says. She come into my kitchen the other day and go through the grocer's book. "What do we do with sugar?" she says, for we had four pound last week, not counting loaf, "stoke the boiler with it?" Well, I told her straight, "when it's rhubarb one day, 'M, and blackberry fool the next, and the French young lady taking cornflakes for breakfast, it's not surprising that it runs through your fingers like sand." Then she says about the eggs, and not using any for my pastry, and I was quite upset, for how am I to make it bind? And as you know, Miss M., I take a pride in my pastry. I've the hand for it, I always say.' She contemplated her worn, red hands with satisfaction. Mary was worried. How much of this was true, and how much was the old blackguard inventing?

'And she said no more gin, did she?' she ventured casually, not wishing to give Mabel an opening by showing too much interest.

'No more than one bottle a month am I to order. How I'm to face the grocer's man, I *don't* know, for we used to 'ave a regular list of orders, and now *she* says not to 'ave this, not to 'ave that——'

'Well, is there any sherry?' cut in Mary, who had heard enough.

'Ah, now you're talking. There's been a bottle in my pantry these last three days, for *she* 'asn't fancied it, and '*e* says 'e'd rather take poison than drink cheap sherry. I'll go downstairs and bring it upstairs for you,' she said, stressing the stairs. 'It's me legs,' she added, with pretended irrelevance. 'I could cry with the pain sometimes, I could really.'

'Oh, I'm so sorry,' said Mary, feeling contrite that five minutes of Mabel's company always left her limp or at screaming-point. 'I'll go down and get the sherry, don't you bother.' She went down the kitchen stairs, with Mabel creeping after her, and when she came up again, with the bottle in one hand and a corkscrew in the other, a key was clicking in the lock of the front door.

As her mother came in, Mary rushed along the little hall and flung her arms round her, thumping her in the small of the back with the

154

bottle of sherry. 'Darling! My Puss!' Mrs Shannon dropped her parcels, handbag, and latchkey, and they hugged each other. Mary had forgotten how small her mother was. There was nothing of her to hold. Was Mabel right? Was there even less of her? She noticed with a shock that her mother was wearing a different perfume—not the subtle, expensive 'Souvenir d'Amour' that had been part of her for so long.

'Mary, you're thinner than ever,' she said, holding her away and looking her up and down.

'About time. I'm just beginning to get a figure, thank goodness. Like my dress? I made it.' She whirled round to show it off, and then began to chatter about Paris and the school, watching her mother with covert anxiety. She did look tired and strained. She was as vivacious as ever, but in a more nervy way, moving restlessly about, her hands never still, picking up the glass of sherry that Mary poured out for her and putting it down untouched. In spite of her careful make-up, her face looked lined. Mary purposely did not ask her any questions. Uncle Geoffrey would not be home until late, so they would have plenty of time alone together after dinner. She would find out then what was wrong.

'You're very grown-up; much older than when you went away,' said Mrs Shannon, oddly voicing Mary's own thoughts, for she had been feeling, with surprise, that she was older than her mother, and must protect her; as if she, and not Mary, were the daughter.

'Paris has done one good thing, then,' she answered. 'I do feel more grown-up, actually. More, sort of—sure of myself, you know.' That was Pierre's doing. She had not yet told her mother about Pierre. That, too, would keep.

Mabel, who wanted to get back to Putney, rushed them through dinner as usual, clearing the table round them, so that it seemed a crime to be eating dessert.

'Don't bother about coffee if you want to get off, Mabel,' said Mary, who could bear no longer the creaking of her shoes and stays. 'I'll make it myself. I've learnt a marvellous way to do it—the real French way. I'll show you some time, if you like?'

Mabel banged the sideboard drawer shut on the salt and pepper pots. 'I'm sorry if my coffee hasn't given satisfaction, I'm sure,' she said.

'Oh, now, Mabel,' said Mrs Shannon, who had never learned not to argue with her when she was taking up an attitude. 'Miss Mary didn't mean it that way. She was only trying to save you trouble so that you could get off earlier.'

'Well, I don't care to stay late, as you know, 'M,' said Mabel, already at the door, and beginning to untie her apron. 'What with my legs and the buses being such a scandal, you'd be surprised what time I get home sometimes. "You are a night-bird," Wilkins says to me the other night.

"You been in all the saloon bars between 'ere and Chawlsea?" That was the night we'd company to dinner, if you remember, 'M, and as I tell Wilkins, though I like to see things done in style, the pile of dirty dishes simply take the heart right out of you. Not that I wish to complain.' She held up her hand. 'I'm only too glad to see you enjoying yourselves, I'm sure,' she said gloomily, and took herself away.

'Well, I'm glad she thought we enjoyed ourselves,' said Mrs Shannon, when the door had closed, and clicked open and then closed again, for Mabel could never do anything, even shutting a door, at the first attempt. 'It was the dullest dinner-party I've ever known. Family,' she added in explanation.

'Oh!' Mary understood. 'How ghastly. Uncle Lionel and Aunt Grace?'

'Yes, and even Winifred. They hate all coming together, I know, but it gets them all over at once, and, honestly, who else could one ask them with? Guy's an asset to any party, but not when Mavis is there. She still goes shrill and brims over at the eyes whenever she speaks of Sarah. What she'll be like at the wedding I tremble to think.'

They went down to the kitchen together to make the coffee and saw out of the window Mabel's black woollen legs disappearing up the area steps with unwonted agility.

'Don't you think the poor old girl's getting a bit past her prime, Mummy?' said Mary, hunting in all the canisters on the dresser for the coffee.

'She's been past it for years, darling.' Mrs Shannon perched on the kitchen table and lit a cigarette. 'But I don't know who we'd get to do as much work for her wages.'

'Well,' said Mary, deliberately, 'couldn't you pay someone a bit more?'

Mrs Shannon blew out a delicate cloud of smoke and looked intently at the end of her cigarette. 'Not at the moment, darling.'

'Mummy——' Mary turned round, with the sago tin that held coffee in her hand, 'what is all this about? Are we getting poor again or something? Has anything happened to the dressmaking business?'

'No, darling,' her mother began, and then broke off. 'Oh, well, I suppose you might as well know. I wasn't going to tell you, but the truth is, I *am* in a bit of a fix. Only temporarily, of course.'

'Go on,' said Mary, taking out the saucepan to the tap in the pantry. 'I can hear you.'

'You know I'm supposed to be paying off Wilkie by instalments. I thought I'd be able to do it out of the proceeds as I went along, for we *were* doing well, but—the fact is, I find I can't pay her. Business has suddenly dropped off for some reason, one of my best customers has gone bankrupt, owing me five hundred pounds, out of which I shall get about ten if I'm lucky, and—oh, well, what's the good of going through the whole dreary list? It's just an accumulation of things, that's all.'

'How much d'you need to pay what you still owe Wilkie?'

'A thousand pounds,' said Mrs Shannon in a deep, gloomy voice. 'A thousand pounds would just about put me straight. The shop'll pick up soon, I know. I'm trying out a lot of new ideas, and you can't expect results straight away.'

'Can't you borrow from somebody?' asked Mary, jigging the saucepan. 'What about Granpa? Or even Uncle Geoff? I wish this water would boil. I believe your gas pressure's too low. They're not going to cut you off, are they, Mummy?' she said, anxiously.

Mrs Shannon laughed, and pitched her cigarette neatly into the coal-box by the boiler. 'Not quite yet, Puss. That comes later. I don't want to borrow,' she said in a different tone, her face drawn and worried over the fresh cigarette that she was lighting. 'I hate the idea. I'd never ask your grandfather. He's done enough for us, and I don't know that Geoff could help me even if I asked him. His last film was a flop, as you know, and he says the one they're working on at the moment will probably never even be finished. He's got nothing more in the offing. He says he's going back to Hollywood to tout himself round the studios; like a prostitute, he says. Poor darling. And that's another thing——' She sighed heavily, and Mary, turning from the stove to see her dismal face, came and put her arm round her.

'What is, Mummy?'

Her mother leaned her head on Mary's shoulder with a little tired movement. 'Sorry to gloom like this, darling. I didn't mean to behave like a Russian play on your first evening. If Geoff goes we shall have to economize here more than ever. He pays me far too much, you see, towards the housekeeping—I never could stop him—and it has been a help. Darling, would you mind terribly if we had to move out of here and go somewhere a bit sordid again? Only for a while, of course.'

'Oh, Mummy!' Mary was aghast. She had not realized things were as bad as this. 'Our darling little house. Oh, we couldn't. I—I was keeping those geraniums to put in again next year,' she said futilely, her voice trailing miserably away.

'Don't pet, don't.' Her mother was fumbling for her handkerchief; she was going to cry. Mary hugged her, terrified. She mustn't cry. Her face mustn't twist with those anguished, difficult tears of a person who seldom weeps. If one's mother cries, there is nothing stable left in the world.

'Look, the water's boiling!' She jumped down from the table suddenly, her voice shaky. She wouldn't let herself cry; she wouldn't. And then perhaps her mother would be all right. 'No wonder Mabel's coffee always tastes so beastly,' she said with forced brightness. 'She keeps a metal spoon in the tin. She would.' She began to ladle coffee into the saucepan, carefully, as if it required extreme concentration. Behind her, she could hear her mother coughing over her cigarette, sniffing a little, then blowing her nose. It was all right. They were neither of them going to cry. The coffee frothed up, and Mary stirred it, pulling the pan away from the flame, smiling to herself, as the fragrant steam whirled about her face. She knew what she was going to do. No more need to worry about Pierre. Her mind had been made up for her. She felt a glow of power as she thought how she would be rich, and would save the family fortunes. It was a dramatic, lovely thought, and it must be that she had been meant to marry Pierre. It had just needed this to show her that it was right that she should. She wanted to tell her mother, and actually turned round with her mouth open to make the announcement, but suddenly thought better of it and turned it into: 'Where does the old fool keep the strainer?'

She would not tell her mother yet, while the question of money was still prominent between them. She would at once connect it with Mary's announcement, and then there would be more difficulty than Mary already anticipated, in making her eventually accept a loan. Besides, Mary wanted to see Pierre first. She had always, at the back of her mind, thought it incredible that he should want to marry her, and supposing, when she got back to Paris, she found that he had changed his mind? She would look pretty silly if she had already announced her engagement to her mother, which was as good as telling half London. Mary could imagine how the telephone wires would hum, and then they would have to hum all over again, with people saying delightedly to each other: 'My dear, isn't it sad? Poor little Mary's been jilted,' and 'If you ask me, I believe she made the whole thing up to create a sensation.' 'Havelock Ellis, you know. A form of sex-repression.' Before they had done with her, she would be a sort of Aunt Winifred, pitied and talked about in whispers and in French before the servants.

Mary enjoyed her four days in London. Every time she looked at her mother, who had revived completely after that momentary slump in the kitchen, Mary felt again the thrill of power. She wanted to be able to say: 'Don't worry any more. Everything's going to be all right. *I'm* going to make it all right.' It was difficult to keep her secret, but she kept it, cautiously. She did not even tell Angela, though she was sorely tempted, after listening to the recital of the 'perfect man' that Angela had collected since she saw her last.

On Saturday Mary went to meet her as she came out of the Rockingham College. She did not dare go in, for it would be too degrading to be treated again like an infectious disease. Had not Rocky said, 'If you so much as show your face again'? The dread shadow of his presence still hung about those peeling double doors, which every now and then opened to let out a dispirited figure, some familiar, some unknown, while Mary hovered guiltily about in the entrance to the draper's shop next door. At last Angela came out, the first person to come through the door with a smile, accompanied by a shabby, adoring young man. He was carrying her books, and if he had been holding them in his mouth, and wagging a deprecating tail, the resemblance to a mongrel spaniel would have been complete.

Mary stepped out from the shelter of the tea-rose brassières.

'Darling!' screamed Angela, and fell on her.

'Come away from here,' urged Mary, taking her arm. 'I'm terrified of being seen.' The spaniel hovered uncertainly on the pavement, as if waiting for someone to say the magic word, 'Walkies?'

'Oh, Dick,' said Angela, and he sprang forward, with his tongue hanging out. Angela introduced him to Mary, and they had to walk all the way to Selfridge's before they shook him off by telling him they were going inside to buy underclothes. 'See you tomorrow,' he said to Angela, practically slavering at the mouth, and stood on the pavement watching them go in, while women jostled him in the ribs with umbrellas and parcels, and trod on his feet with large, low-heeled shoes.

Mary and Angela walked right through the shop and out at the other side, glanced round furtively, and jumped into a taxi. They went back to Marguerite Street, and Uncle Geoffrey was there, reading a boy's school magazine and listening to two programmes on the wireless because he was too lazy to get off the sofa and tune it in properly.

'Hullo, scum,' he said to Angela.

'Hullo, louse,' she said, dumping her books on to his stomach, and going to the mirror over the fireplace. 'Why aren't you filming?'

'They've suspended production—and pay, I need hardly add. Presumably they want to find out whether it would be possible for a chorus girl to dance on the table of the officers' mess, while her friend extracts the secret papers from the Colonel, who is under the table, after the port's only been round once. Me, I think it's the least bit improbable.'

He made cocktails for them, because Mrs Shannon, making the excuse that twelve-and-six one way or the other made no difference to a thousand pounds, had told Mabel to order a bottle of gin after all. He teased Angela as usual, and prattled on inanely about the film, with the wireless murmuring unheeded in the background, but, ever since she had come back, Mary had noticed a difference in him. He was more subdued, oddly anxious to please and be liked. Sometimes she thought he had an almost sheepish air about him. She wondered whether it was because of his films; whether he felt, perhaps, that he had let them down, and whether he knew about his sister's money matters.

159

'Where are you kids going tonight?' he asked, rather wistfully, Mary thought, and Angela noticed it, too, for she answered: 'On a party. Why don't you come too? I wish you would.'

'What, as chaperone? No fear. Thanks, all the same and all that, but I—no, I definitely won't. I ought to get some sleep.' It was obvious that he was pining to go on a party.

'Oh, do come,' urged Mary. 'It doesn't matter about numbers, does it, Angel?'

'Good lord, no. Anyway, Johnny is sure either to pass out or wander off after a Brazilian in red satin, like he did last time.' But he would not yield. He got on to the sofa again, and retired behind his boy's paper.

Mrs Shannon came home in a state of exhaustion. She had been down to Dulwich to see her mother, who had been brought to her bed a year ago with bronchitis, and saw no reason for ever getting up again.

'How was the momma-bird?' asked Uncle Geoffrey without interest.

'Sour.' Mrs Shannon threw her hat on to a chair, and pushed her short, black hair up wearily. 'She complained that you hadn't been down for ages.'

'I'm going on Wednesday,' he said definitely. Mrs Shannon and Mary turned on him, surprised. He never went to Dulwich of his own accord. He had to be goaded and bullied and almost taken to the bus-stop and pushed on to the bus.

'Wednesday? Why Wednesday?'

'Nothing, just Wednesday, that's all. I'm going to see her on Wednesday.' Yes, thought Mary, there was something mysterious about him. He was like a man hiding something.

What he was hiding was revealed on Tuesday, the day before Mary returned to Paris, and the day on which Lucienne Robeau, who had a cheap excursion ticket, came back to London, to sleep on the sofa in the drawing-room. Mary felt that she ought to let her have her room, but she was not going to.

Uncle Geoffrey was still not filming, and on Tuesday afternoon he sneaked out of the house, and returned at about six o'clock with Lucienne. He had met her at the station. He came in at the front door carrying her bag, and furthermore, her umbrella. Neither Mary nor her mother was present to witness this phenomenon, but Mabel related it to them in the hall with bated breath, when they returned together from Sonth Molton Street. Mrs Shannon's eyebrows went up.

'Where are they now, Mabel?' she asked, for the open door to the right showed that the drawing-room was empty. She would not now have been surprised to learn that they were in bed together.

'In the garden,' said Mabel hoarsely, jerking her head with its

160

meagre bun of string-coloured hair. With one accord, Mrs Shannon and Mary went to the other end of the hall, where it narrowed past the gents' toilet, and gave on to the garden by way of a door and a flight of iron steps. They peered together through the glass half of the door. It was true. There sat Uncle Geoffrey and Lucienne, side by side in two dirty deck-chairs. They were holding hands. It was almost indecent.

'Come on.' Mrs Shannon pulled open the door, and clattered down the steps like a hound on the scent, with Mary after her. Uncle Geoffrey sprang to his feet when he saw them coming, a thing he had never done before, and Lucienne got up, too, with one of her slow, placid movements, and stood by him, taking his hand again. Mary was reminded of Greta Daniel.

If Uncle Geoffrey had looked sheepish before, he now looked positively criminal. His teeth were clamped furtively to his lower lip, and his eyes would not meet theirs.

'Who will tell them?' said Lucienne, in her flat, careful English. 'I or you?'

'Oh, you. Go on, you tell them,' said Uncle Geoffrey, snickering and shifting his feet like a schoolboy.

'Geoffrey and I are fiancés,' said Lucienne calmly, a smile appearing on a small portion of her moon face.

'*No!*' said Mrs Shannon with an incredulity that she managed somehow to turn into delighted surprise by changing the inflection before it was too late.

'Yes, we are,' said the happy bridegroom, looking at his feet.

'Oh, Uncle Geoff dear, I am so pleased.' Mary hugged him, and, turning to Lucienne, kissed her too. She smelt quite clean, that was something, but her eyes were dull and sluggish. There was a slow-motion effect about her, a heaviness that made you feel that too much of her company would eventually overwhelm and stifle you, like a mattress.

'Why didn't you tell us before?' asked Mrs Shannon, when she had pecked them both in a dazed way.

'Well, Loocienne had to ask her mother's permission first. Quaint old French custom, something about a *dot*. Not d-o-u-g-h, but the same thing, spelt differently,' said Uncle Geoffrey, laughing unhappily. 'We fixed it up about a week ago, but she wouldn't let me tell you till she came back, would you, dear?'

There was something dismal in the four of them standing awkwardly about on the tiny square of sooty lawn, not knowing what to say.

'Let's go in and drink to your engagement,' said Mrs Shannon, on an inspiration, but when they got indoors it turned out that Lucienne did not drink, and the sight of her sitting squarely on a chair with a glass of orangeade made the cocktails of the other three not a celebration, but merely a waste of gin. Uncle Geoffrey still avoided the eyes of his sister and niece, and was careful not to be in a room alone with them. After dinner Lucienne stated that he was taking her to the cinema, so he got up, fetched her coat from upstairs, and took her.

'Oh, Mummy, why did he do it?' burst out Mary as the front door slammed behind them.

Her mother shrugged her shoulders. 'I suppose it's natural for him to want to get married,' she sighed, cupping her small square chin in her hand, and staring glumly at nothing.

'Yes, and it's high time he did; he must be nearly forty-five. But why *her*?' Mary went to the window and watched the back view of the pair—Lucienne solid and heavy-footed, with short, woolly hair, and Uncle Geoffrey thin and loose-legged, his hair carefully plastered over the thinning patch at the back of his narrow head. They turned the corner towards the King's Road, and Mary looked back into the room. 'Why her?' she repeated. 'His taste used to run to hot Mommas and peroxide blondes.'

'I think it was mostly talk. I don't imagine they ever took him seriously. Poor darling, that's his life's tragedy; nobody ever has. Except Lucienne. That's why he's going to marry her, I suppose.'

'Did you know this was coming?'

'Good heavens, no,' said Mrs Shannon, 'I thought she rather liked him, you know, because she used to go down to the kitchen on Sunday nights and make sardine soufflé, which he adores. He used to take her to the cinema occasionally, with a glass of beer afterwards at the "Brasserie"—no, she must have had tonic water, or something—but I thought he was just being kind. Oh, well.' She clapped her hands on her knees, and got up resignedly. 'Good-bye to any hope I ever had of getting financial help from Geoff.'

Mary longed to tell her now about Pierre. It seemed unfair to let her go on worrying needlessly, but she must abide by her first instinct, which had been to see Pierre first. She contented herself with saying, as she had before, in the kitchen: 'Never mind, Mummy. I've got a hunch that it's going to be all right. Don't worry about it. Old Wilkie can wait for her money. You'll manage somehow, I know; my hunches are always right.' They never were, but that didn't matter. Her mother was not really listening, anyhow.

When Mary told Pierre that she would marry him his smile was wonderful to see, but she had the feeling that he had not been on tenterhooks while she had been away. He had never had any doubts. She met him at the Porte Dauphine that first evening, and they walked into the Bois and sat on two iron chairs and words poured happily out of him, and he joked and kissed her and gabbled on. Mary looked forward to introducing him to her mother. What happened when two people met who hardly ever stopped talking? Did they simply talk on through each other's speech like Uncle Geoffrey's two programmes on the wireless? It would be a lively scene.

She was very happy, basking in the dazzling shafts of evening sun that slanted through the tree-trunks, and in the warmth of Pierre's jubilant, invigorating presence. When you were with him, you were conscious all the time of his aliveness; it radiated from him like electricity.

He was irrepressible that evening. They went to almost every place to which they had ever been before. He whirled her from one to the other, and everywhere his friends had to be told the news—barmen, waiters, guests, members of the band—the drinks were on Pierre, and he was the most popular man in all Paris. Mary, dizzy with excitement, drink, and fatigue, sat back flushed and proud, revelling in the compliments and congratulations that showered on her, and in the conquering charm of Pierre. How thrilling it would be, introducing him to people in London. Staggered, they would look at her with new eyes, as the girl who could get a man like this.

The reaction of the Robeaus was a foretaste of the gratifying reception to come. Madame paused in her serving out of the gnocchis in cheese sauce—cheap and filling—and sat with swimming eyes fixed unseeingly on the dreary picture of Boulogne Harbour on the opposite wall, rapt in visions of wealth and high living, with Mary in a new dress every day, and herself coming in for some of her cast-offs. Jeanne burst into tears of unaffected joy and kissed Mary tenderly, sobbing that it was '*émouvant comme tout*,' and that '*la petite Marie doit être heureuse comme une ange*.' Didi's brilliant black eyes flashed with envy, and she stuffed bread rapaciously into her mouth, as if to satisfy her hunger for something like Pierre. She had always regarded Mary as rather a ninny, because she never wanted to be made to squeal in dark doorways or cheap cars, but henceforth she treated her with a new, suspicious respect.

The girls at the École Flambert twittered like sparrows over the enormous diamond ring that Pierre gave Mary. M. Flambert smacked his saurian lips, and Mme Flambert, with her mouth full of pins, mumbled over her like a beneficent procuress.

In contrast to all this was the terror of being received by Madame Mathieu. It was impossible to tell whether or not she welcomed her future daughter-in-law. Her face was a mask, and when she inclined forward slightly for the necessary embrace, Mary, making a nervous dab at her, felt the hard aquiline nose ice-cold against her cheek. M. Mathieu was different. He was obviously delighted, and took every

163

opportunity of embracing Mary warmly, and talked only of the presents he would give them.

Mary was glad that nobody raised the question of her *dot*. Pierre knew that she was not well off, but she had not told him about the present state of her mother's finances. She imagined vaguely that when she was his wife he would make over some money to her, so that she could help her mother without having to ask him. She knew that he did not like to think of people being poor. As disease is to be flagrantly robust, poverty was to him unfortunate, but faintly abhorrent. He was like a man who picks up a stone and, finding something unpleasant underneath, replaces the stone hurriedly and goes away.

Mary's allowance from home had dwindled, and because she could not borrow from Pierre she had to pinch and scrape in order to save her money for clothes in which to be worthy of him. She discovered absurdly cheap restaurants; second-floor haunts behind the Madeleine, and vaporous cellars at the wrong end of the Boulevards, where the fly-blown waiters expected small tips, and you could get a carafe of wine for a franc. Also, to the horror of Mme Robeau, she used to risk her honour in the third class of the Metro, which was admittedly dirty, but not without interest.

This life when she was not with Pierre was in comic contrast to her other life of taxis and vast, imperious cars; tea at the 'Georges Cinq,' cocktails at the 'Crillon,' dinner at the 'Ritz'; orchids and caviare; champagne ordered as casually as a cup of tea. She often wondered what Pierre would have said had she told him, in the middle of dinner at the most expensive restaurant in Paris, with the *maître d'hôtel* flattering them like a condescending Pope, that she had lunched that day off a plate of spaghetti costing seventy-five centimes at the '*Diable Sous-Sol*,' where a waiter, frowsty as a pit-pony, had asked her what she did on her evenings out. She wondered, too, what he would say when she suggested that they should live in England. When her course at the dressmaking school was finished, he was going to accompany her back to London, and she thought she might ask him then. At the moment she did not want to spoil that carefree, amorous summer in Paris with the possibility of dissension. Life was so gay and so easy that she let everything slide except happiness. Pierre was a difficult person to talk to seriously. He would laugh at her and call her Baby, or tickle her, or make love to her, or play the fool, so that anything earnest she had to say would be drowned in a bubbling stream of giggles, and she no longer wanted to say it.

Life with him was full of new delights. When they went back to England together, he insisted on flying. For the first time she experienced that glorious moment when the bumping rush of the plane changes to a smooth buoyancy as the wheels leave the ground, and you realize that the miracle has happened; you are actually in the air, and rising, rising, unsupported, omnipotent, and ridiculously safe.

Afterwards, Pierre laughed at her, and told her she had had her mouth open all the way across. She had almost forgotten him as she stared out of the window at the motionless, patterned sea over which it seemed that they were hovering, not travelling, until the English coastline suddenly appeared, looking like a travel poster, and was ahead, underneath, behind them, with incredible speed.

Before she even saw Pierre, Mrs Shannon had made up her mind that she was going to like him very much. Consequently, their actual meeting was bound to be a slight anti-climax. He was very polite—too polite; stiff and formal, as if he were wearing spats and white kid gloves, and they made little headway. Uncle Geoffrey, who seemed happier now that he had got used to the idea of his impending marriage, and was by now so French that he called Lucienne *Chérie*, pronounced Cherry, took to Pierre at once, and slapped him on the back and called him *maw garsaw*. Pierre responded with great heartiness and became fearfully English and called him 'old fellow.'

Mary wished that they could have seen him as he was with her, easy and charming and natural, whether he was being the sophisticated man-about-town, or a funny, lovable little boy. He had a business dinner that first evening, so he left them soon to go back to his hotel, and Mary kissed him good-bye at the front door with a tiny disappointment in her heart. They had liked him, but she wanted them to adore him. She had looked forward so much to showing him off. She wished he had not said 'rather' so much. It was incredible that he could be shy, but perhaps he was. She could understand that. Sweet Pierre. She went to sleep that night wishing that they were back at 'Schéherazade' together, and that he was kissing her hair as they slowly waltzed on the dark floor while the violin mourned and soared like a dreaming bird.

Mary had looked forward to showing London to Pierre as he had shown her Paris. She knew that he had already spent a good deal of time there, but he could not know it as intimately as somebody who had lived there all her life. However, it was soon apparent that he knew it better than she did; the parts of it, that is, to which he wanted to go.

As in Paris, he walked into the smartest restaurants as if he and his father's money owned them. That had been all right, even gratifying, in Paris, but here, in London, Mary was not so sure. London belongs to the English, and even if you are Pierre, you can't own Paris and London as well. He did not have time to see much of Mary's family, for he had a lot of business to attend to, and also a lot of friends, whom Mary had to meet. Some of them had familiar, weekly-magazine names and faces, and made Mary feel dumbly inferior, an opinion of herself which she was quite certain they shared.

The wedding was fixed for the end of September, and although Pierre scowled and insisted that it should be in Paris, Mary still had hopes of persuading him to let it be in London. She was beginning to realize that her chances of getting him to live in England were very remote, but about that, too, she still had hopes. If they were married in London, conceded Pierre, the best man should be his great friend, Max Nordberg, whom Mary did not like at all. The only good thing about Max was that his family owned a film company, and he might be persuaded to give Uncle Geoffrey a leg-up. He was a smooth, young Jew, fat, opulent, and—something that Pierre did not seem to notice—distinctly common. He wore his oily, black hair rather long, and brushed straight back from his forehead without a parting, and his hands were soft and white. You could not imagine them ever doing anything with animals; they were made for holding a glass or a cigarette-holder, or for patting young film aspirants on the thigh and saying, 'I could do a lot for you, little girl.' He had an inexhaustible flow of stories that were sometimes funny, but never clean. Pierre thought he was marvellous, so Mary tried to like him for his sake.

Max had a girl friend with red hair and green eyes, who was so svelte that she was practically one-dimensional, and the four of them used to go out together in the evening. Like Pierre, Max owned everywhere, but unlike Pierre, he was offensive to waiters. Mary used to smile at the waiters extravagantly and thank them with unnecessary fervour, to try and make it up to them, although she knew that they probably didn't mind how rude Max was so long as they got his money. Veronica, the green-eyed girl friend, also owned everywhere, in a passive way, particularly the ladies' cloakroom, where she would gyrate and grimace for hours in front of the only long mirror, or run narrowed eyes up and down Mary and say: 'My dear, I think your Pierre's too marvellous. What luck to get a man like that!' As if Mary had won him at one of those 'No skill required' sideshows, and not by her own attractions.

Mary treasured the times when she and Pierre were alone together. She hoped they would be alone a lot when they were married. He was so sweet to her. He always said the right thing. He never said: 'You look tired,' meaning, 'You look plain,' but instead, 'I love you when you're very pale and your eyes are big and dark and sleepy.' They used to walk in the Park in the morning sun, before looking in somewhere for a drink, and Mary did not mind that his hat was rather small and un-English, because it was such fun to be with him. All the same, she could not help saying: 'Why don't you take your hat off and let the sun get at your hair? It's good for it.' She felt somehow that by removing the hat she could remove all the other tiny things which had not mattered at all in Paris, and which ought not to matter here. She wanted everyone else to think him perfect, and more than anything she wanted to think him perfect herself, never to have even the smallest disloyal doubts.

One day they met Angela, walking her Sealyham alongside the Row, and being stared at by sporting old men on rolling cobs and insipid youths on slack-eared, shuffling hirelings.

Mary introduced Pierre, and wished that he had not given Angela one of his undressing looks, nor paid quite so much unnecessary attention to her as they walked along together towards Hyde Park Corner. She wanted him to love Angela as she did, but not in quite this way. When they parted, Angela to lunch with her father at his club, and Mary and Pierre to meet Max at his lavish, unmasculine flat, Angela nearly swooned with delight as Pierre kissed her hand with a perfection of style that Mary also thought unnecessary.

'He's divine!' she hissed into Mary's ear, under cover of a farewell kiss. 'I'm so thrilled for you, darling. Quite divine.'

Yes, thought Mary, but he's mine.

'She is very *élégante*, your friend,' said Pierre thoughtfully, as they waited on the pavement for a taxi, though Mary would have liked to walk farther in the sunshine. 'That hair is stunning, and——' he sketched a slight gesture in the air, 'those beautiful breasts.' Mary sulked. He was being most unnecessary.

Mary's relations kept ringing up and saying, 'When are we going to see your young man?' But so far there had been few opportunities. Pierre's time in London was short, and there were so many other more important or more amusing things to do. At last, however, a few days before he had to return to France to accompany his parents to Juan-les-Pins, Mary pinned him down to attending one of the periodical gatherings of the clan, held this time on Bank Holiday, at the country house that the Ritchies had taken, not far from London.

Pierre did a lot of pouting, and little-boy protesting, putting forward a lot of infinitely preferable suggestions for spending the day together, but Mary was firm.

'You've got to meet them some time, darling,' she said, 'and it's much better to get them all over at one blow.' So in the end he hired a ridiculously smart car and called for her on a hot, hazy morning.

Her mother had already left with Granpa and Aunt Winifred in the Daimler, which looked every year more and more like a hearse, with Linney a tighter fit than ever behind the wheel, and inclined to treat the new traffic lights with a Diehard mistrust. Uncle Geoffrey had taken Lucienne to Whipsnade, with sandwiches, fizzy lemonade, and one bottle of beer, where she and the bison could stare each other out with identical bovinity.

Mary was alone in the house when Pierre arrived with an announcement on the horn that brought the infuriated heads of the late sleepers in Marguerite Street blinking out of their windows. He was wearing an impeccable fawn pin-stripe suit, with a brown silk handkerchief in the breast pocket, a cream-coloured shirt, and a cream and brown spotted bow tie. His shoes were very pointed, and he wore his small-brimmed city hat. Mary was hatless and stockingless, in a white linen dress with a short red jacket. She wondered for a moment whether he was right and she was wrong and under-dressed. She was quite ready to leave when she opened the door to him, but he pushed past her and entered the hall, throwing his hat and gloves on to the table, and drawing her to him in a passionate embrace, that smelt, sexlessly, of expensive eau-de-Cologne.

For the first time, Mary struggled from him, turning her head away the instant he released her mouth, and wriggling out of his arms.

'Hello,' he said. 'Don't be shy, Baby. Come and sit on the sofa with me.' He tried to pull her towards the drawing-room.

'No, Pierre, not now,' she said, patting her hair. 'It's—it's too soon after breakfast.' That was really how she felt, yet she knew it sounded absurd. 'We ought to go, really,' she added, rather wanly. It was the first time she had ever not wanted to kiss him, and she did not like to discover that it was possible.

'Oh,' he said, his Maurice Chevalier lip very assertive, 'so I can't kiss you when I want to, eh?' He was rougher with her this time, and as she resisted him, she nearly cried with annoyance, half at herself, half at him for his untimeliness.

He let her go suddenly. 'My God,' he said, furiously, 'I'm not kissing any woman who behaves as if I smelt bad. Come on.' He picked up his hat and stamped down the steps, holding the door of the car open for her without a word, and banging in himself on the opposite side.

He drove badly and dangerously, screeching down the King's Road, and cutting in and out of the holiday traffic. Red-faced drivers mouthed at him in impotant anger, and Mary sat tense in her seat, determined not to show that she was terrified. When they were on the Great West Road he put his foot down, fuming every time a red light brought them to a shrieking stop. Mary stole a glance at his face, and saw that his jaw was set firmly under the extravagant tilt of his hat. He looked like a schoolboy who has been told that he cannot have a bicycle for his birthday. She thought about saying 'I'm sorry' for a long time before she could actually bring herself to say it. The effort was a tremendous, almost physical one, which grew with every moment of delay.

At last she put out a hand, squeezed his knee, and said, in a small voice: 'I'm sorry, Pierre. I was silly.' He made a non-committal, French noise, still looking ahead.

She abased herself still further, looking for them both to be in sympathy again. 'I'm awfully sorry, Pierre, really. I didn't mean to be like that. You know you can kiss me any time and place you like.'

He came round gradually, triumphantly, and, for the sake of serenity, she let him bask in the Right, while she hovered deprecatingly in the shadowy Purgatory of being in the Wrong. Soon he began to sing, and drove through Staines with contented care, leaning over when a policeman held them up, to kiss her.

How careful she would have to be, she thought, to keep things right between them when they were married. She could not conceive of the sort of marriage that seemed to appeal to some people, based on violent quarrels and exciting reconciliations, but there were so many things in herself that she would have to suppress. She suddenly felt very old, as if she had finished with her youth, which was unreasonable, since she was going to marry someone essentially young and gay. 'You're taking life too seriously, my girl,' she told herself. 'I thought you'd got cured of that at the Dramatic College.'

Pierre sang on, and presently she sang with him, and the country rushed towards them, losing little by little the last stigmas of urbanity.

With the help, or hindrance, of the map that Aunt Mavis had drawn, slightly wrong, with detailed descriptions of all the corners where they were not to turn, they found the Old Farm, Thurley. It turned out to be neither old, nor a farm, but it was quite an attractive house, and smelt pleasantly inside of shabby cretonnes. The plump, sing-song Welsh maid, who opened the door to Mary and Pierre, told them that, 'The party's having cocktails in the garden,' and showed them out on to a wide, informal lawn, where many of familiar shapes were gathered under the shade of a cedar tree.

Uncle Guy came forward, cheerful and welcoming. It was evidently one of his good-form days. He was wearing a tennis shirt, white trousers supported by the Old School Tie, and monk's sandals on his bare feet. He kissed Mary and pumped Pierre's hand, slapping him on his impeccably tailored back. He had met him already, in the cocktail bar of 'Shannon's,' when Pierre and Mary had lunched there one day. Mary remembered that lunch quite well. Pierre had refused to be impressed by the restaurant's expensive dignity, and had belittled the *Sauce Béarnaise*, although Mary kept telling him that all the chefs were French. He now had to be introduced all round, and adopted his usual manner under these circumstances—a mixture of Gallic urbanity and extravagant Anglicisms. Aunt Mavis nonplussed him by saying, 'Ah, the blushing bridegroom!' as she surged towards them in flowered georgette, rather straggly at the hem. Uncle Lionel, who was evidently under the impression that Pierre spoke no English, said, '*Bonjour. Il me fait grand plaisir de vous rencontrer*,' as if he were reciting from a phrase book.

Sarah was there with her husband, the despised Roebuck, who turned out to be called James Robart, and was stringy, but surprisingly likeable in a gentle, unworldly way. Sarah seemed to be very happy. Her hair was properly done, and her legs seemed to have got miraculously thinner. She and Roebuck held hands most of the time, and whispered in corners, like children uncertain of their acceptance.

Mary's mother kissed Pierre, as she always did, but there was still a disappointing reserve between them. She had told Mary that he was 'a lamb, and a beautiful son-in-law,' but she always seemed to be watching him, waiting to see what he would do, as if he were a marionette. Granpa was really the only one who was quite natural with Pierre, and did not treat him like an exhibit. They seemed to take to each other, and soon drew aside and began to talk earnestly about food.

'Where's Denys?' asked Mary. It was easy these days to speak his name casually, but not so easy, she found a moment later, to avoid that old disturbance of equilibrium when she actually saw him.

'He and young Martin had gone to the local to fetch the beer,' said Uncle Guy, and at that moment Denys and his friend from Oxford came through the gate at the far end of the garden. They were both wearing khaki shorts, old tennis shoes, and faded, coloured shirts. Martin had an untidy crest of yellow hair that shone in the sunlight as they came across the lawn, whistling, with a jaunty little urchin of a white dog at their heels. The picture that they made impressed itself vividly on Mary's mind. She knew that Pierre would never look like that. These boys were part of the character of the garden, with as much right to be in it as the grass, or the roses, or the clustering colours of the borders. Pierre would always be a person in a garden; man distinct from nature, instead of the two 'far more deeply interfused.'

Denys and Martin came up to meet him. Denys was as brown as a native boy, and his bare legs were scratched and grazed at the knees, as in the Charbury days. As they shook hands, the contrast between him and Pierre in his pointed shoes made Mary not want to look at them. This mustn't happen. She mustn't think like this. She told herself that it was only the old associations of Denys that troubled her.

'Beer, beer, glorious beer,' sang Uncle Guy, and Mavis, coming out of the french windows that led to the dining-room, winced.

'Lunch is ready, people,' she said. 'Lunch is ready.' She raised her voice and began to go clucking round as if the cold spread indoors were a soufflé. She was a strenuous hostess. Someone collected Aunt

170

Winifred from the kitchen garden, where she had been happily inspecting the vegetables, and they all trooped in to the sudden dimness of the cool, panelled room.

Pierre was a quite a success at lunch. He played up to Aunt Mavis, and flattered her in a way that no man had done since Uncle Guy was misguidedly struck by the handsome figure that she cut while circling an orange on her outside edge on the St. Moritz skating rink in 1903. He pleased Aunt Grace by saying the right things and showing tricks with a napkin ring to her nine-year-old son John, who was used to being treated like the smell of the engine by the other grown-up men.

Denys sat next to Mary. 'You're looking radiant,' he said to her suddenly, and she was furious to find that her heart leapt. 'Must be love,' he went on. 'I ought to try it some time.'

'Do you—so you like him, Denys?' she asked eagerly.

'Who? The boy friend? Looks all right to me,' he said, grinning across the table at Pierre, but she knew that he was lying.

Pierre did not look right in the country.

After lunch the women went out into the garden for coffee, leaving the others drinking brandy, with Pierre calling the older men 'Sir' almost every three words. Mary hoped that he would get on all right with them. He was always at his best in mixed company, demonstrating his prowess at the art of whose existence most Englishmen were ignorant—how to treat women.

Mary sat down on the grass and chewed a clover leaf. It seemed a long time since she had been in the country, and she lolled on her elbow, revelling in the summer haze that hung over the scented garden, and the bubbling song of a lark high over her head, bursting his heart with joy at the blueness of the sky. She wondered, as always, why anyone lived in towns. Her Cousin Julia, who was as obnoxious and precocious as it is possible to be at thirteen, came and tickled her nose with a piece of grass.

'I saw that Uncle Geoffrey of yours at the flicks down here,' she said. 'Gosh, it was a stinking film. He was an awful ass in it. I didn't know whether he was meant to be funny or not.'

'You don't say,' murmured Mary acidly.

'The girl was futile, too. I'm going on the films, you know. I bet I'm better than that. I'll bet you anything you like. What'll you bet?'

'Go away,' said Mary, rolling over on her face. 'I want to go to sleep.' The grass smelt lovely. Julia smacked her on the behind.

'You've got grass marks on your dress,' she rejoiced.

'I don't care,' mumbled Mary.

'Julia!' called Aunt Mavis, 'run in and get the chocolates off the round table in the drawing-room, there's a good girl.'

'No fear,' said Julia. 'Nobody wants chocs. Too hot.'

'Run in and get the chocolates,' repeated her mother sharply.

'They're bad for you in the heat. I read it in a book.'

'Julia!' said her mother, her sharpness blunted already by defeat.

'Oh, Mummy, you know it's not good for me to run about after food. I might get a stroke. A mother shouldn't expose her child to dangers like that.' She always won her way in the end, because she could keep up an argument longer than anyone else.

Aunt Winifred did not speak much, but when she did, she often got straight to the heart of the matter in one simple, penetrating remark. When Julia had gone wandering away, bored with the grown-ups, Winifred said, 'Child wants a good spanking.' Everyone looked at Aunt Mavis, who pretended that she had not heard, so Aunt Winifred, sitting awkwardly on the grass in her waistless fawn silk dress, repeated it very clearly.

'Yes, dear, I daresay,' said her eldest sister, bottling her annoyance. Winifred looked at her as if she were mad, then got up and went away as the men came out of the dining-room.

The afternoon passed in lazy argument about how to spend it.

Pierre actually took off his coat and dozed on the lawn beside Mary in his double-breasted waistcoat. Denys and Martin wandered away to fiddle with a car, and Aunt Mavis, who was not good at relaxing, dragged Mary's mother away to see the garden. Mrs Shannon went, only because it took her away from Uncle Lionel, who was threatening to become too pertinacious about her money matters. Mary had not yet broached the question of assisting her when she was married, but she suspected that her mother already had it in mind, for she had been less worried lately, and had given up chivying Mabel about the tradesmen's books. Sarah and Aunt Grace talked on and on about housekeeping, in an endless monotone, that droned through Mary's half-conscious reverie and mingled with the sound of the bees in the heavy-headed flowers.

Soon it was tea-time, and soon it was time to go home.

'Whew!' said Pierre, as he turned the big car skilfully out of the awkward drive, 'it's nice to be alone with you again, to touch you, to feel you near me. They are all right, but——' he bent to kiss her neck, 'you are better.'

'Look out,' said Mary, as the car swerved towards the hedge.

He laughed. 'I know what I'm doing Baby. You just sit there and look beautiful, and I'll do the driving. Where shall we go tonight?' He began to plan a gay, expensive evening. Mary began to think about what she would wear, but all the way home she could not get out of her head the picture of Denys and Martin crossing the lawn with their huge jugs of foaming beer. It tormented her. It seemed to be imprinted

172

behind her eyes, like the outline of a light that stands out in the darkness after the light has gone out.

'Pierre,' she said suddenly, breaking a silence, 'when we're married, let's live in England, in the country.'

'Good God!' The speeding car shook with the reaction of his dismay. 'What an idea. You and I aren't old fogies yet, my love.'

'Where *will* we live?' asked Mary timidly, feeling her heart beating very fast.

'Why, in the flat that my mother's chosen in Paris, of course. You know that. It's all arranged.'

'Yes, I know, but eventually? Couldn't you work in the English branch of the bank, so that we could live over here? You're awfully keen on England, aren't you?'

'What's all this about?' he said, turning to her with an affectionate smile. 'Have you forgotten you're marrying a Frenchman? You'll be French, you know. Where else should we live but France? I'd die if I didn't live in Paris, anyway. It's in my blood. It's part of me. The same spirit—something in the air—I don't know what it is, makes us both alive. London is so—what'd the word?—*stupefié*.'

'I like it,' said Mary in a small, stubborn voice.

'Oh, of course, you'll come over here and visit your family whenever you want——'

'Yes, of course,' said Mary, and fell silent again. She had known all along that this was what he would say. That was why she had put off asking him.

'Pierre,' she said, as they turned off the Great West Road, trailing a hot, gaseous procession of returning holiday cars, 'd'you mind terribly if I don't come out tonight? I've got a beastly headache and I'm so tired. The family must have been too much for me or something.' He protested for a moment, and then was genuinely concerned, lavishing affection and sympathy on her so that she felt a brute, because she had no headache, and was not particularly tired. Not in her body, but in her mind there was an aching weariness. She had got to be alone, just for one night, at any rate. She wanted to creep away from everybody like an animal; she wanted to go to bed and cry. She wanted to be alone so desperately, that it was like a hunger.

She could think of nothing else until they were home at last, and she had said good-bye to Pierre and gone up to her room, locked the door, undressed hurriedly, and crept into bed. She lay with just the sheet over her, a huddled ball, with wide-open eyes to which no tears would come, although misery pressed behind them like a dead weight.

'I can't do it, I can't do it,' she kept saying to herself, while the light gradually faded outside the drawn curtains and twilight crept into the room. But she knew that she must. She thought of her mother, sitting

173

on the kitchen table, struggling against her tears. She had pledged herself to help her, and she must go through with it. And always the picture was with her that had come now to stand for all the things that were never going to be part of her life any more: a dark boy and a fair boy strolling across an English lawn with great jugs of beer in their hands.

'Well, that's that,' said Mrs Shannon, resignedly, putting the handkerchief that she had been waving back into her bag, and searching for her platform ticket. 'Lucienne in Hollywood is about the most incongruous thing imaginable, but I suppose they'll get along together all right.' Uncle Geoffrey had been married a week ago, and now, after a negligible honeymoon in the Isle of Wight, he was gone from them again, carried away in the boat train, with his bride in a navy blue two-piece and a hat like a coal shovel.

Madame Robeau had come over for the wedding, all in black as if it were a funeral, but wearing a magnificent hat with an enormous wing on either side, torn, perhaps, from some relic of her Edwardian girlhood. She had cried all the time, and Uncle Geoffrey had looked as if he felt like doing the same.

'Cheer up, my Puss,' Mrs Shannon said to Mary, as they walked off the platform, 'he'll probably be back soon. Let's buy a bottle of champagne, and have it for dinner tonight, shall we? You look as if you needed it. You've been looking awfully mopey these last few days, darling. They always say that being engaged is a trying time. Are you fretting for your Pierre? You'll soon be going over to join him, and then, before you know where you are, you'll be married.'

'Yes,' said Mary despondently.

'Let's take a taxi home. You do look tired, darling.' She stopped the taxi at a wine shop, and returned clutching a bottle triumphantly. She had been very chirpy all day, and hummed all the way home, flat, but happily.

'What's wrong with you?' said Mary testily. 'Champagne, taxis, bursting into song——' Her mother shook her head and laughed. 'Today, I feel so happy,' she sang.

Mary was combing her hair in her bedroom when her mother strolled in, ostensibly to look for a pair of stockings that she had lost.

'Darling,' she said casually, rummaging in Mary's chest of drawers. 'You remember my telling you about that little—financial trouble I was having?'

'Yes,' said Mary, pausing with the comb in mid-air and watching her reflection of her mother's neat bending back view.

'Well, I'm not any more. I mean, it's all right now. Isn't it fun?' She turned round with a beaming smile, and a pair of Mary's best stockings in her hand.

174

'What d'you mean?' said Mary quickly. 'Have you paid off Wilkie?'

'You've got it in one.'

'But you said you needed a thousand pounds. You can't have suddenly earned that.'

'I haven't.' Her mother looked slightly guilty. 'It's a—a sort of loan. Anyway, never mind what it is, I've got it.'

'Who from?'

'I'll never tell you, so don't ever bother to ask me, darling.' Mrs Shannon made gaily for the door. Mary still sat with the comb half-way to the top of her head, staring into the glass, while her brain raced madly. 'Hi,' she said, like a person speaking out of a dream, 'you don't pinch my stockings. Put them back.' But her mother had gone.

Months afterwards, long after she had written that difficult, impossible letter to Pierre, and he had ceased to bombard her with telephone calls, telegrams, and, finally, bitter, abusive letters, which she knew were less than she deserved, she came to the conclusion that she could never, in any case, have reached the actual point of marrying him. Now that it was safe to drag their relationship out into the light and examine it mercilessly it was fantastic on what a thin basis they had proposed to build their life. Apart from physical attraction, there was nothing between them but fun and parties, and that was not entirely a taste in common.

Life was like a jigsaw, but if you tried to fit the pieces together yourself, you generally got them wrong. Pierre had money; she needed money. Pierre was lovable and loved her; she would marry him. She had thought that was the pattern the pieces made. But it had been like trying to force two pieces together that didn't fit, and then, suddenly, the jigsaw had been done, in quite a different way, by other hands.

She still did not know who had lent her mother money. Mrs Shannon maintained a jaunty discretion. Mary used to accuse her alternately of being a swindler, a bank robber, or a kept woman, but she only shook her head and laughed. A corner of the jigsaw of Mary's life had been made into the right pattern, by unknown means. It seemed that one had little control over one's own destiny. All one could do was to get on with the one job that nobody else could do, the job of being oneself.

Chapter Eight

'BUT, Mary *dear*,' said Mrs Van de Meyer, 'it's not a question of whether you *like* it, or whether you *don't* like it—it's just a very wonderful building. Stop the car right here, dear, where I can get a good long look. Mm—*mm*.' She raised plump little fur-clad arms to the edge of the door, and resting her chin on them, gazed at the house through rimless pince-nez.

'It's Georgian, isn't it?' said Mary.

'Why, certainly it's Georgian. It just couldn't be more so.'

The house stared back at her from its symmetrical, blind windows. Separated from the main road only by a low wall and a stretch of bare parkland, it was exposed in all its uncompromising squareness. No creepers had dared to outrage the dignity of those red and grey bricks, no ivy blurred that Prussian alignment of jutting wings on either side.

'Mm—*mm*,' sighed Mrs Van de Meyer again. 'That's just the way I'm going to have Sam Howard build my house at White Plains. Why, it's the most English thing——'

'I thought you liked those houses at Stratford today.'

'Well, I did, but then so have a lot of other people. White Plains is lousy with beams and inglenooks. Charlotte Schumacher, the Barnet Summers, Mrs Otto—why, Charlotte's even got a thatched roof! No, this is really going to be something—I might call it Meyer Hall. I'm certainly going to have Mr Howard come down and see this before he starts on the plans. I wonder who owns it. Drive on to the gates, dear, and I'll ask at the Lodge. It'd be fun to have a look around.'

'Oh, we can't very well do that, d'you think?'

'Why ever not? My goodness, if I had a place like this, I'd be only too glad to have strangers admire it.'

'Yes, I know, but these people mightn't like it. You never know——'

It was no good. She would do it, trotting up the flagged path to the Lodge in her high heels and brave little pointed hat, as she had trotted up to so many private gardens, high altars, and even back-stage at the Shakespeare Memorial Theatre—wherever her enthusiasms carried her. With the *naïveté* of wealth, she seemed equally oblivious both of annoyance and ridicule, but Mary suffered agonies of English embarrassment on her behalf. She had become fond of the little Pekingese woman, to whom she was chauffeur, companion, and guide to all the sights of England within a day's journey of the Berkeley Hotel, Piccadilly.

Mrs Van de Meyer was one of Mrs Shannon's best customers. Whenever she came to England, she hopefully bought unsuitable clothes at 'Lilianne,' which, in the two years that had passed since its temporary setback, had grown to be one of the more solvent firms of South Molten Street.

Trying on a skittish black dress trimmed with monkey fur, Mrs Van de Meyer had told Mrs Shannon that her hired chauffeur was a bore, and 'didn't know an Eleanor Cross from a war memorial.' Mary's mother, anxious to keep her happy, had suggested that she might like to have Mary in his place. The American woman had been so pleased with the idea that she had actually bought the monkey-fur dress, which had been a white elephant about the shop for some time, at the price asked for it, which Mrs Shannon had been fully prepared to reduce.

Mary had never even heard of an Eleanor Cross, but between guide-books and guesswork, she managed all right, and she enjoyed driving the big hired Buick coupé. It was a pleasant, effortless change, after two years of taking notes at dress shows all day long, modelling clothes in the shop, and lying on her stomach on her bedroom floor, designing lovely clothes for ugly bodies. Mrs Van de Meyer was sweet too, about money. She was not supposed to pay her anything, but often when Mary got home rather cross and devitalized after a day of American vitality, she would shame her with a five-pound note.

She emerged now, jauntily, from the lodge gate, seen off the premises by a glowering woman in curl-papers, two children eating bread and jam, and a sniffing mongrel.

'It's a Lord,' said Mrs Van de Meyer happily, as Mary opened the car door for her. 'The house is to let and the people are abroad, but she gave me the name of the agents, so we can go and see them right away. They're in that town we passed a while back.'

Feeling suddenly tired, and depressed at the thought that now she would be late for her dinner with Hugh, and he would be sourer and duller than usual, Mary turned the car in the space before the wrought-iron gates, while the unattractive party from the lodge watched in dumb derision. She nosed out into the main road and the smallest child kicked the mongrel, the mother slapped the child, and the other one said 'Yah' and did something very rude with his hands.

Mrs Van de Meyer's unselfconscious persistence achieved miracles at the estate agents, Jowitt, Jowitt, and Sicklemore. Jowitt senior agreed, for a consideration, purely nominal, of course, on behalf of and payable to the owner of the property, or such person or persons as might represent him, etc., etc., to produce the plans and moreover to conduct personally a tour of the house for the benefit of Mrs Van de Meyer's English architect. Mary wondered what Mr Van de Meyer would say to it all. He was never mentioned, so for all she knew, he might be dead, or worse. One of the indigestion pains that she had had lately was starting, and she drove the sixty miles back to London silently and mechanically through the gathering darkness. Mrs Van de Meyer talked about the house as far as High Wycombe, and after that about her operation.

'Keep Thursday then,' she said, as the commissionaire handed her on to the pavement. 'I'll call you later when I've spoken with Mr Howard. Good-bye, honey. Buy yourself something cute, hm?'

Mary felt like crying as she thrust the note on to her lap and hurried away. Would she never grow out of this silly habit of easy tears? She was always crying for nothing at all, even when she was quite happy, and she could never lose her temper successfully. It was so absurd, but she just couldn't help it—like sneezing. She wept gently as she rounded Berkeley Square, for the pain that had been nagging all the way home, was still there. Mastering herself in Grosvenor Street in time to save her make-up, for there was no time to go home before meeting Hugh, she left the car in the garage at Marble Arch and took a taxi to the Café Royal, where she dined on the balcony with a sleek young man, had once had an affair with a minor film star, and obviously wondered, as Mary did, why one let oneself in for such uninspiring evenings.

On Thursday, Mary woke with an agonizing pain in her stomach and cursed all Lobsters Newburg. Was everybody's digestion like this if it wasn't pandered to? It was a worse pain than usual. Mummy—Mummy must give me some bicarbonate or some whisky or gin or something—anything! She swung her legs over the side of the bed and sat for a moment feeling for her slippers and then suddenly scuttled for the bathroom and plumbed the depths of degradation.

The well-meaning head of Doris, Mabel's successor, came round the door. 'Oh, Miss Mary—— Oh, you poor thing. Here, let me hold your head.'

'Go away, go away, I'm dying——' But this was worse than death, and afterwards, when she had collapsed, exhausted on the bathroom floor, the pain was still there, coming in waves, like it must be having a baby, only worse because there was nothing to show for it. During a lull, she got back to her room, keeping her eyes averted from the breakfast tray that Doris had left by her bed. The pain would go soon; it always had before, and she must get dressed or she would be late for Mrs Van de Meyer and whatshisname—curse him. Grim-faced, she roved round the room collecting garments and indulging in the luxury of moaning. 'I'm ill, I'm ill,' she wailed to her pale reflection in the mirror. Thank goodness she had had her hair done yesterday, the dark curls were more or less where they should be, though the ones on her forehead were damp and sticky. Her face looked awful, all bones, and the effort of making-up seemed impossible.

178

Shall I not go? I could easily take them another day, or she could get a chauffeur. Heavenly thought, to climb back into bed and relax, let go everything for the sake of being prostrate. If it gets better though, and I know I could have gone? I ought to go if I can—I must decide soon. I'll see what Mummy says—oh, God! it's starting again—get her to absolve me. Like the Pope, she thought weakly, bending double in the middle of the room while the pain was born, grew, achieved its impossible peak, and lingered away, leaving her wild-eyed and panting.

Her mother was at the dressing-table, dividing her attention between the mascara brush and a sheet of notepaper covered with large, indignant writing.

'Mummy——'

'Oh, hullo, darling. Get the shop number for me, would you, and bring the 'phone over here. They've made a muddle over Mrs Bagot's coat—it would have to be her—and she's simply furious. Sybil gets more trying every day, you know. I told you what she did about that Rodier stuff, didn't I?' Her mother's rattling speech went through Mary's head like machine-gun bullets.

'Mummy,' she said, again, as she dialled the familiar number, 'I don't feel well. D'you think I can put off Mrs Van de M.?'

'Oh, darling, what a nuisance, I *am* sorry. Tell me about it in a second, I must just get this settled.'

' "Lilianne," South Molton Street,' clacked the receiver acidly, as Mary put the white telephone down on to the dressing-table and sank into the armchair behind her mother's back to deal with another pain.

Agony and Mrs Bagot's coat. The two were tangled together for all time, and two more pains had come and gone before her mother had finished with Sybil. Was it her imagination, or were they getting less acute? Perhaps her stomach was getting blasé. 'Numb with great suffering'—the phrase hit her brain, and she sighed and waited, curled up in the chair, for the next spasm.

'Right,' said Mrs Shannon, 'do that, will you? I'll be down in about half an hour.' She rang off and swung round on the stool. 'Now then, darling, what is it? Not that poor tummy again?'

'Well, yes, actually. And I was sick.'

'Oh, poor Mary, how horrid. What had you to eat at Angela's party?'

'Lobster Newburg. And——' she had just remembered—'and rum punch.'

'Darling, that was silly. You really ought to take more care. Still, it's not much comfort to be told that now. Would you like to get back into bed with a hot bottle? I'll ring up Mrs Van de Meyer and explain, if you really feel too bad to go. I daresay she'll understand—after all, there's nothing Americans don't know about dyspepsia. How is it now?'

She tilted her head on one side and screwed up her thin eyebrows, contemplating her daughter anxiously.

'How is it now?' she repeated, as Mary waited while a fresh pain threatened, and died away, unfulfilled.

'So-so. Better than it was, actually.'

'I think you ought to let Doctor Brett have a look at you. You're having too much of this indigestion, darling. I don't like it.'

'Neither do I, oddly enough,' said Mary under her breath while her mother went on: 'I'll try and get an appointment for you tomorrow. What d'you think about Mrs Van de Meyer? If I'm going to ring her up I ought to do it soon, to give her time to make other plans. Would you like me to, or does it feel as if it might clear off?'

'Well, I don't know,' said Mary bleakly. 'I wanted you to decide for me.' The thought of the day before her seemed suddenly so dreary that she was almost disappointed when another little pain died stillborn. 'Need I go, Mummy?' Bed, lovely bed was fading away.

'Of course not if you really don't feel up to it. You do look rather a poor little wreck, I must say. Come on, I'll help you back to bed. I know you wouldn't cry off for nothing, you've never been a hypochondriac. Poor Mary—it is a shame. Here, lean on me if you're shaky. How does the pain feel now?'

'Much better. Quite gone. I'll have to go,' said Mary, and burst into tears.

It was a very cold day. The November sky was colourless and low, and the air was raw and acrid with the scent of coming fog. Mary wore a grey flannel suit with a sweater and her camel-hair coat over that, and Mrs Van de Meyer wore suede bootees and the long-haired fur coat that disguised the never very apparent existence of her legs. Sam Howard wore a blue scarf and a rough sort of overcoat that smelt of Scotland. The three of them sat together in the front of the Buick, with all the windows shut, and as they rushed through the chilly scenery, their breath made mists on the windscreen. Mary had to keep wiping it with the fur paw of her gloves. When she took her eyes off the road, she noticed how solemn Sam's face looked against the far window as he listened politely to Mrs Van de Meyer. She was in full spate conversationally, and Mary was able to be silent, listening idly and revelling in the extra peace that comes after pain. Her stomach was blessedly quiescent. The car and the American voice sped on, and only once slowed down for the noisome streets of Uxbridge.

'Oh, Mrs Van de Meyer,' said Mary suddenly, 'I've discovered why I couldn't change down. You've got your legs crossed over the gear lever.' She giggled and, looking across, saw that the grave lines of Sam's face broke up into complete chaos when he laughed.

'What an attractive smile,' she thought, suddenly aware of him for

180

the first time as more than the potential designer of Meyer Hall. She had got past the age when, on meeting a man, one instinctively visualized oneself standing at his side in foaming white tulle and a dress designed to look well from the back, but she shot another look at Sam and his smile and thought: 'He'd be nice to marry.' He probably had a wife and six children. All Mrs Van de Meyer had said after being introduced to him at the Gregorys, talking to him for two hours and concluding a business arrangement in the middle of a horde of people drinking cocktails, was that he was a 'very lovely person.'

When they stopped for traffic lights in High Wycombe, Mrs Van de Meyer was talking of a park with deer in it. To interrupt her was not a rudeness, but a necessity for anyone who wished to open their mouth at all. Sam looked out of the window and said:

'Do look at that man trying to walk down the pavement without stepping on the cracks.'

How few people would notice that sort of thing. He *is* nice, thought Mary and said: 'D'you play that game, too? I often do.'

'Always,' he said thoughtfully, and Mary, disentangling Mrs Van de Meyer's legs once more as the lights went green, searched for something to say that would prolong the small moment of contact, but the insistent clamour of the deer-park claimed him for its own, so she concentrated on her driving and left them to it.

They stopped for a drink soon after Oxford. Mary, who knew Mrs Van de Meyer's idea of a drink, had slowed down at a bald-looking modern hotel with 'American Bar' written over the door in Neon tubing, but her employer would have none of this. She insisted on a real public-house with *at*mosphere, and then was aggrieved to find, in the private bar of the 'Black Swan,' that the landlord had never heard of an Old-fashioned, and, furthermore, had no ice.

'Can you beat that?' she said, sitting down unhappily with a glass of sherry, and taking no more notice of the genuine old high-backed settle than if it had been a brocade sofa at the 'Waldorf-Astoria.'

'What for you?' Sam asked Mary. She now saw that he was very tall with nondescript hair, and long legs that looked right in grey flannel trousers.

'I don't know. I suddenly feel awfully cold. What's good for a person who suddenly feels cold?'

'Whisky Mac,' said the landlord promptly, reaching for a bottle. He looked like Uncle Lionel, narrow, as if he had been pressed together sideways; much too pinched to be a puller of beer handles, and a tipper of bottles. 'Whisky and ginger wine. Best thing out,' he said.

Mary tried it and liked it, and Uncle Lionel said, 'Don't mind if I do,' to Sam's offer of a drink, so she left the two of them drinking sherry and talking about football pools, and went over to the fire. Mrs Van de Meyer was sulking, quietly, among the old oak and pewter. Mary was half-way through her drink before the awful realization came to her.

The pain was starting again.

So slight as to be hardly noticeable unless your stomach were as sensitive to it as a nervous horse to the first prick of the spur. Perhaps it would go away if she ignored it. It must go away. I can't have agony here, miles from London. I've got to drive, and Mrs Van de Meyer will get so excited if I'm ill, and Sam Howard—well, a tummy-ache's not exactly glamorous. She leaned her elbows on the mantelpiece and tried to concentrate on a celluloid picture of a girl with a 1920 waistline being very arch with a glass of port.

'Let's go, shall we?' said Mrs Van de Meyer. 'I just can't wait to see my house. Coming, dear? Why, you haven't finished your drink. Wasn't it nice? That's too bad!'

'No, it was lovely, actually, but a bit strong . . .' Mary trailed after her to the cold, stony road. They were on the flat top of the Cotswolds and the low walls gave no shelter from the wind that raked the grey-green fields. She shivered and got quickly into the driving-seat, remembering to say, 'Thank you for the drink,' to Sam, before the realization that the pain was getting worse blotted out all other thoughts.

There are moments in life when one ceases to live and merely exists, when physical misery or discomfort become so great that they exclude all other sensations. One goes on, automatically, a body without a mind, like a tadpole, with no thought of the past or hope for the future. The present is eternity and fabricated of despair.

How she managed to drive on until she was told to stop, where they lunched or what the hotel was like, Mary had not the slightest idea. She could manage to talk all right if she kept her voice very quiet, and she just said yes to all the waiter's suggestions without knowing what they were. It was worse than the morning. I'm really ill, she thought with a certain grim satisfaction. When I get home I'll be really ill—bed and doctors and everything. They'll be sorry then, she thought, looking morosely at the other two, who seemed to have plenty to talk about without noticing her stricken silence. Although she was doing everyting possible to disguise her plight from them, she felt aggrieved that she was succeeding.

She dropped her napkin on the floor in order to be able to double up inconspicuously until a spasm of agony had passed. Sitting up, she became conscious, suddenly, between two waves of the pain that bounded her world, that there was a plate in front of her with nameless, formless horrors on it—greasy things, gravy. . . .

She pushed back her chair quickly: 'I forgot to wash my hands,' she mumbled. 'Excuse me.' Once outside the dining-room she broke into a run, up some stairs, along a narrow passage like in a liner, hunting wildly, like a trapped animal. Where, oh, where? Round a corner—Oh, thank God!—Oh, message of hope: 'Ladies' Cloakroom, mind the step.'

She had got through lunch all right. She had managed to toy with the food when the pains began to subside, and had even drunk a cup of tepid black coffee, made by that secret formula known only to provincial hotels which ensures that coffee shall taste of anything— gravel paths, bitter aloes, charcoal, soap—but never of coffee. Never that clean, wholesome, almost wheaten taste, fragrant as the steam that rises lazily above the cup.

Mrs Van de Meyer had looked at her vaguely once and said she had no colour, and had she tried Arden's 'Hibiscus' rouge? Sam Howard had said, 'Not nice?' and raised one eyebrow, as the waiter took away her untasted pudding, and she had had to say, 'I'm not hungry,' very tersely, in order not to cry.

She was sitting now, kicking her heels, on a low stone balustrade that ran along the terrace at the back of Mrs Van de Meyer's dream house. It was, if anything, balder and uglier on this side than at the front, but that unimaginative regiment of windows stared out over a wonderful view. Mary sat with her back to the house and her coat collar turned up against it and wondered what it would be like to wake up every morning and see a gently sloping lawn that merged into a park dotted with bare black trees that became thicker and thicker until they were a wood. The wood ran downhill a short way and then stopped abruptly at the edge of a bright green meadow that led at last to the river. A huge red ball of sun was hanging over the low hill on the other side of the valley. It would be gone soon and then the darkness would come quite quickly.

From time to time she could hear the voices of the other three inside the house. Jowitt senior was very hoarse, and was racked at intervals by a shattering smoker's cough.

Mary had had a look at herself in the mirror at the hotel, and was now resigned to the fact that she had never looked more unattractive. One would have to meet a really nice man under these conditions; life was like that. She had got through without disgracing herself, anyway, and if the pain held off for three hours, as it had this morning, she could get home all right. She would probably never see him again. 'I expect I shall die in any case,' she thought dispassionately.

The wind was blowing straight at her across the valley, and she huddled in her coat, feeling forlorn. Bed would be nice, and somebody to cosset one. She wished suddenly that her mother were a slow, dowdy old thing with an enormous lap.

It was too cold to stay on the terrace any longer, so she got down and went round the side of the house in search of the voices. Sam and Mr Jowitt were in the shrouded dining-room, poring over vast sheets of plans that littered the oval table. Mr Jowitt had a cigarette hanging from his lower lip, which he only removed to cough, and sometimes he coughed without removing it, and choked like a dying man. He was very messy, with sticky hair and eyes like hard-boiled eggs. 'Now take your ground plan,' he kept saying, 'take your ground plan—fifty-five by thirty. Never mind that other, take your ground plan——'

Sam had a pipe stuck in the side of his face. He looked up and smiled at her when she came in, and they exchanged a glance of horror as Jowitt senior had another repellent seizure. Mary felt better and wandered off to help Mrs Van de Meyer, who was kneeling in the dust of the hall trying to measure the circumference of a pillar with a handkerchief.

At last they were ready to go, and Mr Jowitt rolled up the plans and they all trooped out to where the car stood on the gravel sweep outside the front door. Mrs Van de Meyer was loth to leave, and kept darting back to have another look at something, and just as Mary thought she was really coming at last—she actually had one foot on the running-board—she saw a chimney and dragged Mr Jowitt off across the gravel to get a better view of it.

Mary slumped against the car with her hand in her pockets and sighed. Sam came and stood in front of her, quite close, so that she could see all the stitches of his blue pullover.

'Look here,' he said, 'are you all right? I hate to interfere, because you obviously like to be left alone when you're feeling like death. You are feeling like death, aren't you? At least you were at lunch.'

'Oh, dear, did you notice?'

'I couldn't help it.'

'Oh!'

His sweater was hand-knitted. Someone had made a mistake half-way up, and one of the stitches was bigger than the rest. She wondered who had knitted it for him. I hope it was his mother.

She went on talking quickly without looking up: 'I had the most ghastly pain, that's all. I get it sometimes. But I'm all right now, actually. I didn't want Mrs Van de Meyer to notice; she'd have made such a fuss.'

'She didn't. She's so keen on this hideous place, she wouldn't notice if you were dying. Look here, are you really all right? Why don't you let me drive the car home, I'd love to.'

'Would you really? That would be marvellous, I——' Footsteps crunching on the gravel, and Mr Jowitt came coughing round the back of the car. Sam put out a hand and pulled her upright.

184

'O.K.?' he said, still holding her arm. 'All right, soon be home. I say,' he whispered before he let her go, 'isn't he foul?'

'Revolting,' she said, and beamed up into his eyes.

They drove Mr Jowitt back to his office, and he sat in the back of the car with his elbows on the seat in front, and breathed down Mary's neck. After he had got out, Mrs Van de Meyer kept him standing on the pavement of the High Street while she thought of several last-minute things to say to him through the window. Then he tipped his bowler hat and said, 'Good-bye, all,' and Mary, looking through the back window, saw him spitting in the gutter as they drove away.

She was sitting in the middle this time, nobody's idea particularly, it had just happened like that, and she sank down on the comfortable seat and leant back while Mrs Van de Meyer and Sam talked across her. His hands on the steering-wheel were long and brown, with knobbly joints.

They drove through the short twilight, and the falling darkness brought fog with it, only a thin, swirling mist at first, but as they got nearer London, it got thicker and closed in ahead of them, throwing back the light of their own headlamps. A pinpoint of red light seemed to be quite far away until, suddenly, Sam had to swerve to avoid the stationary lorry that loomed almost on top of them. Mrs Van de Meyer screamed and Sam said:

'For the love of mud——' and slowed down to a crawl.

'I shall ignore you this time,' said Mary to the rat that was beginning to nibble at her inside.

Sam had the window down and was leaning over to peer out at the road ahead, so when the nibble became a gnawing, not in waves this time, but insistent, she was able to turn her head to the right and moan into his coat unnoticed. Mrs Van de Meyer was perched right forward on the edge of the seat, rubbing vainly away at the windscreen with a scented handkerchief and saying, 'But I can't see a thing, d'you know it?'

'I'm afraid we'll have to have the windscreen open, I can't see the kerb,' said Sam, drawing in his head and shoulders suddenly so that he nearly squashed Mary's head against the back of the seat. She jerked upright guiltily.

'What's up?' he said.

'It's beginning again——' she whispered.

'Oh, God! Can you stick it till we get home? It won't be much longer.'

'Yes, I'm all right.' She sat with hunched shoulders, bending double over her folded arms. A choking, icy rush of air came in when the windscreen was opened, but Sam was able to drive a bit faster and soon they caught up with a procession of cars, playing a groping follow-my-leader along Western Avenue. There was no hope of passing them,

185

nothing to do but stay in the line like a truck in a goods-train. They would never get home, and the gnawing would never stop. Mary made a little sound and Mrs Van de Meyer's pince-nez glinted at her out of the swathes of fur coat with which she was trying to keep the fog out of her throat.

'What's the matter, Mary, aren't you well? Oh, my goodness, you look terribly, dear. You poor child, tell me what it is and I'll——'

'I'm all right, honestly—I'll be all right when I get home. It's nothing, honestly, Mrs Van de Meyer, please——' She began to be so kind and sympathetic, and to make such a disturbance over it, that it was over-powering. 'Please,' said Mary again, faintly, as Mrs Van de Meyer bounced on the seat, and leant across her to say: 'Oh, Mr Howard, Mary isn't well. Stop at a drug store, quickly, we must do something.' Sam managed to still the commotion slightly by saying that they were nearly home, but she kept bouncing about, now peering out through the windscreen, now turning back to smother Mary with solicitude, talking, conjecturing, exclaiming all the time, and still harping on the drug store. . . .

'Oh, God! Mrs Van de Meyer,' said Mary under her breath, 'don't you ever stop?'

'Apparently not,' muttered Sam, still concentrating, gravely, on the road ahead. Unseen voices shouted suddenly outside the car and were lost, and once a flare lit the fog for an instant, and a man's face loomed disembodied, shouting helpful, indistinguishable things. It was an eternity before they got right into London, and were able to leave the line of cars. It was clearing a little, and street lamps were piercing the thinning fog. Sam speeded up, nipping round corners, pulling up short at cross-roads and then roaring away. He seemed to know his way well. Mary leaned back, and closed her eyes. The rat was going round and round now and so, funnily enough, was her head.

'Where are we?' said Mrs Van de Meyer. 'This looks like somewhere I ought to know.'

'Berkeley Square.'

'Oh, but no, you should have taken Mary home first. That's too bad. Go to Sloane Square now and I'll get back to the hotel afterwards. I must see her home. I can't leave her like this. Please drive on, Mr Howard,' she said as Sam stopped, and the door was opened magically, from outside. She protested, half in and half out, but Sam was firm and reassuring and Mary said, 'I'm all right, honestly, and my mother'll be there—it's all right, I'm——' her teeth were chattering so that she could hardly speak, and she wanted to scream and yell and have hysteria.

At last they were driving off and the anxious voice on the pavement faded into oblivion as if it had never been. Her body was the centre of

186

circles of pain that concentrated and expanded, sometimes reaching her brain, and oscillating there like a humming top. Agony and Mrs Bagot's coat—the two whirled round together.

'Sloane Square?' said Sam. 'What's the address?' and someone, perhaps it was Mrs Bagot, said, '44, Marguerite Street.'

When the car stopped again, he got out, and she looked after him and saw him run up the three steps to her own red front door. She wanted to call out and tell him that it was no use ringing because it was Doris's day out and Mummy wasn't coming back till late, but she couldn't be bothered. She was only a passenger now, with no will of her own. Someone, some time, would put her to bed, and then she would die.

He was back. 'No answer. The telephone's ringing; probably Mrs Van de Meyer. Where's your key?' He took her bag and fumbled about. 'Hell, it's not there, you silly idiot.' The door slammed and they were off again, driving, driving, never anything but driving.

'Hang on,' he said. 'Agony?' Agony! when everything in your body that could possibly hurt was in action! She groaned, and then she thought she heard him say, 'You poor darling,' but she was so dizzy that she couldn't be sure. A gust of pain swept right through her and she knew she was either going to faint or be sick. She never knew which she actually did.

She was lying on a bed. The pain and confusion had disappeared and with them the little pointed grey face with the enormous eyebrows like prawns, and the low, rumbling voice. No, there was the voice again, in another room: 'If you'll see her into the ambulance, I'll just nip down to the hospital in my car to make sure they're ready for her.' Who on earth were they talking about?

'Right, doctor.' That was Sam. He came in holding her coat—she couldn't remember having taken it off—and sitting down on the bed, lifted her up to put it round her shoulders. She put her arms round his neck and kissed him by way of expressing gratitude that the pain had gone and her head was clear.

'Thanks,' he said, and laughed, and her head suddenly cleared completely and she realized that she shouldn't have done that. Where was she, anyway? She sat up and looked around the room. It was untidy and old-fashioned and masculine; nice in a way, but not like her own blue and white bedroom.

'I want to go home,' said Mary. He was buttoning her coat round her throat, looking very serious about it.

'You will,' he said, 'but you've got to have your appendix out first.' He stood up, bending over her, and smiled. 'Come on,' he said, and picked her up carefully, as if she were an egg.

When she came round from the anæsthetic, she had kissed the surgeon, a thin-lipped man with a blue chin, who in the normal course of events would be quite unkissable. At the sudden remembrance of having done the same, unpardonable thing to somebody else, she had burst into tears and sobbed desperately and uncontrollably until she was exhausted, long after she had forgotten what she was crying for. Her mother had tried to comfort her, but one of the nurses had said: 'Oh, they always do that, Mrs Shannon, when they come round. Either that or laugh like a drunkard. It doesn't mean anything.'

Mary had a nice little room, very clean and white, with a blue arm-chair and a most pleasing picture on the wall opposite the bed. It was of a clearing in a very green wood, with the whole ground covered with a misty sea of the bluest possible bluebells, and a woman with a red parasol among them. She used to lie for hours, contemplating the simple colours of the picture and letting her thoughts wander in an idle, luxurious way for which one never had time in ordinary life. She had hardly any pain, and they used to give her things to make her sleep blissfully at night. It was very peaceful, for even hospital nurses cannot talk for ever.

She was not allowed to see anyone at first, except her mother, who visited her whenever she could get away from the shop.

'You can expect a rush of aunts and cousins later on, I'm afraid,' said Mrs Shannon rather grimly. 'They keep ringing up all day long. It's really rather trying, though they are so kind.' She moved restlessly about the room. She was no good at sitting still and relaxing, and she would wander about, picking up things and putting them down again, rearranging a flower here and there, bending over the dressing-table to powder her nose or dab at a flat curl with a wetted finger.

'Tell me some family gossip,' said Mary, following her with her eyes from the bed. 'There must be some.'

'Let's see—— Oh, yes, I knew I had something to tell you. Mavis—poor Mavis, she does have the worst luck with her children—says that Julia has fallen in love with a crooner in a band. He passes notes to her and whispers things down the back of her neck while she's dancing.'

'I don't call that so bad,' said Mary. 'She'll be lucky if that's the worst thing Julia ever does.'

'Yes, I know, but you know what heavy weather Mavis always makes of everything. She says Julia's fascinated by the glamour of the man or something, and might do anything. "But *anything*, Lily!" I think it's absurd. I can understand anyone being in love with a crooner because he was a man, but not being in love with a man because he was a crooner.'

Mary smiled half-heartedly. She wished her mother would sit still, and not make the tiny hole in the net curtains bigger by twiddling her finger in it while she looked down at the street. 'What else has happened?' she asked, not because she was particularly interested, but because one must talk to one's mother when she came to visit one, however tired and dispirited one felt.

'I had a letter from Geoff to say that Lucienne's baby is still bright yellow, but otherwise the spit of old mother Rombeau. It's going to be called René—I knew Lucienne would get her way—and be christened in some impossible place called the Wee Kirk o' the Heather. Really, the Americans are quite mad, aren't they?'

'Aren't they what? Sorry—I wasn't thinking. . . . Oh, yes, quite. I say, Mummy——'

'What, Puss?'

'Nobody's—rung up or anything, about me, have they?'

'I don't think so. Mrs Van de Meyer, of course. She never stops. Oh, and Hugh rang up last night and wanted to speak to you, but he didn't seem particularly concerned when I told him where you were. He was full of some house-party he'd been to; he's rather a bore. You never would fall for that profile, would you, darling? I'm always afraid he might become a second Pierre to us, and really, the expense of having to put two notices in the engagement column of *The Times*——'

'Nobody else then? Only Hugh.'

'Wait a minute, there was a man the other day, when I was out. He's rung up twice, Doris says, but I don't know who he was.'

The brightest and tritest of the nurses, who was called Bonzo, came staggering in under a huge sheaf of flowers. 'Aren't you the lucky one? I'm afraid she's very spoiled, Mrs Shannon. Ee-normous chrysanthlybums; I had a tiny peep through the paper.'

Mary tore off the wrapping. They were lovely. Huge, white snowballs with strong, tightly-curling petals—just the sort of thing a man might choose. She hunted quickly for the card.

'Oh,' she could not keep the disappointment out of her voice. 'From Gerald.' Her mouth dropped.

'How sweet of him,' said her mother, coming over to the bed. 'Oh, they are beauties; he must have wired for them. Don't forget to write and thank him, darling——'

Mary made an irritable exclamation and slumped down in the bed.

'Well, there's no need to be crusty about it, even if you are an invalid,' said her mother patiently, as if she were speaking to a petulant child. 'Here, here, don't cry, you ninny, there's nothing to cry about. Weak,' she mouthed to Bonzo across the bed.

'Oh, she wouldn't cry,' said Bonzo breezily, although two tears were even then rolling down Mary's cheeks on to the sheet. 'We don't allow mopey Muriels here. We give 'em a good smacked bottom, don't we, Mary?' She roared with laughter, and went crackling and rustling away on her large squeaking rubber soles, to arrange the flowers with less artistry than was humanly possible.

It would have to be Auntie Fanny who was there when he came. She was a great-aunt, actually, Granpa's decrepit, unmarried sister, who seldom left her eyrie in the Cromwell Road, except to visit cemeteries. When she had exhausted her collection of graves, she would visit the sick, which was the next best thing.

It was so long since she had talked to a personable young man that she got about ten years younger, which still made her seventy-two, when the pink-eyed Scotch nurse came giggling in with Sam.

It was sickening. There she sat—two beady eyes in a dusty bundle of clothes, overrunning the conversation like blight on a rose bush. Sam was a stranger, infuriatingly polite to Mary as well as to Auntie Fanny. He had obviously come only out of politeness. He would always think of Mary as the girl with the shiny face and the tummy-ache, so what did it matter that she was wearing her prettiest bed-jacket and had dry-shampooed her hair that morning? There was no trace of the intimacy that had been born of the nightmare urgency of that foggy evening. It might never have been, thought Mary, lying back miserably, making no effort to cope with the hopeless situation.

Once or twice, Sam tried to say something to her, something about Mrs Van de Meyer or the house, but Auntie Fanny cut in like a grating bread-saw and he dried up. Why didn't he take the old lady by the scruff of the neck and dump her outside the door, instead of sitting listening to her stories of tumours at the Hospital for Women, Soho Square, or the incompetence of a gardener at Putney Vale Cemetery? Sitting so seriously on that small hard chair, clasping and unclasping his hands between his knees. His hands had not changed. They were still long and brown, with knobbly joints, like they had been in the car. Mary had not even thanked him yet for all he had done that day; it was impossible with Auntie Fanny ready to pounce on any topic like a vulture. Nobody knew that she had been at his flat, they thought he had taken her to a doctor, and Mary had not thought it worth while to embark on explanations afterwards. She could imagine her mother saying: 'But what were you doing in his *bed*, dear? What can the doctor have thought? Why didn't you ring me up?' Who had paid the doctor's bill, by the way? Oh, she must ask him that. Would Auntie Fanny never go? Not a chance. This was a rare treat for her and she had nothing to go home to but a poached egg on baked beans and the B.B.C., imperfectly materialized through the medium of a small, second-hand wireless, for what Auntie Fanny did with her money, no one knew.

When the nurse came in with Mary's supper, she turned both the visitors out together. Mary was almost in tears as Sam said good-bye, getting up obediently to go, and even calling her Miss Shannon. She did not dare ask him to come again, and he did not suggest it. Oh, it was sickening.

The days passed in an endless procession of people she didn't want to see, books she didn't want to read, and wireless programmes she didn't want to hear. The doctor said she might draw, so her mother brought along her things, and she started to design a wedding dress in which Lady Sachs' daughter should renounce her maidenhood at St George's, Hanover Square. Mary used an idea that she had got from a production of *A Merchant of Venice*, and the dress began to evolve into one of the best things she had done. She could not bear to think of Eularia Sachs with her fat arms and hempen hair, walking down the aisle in it on the arm of an elderly stockbroker. She would design something commoner, and keep this dress for someone more worthy of it. It ought to be worn by someone slight and dark——

The door opened a crack, and Fergie, the Scotch nurse, put her head into the room. 'Will you see a visitor?'

'Oh, Lord,' said Mary sulkily, turning the board face downwards on the bed. 'I suppose I'd better.'

Sam walked diffidently in, looking round the room for great-aunts, before he came up to the bed.

'Hullo,' he said. 'I hope you don't mind me coming again. I saw these violets, and I thought you ought to have them, because they're the same colour as your eyes are sometimes.'

He had noticed her eyes! They were never violet; that was impossible. Nobody ever had violet eyes except in magazine stories, but never mind. He had been interested enough in them to think that they sometimes changed colour. He had remembered them.

After he had gone, twiddling his hat at the door and saying, 'I say, am I an awful pest if I come again?' she lay back against the pillows with a sigh, a smile spreading from ear to ear, and went carefully over all the things that he had said, during their half-hour of quite ordinary, but incomparable conversation.

He had turned over the drawing-board and said, incredulously: 'But that's good! Is it for you? It ought to be. You've made the girl look rather like you.' He had been genuinely, not politely, interested in hearing about her work, and had compared it to his as if they were in the same sphere, and she not merely a sketcher of decadent, leggy women, while he was a creator of real, permanent places where real people would live.

He had said, quite seriously, when she apologized for Auntie Fanny, 'That's all right; but I was terrified at first she was your mother.'

Each time he came to see her she had to keep saying: 'Don't make

191

me laugh. Don't make me laugh, for heaven's sake, it's agony.' Each time before he came she thought he could not possibly be as marvellous as she expected, and then he always was. He must like her. He wouldn't keep coming to see her if he didn't. No man could be as charitable as all that.

It was on her last day in hospital that he suddenly said, *a propos* of nothing, 'I love you.'

'*What?*'

'Don't sound so staggered, darling. I've been wanting to say it for ages. Well, it's out now. I can't take it back.'

'For ages——'

'Remember that time when you sat up in my bed and kissed me? Well, I'd just said it then, only you hadn't heard.'

'You couldn't have. I was ghastly.'

'You were divine.'

'You were so sweet to me.'

'I was miserable for you, darling. I didn't know what to do. God, when you kissed me. I nearly went through the roof! But the look on your face when you came to and realized what you were doing——'

'I felt such an idiot. Oh, Sam, why didn't you say this before?'

'I didn't dare. I was terrified of you when I first came here. You were so damned upstage.'

'Oh, I wasn't. *You* were.'

'You've got a funny little way of being suddenly very cool and silent and detached—quite terrifying.'

'That's when I don't know what to say.'

'I thought you were so lovely. That day when I first met you—your figure, and the beautiful shape of your face—I had to keep looking at your profile all the way down in the car. I couldn't believe it was true.'

'I kept looking at you. Didn't you see me?'

'God help you.' He laughed. 'Then when I came here and saw that your eyelashes were even longer than I'd remembered, and your hair all curling on the pillow in the most devastating way, and then that bloody old woman sitting there like a carrion——'

'Oh, don't make me laugh. Oh, Sam, stop me laughing. Oh, darling —look out, don't lean on my stomach——'

'Pardon me if I intrude,' said Bonzo at the door, but nobody took any notice of her, so she went away and wished she had a man, and determined either to diet or to buy a new pair of corsets.

Mary left the hospital a week before Christmas. 'Good-bye and good riddance!' said Bonzo in the corridor, and gave a yell of laughter that woke a man out of the first real sleep he had had since he fell off his bicycle under a lorry.

After a few rather tottery days at home, Mary and her mother were ordered down to a hotel in Cornwall for ten days of recuperating air.

'Do ye both good,' said old Doctor Brett, drawing a scrubbed fore-finger along his yellow-grey French general's moustache. 'Lilian's been overworking at that shop. Ye look a pair of wrecks. Horrible sight.' He drew the finger back again, so that the moustache was fluffy on one side and smooth on the other. He was an engaging old man. Mrs Shannon had been trying unavailingly for years to marry him off to a succession of suitable spinsters and widows, but all he wanted was his rock-garden.

Once she was really away from the shop and had resigned herself to leaving it to the mercies of imbeciles like Sybil, Mrs Shannon began to enjoy herself.

'D'you know,' she said to Mary on the way down, as they faced each other over the Great Western Railway's tomato soup, 'I've just realized I haven't had a real holiday for ages. Even when we've been abroad there's always been incessant worrying, and dress shows to go to, and new clients to cultivate. This time I'm going to cut free. I'm going to forget there's such a place as South Molton Street, or such a number as Grosvenor 1354. I've only brought down awful old rags, and I'm going to tramp the moors in a sack-like skirt and hob-nail boots, making hog-calling noises.'

'Very nice, darling,' murmured Mary, who had seen some exquisite tailor-mades going into her mother's suitcase.

'All the same,' went on Mrs Shannon, refusing boiled hake and egg sauce with a slight shudder, 'I can't help being a bit worried about Sybil. I'll have to ring up as soon as we arrive, to find out whether everything's all right, or I shan't get a wink of sleep. No—I mustn't, though. I said I was going to cut free, didn't I? You'll have to help me to be strong-minded, so if you see me being drawn like a magnet towards the telephone, pull me in the opposite direction and send me out to look at the sea.' She prattled on, and Mary listened apathetically, for the prospect of the holiday filled her with none but the gloomiest thoughts. She had not seen Sam since that last dream-like day in the hospital. His work had taken him up north the next day, and he was not back yet.

He had written to her. She could hear his voice in his letter, for it was written just the way that he talked. He was coming back to London tomorrow, and she would not be there. Worse, even, than not seeing him, was that he expected to find her there—had specified in his letter some of the things that would happen when they met again.

It was all right though. She knew he was sure of her, just as she was sure of herself and of him. She knew him so well, even though they had only been together five or six times, and only really close at the last.

She knew his generosity and his perfect sense of humour, which was the essence of all the things that she had ever thought funny in her life; his quick perception of atmosphere, and his intolerance, which never prevented him from being devastatingly polite to the people to whom he most objected. She knew things like the way he loved to work, and how he hated to make plans, and how he clung to certain expressions that fascinated him, like, 'For the love of mud.'

She knew what he looked like. Tall and dark, but not handsome; only just incredibly *right*-looking, with clear brown eyes and a kind mouth that lifted like wings when he smiled. A face that was strong without being tough, clever without being ascetic—the sort of face that would stand looking at for ever.

She smoked a cigarette and gazed out of the window at the frozen floods of the Athelney Marshes and ached for Sam.

'Cheer up, darling, only ten days,' said her mother, who was almost bursting with unsatisfied curiosity and the effort of not asking Mary about the tall, polite young man that she had met once or twice at the hospital. He obviously must mean something, as he was never mentioned. He figured largely in Mrs Van de Meyer's disjointed telephone conversations, and she knew that his name was Sam Howard.

She could not help nosing delicately round the subject.

'You know, Mary,' she said, drinking coffee with a difficult, bird-like motion, as the train rocked over some points, 'I've been a pretty good mother on the whole.'

'I know,' said Mary, 'but why suddenly?'

'Nothing particular. I was just thinking, though, there aren't many mothers who'd let their daughters get away with keeping them in the dark like you do.'

Mary knew what her mother was trying to get at. 'Never tell anybody anything,' she said. 'That's the only safe way.'

'Oh, I know. It's not that I mind, but—well, even Julia tells her mother when she falls in love with a crooner,' said Mrs Shannon wistfully.

'Oh, Mummy, I *am* sorry. Would you have liked us to have had girlish talks, with me saying, "Mother, I love him," and you saying, "Dear heart, a mother knows best"? Goodness knows, we could have had some comic ones. I've loved some pretty odd people in my time.'

'You never even told me you were going to break it off with Pierre until you actually asked me to post the letter to him. I mean, one likes to know where one is.'

'Never tell anybody anything,' repeated Mary. 'It only makes one look such a fool if the thing that one's planning doesn't come off.'

'*I* wouldn't think you a fool,' said her mother. 'Why on earth do they complicate life by making these cups this shape? But seriously, darling, if ever you are pining or anything, I wish you'd tell me. You never know, I might be able to help.'

'You'd tell everyone in London and all the girls at the telephone exchange first,' said Mary, getting up. 'Come on, let's go back while we're in this station. And you needn't look at me quizzically like that. I'm not hiding a secret sorrow from you. If I look pale, it's because I didn't put on any rouge today, and if I've got circles under my eyes, which I know I have because I saw them this morning, it's because I'm tired. That's all. Honestly.'

She was tired, too. Even the effort of packing and catching a train had left her limp, and with a dull ache where her appendix had been.

She spent the first few days at St Justins sleeping and resting and being thankful for a good book, and wondering when Sam would write again. Her mother tied a fuchsia-coloured handkerchief round her smooth, black head and started manfully out for a country walk on the first morning. The hotel stood on a hill, high above the sea, and after walking half a mile down the drive and back in the salty Atlantic wind, she came in again, with her neat ghillie shoes unsoiled, peeled off her hogskin gloves and ordered a cherry brandy. After that, she flipped distractedly through the fashion magazines, and when she could bear it no longer, put through a call to the shop. Then she was much happier and spent the rest of the time telephoning and wiring to London and playing bridge with various desiccated people that she picked up, for she would rather talk to anybody than not talk at all.

Mary began to feel stronger, but bored. She was not allowed to ride, or even to drug her restlessness by long, satiating walks. There was hardly anyone in the hotel between jolly young folk of sixteen and old, old men and women who had crawled to St Justins to die. She learned the life history of the barman, which could not have been duller, exclaimed over the photographs of the chambermaid's children, who could not have been plainer, wrote letters, or wandered down to the intriguing little harbour, where the gulls cried all day long round the shut-up Tea Shoppes on the quay.

She was dressing for dinner when the page with the breaking voice knocked on the door and squeaked and growled, 'Phone call for you, Miss.'

Her heart thumped. She flung her dress over her head, wrenched up the zip fastener, crammed on any old shoes, and flew along the corridor and down the stairs to the telephone box, with her hair uncombed and her face naked. When she heard a woman's voice at the other end of the line, her heart sank like a stone, but it was only the telephone girl.

'Hold the line, ple-ase,' and then there was Sam's voice, very distant and rather impatient.

'Hullo! Hullo, operator——'

'It's me—it's Mary.'

'Oh, darling, Hul*lo*! God, it's good to hear your voice. Listen, what on earth are you doing in Cornwall? Why didn't you tell me you were going? When are you coming back?' He fired questions at her without giving her a chance to answer. 'Listen, Mary darling, I've got some free days over Christmas. Could you bear it if I came down and spent it with you?'

'Could I bear it? Oh, *Sam*, how heavenly. I'll get you a room.'

'Angel. I can't wait to see you. I'll drive down, I think—be there about six tomorrow. Sure your mother won't mind?'

'She'll adore it. What about your father though? Oughtn't you to spend Christmas with him?'

'The old devil's still abroad. Staying with a mad countess in Austria. Look here, it'll be three minutes in a sec. and I haven't got any more money—I'm in a box.'

'Does it smell?'

'Yes. But that's not the point. I haven't said what I wanted to.'

'What, darling?'

'Pip, pip, pip,' said the telephone.

'I love you.' His voice was cut off and Mary went out of the box and walked through the corridor lounge, smiling a foolish, secret smile to herself. All along the gauntlet of armchairs, from behind the camouflage of knitting-needles and library books, peered the old eyes that never missed a thing.

Mary's first waking thought on Christmas Eve was, 'How can I possibly wait until six o'clock?' She grudged every moment of the nine hours before they could be together. The people in the hotel seemed more futile and more tragic than ever. She had finished her book, and the country and the sea outside were hung with a streaming curtain of rain.

Once the morning was gone, however, there seemed more hope of its ever being six o'clock, and she lay on her bed and did her nails, and then it was tea-time. Mrs Shannon was incarcerated in the fug of the card-room, so Mary had her tea alone, and remained glued to her chair at the end of the lounge nearest to the front door, pretending to read a paper and looking up with a quickened heart-beat every time she heard a car. Several people were arriving to spend the Christmas days, and she hated them all for not being Sam. Once the bus arrived, bringing people from the London train: a family who looked quite nice until they opened their mouths, an attractive, curly-haired man who awakened not the smallest interest in Mary, and a colourless woman with such negative clothes and features that she might just as well not have existed at all. Mary stared at them, as people had done at her and her mother when they arrived, and they stared back uncomfortably, with the disadvantage of newcomers.

After that a square, golfing couple arrived in a car, and then came a pitifully lost-looking little pair who might have been on their honeymoon, but should never have been allowed to get as far as the altar. But still no Sam. The curtains were drawn across the big windows of the lounge, and Mary could hear the wind hurling spatters of rain against the glass outside. Sitting in the warmth of the hotel, she thought of Sam driving along a road towards her, with the wind hurling spatters of rain against his windscreen. He was coming to her. To *her*—it was incredible.

It was after seven o'clock. Most people had gone up to their rooms to dress, but Mary still sat on. An enormous family of children arrived, with a jolly, open-shirted father, and a mother like the German ideal of motherhood. They were all frank and freckled and free from inhibitions, and their luggage consisted mostly of hold-alls and cardboard dress boxes. Mary wondered how they could afford to stay here. She was just deciding that the mother probably had a rich sister who felt it her *duty* to help poor Norah, when she heard the deep roar of a car coming up the drive, and she was so certain that it was Sam that she got up and went outside.

There was a big two-seater, and there were some legs getting out of it, and as soon as he saw her he drew her into the darkness between the headlamps and the light from the front door, and kissed her as if he had been thinking of nothing else all the way down from London.

Suddenly he held her away from him and said quickly, 'Darling, you will marry me, won't you?'

'Of course.'

'Thank God,' he said, and kissed her again.

The porter cleared his throat like a fog-horn. 'Any luggage, sir?'

'Yes, please. In the back there. Come on, darling,' said Sam, 'you oughtn't to be out in this rain.' They went into the hotel holding hands, and the eyes of the *tricoteuses* nearly came out of their heads, and the less hardened of them dropped a stitch.

There were several stitches dropped at the St Justins Bay Hotel during the next three days, for two people as blatantly in love as Mary and Sam had not been seen there since the days of the great scandal of the head porter and the second-floor chambermaid.

They had found Mrs Shannon in the bar that first evening, drinking a solitary dry Martini to drown the memory of her bridge losses, and

197

when they told her, she had fallen off her stool and said, '*Darling!*' and hugged Mary as she had not done since she was a little girl. Then she stood on tiptoe and kissed Sam, who laughed rather shyly and said, 'Thanks awfully.'

'Why didn't you tell me before?' asked Mrs Shannon, clambering back on to her stool. 'Three champagne cocktails, please, Albert, and one for yourself. This is an occasion. You might have told me, Mary, I think it's very mean.'

Mary looked at San. 'Well, there wasn't really anything to tell, until a minute ago, was there?'

'Quick work.' Mrs Shannon was obviously rather flummoxed, but was bearing up jauntily. She kept darting glances at Sam, trying to take him in all in a moment as a son-in-law.

'Bless you both,' she said, raising her glass, and Albert raised his tumbler, for he had said, 'Thank you very much, Madam, I don't mind if I have a beer,' and said now, 'May I take the liberty of congratulating the happy pair?'

After dinner, there was dancing to Col Collier and his Truro Trio, and gaiety was unbridled. There were paper chains and holly and balloons, and a Christmas tree with coloured lights and spangles and glass balls, but no presents. Matrons in brown lace with artificial roses on the shoulder were trundled round the room by clammy adolescents, and toothy girls in pink taffeta blew squeakers at retired colonels, who danced with very high knees and felt no end of dogs. Mrs Shannon wore diamond shell ear-rings and looked like a sophisticated mermaid in a green crepe dress that clung to her all the way down and then kicked out in a fish-tail train at the back. Mary wore a dress she had designed for herself—pale grey chiffon with a draped top and a cloudy skirt, clasped at the waist by a wide, flame-coloured belt.

She did not care whether it was a State ball at Buckingham Palace or a village hop. She moved in a daze of happiness. It was thrilling to keep discovering new marvels, to do things like dancing together for the first time, and to find that Sam danced just the way he should for her, and that he loved to waltz. Even the Truro Trio's breathless rendering of the 'Blue Danube' could not spoil the swirling heaven into which she floated, with Sam's arm behind her waist the only thing that kept her on the earth. When the music stopped, her lips were still parted in a huge smile, and she swayed a little, giddily, leaning against him.

'Come on, darling,' he said. 'Let's get out of here. Come up to my room, or yours, or somewhere.' As they threaded their way out, Mary had a fleeting thought of pity for all the dim people who had nothing better to do all evening than to dance to Col Collier.

On Christmas morning the three of them went to church, and Mrs Shannon, being deeply affected by the carols, got her annual religious mania, and walked trancily down the road afterwards, talking about the peaceful life of a nun. She left them at the corner where the High Street branched down to the sea, and drifted back to the hotel alone with the angels. Sam and Mary walked down to the harbour, and rounding it, climbed the hill on the other side to the high, grassy peninsula that divided St Justins' two bays. Mary pulled off her hat, and they ran when they got on to the open space, laughing and shouting and taking great gulps of the ocean wind. When he kissed her, Sam's lips tasted salty, and the skin of his cheek was smooth and cold. Mary's long, tangled curls blew across his face and he said they smelt like seaweed.

Since yesterday the weather had cleared completely, and broken clouds were being swept across the clean sky. The sun kept bursting out and making a glorious sparkle on the tops of the waves, and the wet grass at their feet glittered like broken glass. They stood at the edge of the cliff, watching the dark sea crumble into foamy spray on the rocks of the opposite point.

'Not cold?' said Sam.

'Of course not. It's heavenly.'

'How about coming and sitting out of the wind for a bit? I'm scared of your mother if I get you tired.' They went back a little way, and found a flat rock sheltered by a larger one. 'Here,' he said, suddenly remembering something as they sat down, 'I've got a Christmas present for you.'

'Oh, darling—and I haven't got anything for you!'

'This isn't only a Christmas present, though.' He pulled his hand out of his pocket and opened it. In the palm lay a little ring; a twist of dull gold, intricately carved in the shape of two clasping hands, quite different to anything Mary had ever seen.

'Oh, Sam,' she said breathlessly. 'It's lovely.' She twisted and spread her hand to admire it on her finger. 'Oh, thank you, darling; I do love it. Where did you find it?'

'I saw it in a comic little shop ages ago, and I went back there the day before yesterday to see if it was still there. After I'd bought it, of course, I suddenly remembered I hadn't even asked you to marry me. I'd sort of taken it for granted, and I was in an awful panic all the way down in the car to get to you and make sure.'

'How could you know I'd like something like this?' said Mary, spreading her fingers on his knee and gazing dreamily at her ring.

'It just looked absolutely us, somehow. Darling, you wouldn't have liked diamonds or something to swank with to your girl friends, would you? No, I knew you wouldn't. I'll load you with diamonds later on if you like—and women like Mrs Van de Meyer go on existing—but not for something that means something.'

'I never liked the ring that Pierre gave me,' said Mary, thoughtfully. 'When I broke it off I threw it into the Thames off Westminster Bridge. Awfully dramatic gesture, wasn't it? I was young then. I'd have pawned it now. Darling, I haven't told you much about Pierre—or anybody. Does it matter? Ought I to?'

He shook his head. 'I don't want to know,' he said seriously. He was holding her against him so that her back was against his chest. She could feel his heart beating against her shoulder. 'Don't tell me things,' he went on. 'What happened before we met doesn't matter. It doesn't affect this thing we've got between us. That doesn't mean, of course, that I'm not jealous as hell of any man who's even looked at you; I could slay the whole lot. But, it's funny, I don't want to know about them.' Mary was silent, listening to his dear, calm voice talking quietly on.

'I'm not going to tell you about me,' he said, 'because it doesn't matter either. One thing I'll tell you, though. It's odd, but all through everything it's as if I'd known about you. I always kept a bit of myself back, because I knew that it wasn't the ultimate thing—that I still had to find you.'

'Oh, Sam,' she twisted round to look at him. 'That's exactly how it's always been with me. I always knew God had something special up His sleeve. There I was, going round with a lot of love to unload on to you, and I dumped it on to one or two of the wrong people on the way, by mistake, that's all.' She stared and stared at his face as if she could never get enough of looking at it. 'Darling,' she said, 'I wish we'd been together from the day we were born—or from the day I was born and you were ten years old. Let's make up for it now. Don't let's ever waste time——'

'We won't. We've got loads of time, too; all our lives in fact.' He kissed her. 'Come on, darling,' he said, pulling her to her feet, 'it's too cold for you here. We'd better go, or your mother'll get excited and start thinking you've got adhesions.'

On the way home, they stopped at the tiny public-house on the quay, with its panelled tap-room that was like a little dark box, hung with paintings of the harbour, realistic, surrealistic, or frankly bad.

St Justins was 'an artist's paradise,' which simply meant that, if you wanted to, you could wear pea-green trousers and a blue Russian blouse and no questions asked. When Sam and Mary ducked in under the low door, there were two young men in the bar, wearing clothes that would have got them arrested in Hyde Park for soliciting. There was also a filthy old man with a beard, and a hat that was as battered as his teeth, and a couple of old salts who looked as if they had been thrown in by a film director to make up the quota of local colour.

200

The old man, who had been there since opening time, insisted on introducing everybody, so Sam stood drinks all round and told them that he and Mary were going to be married. This was a great success, and there had to be more drinks. The old man nearly wept over them, and the smallest and palest of the artists kept repeating excitedly, but a little wistfully, that it was all too unswervingly normal. It turned out, before they left, that the dirty old man was the only real artist in the place. He showed Mary one of his pictures—a lovely painting of a fishing smack sliding across the harbour in the sunlight. It had a clear delicacy of colour that made it impossible to believe that it was the work of this man, whose clothes looked as if they were growing on him like a disease.

Mary liked him. She didn't even mind when he patted her knee with a horny hand and called her little girl. She liked everybody in this funny, smelly little place, because it was such fun being with Sam. He made life so easy by always knowing, not deliberately but intuitively, how to treat people. It would always be like this now. Secure. Never again that feeling of solitude in a crowd that made one sometimes begin to think furtively of escape. It was fun to be among people with him and lovely to leave them afterwards and go out alone together. Lovely to walk away in the cold sunshine discussing the people you had left behind with someone who might have been yourself, so identical was his perception.

They went back to London on Boxing Day. Mrs Shannon went alone in the train, with a packet of sandwiches for her lunch, for consistent losses at bridge had brought on one of her spasmodic economy campaigns. Mary went in the car with Sam. She sang most of the way in her small, flat voice that nobody before him had ever wanted to listen to. She took the map out of the cubby-hole and spread it all over the steering wheel and across the windscreen in her efforts to study their route. He pushed a corner of it politely aside in order to see his way round a left-hand turn.

'Darling,' she said, flapping it back again excitedly, 'we shall pass quite near Charbury! Oh, let's go round and have a look at it. I'd love you to see it, and I think I could bear to see it again myself. I shall probably get beastly sentimental; will you mind?' He said no, and she prattled to him about the marvels of Charbury until they stopped for lunch at Taunton, where she was thrilled to discover that he liked prunes, a taste of which she had always been faintly ashamed until now. After lunch, she was silent, staring out of the window at the increasing familiarity of the road. It was not so long since she had travelled it, but all the things that had happened in those seven years between had driven its memories far into the back of her mind and they came forward slowly, as if from another life.

Then, before she was ready for it, they drove into Yarde. There was the station, comatose in the desertion of a holiday afternoon; there was the police station, with the air of leniency given it by the creepers and window-boxes and the blue gingham curtains of the sergeant's wife; there was 'Stationers, J. G. Ingledew, Newsagents,' shuttered now and with the revolving postcard stand taken indoors, but looking as though it still smelt of gum and string inside. She wished she could have taken Sam in and shown him the corner of the bookcase where Mrs Ingledew used to mark their growth every holidays with an indelible pencil. There was the sweet-shop where they used to buy those red sweets which had been the unattainable criterion of all sweets ever since. Yarde was the same—yes, it was the same, and yet the people seemed to be moving faster and to be more urbanely dressed. There was a red motor bus standing in the square exhaling blue fumes, and outside the hall where Mary had once seen the Star players in *Under Two Flags* and *Sweeny Todd the Demon Barber of Fleet Street*, there was a highly-coloured poster of Claudette Colbert in *It Happened One Night*. It was not quite the same. Nothing ever stayed the same. Why couldn't it when it had been perfect?

'Which way?' asked Sam.

'Left at the bottom of the hill . . . then right . . . now left again by that church, and straight ahead. . . .' She could have travelled the road with her eyes shut. All the memories came rushing forward from the back of her brain, and she began to sing the old song that went to the tune of the 'Keel Row.' She had to sing it very fast, because the landmarks came crowding on top of one another sooner than she expected. Was it because Sam's car went faster than the Lancia, or had the distance really dwindled? It couldn't be the Avenue and the signboard yet. From Yarde to Charbury had been quite a journey—miles to walk, and a long enough ride in a car. Disputes had been begun and wrestled with, long stories had been invented, momentous incidents had come and gone on the road between Yarde and Charbury. Yet now the corner where the Avenue turned away uphill was upon them almost before they had left the last straggling cottages of Yarde.

'This is it,' she said excitedly to Sam. 'Let's drive up the Avenue to the gates. The people couldn't mind us just looking through.'

The old illegible notice-board had gone and in its place a smug creation of black and white stood in front of the fir trees and pointed the way efficiently to Charbury House.

'Go slow, darling,' said Mary as Sam turned up the Avenue where one had once had to push one's bicycle, but that was now hardly a hill at all. They crept up between the bare branches of the elms, and Sam said, looking out to the right, 'Nice bit of meadowland there.'

'It's not a meadow,' said Mary vehemently, 'it's a park.' In no time

202

at all, they were at the top of the Avenue, level with the iron gates that Mary had never before seen closed. 'Stop here,' she said and, leaning across him to look through the gates, she stared and stared, unable to believe her eyes.

'But it's so small,' she kept saying, 'it's so *small*.'

The gravel drive, where even a tired horse used to jog-trot because his stable was near, was ridiculously short. The house at the other end was closer than it had ever been, and, compared with Mary's memory of it, a miniature.

'What a gorgeous old place,' Sam was saying. 'I'd love to see it nearer to. Those chimneys are perfect.'

'D'you think they'd mind if we drove up and just asked if we might look round?' said Mary hesitatingly. 'We needn't go indoors. I wouldn't want to, with the furniture all different and everything. We could explain that I used to live here. Would it be awfully Van de Meyerish?' It was dismal to be on the outside looking in, like a child at a sweet-shop.

'Let's risk it,' he said. 'I want to see the place where you were a kid. I'll open the gates.'

'No, I will.' She got out of the car, and went up to the gateposts in the grey stone wall. It was uncanny to lay one's hand on the exact mossy spot where one had sat so often and watched the cows going past on their way to the farm, or waited for a car or the pony trap to give one a lift up the drive. Imagine bothering to save oneself that negligible walk! But the stone had been warm and smooth to sit on, and—yes, here was the crack into which the heels kicked so comfortably.

When they reached the house, she knocked on the door—that door that she had hardly ever seen shut—with a pounding heart. Nothing happened. Silence. It was like: ' "Is there anybody there?" said the traveller, knocking on the moonlit door.' She looked back at Sam, lighting a pipe in the car, and he smiled at her encouragingly. She knocked again, thinking: 'He smote upon the door a second time. "Is there anybody there?" he said.'

Silence. ' "Tell them I came and no one answered. That I kept my word," he said.' But now there was the sound of feet on the other side of the door, and a bolt slid back. A woman with a face like a cold boiled pudding tied up in a dirty white handkerchief opened the door and said at once: 'If it's to collect for the jumble sale, you're please to come to the back, as I'm sick and tired of saying.'

'Oh, I'm sorry,' said Mary, taken aback. 'It's not for the jumble sale. It's just that I wondered—I mean, could we possibly——' She explained as well as she could to that expressionless stare.

'Well, I must say.' The woman scratched her head, dubiously, through the handkerchief. 'I don't know, I'm sure. I'm the caretaker here, cleaning and minding while the place is empty. It's not for me to say do this, do that, or the other. I'm sorry.' She may have been, but her face did not show it.

Mary had an inspiration. 'Is Tom still here?' she said. 'Tom Lawley. He knows me.'

'Never 'eard of him.'

'Well, what about Bates then? Bates and Mrs Bates. Do they still live at the lodge on the back drive?'

'Ah, well.' The face showed the embryo of a smile, like a lump of dough prodded gently with a finger. 'Now you're talking. If it's Bates you want to see, why didn't you say so before? He's down to the kitchen garden, breaking his back over the 'taters. 'E don't have visitors in a month of Sundays,' she said, looking with slow disparagement at Mary and the car.

'Well, if he says we can look round the grounds, may we?' asked Mary humbly. The woman shrugged her heavy shoulders and prepared to shut the door. 'Don't ask me,' she said. ' 'E can take it 'pon himself *if* he likes. Cleaning and minding, that's me. *I've* no say, I'm sure. 'Darternoon.' She withdrew her indigestible personality and rebolted the door.

Mary drew a breath of relief and spun round to Sam. 'Come on, darling. I'll take you to see the man who taught me my demon roundarm bowling.' They walked round the house and up the stable hill towards the walled kitchen garden, every step taking Mary further back into her childhood. 'This is where we . . .' 'This is where Denys . . .' she kept telling him, and hung on to his arm, tightly, because it made her feel sad. There was something so wrong about being intimately bound up with a place and yet walking through it as a stranger, trespassing on one's own ground.

They found Bates sure enough, in the potato patch, and the slow, unbelieving grin that spread over his face was worth coming miles for.

'Miss Mary!' he said, straightening up and dropping his hoe, and she rushed at him, and would have embraced him as she often had in transports of childish delight, but at the last moment he drew back, and lifted his cap, suddenly embarrassed to find her grown-up. He stooped and picked up his hoe, wiped an earthy hand on the seat of his trousers and gave it her when she held out hers. The grin was still plastered on his dark, rutted face.

'It's like old times. It's like the old days to see you,' he said, shaking his head from side to side with slow delight. Mary introduced Sam, and there was more grinning and head-shaking when he heard they were engaged.

'D'you mind if I show him round a bit?' Mary asked.

'Course not. Go anywhere you like. Don't you be running on my seedlings now!' he added, and Mary was moved almost to tears by his remembering that old joke between them. She had once chased a dog over some infant peas, and he had never forgotten it.

'What are the people like who live here?' she asked him as he walked with them to the gate in the wall.

Bates looked furtively round him, put his hand to the side of his mouth and made a wordless, most expressive articulation of disgust.

'*No!*' said Mary. 'How awful. Do they live here much?'

'Not when they can help it. She——' He pushed the end of his nose upwards with a thick forefinger. 'And 'e——' He pushed it down again on to his upper lip. 'Jew,' he said hoarsely, looking round the garden again for spies.

When Mary and Sam left him, they went up to the stables and Mary was aghast. Some of the loose-boxes had been made into garages and others held coal and stacks of wood. There was no sign or smell of a horse anywhere.

'Oh, Sam,' she said tragically. It was no use telling him what it had been, it only deepened the hurt. They went down to the Play House, which was locked up and dilapidated; the lily pond was empty of goldfish and had been made formal, with a fountain; the ha-ha wall—how could she have hurt herself jumping from that low height?—had been rebricked with glazed grey stones like a public-house. 'Oh, darling, I wish we hadn't come,' Mary said. Sam was right. The Park was no more than a glorified meadow, empty now of the woolly backs of grazing ponies.

'I'll show you the swing tree,' she said. 'That was one of our favourite places. Let's see, where on earth is it? It used to be just here, surely.' She walked a few yards, looking about her, mystified. Funny how one forgot some things and remembered others so exactly. Surely they used to climb down the wall, jump that ditch, run past that big oak tree and then——She stopped, staring at the ground before her in horror.

The swing tree had been cut down. Its terrible, pathetic stump was flat and clean, like a new tombstone. What had happened to the tree? Was that it, stacked in the loose-box where Joy had once stood in her winter rugs and blown warm, apple-smelling breaths over the door? Had the very branch that had supported Mary through so many summer afternoons been thrown into the hall fireplace that a rich Jew might toast his toes?

Mary clutched Sam's arm. 'Come on. Let's go. Let's go away. I can't bear it.' She ran with him across the Park, stumbling over the rough grass and thistles. As they hurried up the three terraced lawns, she seemed to feel the house and garden tugging at her, begging her not to desert them, but to stay and make it as it had all been before.

'It's all right, darling. Don't cry. Don't cry, my love,' Sam was saying, but he knew that she wanted to get away. He pulled her up the last slope, bundled her into the car, and swung off at once down the drive without looking at her. When they were through the gates, he got out to shut them, and got back quickly into the car.

She looked back once, just before he turned to go down the avenue.

'But it's so *small*,' she said helplessly.

Chapter Nine

'HAPPY the bride the sun shines on,' said Doris, rattling up Mary's blinds on a day of pouring, relentless rain. 'You wouldn't think it could rain in July, would you?'

Mary was wide awake; she had been since six o'clock, but she burrowed under the sheets and pretended to be still asleep. Undiscouraged, Doris came over to the bed, falling over Mary's slippers on the way.

'Madam says would you fancy a little scrambled egg just this once. Coffee and grapefruit aren't sustaining enough, she says.'

Mary pushed back the bedclothes an inch and looked at Doris with one eye. 'Doris, is it really raining?'

'Sheets,' said Doris succinctly. 'Never seen the like.'

It was a nasty thing to hear on the morning of one's wedding day, but it couldn't stop one getting married. It would take an earthquake to do that. Mary pushed the clothes right back and sat up, pulling the old teddy bear that still went to bed with her out from the small of her back and plumping him on top of the eiderdown.

'I'm not crazy about scrambled eggs,' she mused, feeling suddenly so well-disposed towards Doris that she could have embraced her, wall-eye and all. 'What do people generally have on their wedding day? What did your sister have when she married Cecil?'

'Well, I believe she fancied sardines. She was always a great one for sardines, our Nell was. Not Cicil, though. 'Eh can't touch them, Mums says if the way to a man's heart is through 'is stomach the way to Cicil's isn't paved with sardines. Laugh! You should have seen me——'

Doris' wall-eye had taken on its reminiscent glaze. She would gossip all morning, if given half a chance.

Mary cut in hastily. 'I don't know that I could face a sardine, actually. I say, I couldn't have a sausage, could I? I haven't had them for breakfast for years. Have we got any?'

Doris nodded. 'They lay heavy enough,' she said with interest.

'Not on me.' It was a lovely idea. When she had finally got rid of

206

Doris by pretending to hear the back-door bell, Mary rang up Sam, and was not surprised to hear that he had just ordered sausages too. They were always coinciding in things like waking up at the same time in the morning, choosing the same food when they were not together, and sometimes they both started to speak at once, in exactly the same words. When he had been in America, those long, lonely weeks when he had been panting about over White Plains in the wake of Mrs Van de Meyer, it was always happening. They discovered it by comparing notes afterwards when they were together again. Once, Mary had woken up to the clatter of the milkman, with a song running through her head that she had not heard for years. It was one of the sad little French tunes that the Russian used to sing at *Schéherezade* in Paris. She found out afterwards that Sam had been listening to the same man singing the same song in a New York night club at that time—two o'clock in the morning for him. These things were no longer surprising. It would have been odder now if they had not happened.

When Doris brought in her breakfast, there were several letters on the tray, and some telegrams. Life was exciting. One of the telegrams came, surprisingly, from Dulwich. Gran had sent a stock greeting—cheaper that way. Poor old Annie must have had to totter all the way down to the post office in the rain, with her shoes turning over at every step, for her ankles were weak.

For years, Gran's world had been bounded by the walls of 'Laureldene.' Since her illness, it was restricted to the airless museum of her bedroom. On her high bed, that looked as though it were designed for a lying-in-state, she lay in a sort of limbo: alive, and yet getting nothing at all from life. Annie was wont to mumble that 'the poor old lady still had her faculties,' but then they had never been remarkably acute before she took to her bed in her cock-eyed lace cap.

When Mary had taken Sam to Dulwich to introduce him to her grandmother, she had pretended to like him, but Mary had seen that old, watching look in her eyes as she talked irrelevantly, which was a sure sign that she was thinking dark thoughts.

'What a pretty ring,' she had said, peering disparagingly at it from under the random ribbons of her cap. 'Take it off and let me look at it.'

Mary had looked enquiringly at Sam, standing uneasily on the other side of the bed, for she had not taken it off since he put it on her finger on that Christmas morning. He had shrugged his shoulders helplessly, resigned to anything that might happen in this horrid room with its menacing furniture and curtains that looked as though they would crumble into dust at a touch. It might have been a setting for an Edgar Allan Poe story, and Mary, looking apologetically at Sam as she pulled off her ring, thought how inappropriately healthy he looked.

When she handed the ring to Gran, the old lady had fumbled with it for a moment, and then dropped it on the floor. Mary knew that she could not help it, but as she crawled on the worn carpet looking for her ring, she was choking with dust and fury. Why did she ask for it if she knew she could not hold it?

When she stood up again, Gran said: 'Let me look at it,' and held out her hand as if nothing had happened. The next time she dropped the ring, it rolled under the bed.

Mary bit her lip, shot a smouldering glance at her mother, and dived down into the dark, infested cavern, whose roof creaked and groaned as Gran moved on the protesting springs. There was room to get her head and shoulders under, and she groped about, shrinking from the accumulation of years of Annie's sweepings. Her lovely ring—she would never find it. Her searching hand touched nameless, repugnant things and suddenly, to her horror, she felt the yielding warmth of human flesh.

Then she heard Sam, laughing and choking, quite close to her. He had crawled under from the other side.

'I've got it,' he said, and kissed her, there in the unspeakable vault under Gran's bed, that no longer seemed quite so unspeakable. When he crawled out again, he had a bit of fluff in one eyebrow and a trace of lipstick on his mouth. Gran watched him more darkly than ever and called him Mr Hubbard.

Annie staggered in with tea, black and bitter, on an old tin tray. She went out again and returned defiantly with a plate of bread and butter, dry as cardboard, and half a fossilized Swiss roll. Gran had to be helped with her eating and drinking.

'I can do it, I can do it,' she kept clamouring, as Annie held the cup to her lips, ignoring the clutching hands.

'No you can't,' retorted Annie acidly. 'I ain't forgotten what come of letting you 'andle your soup bowl the other day, even if *you* 'ave. Who 'ad to change the sheets, I might ask.' She would have tossed her head, if her neck had not been so stiff.

Mary kept prodding her mother in the ribs and whispering: 'When can we go?' but there was a further ordeal to be gone through, and Mrs Shannon had not yet plucked up the courage to plunge into it. She as well as Mary had something to tell Mrs Payne.

It was simply this: she was going to marry Gerald Rigley.

For years, his wife had lain palely on her *chaise longue*, refusing to divorce him, and having one of her nerve storms if he even touched on the subject. Then one day, having exhausted the medical books in the house and unable to think of any new ailments, or feeling, perhaps, that she had done a good job of spoiling Gerald's life, and ought to start on somebody else, she had run away with the interior decorator

208

who was supposed to be designing a new colour scheme for her bedroom. Not run literally, of course, but driven exhaustedly away in a cream-coloured coupé, according to the cook who had been slicing beans at the kitchen window and had seen her go.

When her mother showed Mary the cutting from the Southampton paper, which said that Mr G. E. V. Rigley, F.R.C.S., of Hill House, Wickham, orthopædic surgeon to the King's Hospital, had been granted a decree nisi with costs on the grounds of the adultery of his wife with Mr Munroe Stevenson at the Royal Hotel, Droitwich Spa, Mary had said, good riddance for him.

'I'll allow you to go out with him now,' she had added, laughing, and then her mother had burst out, with a funny little air of deprecation: 'What would you say, darling, to having him as a step-father?'

Mary was staggered at first. Her mother to marry Gerald? Gerald, the faithful Airedale, the unfailing applauder of banana-skin humour, the invariable treader of trains as he followed you through a door in evening dress, the man who fell into the aisle at the Palladium and sat in somnolent misery at the Queen's Hall. She knew that her mother was fond of him. He was to her as Bingo, the Cairn puppy that Sam had given her, was to Mary. But then, Mary wasn't thinking of marrying Bingo.

However, when she got used to the idea, and saw that her mother was positively juvenile with happiness, and was not even taking seriously the world-shaking question of crinolines for débutantes, Mary began to think that she could not have thought of a better thing if she had been arranging her mother's life herself. In the midst of her own happiness, she had been worried about deserting the shop and leaving her mother to live alone. Now it seemed that Mrs Shannon was going to sell 'Lilianne' as soon as she could find a buyer, and retire to the lush peace of the Meon Valley, there to keep house for a man with a ginger moustache that was like a nailbrush to kiss, whose favourite reading was Sapper and E. Phillips Oppenheim.

Incredible but true. It also transpired that it had been Gerald who had lent her that thousand pounds, three years ago. Life was full of surprises; but now, as then, the pieces of the jigsaw puzzle were slipping into place with uncanny independence.

When Mrs Shannon, no longer able to resist Mary's nudges and Sam's grimaces, stood at the end of Gran's bed and said rapidly: 'By the way, Mother, I'm going to marry again. A man called Gerald Rigley. But you mustn't say anything about it yet,' there was a deathly hush.

'And why may I not say anything about it?' asked Gran, as one coming to from a knock-out blow.

Her daughter took a deep breath. 'Well, not until his divorce is made absolute, you see,' she said, with a brave attempt at airiness, that dwindled and died among the shrouding shadows of the room.

Gran recovered consciousness for the second time. 'You are going to marry a divorced man,' she said. 'Tell Annie to get my tablets. You have made me feel very ill indeed.'

She did not really mind at all. She was acting a scene from a book she had once read. Mary recognized it, for she had devoured it one Sunday afternoon, when it had seemed, as today, that it would never be time to go home. The book was called *The Fortunes of the Faulkener Family*, and the high spot was where the old mother was given her death blow by learning that her manly, curly-haired son had forgotten himself with the barmaid of the Rose and Crown.

'But a common village wench'—Mary could remember it as well as Gran apparently could—'a hireling girl. . . . You will marry her, Hugo. You are still a gentleman, nothing can alter that. No Faulkener babe shall want for a name. . . . Quick, the draught! I grow weak!'

Gran enjoyed herself tremendously, and Mrs Shannon who, not having read the book, was inclined to take her seriously, made a few hopeless attempts to reconcile her. At length, however, she gave it up, and they left the old lady trying hard to make herself faint. On the way downstairs, Mary nipped into the drawing-room, submerged at last by the macabre tide of dust-sheets, and stole *The Fortunes of the Faulkener Family*. She read it aloud to her mother and Sam, as he threaded them home among the tram-lines of Streatham, and they both agreed that Gran had put up a very good show.

The most welcome telegram that Mary received on her wedding day was from Uncle Geoffrey, 'BE HAPPY,' it said, 'IS HE NICE IF NOT I'LL COME STRAIGHT OVER AND PASTE HIM STOP WHY DON'T YOU BOTH COME AND VISIT WITH US STOP THE APARTMENT IS SWELL AND RENE NOT BAD STOP LUCIENNE SENDS LOVE YORS TILL DETH.'

Mary wished he could have been there to give her away, but he was too busy to come home at this time. Gone was the heyday of Lord Footle and the Young Gentleman of Oxford, but though the younger generation had to be taken seriously these days, the older generation could be as footling as you pleased. To have an English father gave a heroine background, and Uncle Geoffrey, complete with monocle and snow-white hair was coming once more into his own.

In and out of Mary's bedroom whirled her mother, fussing, planning, exclaiming, excited.

'Darling, you're not taking this repellent old creature with you!' She plucked out of Mary's suitcase the mangy, eyeless teddy-bear that had never squeaked since the day Uncle Geoffrey threw him out of the window at Clifford Court, trying to hit a policeman. 'Sam'll think you're mad,' she said. 'Look, I can't find my comb anywhere; my room's simply in a turmoil of wedding presents. Can I borrow yours? Where is it? Oh, here—oh, darling. I *am* sorry, there goes your scent. No, not broken. I've spilt some powder, too; never mind.' She giggled and whisked out of the room, calling: 'Doris! Doris! Have you found my gloves yet? I've simply no idea——'

'She's got the jitters, that one,' said Doris, pausing open-mouthed in the doorway to gape at Mary in her exquisite cami-knickers. 'Anyone'd think she was the bride, not you. When our Nell was married, she was taken queer,' she added proudly. 'It was cups of tea, cups of tea, before we could get 'er to the church at all.'

'Perhaps it was the sardines,' murmured Mary. 'Be a dear and get my dress, Doris. It's on the spare room bed.'

When it was all over, the business of dressing and doing one's face and having one's hair done by M. Louis, with his little black bag and bright orange shoes, Mary stood on a dust-sheet and looked solemnly at herself in the long mirror.

She was alone in her bedroom. Her mother and Doris had left for the church; Mrs Shannon in a tomato-coloured two-piece, orchids, and a hat like a small, straw saucer, and Doris in her navy costume and a hat that had brought forth fruit. There had been a lot of banging of doors and rushing back for forgotten handkerchiefs, and then they were gone. In a few moments, Mary must go down to her grandfather, who was fortifying himself with a brandy and milk in the dining-room.

She was wearing the dress that she had designed in the hospital, the dress that Sam had said should be for her. It was of dull, parchment satin with a heart-shaped neckline and a high waist that came up in a point and moulded her figure closely before it merged into the smooth, heavy fall of skirt that flowed out into the train now lying coiled about her feet. On her head, a tiny coronet of gardenias, tipped forward, with her hair curling loosely under the cloudy veil, and in her arms more gardenias, with their swooning, haunting scent.

'I'm sorry about all this, Sam,' she thought, bending to pick up her train, 'but I'll be Mary again afterwards.'

Granpa had got a new car. It had been the family event of the year. Linney, to whom every trick of the old Daimler had been as familiar as his wife's varicose veins, was not entirely happy with it. He did not trust its faultlessness, and drove it rather as if it were a high-explosive bomb.

He now stood by the car, wearing a huge white buttonhole and his water-melon grin as Mary and her grandfather came out of the red front door and stepped between the cheering throng of one perambulator, a small girl in battered tin spectacles and a contemptuous errand boy with the cutlets that somebody was anxiously awaiting for lunch.

The rain had stopped, contrary to Doris' prediction of, 'Rain after May, rain all day.' In the car, Mary sat carefully upright and exchanged distrait remarks with Granpa. He kept fingering the pearl pin in his cravat, pulling his lavender waistcoat outward and downward, drawing out his watch and grunting at it. The feel of his hand holding hers and the vast red back of Linney's neck were the only familiar things in this strange situation.

In the Park, the discoloured, thundery clouds were rolling away over Marble Arch. The sun might yet shine. Suppose Sam were not there. There was no reason to suppose that he would be. Anything might have happened. When they stopped at traffic lights, people on the pavement stared and peered and said, 'Look, Gwen, a bride!' The sun was trying to come out. It would be nice to be in the country now, in a field, watching the sun race towards you over the grass, blaze over you, and chase the shadows in which you had stood, away behind you to darken someone else's county. One of her gardenias was going brown at the edges. Poor thing. No wonder, with bits of wire torturing its stem.

The car stopped cautiously, so as not to disturb the time-fuse.

Granpa cleared his throat. 'Well, here we are,' he said, and heaved himself out of the door. Mary stepped out after him. What was all this crowd for? They couldn't have come to see her; this must be the wrong church, or a Cabinet Minister's funeral—no, not with the red carpet. Wait for me, Granpa. She was momentarily aware of bobbing faces on either side, of indrawn breaths and lugubrious cries of 'Oh, isn't she lovely!' and then she was into the blinding obscurity of the church. The dim space behind the back pews was filled with a fluttering crowd of women, telling her which side of her grandfather to stand, dabbing at her veil, arranging her train behind her—that was Sybil, she saw with surprise. She turned to look for her bridesmaids. There they were, in billowing white chiffon, Angela looking unbelievably lovely, and Margaret earnest and unhappy, with her wreath at the wrong angle. Angela gave her a beautiful, all-comprehending wink, and then, just as Mary turned forward to realize that the triumphant, swelling organ tune was 'Lohengrin,' Granpa put his hand across to squeeze the hand that lay on his arm.

'God bless you, my poppet,' he whispered, and they started forward.

Oh, she couldn't cry now! Oh, Granpa, why did you have to say that? Everything in front of her was blurred as they raced on between the surreptitiously turning heads, with the sibilant rustle 'Here she comes, here she comes,' whispering before her like the wind through reeds. The moment passed, mercilessly, and the tears receded from her eyes as quickly as they had welled up. She suddenly saw Sam. Did any man ever have such a touching back to his head? Did he know she was coming? Sam, here I am. As she came up to his side, not daring to look at him, the organ swelled to a finale. Sam, Sam, here I am. Granpa stepped back, the fat white cassock of the clergyman stepped forward, and the silly jingle kept on dancing in her head. Sam, Sam, here I am.

Trying to sort out afterwards her impressions of her wedding was like trying to put order into a kaleidoscope. The chief thing that had struck her was that Sam's name was Samson. She had not recovered from this shock all day. It kept coming back to her at intervals, and in the hushed, small hours of the next morning, she woke up saying plaintively, 'Why didn't you tell me your name was Samson?'

'Would you rather it was Samuel?' he had said, and they had snickered into the pillows, because there was someone in the next room who kept thumping the wall.

Other random things stood out. Aunt Mavis' hat—very large and, for some inexplicable reason, mauve.

A sudden, dispassionate impression of Denys. Why, he was really hardly attractive at all! Charming and good-looking, but there was no strength in his face; his features were too small. She wondered what he would say if she told him that she had come upon that crumpled handkerchief of his in the back of a drawer when she was packing, and had washed and ironed it for Sam's future use.

Sam calling her 'my wife' in his scrap of a speech after the toast.

The best man, Sam's childish friend Nobby, falling like a log for Angela, haloed in the glamour of her first West End part—the sex-interest in a comedy thriller.

Auntie Fanny, creeping about among people's legs like a bedraggled water spaniel.

Gerald, in a suit that looked as though he had worn it in his slighter days as a bridegroom, being elaborately unproprietary towards Mrs Shannon.

Aunt Winifred, with her petticoat showing three inches at the back and endless, champagne-coloured shoes, producing a smile for Sam that Mary had never seen before.

A perfectly strange woman following her about trying to snatch bits off her bouquet.

The realization, when she went into the old-fashioned room where brides at Shannon's had changed for half a century, that she had indeed had too much champagne.

Sam's father, distinctly tiddley, his long legs wobbling in the sponge-bag trousers but his ribald eye bright as a bird's.

Sam's sister, who had said before: 'Let's see a lot of each other; we're going to be terrific friends,' staring and staring, determined to find some fault.

213

Last of all, Linney, shaking hands with her at Croydon Airport, and saying: 'Good luck, Miss—Madam. Being married's all right, being married is.'

Everyone had said: 'Venice in August! My dear, you must be mad. You'll never stand the heat—and the smells!'

It was hot, but when you did nothing much except drift about in a gondola, what did it matter? Mary got a little paler and Sam changed his shirt six times a day; that was all. Mary did not remember afterwards that there had been any smells. She remembered chiefly the deepening discovery that another person could be oneself. That being with him could be like being alone without the loneliness. She remembered Sam saying once, when they were dining on the terrace over the water, with a hot little evening breeze stirring the tablecloth and the awning above, 'Don't you ever get sick of never having an argument? In books, the man and the girl always have terrific disputes about ethics or Walt Whitman, or Baroque architecture, sitting on the floor for hours and hours, when they might be in bed. That waiter—the one who's always rushing about to find black figs for you—if he were to write a book about us, no one would read it. People don't want to read about people in heaven. They like to lick their lips over them in hell.'

He tried to cure her of her ridiculously easy tears. He had promised her a pound for every month that she could go without crying. A week was the longest she had held out so far against her weak tear-ducts; she was always having to start again. One night she had been lying awake in the stifling heat, when she had heard a sound, faint at first, and then approaching, that had made her steal out of bed and go to the window. Leaning her bare arms on the deep ledge that was the thickness of the wall, she looked out, and saw a solitary gondola drifting down the moonlit blackness of the Grand Canal. In the prow, a man was playing a violin. The single sound rose up from the water with an unearthly sweetness while the gondola floated away between the silent places like a dying swan.

'You'll never win that money in Italy if you're going to cry for every beautiful thing,' said Sam coming up behind her, and he held her close as they leant on the stone ledge together and gazed at unreality.

After Venice, they took a small white steamer down the Adriatic to the Bay of Naples—a week of soaking in sunshine and bright, inconceivable blue. They had called on the way at Malta, arriving there in the morning to find the harbour blazing with that curious dry yellow light. Mary had sent a telegram to Uncle Tim, and she nearly fell over the rail with excitement when she realized that the naval launch that was going phut-phut alongside the gangway had come for her and Sam. Mary hoped that the other passengers were watching as Sam and she, in her best white hat that he said made her look like an angel, were taken off the steamer in such style. Mary had seen the Naval Review from Uncle Tim's ship, and had sometimes had tea at Portsmouth with Michael on her way over to the Isle of Wight to stay with Angela, but she had never yet solved the problem of what to do when saluted by an officer as she stepped on board. Did one pretend not to notice, bow graciously, smile, or what? Mary always wanted to salute back, though the only one she was qualified to give was the Brownie salute from the far-off days when she had been Sixer of the Pixies at Manton House. Somehow, though, with Sam, nothing was embarrassing any more. There had been a time when she had nearly died if she had to walk into a restaurant alone, or go to a cocktail party, where everyone except her knew everyone else, and shouted about it. She had far more confidence now. She could go about calmly. Sam thought she was all right, so perhaps she was.

In the captain's cabin were Uncle Tim, a lot of cocktails, two clean-living young officers and one rather common one who was not so clean-living but much more amusing, and the phenomenon of Uncle Tim's wife.

She was, as Sam remarked afterwards, 'a walking Gieve's.' A naval brooch pinned back the brim of her determined hat and another fastened her blouse; her cigarette-case, flapjack, and watch bore the crest, and down one lapel of her sensible linen suit was a string of little enamel flags—her initials in naval code. She also knew more about the Navy than any of the men present.

Uncle Tim seemed to be perfectly happy now that he had got over the shock of finding himself married to her, and had learnt to leave her to her own devices while he attended to his. Mary, being instructed about Malta by one of the clean-livers, saw that Sam and Uncle Tim were getting on very well over pink gins. Sam was mad about the Navy and knew almost as much about it as Aunt Annabelle. He kept his own sailing yacht at West Mersea near the little cottage that Mary was going to spring-clean and rejuvenate when they got home. She would have liked to listen to the talk about sailing, but the other clean-liver, to whom everything that was not a 'bright wheeze,' was a 'poor show,' had joined her in conversation with the guide-book one.

Mary sat opposite Sam at lunch, and wanted to giggle all the time. After two strong cocktails and a glass of hock it was hard to control oneself at the sight of Sam's expression when he first heard Aunt Annabelle address one of the officers as 'No. 1.' He was still engrossed in what Aunt Mavis called 'man's talk' with Uncle Tim, but every now and then he would shoot a look at Annabelle as if to satisfy himself that she was true, and then twitch the corner of his mouth at Mary, which was their private signal when a wink was too obvious. A sailor appeared in the doorway and came prowling in with a message for Uncle Tim. Aunt Annabelle interrupted his exit with: 'Oh, Mason. I brought the Captain's mess kit down in my car. He's going to shift on board tonight. You'll find it there—stowed aft.' Mary thought that Sam's eyes would come out of his head.

'But Mrs Howard,' Guidebook was saying to her, 'you really ought to see the fortress before you sail. It's jolly fine, really. Perhaps we'd have time to show you round after lunch. I've got an old tin Lizzie.'

On her other side, Bright Wheeze was saying to Uncle Tim: 'Yes, sir. By Jove, no, did you really, sir? Ha-ha-ha.' He was very shy and had big clumsy hands, and a fair skin that blushed easily. Mary suddenly noticed that his cuffs were frayed, and could have wept for him. She was sure he was engaged to the daughter of a retired naval officer at Alverstoke, and they were too poor to get married, and when they did, the girl would probably turn into an Aunt Annabelle and Bright Wheeze would not have the gumption to stop her.

Mary was longing to get away with Sam and discuss them all. That was the only point now for her, of going to any party.

They refused Aunt Annabelle's invitation, which was more like an Admiralty order, to cruise along to her flat and see the young. The Captain of the *Piccolino* had a carefree habit of weighing anchor according to whim rather than schedule. In consequence, three German *Vandervogel* had been left behind at Bari, and though this was no tragedy, Mary and Sam had no intention of letting the same thing happen to them.

Of course, the *Piccolino* did not sail for three hours after they had gone back on board, and they lay in deck chairs receiving periodic wireless messages from Aunt Annabelle telling them to jump into a *dhiassa* and come ashore. 'Just sailing' was their consistent answer, with the *Piccolino* anchored firmly and blatantly at both ends, without a wisp of smoke rising from her funnel.

At Naples, they left the *Piccolino* in the smoking shadow of Vesuvius and took another boat round the southern corner of the bay to Amalfi, where the rock dropped sheer from the terrace of their hotel into the sea. All day, the little white sails wandered by below, and at night sometimes the breaking melody of 'Santa Lucia' would climb from the sea to the stars. If you looked out of the window, you could see the spotlights of the fishing boats scattered over the dark water like glow-worms.

Mary lost count of days. Each day was an idling dream of sailing in the slim blue boat that they grew to regard as their own, sunbathing on their balcony, or lying all day on the flat rocks at the seaward side of the harbour mole, slipping like seals into the transparent water when they could bear the heat no longer. Sometimes, in the evening, they walked up into the hills towards Ravello and looked back to see the legacy of the departed sun like an Alpine glow on the white climbing houses above the harbour, whose water was streaked with deep rose, like silk.

When was it that it had first begun to matter when *The Times* came three days late? When had they first begun to puzzle out the news in the *Roma*, to try and get Daventry on the proprietor's wireless, crackling through storms in the Alps? Mary had not been bothering about the world. Her only worry up till now had been whether or not her shoulders were going to peel. From one day to another it seemed there was a crisis, and the English people in the hotel actually spoke to one another.

'That good old man,' they said, as the news trickled through that Chamberlain was rushing back and forth to Godesberg. 'He'll put things right.'

Sam wandered despondently out on to the balcony, with his hands in the pockets of his shorts. Mary thought his legs were heavenly. He had just been talking to a Frenchman downstairs, a man who had a lot of confidential information and was not loath to impart it, with a finger to the side of his nose to show that it really was confidential.

'Anything may happen you know, darling. I wonder if we ought to go home.' They had planned to have two weeks more at Amalfi.

'Oh, *no!*' Mary had been talking to the head waiter, and he had convinced her that *Il Duce* would not allow anything to happen.

That evening, down in the town, *Il Duce* did indeed blare out a message of confidence to crowds of Italians, grouped spitting round the doorway of every shop that had a wireless.

A wire from Mary's mother: 'Think you should come home,' followed by another: 'Everyone says definitely you should come home,' made them want to stay more than ever.

Then she rang up. 'Come now while you can. It's peace or war,' she kept saying. 'Gerald says it's peace or war!'

'I could have told her that,' said Mary, coming out of the telephone box into which she had been jammed with Sam, listening to the transcontinental hysteria. It seemed impossible to think that anything really was the matter, when the sea off the Amalfi coast was bluer than it had ever been, and the purple bougainvillæa was draped like a panoply over the terrace wall. Mussolini and the Italian papers were still soothing and discreet.

Sam poked about trying to get information, and Mary, watching his serious, sunburnt face as he said: 'I really think we ought to go, darling; I'll see if there's any chance of getting on the train,' saw that he hated the words.

217

'Oh, don't do anything yet,' begged Mary, who had been talking to the chambermaid. 'Let's wait a little longer and see what happens.'

Then Sam's father rang up, excited and incoherent, and talking about rejoining his old regiment, at the age of sixty. Chamberlain was going to Munich.

'It'th a crithith all right,' shouted Sam's father faintly, with the lisp that so endeared him to elderly *connoisseuses*.

The porter came up with the news that at great trouble and, of course, extra expense, he could secure two sleepers on the Rome Express.

'What about it?' said Sam. 'Life's hardly going to be worth living if we're going to be bombarded with wires and telephone calls all day long. Next thing'll be, your mother will arrive in a fast 'plane, piloted by Gerald.'

'Oh, dear,' said Mary, and went to the terrace wall to look at the sea.

Chapter Ten

LYING in her bed at Little Creek End, Mary listened to the straining creak of the poplar outside the window, as the wind dragged at its bare branches. She could imagine how it must be bent over in a long, tortured curve, its trunk dark as sealskin in the streaming rain. Was it her imagination, or was the wind really dying down at last? The night and the storm had been going on for so long.

Had ever a night been so long? Long enough for a lifetime to pass through her mind. Timeless. They say it's like that when you drown, only it's just a second or two then. Don't, don't. Think of something else quickly.

But it would be so cold in the sea. . . .

She forced her mind back to Italy, and to that anxious journey home which had ended in the anti-climax of Chamberlain and his bit of white paper. Why couldn't the war have started then instead of a year later? Sam would not have been already in the R.N.V.R. He would not have gone to sea at once. He would not have been in the *Phantom*.

He had joined up soon after they got back. Mary remembered him saying: 'That bastard Hitler cut short our honeymoon. I'm going to see he doesn't get away with a thing like that again.'

She remembered him saying, two months ago: 'When this business is over, we're off to Amalfi, you and I. D'you know that?' That had been at King's Cross, just before the train went.

> '*Oh love, we two shall go no longer to lands of summer across the
> sea.*'

His cap had been on one side. It was important to remember things
like that. A lot of little things. They were going to have to last her a
long time.

Downstairs, the blue-and-white china clock chimed once more. Seven
gentle notes. In an hour's time she would be going down to the end of
the lane, to catch the bus as it passed on the main road. She could
see quite clearly how it would all happen. A quarter of an hour to
Weatherby village; the usual delay in getting through on the telephone,
with old Mrs Munday, the post-mistress, watching her through the
glass of the telephone box. Half-past eight. The maid waking Angela,
sleepy and stupefied in her big satin bed. Would she have heard about
it, or would Mary have to tell her? At least another half-hour for her
to get dressed and hum her car down through Regent's Park, through
Hyde Park, across Eaton Square and into Marguerite Street. In at the
back door, up the back stairs, pick up the telegram lying on the front
door mat, and ring through again to Mary at Weatherby Post Office.
'Your call, Mrs Howard,' Mrs Munday's daughter would shout
from the back room where the switchboard was, and Mary would stop
reading the notices of gun licences and 'lost, a small black-and-white
terrier,' and go back into the box to hear what she knew already.

That poem—what was it?

> '. . . *Then said she, "I am very dreary,*
> *He will not come," she said.*'

That was how she felt. She knew. You couldn't be as close to a
person as she had been to Sam and not know. She was as certain as
she had ever been of anything, even of him, that he was not coming
back.

> ' "*He will not come," she said;*
> *She wept, "I am aweary, aweary,*
> *Oh, God, that I were dead!*" '

But Mariana was wrong. You couldn't die. You had to go on. When
you were born, you were given a trust of individuality that you were
bound to preserve. It was precious. The things that happened in your
life, however closely connected with other people, developed and
strengthened that individuality. You became a person.

Nothing that ever happens in life can take away the fact that I am
me. So I have to go on being me. There's only me now.

219

Funny that she couldn't cry. If she didn't cry now it would make a full month since the last time. But there was nobody to give her a pound, so it didn't matter, really, whether she cried or not.

That dog across the marsh had started his meaningless barking again.

'It's all right, Bingo,' said Mary, as the little dog suddenly raised his head, wide awake out of a sound sleep. 'It's all right. He's not saying anything.'

The dog stopped barking, but Bingo still listened. She could feel his body taut against her legs. Bingo, you mustn't ever listen for Sam. That will be one of the things I shan't be able to bear.

When she got out of bed, with her head and her eyes and her body aching and leaden from the sleepless night, she went to the window and looked out, her teeth chattering with cold. The wind had dropped since last night, but the rain was still falling steadily, as if it were trying to turn the marshland back again to water. It was still dark, but the beginning of a grudging light was creeping in from the sea.

She lit the lamp and fetched the paraffin stove from the spare room and huddled over that while she dressed. But it was hopeless trying to be warm, even though she put on her trousers and two thick sweaters. The coldness was coming from inside her; that was why her teeth would not stop chattering.

She tied her head up in a red handkerchief, and going downstairs, she had to go to the cupboard by the front door to get her sailing mackintosh.

That will be the worst part you see. There'll still be his things.

She could hear Bingo in the kitchen, drinking water as if he had thirsted for a week. A quarter to eight. She had better go, just in case the bus was early. It never was, but just in case.

'Come on, Bingo! Walkies!' He came scudding over the wooden floor and they went out together into the sodden garden. There was still plenty of wind. It tore at the skirts of her mackintosh, while the icy rain stung her face as she turned into the lane. She and Bingo floundered along through the puddles. There was no freshening exhilaration in being buffeted like this, only a soaking chill that seeped through to meet the chill inside you, so that you felt small and shrunken.

Bingo had shrunk too. He was about half his usual size when his thick coat was lank and plastered. Mary picked him up when they reached the cross-roads, and the little barrel of his ribs was like a rat's and his legs were not stubby any more, but spindly, like a rickety child.

They waited, shivering under a tree for what seemed like hours before the blurred head-lamps came wavering up at last through the streaming gloom. Mary stepped out into the road, the unseen driver saw her and stopped, and she climbed in at the back of the small yellow bus with

220

Bingo under her arm. There were not many people inside, but the atmosphere was thick with the smell of wet clothes and mackintoshes and there was steam on the windows. Mary rubbed a space with her hand, but you couldn't see anything. It was barely light yet and the rain was streaking the glass.

She kept peering out, trying to see where they were. They must be more than half-way by now; that white blur couldn't have been only the 'Teas with Hovis' cottage. This was surely the slowest bus ever.

Oh, hurry, bus, hurry. I've waited a whole night. I can't wait much longer.

When the bus stopped at last at the Red Lion Corner at Weatherby, she had to wait until the driver climbed down from his seat and came inside, red in the face, with rivulets sliding down his tarpaulin cape, to take the money. Mary grabbed her ticket, fumed behind a stout woman who was making a great labour of descending from the bus, jumped out almost on top of her, and ran down the main street with her soaking trousers clinging to her legs.

The Post Office was open. A faint light shone through the window on to the wet pavement. She banged in through the door, and there was doddering Mrs Munday, crouched behind the frail wire barrier, trying to add something up.

'I want to make a call to London,' said Mary breathlessly, leaning on the counter.

'. . . and seven is forty-nine, and sixteen is fifty—sixty-five, is three pound five,' mumbled Mrs Munday keeping her finger on the place while she peered up at Mary through the top half of her narrow spectacles.

'Oh dear, oh dear. You are wet, aren't you, Mrs Howard?'

'Yes, I want to make a London call, please, Mrs Munday. I'm in a hurry.' It would be ghastly to cry now from annoyance. Oh, Mrs Munday, quick, quick, quick. I could take you by your old neck and shake you till your teeth rattled.

'Your line's down, to L'il Creek End,' said Mrs Munday informatively.

'Yes, I know. That's why I want to make a call from here. Please ask Ethel to put it through quickly. Primrose 14892.'

Mrs Munday turned very slowly on her stool. 'Ethel, dear!' Her voice cracked as she raised it to carry through the open door to the switchboard. 'Could you get London for Mrs Howard?'

'Is that Mrs Howard?' Ethel's voice floated back, adenoidal, unhurried. 'Tell her her line's down,' she said in an aggrieved tone.

'O-oh, yes.' Mrs Munday turned slowly back again. 'What a time poor Ethel had last night. We 'ad a call come through for you time and again.'

221

'A call for me?' Mary's heart stopped beating and then began to race, thudding so that she could hardly speak. 'From London?' Angela must have heard the news and gone straight round to the house. 'What time was it? Did they . . .'

'Dunno.' Mrs Munday had gone back to her column of figures. 'All I know is, they wouldn't accept that Ethel couldn't get through to you. Ever so rude they were; she was quite upset. Weren't you, Ethel dear?'

'That's right, Mum. You'd have thought it was my fault from the way he was carrying on. "For the love of mud," he kept saying, "Well," I said . . .'

'. . . and six is three pound eleven . . .'

Bingo sneezed and his nails rattled on the linoleum like hailstones as he shook himself all over the floor.